INTO the STORM

INTO the STORM

Into the Storm Trilogy
Book One

Serene Conneeley

Blessed Bee Books

INTO THE STORM: Into the Storm Trilogy Book One

Conneeley, Serene
Into the Storm by Serene Conneeley
ISBN: 978-0-9945933-8-2

Website: www.SereneConneeley.com
Email: serene@sereneconneeley.com

Published by Blessed Bee Books
PO Box 449, Newtown, NSW 2042
Australia

Cover artwork: *Eye of the Storm* by Selina Fenech
www.SelinaFenech.com
Illustrations: Daniella Spinetti and Justin Sayers

Fate whispers to the warrior:
"You cannot withstand the storm."
The warrior replies:
"I am the storm."

Contents

01	Into the Night	03
02	Shelter From the Storm	09
03	Making Friends and Falling Hard	18
04	Fear and Loathing	31
05	The Fault In Her Stars	37
06	Heart Connections	47
07	Darkness Falls	61
08	After the Storm	73
09	Healing Her Heart	81
10	A Sad Charade	91
11	The Final Farewell	102
12	Love and Friendship	122
13	The Rain In Her Heart	129
14	The Twist Inside	137
15	I'll Be Your Magic	144
16	Storm Witch	154
17	And Life Goes On	161
18	A Sacred Heart	173
19	A Yuletide Miracle	184
20	A New Hope	195
21	Written In the Stars	204
22	Wake Me Up Inside	221
23	Looking Forward	229
24	True Love's Kiss	240
25	Another Storm Rolls In	255
26	The Green-Eyed Monster	266
27	A Deal With the Devil	272
28	A New Light	287
29	Into the Magic	296
30	A Spell On You	310
31	Into the Mists	318
32	Embracing the Magic	337
33	How To Break A Heart	356
34	Un-Happy Anniversary	370
35	Eye of the Storm	377
36	A New Storm Breaks	386
	Epilogue: Out of the Storm	396
	With Thanks	403
	About the Author	405
	Other Books	406

She fell.
She crashed.
She broke.
She cried.
She crawled.
She hurt.
She surrendered…
And then she rose again.

Chapter 1

Into the Night

The mists reached out long fingers to the girl in the velvet cloak, frightening her as they lingered around her ankles, then twisted up her body until they were weaving around her throat and through her hair. Shivering, she clutched the edges of the soft black material more tightly around herself, and tried to get her breathing under control. Tried to stop the hammering of her heart that she felt sure could be heard all through the dense woodland.

The full moon overhead usually calmed her, but tonight its light only added to her fear, revealing shadowy silhouettes of twisted trunks and shining creature eyes that offered no comfort. The dark moon would have been easier, because the glimpses of movement she could just see out of the corner of her eye made everything more frightening. Sometimes it was better not to know what was out there.

But eventually she saw the warmth of candlelight ahead of her and quickened her pace, relieved beyond measure. For a moment she'd thought her best friend's older brother had sent her out into the woods late at night as a prank, or a test, but he was here as promised. For the past three weeks she'd been studying the notes he'd given her, the books he'd lent her, and practising with him when they could slip away from friends and family. And tonight, the night of the full moon, they would finally work real magic together – casting a spell to heal her mother.

Her breath caught as she stumbled into the clearing. A circle of tealight candles in pretty glass lanterns marked out the space they would work within, and scattered rose petals between each of the golden flames filled out the magical boundary. On the altar in the centre, several ritual objects were set up around a vase of deep red roses. The scent swirled around her, making her momentarily giddy.

"Rhiannon, beloved, you are here," Evan said, and in the flickering light he looked much older than he was, the dark shadows dancing across his face hollowing out his cheekbones and adding a sinister flare that made her pause. *Beloved?*

He strode from the middle of the circle to the entry point he'd marked with clear quartz crystals – to amplify their working, she remembered – and smiled at her.

"It's a magical night, a powerful night, so our spell will work, I promise," he told her, confidence obvious in his manner and his tone. Her shoulders sagged with relief, and she let out the breath she hadn't realised she was holding. When he reached out his hand to her, she swallowed her hesitation and took it, allowing him to draw her into the space he'd created between the worlds. Voice strong, he welcomed the deities and the directions, using words they'd practised earlier that week. The familiarity soothed her.

But suddenly he pulled her closer to him, right up against his body, and she gasped – he seemed taller now, and broader of chest, and she faltered again, his new proximity to her far more intimate than she was comfortable with.

"Come Rhiannon, let me anoint you, and we will stand before the goddess together."

Quickly he took a small bottle from a pocket in his cloak, then untied the ribbon fastening it at his throat so that it fell to the ground. Her eyes widened in surprise, but she was trapped by his gaze, and by the magic he'd promised her, and so she stood there powerless, clinging tightly to her belief that this was the only way her mother would become well again.

Unscrewing the lid of the bottle, he tilted it so that a single drop of oil splashed onto his finger, then he rubbed it into the centre of her forehead, its rich scent, combining the heaviness of frankincense with the lightness of lemongrass and the sweetness of peppermint, adding to the dreaminess of the moment. And then he spoke.

> *We welcome you god and goddess, under this beautiful*
> *full moon light,*
> *Please come into our circle on this portentous night.*
> *Bless us with your strength during this rite,*
> *And imbue us with the immense power of your healing*
> *magic and might.*

His voice was deeper than usual, and reverent, and Rhiannon stared at him in wonder as light seemed to glow from within him. When his fingers moved to her throat and untied the ribbon that held her cloak in place, she felt it fall to the ground, leaving her totally exposed. Yet the power she saw glinting in his eyes, the presence of the god within him that she convinced herself she could sense, made it feel almost natural, almost normal, in this heightened reality, that they stood here together, their naked bodies caressed by the golden moonlight.

She shivered as he rubbed the next drop of oil onto her chest, between her breasts, and her breath caught as goosebumps rose on her skin and the first inkling of fear and suspicion rippled down her spine. Desperately she sought comfort in his next words.

> *God and goddess, as supplicants we stand before you,*
> *Please come into our bodies so we may ease Beth's pain.*
> *Lend us your power so we can help her move through,*
> *Darkness into light, illness into health again.*

His words made her ashamed of her suspicions, and when a soft golden glow shimmered around him, she was awestruck by the immense power emanating from him. For the first time she allowed herself to believe that this would actually work, that he really did know how to heal her mum, and she felt tears welling in gratitude.

It was so kind of him to be helping her like this, instructing her over the past few weeks in his own time, facilitating this ritual tonight, and asking for nothing in return.

She allowed that sentiment to lull her into a place of calm, to fill her with a sense of security and safety, yet her body trembled when he rubbed a drop of oil onto her solar plexus, and this time she wasn't sure whether it was from the cold, from her fear, or from the naked desire she saw in his eyes.

Time seemed to slow as she stared up at him, trying to read his intentions, to sense whether she should be worried. Surely she was just being a prude, because magic was supposed to be intimate, and raw. It was a stripping away of the physical self and a merging with another's spirit, and with the spirit of the earth and of the god and the goddess.

An owl hooted overhead, making her smile, and the sound of a small creature scrambling through the underbrush nearby distracted her for a moment. As she turned towards the noise, she felt Evan move even closer, felt his leg push against hers, felt his breath on her face. Panic made her heart race.

"What are you doing?" she whispered, suddenly frightened as his hands clamped down on her shoulders and his mouth came down roughly on hers.

"Shh, Rhiannon, shh," he crooned, as his tongue traced a path down her neck. "We have to *be* the god and the goddess, and come together as they do, to power the spell."

Part of her mind accepted this, so desperate was she for their magic to make her mother better, and she tried to breathe through her fear, to accept that this sacrifice would fuel the working.

Yet another part of her resisted. Tried, as his hands moved from her shoulders down to her chest, then lower, to scream out against it. Prayed, as he crushed her to him, that she could somehow stop him. But physically she was frozen, rooted to the earth, to the woodland, trapped by the heavy scent of the oil burning on her forehead. And even the sound of an approaching storm did nothing to dampen his ardour, or help her find the strength to move and get away from him.

Vision clouding, she tried to float out of her body as panic threatened to overwhelm her. Filled with despair, she wondered how this would affect her friendship with

Debbie. Would she be able to look at her friend in the same way, talk about boys so innocently, share her secrets with her? Would she still feel comfortable going to her house for dinners, let alone sleepovers?

Her heart pounded in time with the roll of thunder overhead, and her eyes were squeezed shut – but when she heard him swear, she opened them wide, and was surprised to see a beam of torchlight dancing through the trees behind him.

Hope flared in her heart as she heard the soft but steady tramp of someone moving towards them, and she almost collapsed in relief when Evan released her, knocking the candles over and fleeing into the darkness. He didn't even pick up his ritual tools or close the circle, so she did her best to unwind it, but it was one thing to watch someone else perform a ritual, and quite another to replicate it herself.

Shrugging, she sank to the ground, blindly groping for her cloak, then stood up, wrapping it around her body and clutching it nervously to her chest. Listening intently, she tried to centre herself, to control her breathing, and to work out what new challenge faced her. Who else could be out in the woods tonight? The steps got steadily closer, but she couldn't get a fix on the direction they were coming from, as gusts of wind buffeted the trees from all angles.

When she heard a twig break behind her she stilled, terror racing through her veins and chilling her blood. Visions of darkness, of nightmares come to life, flooded her mind, and she tried to shut out the flash of intuition that was telling her to run. Where would she go?

When a hand closed over her shoulder, she screamed and tried to twist away, but the bony fingers held her fast.

"Rhiannon," the voice said, gentle and full of love.

She spun around, hand flying to her mouth, which was hanging open in shock.

"Mum?" she gasped, voice quavering with the remnants of fear that clouded her mind. "What are you doing out here?"

"I could ask you the same thing," Beth replied, drawing her daughter close and holding her still-shaking body in her arms. "Are you okay? What's going on? Honey, you must be so cold," she added, as Rhiannon's cloak slid open and revealed that she was naked beneath it.

Blushing furiously, she pulled the dark cloak more tightly around herself, then slowly raised her eyes to her mother's face. Beth sighed as she heard the sharp intake of breath, and saw the mingled emotions of fear, relief and love, and a sliver of disgust, that flashed through her eyes before she steeled herself and was able to meet her mum's gaze.

"Come on, you'll freeze to death out here. How about we go to the cafe for a hot chocolate, and you can tell me what's going on before we go home to your dad."

Rhiannon blushed again, and Beth looked at her quizzically, before understanding crossed her face. "Where are your clothes darling?" she asked gently.

Tears fell down Rhiannon's cheeks as regret settled on her brow. Her mouth tightened as she shook her head, and her mum knew she wasn't ready to talk just yet. Taking off her own long, thick coat, Beth handed it to her daughter, who gratefully pulled it on and did up every single button, not caring that her cloak bunched uncomfortably at the back. Modesty finally assured, she relaxed slightly and nodded that they could leave.

Beth took her hand, then switched the torch back to full so she could lead them out of the closely growing trees and back to the road. They trudged along in silence for a while, each lost in their own thoughts, but when the street lights brightened as they approached the village, Beth felt Rhiannon's steps slow, and could sense the growing reluctance and shame radiating outwards from her stiff body.

"So, would you like a hot chocolate first, or would you rather head straight home?"

Fear flashed across the young girl's face as a clap of thunder boomed overhead, and her mum took her hand again and turned in to the High Street. Glad that she could still sense her daughter's moods, Beth smiled to herself. Her husband Mike was the least scary man she'd ever known, but it was clear that facing her father was the last thing the shivering girl next to her could deal with right now.

Chapter 2

Shelter From the Storm

A bell tinkled as they opened the door to their favourite cafe and rushed inside into the warm and cosy dimness. Rhiannon scurried to the small table at the back of the room, close to the fire and more shadowed than the others. Beth smiled in greeting to her friend Kylie, who ran the cafe, and made a subtle gesture to ensure she didn't ask Rhiannon any questions when she brought over their drinks. Then, with a sigh of relief, she collapsed down into the soft, comfy chair opposite her daughter.

Now that the adrenaline rush of her search had drained away, she felt the weakness within her body and spirit, and cursed her illness. A shiver went through her, part anger, part cold, part deep sadness.

"I'm so sorry Mum, you must be freezing," Rhiannon said, embarrassed, as she saw Beth shivering by the fire. As much as she'd like to though, she couldn't return the coat, and the thought that she was making her mother suffer even more than usual through her stupidity broke her heart.

Forcing a smile, Beth waved away the apology, then waited for Kylie to bring their hot chocolates over then leave them in relative privacy before she spoke.

"Oh my darling, what were you doing out in the woods this late at night, with no clothes, no torch, no coat, nothing? Are you okay? Did anyone hurt you, or pressure you? And where are your clothes?"

Rhiannon shuddered, a flush rising in her cheeks as she wrapped her arms around her body, seeming to shrink in on herself as she huddled miserably across from her mother, and looking suddenly so young, so small, in the huge old armchair.

"It was just a prank with Debbie and Sue," she whispered, but as her mother's shrewd eyes raked over her, she knew she couldn't lie to her. Beth was immensely intuitive, and her disbelief was obvious.

"Okay, that's not true," she mumbled, resigned to having to reveal the truth, no matter how mortified it made her. "Only please don't tell Dad, okay? He'll ground me for months, for *years*. And I have definitely learned my lesson, I promise. *Please?*"

Beth took a sip of her hot chocolate, visibly enjoying the sweetness of the drink and the heady aroma of the steam wreathing around her face. It reminded Rhiannon of the mist that had reached out to wrap around her neck though, and she felt a chill rush up her spine.

Her mum leaned over and took her hand. "Oh honey, you don't have to be afraid to tell me anything. I'm not going to judge you, or be angry with you."

Tears pricked Rhiannon's eyes as she felt the truth of the statement. In some ways the fact that her mother understood her and would forgive her anything made this even harder. "Fine," she grumbled, but her voice shook a little as she tried to gather her thoughts. "I was trying to do a ritual, a healing ritual, to make you better," she finally admitted, voice a wisp.

Beth felt the words like a dagger in her heart. She doubled over, the pain almost physical, as she lamented again at what her illness was doing to her family. It devastated her, that her daughter felt that she had to take care of her now. She was the parent, the adult, *she* should be protecting her children, not the other way around.

Finally noticing that Rhiannon had stopped talking and was looking sharply at her, not sure whether to continue her explanation, she took a deep breath and motioned for her to go on, trying hard to mask her physical and emotional suffering.

"I've just been so worried about you, and so frustrated by my inability to cope with your sickness, or help in any way. But, well, Debbie's brother is home from travelling, and when I was there a few weeks ago, he told me he was an apprentice witch, and he could help me weave a spell," she revealed.

"So I've been meeting him after school, learning from him, studying this book of magic that he lent me and trying to impress him with my knowledge, so that he would teach me the spell. We did a practice ritual, and it was like the ones that Rose does, with candles and incense and the building of energy," Rhiannon explained. Her words tumbled over themselves as she tried to make her mother understand her intentions, and to defend her actions, and those of Debbie's brother too.

"So, you've been learning magic from this *man*?" Beth asked slowly, and her tone made Rhiannon feel like she'd been doing something wrong.

"He's not a man, not really," her daughter stammered. "I mean, well, I guess he's nineteen or twenty..." she trailed off.

"And does Debbie know that her older brother is meeting up with her *young, teenage* friend for magic lessons?" Beth continued, and the emphasis she placed on the words made Rhiannon feel dirty and ashamed, and judged, despite her mother's assurances to the contrary.

A blush stained her cheeks. "Well, he said the working would have more power if it was our secret, that it would contain the energy we raise in a purer form," she insisted, but even as she spoke the words, she began to doubt him, to doubt herself. And as it became clear just why he had sworn her to secrecy, she felt like an even bigger idiot.

She'd believed him, that talking about the spell with others would dilute its effectiveness. But now it was dawning on her that he'd just wanted to take advantage of her, and not let her have any allies, anyone who would question him, or encourage her not to go through with it, not to trust him. She'd been so distraught, so focused on her mum and the spell she wanted to weave to make her well, that she hadn't thought of anything outside of that.

Suddenly she looked up sharply at her mother. "How did you even know where I was?" she asked, and the look of anger on her mum's face made her quail before her.

"You mean, because you told me you were staying the night at Debbie's?"

Rhiannon shrugged her shoulders, her gaze slipping to the mug of hot chocolate in her hand, unable to meet her mother's eyes. Embarrassment swept over her, that she'd been caught out lying, yet she desperately wanted to know how Beth had known where she was, and that she needed saving.

"Debbie came over to borrow your history notes," Beth revealed, and Rhiannon cursed herself for her foolishness. Clearly saying she was with Debbie when she was actually with her brother was stupid – she should have said she was staying at Sue's, and let Sue know about it. Now she'd be in even more trouble – sneaking out with a boy and lying about it, lying about her friend, and Debbie knowing she'd lied about her too.

Trembling inside, she finally lifted her eyes to her mother's face. She still looked angry, but Rhiannon had to know everything now. "What did you tell her?"

"I told her that you were out with your dad, so she didn't know you'd used her," Beth snapped, and Rhiannon felt tears well, of gratitude but also of shame. Disappointing her mother, especially now, was the last thing she wanted to do.

"Honey, I'm not angry at you, I'm angry at him. And I'm trying to understand," her mum continued, and this time her voice was gentle. "What were you doing out in the woods? And why did you have no clothes on?"

"He told me that I had to come naked to the circle within the woods, so I was pure enough that I could draw down the goddess and borrow her power for the spell," she muttered, her earlier defiance fading away. "And that I had to do everything he asked of me, no questions asked, in order to please the gods and achieve my goal."

As she spoke she realised how ridiculous it sounded, how naive she'd been. Tears began to fall, and Beth reached over to take her daughter's hand and offer what comfort she could. But nothing could erase the mortification in Rhiannon's eyes.

"How could I be so stupid?" she cried, the force of her words making the hot chocolate spill out of her cup and on to her mum's coat. "Oh god, I'm so sorry!" Clumsily she tried to mop it up, but Beth's hand touched hers again, stilling her.

"Darling, the coat doesn't matter. I'm just scared for you, scared that you would trust some older guy and play into his hands like this. You've been to a couple of Rose's rituals with me, so you know that when you're working magic with others you should only ever do something you feel totally comfortable with, and that anyone demanding that you be naked and submit to their will is not a genuine practitioner. My goddess, I want to find this man and rip his heart out, that he could prey on a young girl like this."

"I'm not *that* young," Rhiannon snapped, trying for defiance again. She pushed her shoulders back and sat up straight in an attempt to regain some of her own power, her own confidence, but she couldn't convince herself, and at a sharp look from her mother, she slumped back into her chair.

"You've just turned sixteen Rhiannon," Beth said sternly, and she quailed at the use of her name. That always meant she was in trouble.

"I know that you feel grown up, that you're testing your boundaries and wanting to experiment and experience new things, but being naked in the woods in the middle of the night, all alone with a man who is clearly using the promise of helping you with magic as a way to make you vulnerable, is not going to teach you anything useful. He wanted to have sex with you, and how could you have fought him off all on your own?"

Rhiannon blushed scarlet. She hadn't fought him off, she'd been frozen, unable to move or do anything to get away, but she couldn't bear for anyone to know that. "Mum, it wasn't like that, I promise. He just wanted to help me help you," she implored, trying hard to believe that what he had done to her was part of the spell, and still had to be protected.

But with a shiver of fear she remembered the feeling of his hands on her body. And the chapter on sex magic he'd made her memorise. And the overtly sexual comments he'd made about her and others. And his promise to "initiate" her into magic. She was embarrassed to have to admit that she'd felt flattered by his attention, and all grown up – for once not the girl with the dying mum, but the girl with the power to *save* her mum.

Beth placed her mug back on the table with shaking hands. "Oh honey, it's not your fault. He took advantage of you, he knew how to flatter you to gain your trust. And magic is a powerful force, an intimate force, and it's easy to confuse the sense of connection you share with those you work magic with for a relationship of sorts. Did it really feel like one of Rose's circles when you worked with him?"

Shaking her head, Rhiannon stared morosely into her empty cup. How could she have confused the two? And how had her mother known that she needed saving, let alone where she was?

"It's a mother's intuition I suppose," Beth said quietly, startling her daughter, that she could read her thoughts.

"Seeing Debbie on the doorstep had me worried, since you were supposed to be at her place, so I meditated a little and took a chance that the vision I saw was a true one. But it was just luck that you'd left a trail between the trees that I could sense, and that Debbie came when she did, because goddess knows what would have happened if I'd been any later."

Rhiannon shuddered. She'd been late enough.

"It sounds like he's a smooth talker, and knew exactly how to make you feel comfortable with him, enough to reveal what you wanted so that he could pretend he could give it to you," Beth continued, and Rhiannon felt a deep unease that her mother seemed to be able to see into her mind.

"But darling, no one can do that. There is no spell to heal me — don't you think Rose would have already cast it if that was possible? That *I* would have?"

Rhiannon nodded, kicking herself that she hadn't realised even that simple truth. How could she have possibly thought that a teenage girl just learning magic would be able to do what even long-time priestess Rose Tyler could not?

"It's just my time honey, or it will be soon, and we all need to accept it," Beth said, heart breaking as she saw the fear and the grief etched so starkly in her daughter's face.

"I can't accept it," Rhiannon whispered, her voice cracked with pain, her eyes deep pools of hurt and anger.

"Well, we need to *face* it, even if we can't accept it," her mother said sternly. "And I need to know that you're going to be okay without me, that you will make wiser choices than you did tonight, because I won't be around to save you next time."

The cafe owner came over then with fresh mugs of hot chocolate for them, and Beth took hers from Kylie gratefully, her thin hands curling around the cup as she tried to warm herself. She wondered if her now-constant chill was a presentiment, a sign that death was fast approaching and the grave was calling for her. Railing at destiny and fate, she tried to pull herself back together, to be strong for her daughter. But her wander through the trees on such a cold night had really taken it out of her, and for a moment she wasn't sure she was going to be able to stand up from this comfortable chair by the fire and walk out into the sudden, unseasonable storm to get home.

It made her want to scream and shake her fists at the gods, to broker any deal with any devil to be granted just a little more time – time to see her beautiful daughter grow up. Right now their teenage girl was poised on the cusp of womanhood, and Beth was scared for her, and scared for her husband Mike too. He was a wonderful father, a wonderful man, but perhaps too soft and compassionate, too endlessly patient, to set any boundaries for their perfect yet precocious daughter. She didn't have the same fears for their son Brodie, knowing he was young enough to accept and adapt to the approaching splintering of their family. But her daughter…

As Beth's thoughts swirled, Rhiannon stopped obsessing over her own failings and really looked at her mother. She'd been trying to avoid that for the last few weeks, had thought she seemed fine. But as she peered at her across the table, she wondered how on earth she'd managed not to see the gaunt cheeks and sunken eyes, the grey tinge to her skin, the extreme fragility of her bones, and the skin pulled so tightly over them.

Was it the shock of her own situation and her narrow escape from it tonight that was making her so horrifyingly aware that her mum was wasting away before their very eyes? Making her even more afraid that she would soon leave them? How would she, her brother and their dad survive without her? Beth was the warm centre of their family, the glue that stuck them together, and Rhiannon doubted her own ability to step up, let alone her little brother and their father Mike's, to keep the family together.

It had shaken them all when Beth had gone to the doctor four months ago to get a migraine prescription, and mentioned in passing that she'd been feeling more tired than usual. All she'd expected was a lecture on her sleep patterns, instructions to meditate, and perhaps some iron and B12 supplements. Instead a routine blood test had seen her rushed off to hospital to undergo a gruelling round of chemotherapy, which had ravaged her body and broken her spirit.

But after six weeks of chemo sickness, she had rallied. Her doctor declared the treatment a success, and Beth looked and felt much better. They'd all headed to Scotland at the beginning of the summer holidays, and the sunshine, break from work, relaxation and family time seemed to have been just the tonic Beth needed. They'd all breathed a sigh of relief, and thought her illness was something they could put behind them.

Until four weeks ago, when the new school year had gotten underway, and Beth collapsed on her first day back at work. This time the treatment didn't work, although it had still ravaged her increasingly frail body, and she'd been sent home with medication to make her more comfortable, but little hope of being alive by Christmas.

The fierce warrior in Beth refused to accept it though, and she'd tried everything over the past month – from the herbal potions Rose brewed for her to acupuncture, reiki, a raw food diet and dozens of other supposed miracle cures people recommended – because she was desperate to survive for her children's sake. And she'd done a spectacular job of reassuring her kids and her husband that she was on the mend. Her skin was rosier, her body filled out, her attitude far more positive, and she'd promised she was getting better. But as Rhiannon gazed at her mother now, she suddenly wasn't so sure.

"You said after you saw the doctor this week that all your test results were better, and you were starting to improve, but that was a lie, wasn't it?" she demanded, while praying her mum would deny it.

Beth gazed at her serenely, managing with a great act of will to maintain a cheerful expression, before she slowly let out a breath and allowed her shoulders to slump, instantly looking older, sicker and even more gaunt than she had moments before. Rhiannon gasped, and Beth managed a tired smile.

"A simple glamour," she whispered. "Just a small trick, so that I didn't scare you and Brodie with my illness-ravaged body, and I didn't upset Mike even more than I already have."

For a moment she looked as though she would dissolve into tears, but Beth was clearly more practised in the art of magic than her daughter had known. A blush of colour returned to her cheeks, then they filled out again, and her air of reasonable health returned.

"I'm scared honey, scared that your dad will fall apart without me," she confessed. "How can I leave you all?"

Rhiannon leaned across the table and gently took her hand. "Oh Mum, please don't waste your energy on this! You need to be letting your body heal, not pushing it past its limits just to make it easier for us. Besides, you have been looking better, and that naturopath said her tonics would start to kick in now, and their effect will increase week by week, so I know you're going to be all right. You *will* get better, if you let yourself. If you stop wasting precious energy on glamours, whatever they are."

Beth smiled, and squeezed her daughter's hand. "You're right, of course," she said meekly. "And thank you my darling, you've been so strong, which is a huge help. Brodie is lucky to have you, and so am I."

Kylie walked over to them to ask if they needed anything else, but Beth shook her head as she thanked her. "We should be getting home, because it is a school night after all," she replied, with a pointed look at Rhiannon. "But thank you so much, you know how much I love your hot chocolate."

The cafe owner leaned over and helped Beth stand up, disguising it as a friendly hug, and Rhiannon smoothed her mother's coat over her hips and thanked Kylie for the drinks, before putting an arm around her mother's shoulder and walking with her out into the chilly night. Desperate to distract herself from the present, from reality, Rhiannon turned to her mum.

"Tell me again about when you and Dad fell in love..."

Chapter 3

Making Friends and Falling Hard

Beth... Twenty years ago...

The tall blonde woman stood alone, gazing out the window, lost in her own little world. There was an air of melancholy clinging to her, and a shred of anger radiating from her, that kept the other guests from approaching her. She'd known the people milling around her family's formal lounge room all her life, and she was not in the mood for any of the usual cheek pinching and "my you've grown up since last time I saw you" cliches she knew she would be subjected to.

It burned her with a cool rage that she even had to be here. Two years ago she'd left this small English town, and her narrow-minded, money-loving parents, determined to escape their influence and find out who she was when she was out of the shadow of her perfect sister Jennifer, and no longer under the control of her cold, cruel and brittle mother Patricia.

A year spent working and studying in London straight out of school had allowed her to spread her wings, but her heart had really opened up, and she'd discovered new aspects of herself, when she'd moved to France. She'd travelled around the country for months, from glamorous beaches to ancient forests and sacred standing stones, from the tiniest villages to the bright lights of Paris, the City of Love, learning the language, making exciting new friends, and soaking up the culture and the history of this fascinating country. Her time there had given her new confidence, revealed her independent streak, and helped her glimpse the potential she had within her.

So the swell of boring conversation around her, delivered in boring accents by boring people over boring food, had her gritting her teeth in frustration and longing for escape. She'd loved the job she'd found six months ago, as nanny and English tutor for a chic Parisian couple and their two cherubic young daughters. Why had she put that on hold to come home?

Cursing herself again for her stupidity in caving in to her mother's demands, she paused mid mental mind lashing, then froze as she sensed said nemesis approaching. Jaw clenched, she turned to face her, steeling herself for another lecture about what a disappointment she was, how much worse her attitude had become, and why she must definitely not embarrass her father at this most important social gathering.

"Elizabeth, *darling*," Patricia said, the fake smile on her face doing nothing to distract from the fierce chill in her eyes. "I thought you were going to wear the beige dress," she hissed, and Beth felt a sliver of satisfaction at her tiny effort at rebellion.

"Sorry Mother, I thought the pearls you insisted I wear went better with the black dress," she replied, voice as insincere as the smile she pasted across her own face. Her amusement died quickly though, in the wake of the older woman's scornful expression, and she wondered why she bothered.

Her moments of defiance never gained her anything, and she felt the oppressive weight of family expectations closing in on her again. In Paris she had been herself, had been free, but all that was gone now. Across the room her older sister laughed, and Beth shrank back into herself, her carefully constructed independence and sense of self falling from her as the guests swooned over perfect Jennifer.

Why her parents persisted in trying to mould her into their image of the ultimate daughter she had no idea – her sister was everything they'd ever wanted in a child. Couldn't she be enough for them? Jenny had just graduated from university with honours, and topped her year, but even more importantly, to their mother at least, she was about to marry the perfect son-in-law, and would no doubt soon produce the perfect grandchildren, at the perfect time no less.

A spark of bitterness flared within her as she looked across at her sibling. It was Jenny's fault she'd had to leave her magical life in Paris, with a job she loved, friends who liked her for herself, and even a passionate romance.

Then she sighed. She couldn't hold on to her rage at her sister. She'd never been anything but kind to her, albeit aloof, and it wasn't *her* fault that their parents liked her better. Jenny had even let her choose her own bridesmaid dress, a black one they knew their mother would hate, but Jenny had stood up for her, insisting it was not negotiable. Reluctantly she acknowledged that her sister wasn't to blame for the fact that she was stuck here. Her mother on the other hand...

"I need some air," Beth muttered, turning to go, but Patricia clutched her arm in a vice-like grip and glared at her.

"We talked about this, and you are going to be sociable," her mother said sternly. "Now come and speak to the Starks. You know your father is trying to close the deal with them, so make an effort for god's sake!" Then, pasting on her dazzling but hideously fake smile again, Patricia turned back to the room and dragged her daughter with her.

"Anne, darling, how have you been?" she purred. "You remember our daughter Elizabeth don't you, the one who's been away travelling?" The disdain in her voice was impossible to miss, but the smartly dressed woman she was addressing held out her hand to Beth, a genuine smile on her face.

"Of course sweetie, how have you been? Your father mentioned that you'd been off on a grand and wonderful adventure. Paris, wasn't it?" she asked kindly, and with real interest. "That would have been incredible."

Beth took a deep breath and tried to relax her racing heart, nodding as enthusiastically as she could in response.

"Et j'espère que vous avez rencontré aussi de charmants garçons français," Anne said, grinning, and Beth was amused to see her mother's horrified expression as she and Mrs Stark spoke to each other in a language she couldn't understand. It also made her smile that this woman would want her to have met some lovely French boys – a thought that would horrify her mother if she knew.

"Un ou deux," she replied cheerfully. "Et j'ai fait de merveilleux amis. Mais je ne pouvais pas manquer la véritable roman de Jenny, alors je suis ici." She *had* made some wonderful friends, but sadly she couldn't miss Jenny's true romance, so here she was. She tried to keep her tone light, tried to keep the anger and bitterness from her face, but it was tough.

Anne laughed, which cheered her up, but Patricia looked uncomfortable and ready to lash out at both of them for being so rude as to exclude her from the conversation. God, did she *always* have to be the centre of attention?

"Is Mike here too?" Beth asked Mrs Stark, switching back to English so her mother would know she was doing her bit for the family plan. "I haven't seen him for more than two years, which sounds crazy. Where did that time go?"

Taking her arm, Anne smiled at her, eyes twinkling with mischief, and led Beth over to the other side of the room, leaving Patricia stranded and momentarily lost for words.

"Mike sweetheart, you remember Beth don't you?" Anne asked her son, and Beth could have kissed her for using her preferred name, instead of the formal version her mother used, which always filled her with dread.

"You used to keep each other company during those infernal business conferences our families attended – although she's all grown up now, and has been living in London and Paris and thoroughly enjoying every minute. Beth, I salute you for your courage in leaving the safety of the village, of the familiar, and going off to create your own life."

Gratitude swept over her at the recognition and acceptance in this woman's tone, and for the first time since returning home she felt somewhat understood. Her good mood stayed when Mike turned to face them, hand extended, and a cheeky smile lighting up his face.

"Of course I do, but I'm not sure Beth would remember me. I was just a kid when she headed off to see the world," he replied, voice friendly and a little deferential, and much deeper than it had been the last time she'd seen him.

Beth held out her hand too, and muttered that of course she remembered him – then as their eyes met and their fingers touched, she froze, jolted by the spark of electricity between them. *What the hell was that?*

Confused, she stared at him. He was right. When she'd been stuck talking to him in the past, he'd seemed so much younger than her, thin and gangly and obsessed with comics and skateboards, and perfectly content to live in this village forever. She'd thought that terribly lacking in imagination – she couldn't wait to escape their small town, and meet new, older guys. Now though, he had definitely grown up, and filled out too. And irony of ironies, he was more attractive and seemed far more mature than any of the guys she'd met in London or Paris, not counting her supposed boyfriend.

A stab of pain shot through her as she recalled their last meeting, but she masked it with a smile. "It's good to see you Mike," she said, as soon as she'd composed herself a little. "Do you want to leave the oldies for a while? I've got some new music we could listen to."

Nodding happily, he followed her upstairs, then blushed as she opened the door to her bedroom. Grinning wickedly, she pulled him inside, then took pity on him and pointed to the purple beanbag near the window.

"Don't worry, I'm not going to drag you into bed with me and have my way with you," she teased, although she realised it wouldn't be the worst choice she'd made of late. Instead she handed him a pile of CDs and told him to pick one, then sat down on the floor opposite him.

Once the music started they both relaxed, and she spoke about her travels, and some of the places she'd been to and the people she'd met, while he told her his plans for university and what he dreamed of doing with his life. He seemed genuinely interested in her and what she thought, which was so nice after her last... well, was boyfriend even the right word?

She'd had a passionate love affair with Andrew, an English guy she'd met at an alternative music festival in Brittany. They'd been together for five months, her falling deeply in love with him, and he making all the moves and acting as though he felt the same way. Then a week ago, out of nowhere, he'd told her that he had to return to London, effectively ending their relationship.

She'd been totally heartbroken, so when her sister invited her home for five weeks of festivities – a bridal shower, hen's weekend, kitchen tea, dress fittings, rehearsal dinner and eventual wedding ceremony – she'd agreed. Admittedly it had been with an ulterior motive – she'd managed to bury her dread at being with her family under the excitement that she would be able to continue her romance with Andrew. But he'd been less than thrilled when she'd told him she'd be going back to England too and could still be with him – and he'd disappeared from her life as quickly and mysteriously as he'd entered it.

"Are you okay?" Mike asked, breaking into her reverie.

Slowly she became aware of her surroundings again. God, had she just totally zoned out? "I'm so sorry Mike," she stammered, and was surprised to realise that she actually was. "That was rude of me, I apologise. It's been quite a culture shock to come back home – and back into my old childhood bedroom no less," she shrugged. "But tell me more about your life. What do you do around here for fun these days?"

Three nights later, Beth found herself standing at the bottom of a staircase in a new age store filled with crystals, candles, cauldrons and velvet robes. Soft golden light spilled out onto the landing from a room at the top, and the gentle murmur of voices seemed to beckon her forward.

But she halted. What the hell was she doing here in some hippie shop, about to climb the stairs to spend time with the very villagers she'd been so eager to escape? This was madness, surely, trying to fit in here.

Cursing under her breath, she spun around, determined to flee – and walked straight into a woman dressed in a long and floaty deep green gown, dark hair tumbling loose and wild around her kind face, and a beautiful pink crystal nestled above her heart. She was probably around her mother's age, late thirties or early forties, yet she couldn't have conjured a person more different than the uptight Patricia if she'd tried.

"Welcome," the woman said softly, with a smile that filled Beth with a sensation of joy and comfort. *How was she doing that?*

"I'm Rose, the priestess leading the circle tonight," she continued. "Are you here for the ritual? It's just up here," she added, shepherding her back towards the base of the stairs.

Beth shook her head. "I was just leaving. I'm, well, a friend told me I should come along tonight, but I don't want to intrude. I should go," she stammered.

"Nonsense Beth, you're more than welcome," the enigmatic figure replied.

Shock crossed the younger woman's face, but Rose chuckled. "Don't worry, it's no magic trick," she said, her voice soothing her fears. "Mike mentioned that you might be coming. He's upstairs with Violet. Come on, we can go in together," she added, taking her arm and steering her up the first steps. "You'll see that there's nothing to be afraid of."

And despite Beth's misgivings, Rose was right. It was one of the strangest yet most magical nights of her life. Suddenly she didn't miss Paris any more, or yearn for Andrew, or feel stressed about her overbearing mother. She felt understood, and a part of something, welcomed with open arms into a community of warmth and caring. How was that possible?

When she entered the sweetly scented candle-lit room with the priestess, everyone was standing in a circle, hands linked. Beth looked around wildly, heart beating in panic, with no idea of what to do. They all looked so natural. Like they belonged.

Again she turned towards the door, determined to leave this time, but her companion gently propelled her further inside, guiding her over to two women with long, loose hair who were wearing flowing gold dresses. Unlinking their hands, Rose walked between them into the centre of the room, then beckoned Beth forward, smiling as the gold-clad women each took one of her hands, including her in the circle.

The priestess made her way to an altar piled high with fresh flowers and golden candles. Then, raising her arms above her head, she began to speak, and Beth stared at her, awestruck by the air of power that was swirling around her, and through the room. She could even feel it touching her.

Most of them went over her head, yet Rose's words, as she welcomed everyone then explained that she would invoke the god and the goddess and call in the elements and the directions, touched a part of Beth's soul that she hadn't even been aware of, and she felt her heart breaking wide open and filling with joy and light. Despite her nerves, and her fear that she would do something wrong, she felt herself falling into the enchantment of the ritual, and opening herself up to all the potential and possibilities of her life, things she'd never dared to contemplate before.

When people started to move, she nervously copied the women who'd been holding her hands, as it seemed that each person was taking it in turns to leap over a huge pot. Or was it a cauldron? That sounded far more witchy, she thought with a giggle. It was burning fragrant herbs in the middle of the room, and the sweet scent spiralled around Beth, weaving itself into her mind and imagination.

But nerves shot through her too, as she watched each person speak aloud their wishes and hopes for the coming month as they leaped over the fire. Just as she thought about slipping away again, she felt Rose's eyes on her, and would swear she heard her voice in her head, telling her to relax. And the next person who jumped over the flames did so in silence, with a dreamy look on his face as he sent his wish skyward, which gave her enough confidence to leap across the fire, as gracefully as she could, and offer up her own silent prayer.

Later, as the evening wound down, Beth sank into the meditation the priestess led, no longer worried that she might appear foolish. And when the deities were farewelled and the circle was closed, she felt warm and floaty, stripped of stress and expectation. She hadn't noticed just how weighed down she'd been feeling this week, how trapped, until some of the load had lifted, like magic, during the ritual. In this moment, a sensation of joy and peace enveloped her.

Self-conscious again as people broke into groups, she anxiously searched for Mike. He was talking to someone across the other side of the room, and Beth wondered whether it would be okay to go over and say hello, or if she should wait. She didn't want to interrupt him, or annoy him in any way, to turn him off her before they'd had a chance to take anything further.

Before she could decide what to do, a pretty, faery-like girl with long dark hair and a vibrant green and gold dress skipped over to her corner and held out a hand to her.

"Hi, Beth?" she asked, voice kind and welcoming, and just a little unsure. When Beth nodded, the girl scooped her into a hug. "I'm Violet, Rose's daughter. Mike said you might be coming tonight, so I wanted to say hello."

A rush of jealousy stabbed at Beth, as she thought about how wonderful it must have been for Violet, growing up with such an amazing mother. She couldn't bear to be in the same room as hers, the same house, but here Violet was, working magic alongside hers. Clearly she loved and respected her mum, and the feeling was obviously mutual. Who'd ever heard of a teenager wanting to spend time with their parents?

She bet Rose understood her daughter too, and encouraged her and accepted her and loved her. She probably even got on well with her friends and approved of her boyfriends. For a moment her resentment boiled over, until she realised Violet was still speaking, and tried to shake off her bitterness and pay attention.

"Come and have something to eat – you need to ground yourself after a ritual," the girl was saying, and although Beth didn't understand what she was talking about, she obediently followed her over to a long table laden with food.

"I feel all weird and floaty if I don't have a cookie straight away," Violet explained, grabbing Beth's hand and dragging her to the end that was filled with sweet treats. Taking a bite out of a piece of shortbread, and motioning for Beth to do the same, she poured cups of tea for the two of them, raised an eyebrow to enquire if she wanted milk, then grinned.

"Mike won't be long, he's just talking to our history teacher – trying to get another extension," she explained, rolling her eyes in mock horror. "But he told me that you've been living in France. Is it amazing? Do you think you'll go back? Are the people as wonderful as I've heard? Oh, I'd love to go there some day," she continued wistfully, leaving no space for Beth to answer, but amusing her with her bubbly personality and sweet, innocent smile.

"I want to walk through the countryside there, clamour into the ancient burial mounds, dance in stone circles..."

The girl's eyes had a faraway gleam in them as she finally paused for breath. "Gosh, I'm so sorry, here I am babbling on at you without pause, asking you questions but giving you no time to answer them. And you might want some quiet time after the ritual?" Violet offered, although she was clearly eager to keep chatting.

Beth surprised herself by shaking her head. "It's fine, really. I am a bit spacey, but I'm glad you came over. I was feeling a bit shy, not knowing anyone," she admitted. For some reason she liked this kind young woman, who looked so vibrant and alive with her crown of ivy and flowers woven through her hair, so she cheerfully answered her queries about France, while furtively casting her eyes over to Mike every minute or so.

"Everyone here is really friendly and welcoming," Violet said, breaking into her thoughts, and Beth realised she'd been gazing at Mike and daydreaming about him again. *Oops!* Reluctantly she brought her attention back to the girl she was standing with, and was supposed to be conversing with.

"You'll have a room full of friends in no time," she continued, and Beth smiled with relief that Violet didn't seem offended by her vagueness and lack of attention.

"So are you and Mike school friends?" Beth finally asked her, casting another wistful glance in his direction, and hoping to get a bit more information about him.

A strange look flitted across Violet's face, but it was gone before Beth could identify it, and her bright smile returned. "You could say that. We've been dating since... I don't know. Mum loves telling everyone that we declared our engagement when we were six years old, and planned how many kids we'd have by twelve, but I think she's exaggerating a little," she revealed, laughing and rolling her eyes. "But it seems that he's finished hassling Mr Arthur," she added, and took Beth's hand to lead her over to Mike.

Struggling to control the fiery blush that lit up her face at this admission, Beth barely heard Violet's next words. *He had a girlfriend.* Panicking that she would give away her distress, she quickly tuned back in to the conversation.

"Hey you, you're neglecting your guest," Violet scolded Mike, but her voice was gentle, with a smile in her words, and he glanced up at her with such a loving expression that it pierced Beth's heart. "I've got to help Mum pack up, but it was lovely to meet you Beth. I hope you'll come to more rituals, and maybe hang out with us sometime?" she asked, leaning in to give her a quick hug.

"And I'll see you tomorrow," she said to Mike, with a grin and a hurried kiss on the cheek, before flitting off to Rose's side.

Beth was amazed. She wouldn't be leaving her boyfriend alone with a strange woman, who'd been invited to the event by said boyfriend, for even a minute. Yet what did that say about her in comparison to Violet? Was Rose's daughter so secure in her relationship with Mike that she didn't feel threatened by a pretty girl coming along to spend time with him?

Or did it mean that it had never occurred to Violet to cheat on Mike, and so she assumed that everyone else was as principled as she was, and it simply hadn't crossed her mind that she had anything to worry about? And what did it say about *her*, that she assumed every man would cheat?

Feeling foolish, Beth admitted to herself that when Mike had invited her to the ritual, she'd assumed it was, well... not a date necessarily, but an expression of some kind of interest. Yet sadly that seemed to simply be wishful thinking on her part. And a sign that he was just so kind and lovely that he'd welcomed her into their circle, as Rose and Violet had, because she so clearly needed friends here. Oh god, did he feel sorry for her?

Desperately she tried to remember what he'd actually said, and turned beet red when she realised his invitation *had* been totally innocent, a friendly gesture to someone who had been away from the village for two years, and a friend of the family no less. It seemed that it was only her that sized up every guy she met as a potential partner, and only her who didn't trust people. Who assumed a boyfriend would cheat if he was left alone to talk to another girl for five minutes, in public no less.

Not that she had, but did this indicate that she thought *she* would cheat on someone, and thus expected that everyone else was capable of doing the same thing? It wasn't like Mike had been sneaky in any way – he'd told his girlfriend all about her, and let her know that he'd invited her along tonight. Hell, even Violet's mum Rose knew who she was. And both women had welcomed her with open arms, as a potential friend, and allowed her into their magical circle. And yet here she was, tainting their kindness with her suspicions and bad intentions. *What was wrong with her?*

And the stupidest thing of all? She didn't even want a boyfriend, did she? After the heartache of Andrew letting her down, hadn't she vowed to be single for a while, to concentrate on making female friends and considering her future? Well, when she wasn't trying to figure out how to get in touch with her former flame and somehow win him back.

Besides, Mike wasn't even her type. He was younger than her for a start, which she'd never liked the idea of. It would be fine in your late twenties or your thirties, but he was still in high school for god's sake, and at this point even a couple of years seemed like such a huge gap of life experience and maturity. Not that he or Violet came across as young by any means – and really, of the three of them, it was she who had acted the most immaturely in this situation.

Mentally shaking herself, she met Mike's eyes. He was offering her friendship, and she knew that was precious.

It dawned on her suddenly that before she'd been with Andrew, she would have been honoured to have been considered a friend by these people. His abrupt change of heart had made her suspicious, cautious and paranoid, destroyed her self-esteem, and left her wondering why anyone would like her.

Although that wasn't fair, she reluctantly acknowledged. Her mother had done all of that to her long before she'd fallen for Andrew, and she'd felt as though she was in competition with her sister – for attention, for love, for praise – her whole life. Sighing, she decided it was time for her to rediscover herself, and to be a person she could be proud of. A person that people would like for who she was.

"Hi Mike, it's lovely to see you again," she began, forcing cheer into her voice. "Thank you so much for inviting me. I met Violet and Rose, and they're both so lovely, and so welcoming. As I'm sure you've gathered, I haven't exactly been thrilled to be back in town, so I really appreciate it. You have no idea how good it felt to be part of something so inclusive," she added, and was embarrassed to hear her voice tremble.

Mike smiled at her, and she felt a pang of sadness and regret at the openness and innocence of his expression. She really wished that she could view the world from such a positive and non-bitter perspective.

"So what did you think?" he asked nervously, and she was surprised to see worry in his eyes. "It wasn't too weird for you, was it? I know it's not everyone's cup of tea, and I was a little afraid of exposing Rose to ridicule if you thought... well, *was* it okay?" he finished hopefully.

"Oh my god, it was amazing," Beth gushed. "And really touching and inspiring. I'd love to be part of any more ceremonies or gatherings that take place while I'm stuck here, if that's all right?"

Chapter 4

Fear and Loathing

Rhiannon... Today...

Finally they were walking up the path to their front door, and Rhiannon trembled with fear as she saw the lights still on. She couldn't face seeing her father, not right now. Not in her mother's coat, when there was no way she could explain why she was wearing it. Beth squeezed her hand.

"It's okay honey, your dad is out in the kitchen. I'll go through and see him, and you can go straight upstairs."

"Please don't tell him," she begged her mum again, as lightning flashed overhead. "I couldn't bear it if he knew." She started shaking, and Beth drew her into a soothing hug.

"I promise I won't tell him," she assured her, and although she could see it pained her, Rhiannon knew her mum would keep her word. "It's your story to tell, and I hope that you'll feel able to share it soon, so your dad can help you too. But right now you need your own clothes, your own bed. Not more questions, not more retelling and remembering."

Sighing with relief, a little of the stress left Rhiannon's body — then she stumbled on the first step, and would have fallen to the ground if Beth hadn't caught her. Remembering too late just how weak her mum was, guilt shivered down her spine as she felt her stagger under her weight. God, she just couldn't do anything right. She was a total mess.

"I'm so sorry," she whispered, voice choked, but her mum smiled bravely and shook her head. Taking a deep breath, Rhiannon pulled herself upright and offered her mum a shoulder to lean on, then helped her up the last few steps, through the front door and into the darkened hallway.

"Do you need me to –" she whispered, but Beth cut her off.

"I'm okay my darling, I promise. Your dad will help me upstairs. Now you go up to bed, and get warm, and try to get some sleep. Everything will look brighter in the morning."

Beth kissed her on the cheek then shuffled her way slowly through to the kitchen, where Mike was making school lunches and washing up their dinner dishes. They were such ordinary, everyday tasks, taken so much for granted, yet who knew how many of them she would still be around to take part in?

Rhiannon stood where she was for a moment, wincing at how painful it looked for her mum to walk even that short distance unassisted. Her heart constricted with fear as she heard her dad asking where she'd been, but Beth did as she'd promised, telling him they'd been out for a hot chocolate, and how wonderful it had been to spend some girl time together.

Smiling grimly, Rhiannon dragged herself up the stairs and opened her door. Seeing her bedroom exactly as she'd left it shocked her, as though she'd expected it to look different now that she was so changed. Grabbing her warmest pyjamas, she headed to the bathroom and turned the shower on as hot as it would go. Then she stood under the steaming water, shivering despite the temperature.

Tears spilled down her face, mingling with the water, as she felt his hands on her again. She'd managed to deceive her mother, to pretend that nothing had happened and she'd been able to save her foolish daughter in time. Save her honour, prevent her shame. But that was a lie.

Now, with no one watching, Rhiannon leaned against the cold tiled wall and sobbed as each awful moment played itself over and over in her mind. She hadn't had a chance to reflect on what had happened until now, too busy putting on a brave face in the cafe, pretending she was fine for her mother, pretending she was fine to herself. She wasn't fine though.

Her stomach churned as new memories swamped her. And as she recalled the look on his face, the cruel twist of his mouth and the bite of his fingers on her flesh, she bent over and threw up, the milky chocolate drinks she'd gulped down swirling over her feet and down the drain.

Her shivering became more violent, and although there was soon nothing left in her stomach, she couldn't stop the retching, or the bitter bile burning her throat. But eventually that passed too, and she slid down the wall and crouched in the tub, hot water still streaming over her, needling her, a kind of pain that was somehow soothing.

Shuddering again with revulsion, she picked up the soap and scrubbed at her skin, trying desperately to wash away the touch of his hands, the stench of his breath, and the bite marks on her neck that made her flesh crawl to think of them. Would she always feel there was some kind of sign above her now, letting everyone know what had happened to her, marking her out and showing the world her shame?

Finally she became aware that the water had turned cold, but she stayed stubbornly under it, enjoying the discomfort, until her dad knocked on the door and asked if she was all right. After shouting a vague reply, she jumped out and dried herself, then pulled on her pyjamas and brushed her teeth, carefully avoiding the mirror. She couldn't face the sight of herself, and didn't want to know if she looked as changed as she felt.

Back in her bedroom, tension thrummed through her as she walked over to the window and stared out into the raging dark. It felt as though the room was shaking, that the earth was moving under her, but it wasn't that. It was her.

The anger rushed through her blood, pounding through her veins, and she felt her heart quaking, roaring, hammering and darkening with deep red rage and quivering purple shame. How could she face her father now? And how could she ever look her mother in the eye again after what she'd seen of her tonight? Her weakness. Her fear. Her total vulnerability. And – there was no way around it – her complete stupidity.

When Evan's face flashed into her mind, her blood boiled again, and she sensed before she heard a booming clap of thunder as it exploded overhead, perfectly matching her fury. Saw a bolt of lightning as electric as her emotions crackle across the sky. Listened to a roar of agony that had been torn from a throat or heart she didn't immediately recognise as her own.

Her vision was painted blood-red with anger, with danger. A small part of her marvelled at how similar the two words were, how intrinsically linked, but the rest of her was noticing the corresponding flashes of lightning and booming of thunder that hit whenever her emotions threatened to overwhelm her.

Panic rose in her mind, in her chest, closing tight fingers around her throat, cutting off the air she so desperately needed. She clawed at the invisible bonds, but when she was unable to shift them, she almost laughed. Tonight she had feared she would die in the woods – yet now here she was, about to be strangled by her fear in the safety of her own home. Drowning in this storm that wouldn't give her even a single moment to come up for air.

Abruptly she felt herself wrenched from her body and thrown out into the raging downpour. As rain splashed down on her, she struggled to comprehend how she could be outside in the wildness of the storm when she'd been in her bedroom just moments before. Sucking in a desperate breath that seared her throat, she tried desperately to understand what was happening. It didn't make sense, yet here she was, standing in the back garden in the savage fury of nature, dripping wet, wind battered and rain sodden, and freezing cold.

The air around her crackled with electricity, and with a growing sense of doom, she somehow understood that a lightning bolt was about to flash across the stormy sky and fry her. Even more scary, she couldn't bring herself to care.

It wasn't that she wanted to die, but tonight's events coming on top of her mum's battle with mortality had pushed her to a dark place she wasn't sure she could make her way back from, or even wanted to try. It was that part of her that somehow knew that *she was the lightning, she* was the thunder. *She was the storm.*

As she raised her arms to the sky and prepared to become one with it all, the hammering of desperate knocking reached her. She was wrenched back into her bedroom, where she found herself standing by the window, paralysed with shock. How did she get back inside? How had she been transported outside in the first place? *How had she created a storm?* Fear washed over her, and confusion clouded her heart. She was so totally, terribly scared.

There was one more loud bang on her door, then it swung open, and a flash of lightning illuminated the frail silhouette of her mother leaning against the door frame, looking even smaller than she had in the cafe.

"Oh my darling, I'm so sorry," Beth said, dragging her back from the window and drawing her shivering form into her arms. A shivering form that was suddenly dry. How was she not dripping wet? And what was her mum sorry for?

"Do you need to talk about it more?" Beth asked softly. "I'm here if you need me. And we can find someone tomorrow, a counsellor or something, if you'd rather not confide in me."

Rhiannon stared at her mother, at her gaunt face and black shadowed eyes, and tried to comprehend what she was saying to her, to comprehend what was happening to her, but nothing made any sense. Before she could ask any questions though, her father stuck his head around the door and smiled at her across the room.

"Hey Rhi, I'm glad you and your mum could have some girl time tonight. And I was thinking, maybe this weekend you'd both like to go over to Smithfield, have high tea at the hotel, go shopping? Brodie and I have been talking about a boys-only fishing trip, although I'm not sure he really understands what that entails, or that we'll be out in the boat all day. But it sounds like fun."

He grinned, not seeming to notice how deathly quiet his wife and daughter were as they stood together in the darkness by the window. "It's getting late though, so we should probably all hit the sack, yeah?"

Numbly Rhiannon nodded, and her mum gave her one last hug before she followed her husband out into the hallway.

"I love you my darling. Thank you for tonight," Beth said softly. "And it will all be okay, I promise."

As her door clicked shut, Rhiannon threw herself down onto her bed and pulled the quilt up over her head. The tears came again, but this time she managed to muffle them, scared that she would wake her brother in the room next to hers.

For a while she prayed for an escape from the awful images that were playing over and over again in her mind, then she prayed for sleep – but her dreamscape was even more terrifying than her waking visions. During the long night she woke often in panic, then drifted back to sleep before waking abruptly again, until soon she couldn't tell what was real from what wasn't, as the awful flashbacks of her time in the woods melded with her nightmares of creatures chasing her and wanting to eat her.

When her alarm forced her back to consciousness the next morning, her pillow was wet, soaked with tears, yet her throat was dry and her mouth was parched. Her bones ached too, and her skin tingled and burned.

The storm had shattered her. She was broken, like fallen twigs, fallen leaves, fallen honour; strewn across the ground, across her bed, across her life. Broken and lost in the wreckage.

Chapter 5

The Fault In Her Stars

For long moments the next morning Rhiannon lay in bed, trying to think of an excuse not to get up. Couldn't she just stay under the covers for the rest of her life, hide away from the world? After last night's fiasco, she was terrified of facing her mum, of seeing the disappointment and fear in her eyes, and more embarrassed than she'd ever been.

But slowly, reluctantly, she dragged herself out of bed, avoiding making eye contact with herself in the mirror again. She picked up the velvet cloak she'd been wearing the night before, wincing as she felt the scratches on her back sting, and scrunched it up tightly, angrily, and buried it under a pile of old clothes she'd never wear again in the back of her closet.

Then she hastily pulled on her school uniform, choosing the long-sleeved shirt even though it was a warm day. There were dark purple bruises on her arms and shoulders from where he'd held her in a vice-like grip, and she was in no mood for explaining, no mood for questions – and in no fit state to see them herself and be reminded of what had happened.

Not that she needed anything physical to make her remember. Her mind recoiled in horror as she saw his face again as he'd lurched towards her, and her skin crawled as she recalled the sensation of his large, rough hand on her naked waist, pulling her towards him.

Desperately she tried to think of something else – but the alternative wasn't any better.

The fragility of her mother's body as she'd sat in the huge armchair in the cafe the previous night, dwarfed by the high-backed brocade and momentarily stripped of her glamour, tortured her. How could the human body be so delicate? So easily ravaged by illness, by injury... *by assault?*

"Life is good, people are good. I choose to see the good in every person and every situation," she muttered, her mind latching on to a mantra she vaguely recalled from a ritual she'd attended with her mother a few months ago. It didn't seem to help, but she doggedly kept on, repeating it over and over in her mind as she forced herself to pick up her school bag and walk downstairs, dragging her feet and dreading who she would have to face.

Tentatively she tiptoed into the kitchen – and breathed a sigh of relief when she found it was empty. It took her several moments to realise how weird that was. Where was everyone? Had her clock stopped in the night or something?

Shouldn't her mum be up, forcing a glass of wheatgrass juice down her throat and trying not to gag? Shouldn't her dad be trying to slurp down one final cup of coffee before he left for the office? Shouldn't her brother Brodie be spilling his breakfast all over the table and laughing at the comic he was reading?

Lost in thought, she jumped when she heard a crash from her parents' bedroom. Her bowl of muesli slipped from her hands, milk splashing all over her uniform before the crockery smashed around her feet, but she didn't even register it happening before she was running up the stairs. "Mum? Are you all right?" she called out, panicked. "Dad?"

Her father peered out of their room, face white. "Darling, find the car keys would you? No, wait... um, where's Brodie?"

Distracted, she shrugged, her mind racing, before she finally recalled the answer. "Didn't he stay at Ben's last night?"

"Of course," her dad muttered. "Thank god."

"What's wrong? Is Mum okay?" she begged.

He stared at her, expression vague. "Hmm?"

Snapping into action at last, he turned back, then came to the door holding Beth in his arms. Rhiannon stared, aghast. Her beautiful, vibrant mum was a shell of her former self. Last night she'd looked like a wraith when the glamour had slipped, but today she was twice as pale, twice as frail, twice as deathly ill. Her face was grey-tinged, and she looked like she weighed no more than a child, no more than her five-year-old son Brodie, so thin had she become, so small did she look crushed against her husband's chest. And he was clearly terrified, and terribly unsure of himself.

"She passed out," he finally whispered. "And… I can't even tell if she's breathing." There were tears in his eyes, and he was gulping in air in desperate, ragged gasps.

Rhiannon's heart lurched at the horror of how fragile her mother had become. Yet she was so brave. What had happened to her in the woods last night was nothing compared to what her mum was going through every waking moment, battling this illness, battling her mortality, battling her fear – and on top of all that, trying to convince them all that she was okay, to save them any pain.

She really had to get over herself. Stop feeling like a victim, and being so selfish, and focus on what was important. Her mum was in pain, was in hell, and the last thing she needed was to deal with her daughter's stupid drama on top of everything else.

Something switched over inside Rhiannon, as she accepted that she would have to take control of the situation. Brushing past her dad, she walked into their room and gathered up her mum's coat, the one she'd let her daughter wear the night before, and tucked it gently around her frail body.

Then, trying not to breathe in the scent of illness that pervaded the room, she picked up her mum's largest handbag and threw one of her favourite dresses into it, along with her hairbrush and the blend of essential oils she loved. After that she raced into the ensuite, opened the cabinet above the sink and grabbed a new toothbrush, some toothpaste and the pain meds she'd seen her mum taking.

It was all done in a moment, then she was leading her dad out of the room and down the stairs, picking up the car keys from the hall table and marching them outside. Opening the back door of the car, she pushed her dad, still holding her mum, inside, and shuddered at the fear etched deep in his face.

"It will be okay Dad," she murmured, although she was no longer sure that was true. "Put the seatbelt on, it should wrap around both of you," she added, feeling another shiver of horror at just how tiny and insubstantial her mum had become. So frail and fragile, as though she was shrinking before their eyes. Not planning a dramatic exit, just resigned to fading slowly away, until she disappeared altogether.

Not bothering to put the L plate on the back window, Rhiannon slid into the driver's seat, muttered a quick prayer, then reversed out into the street. Fortunately there was little traffic, and the hospital wasn't far, because she didn't know how long she could maintain her confidence. She'd only had a few driving lessons, and she breathed a sigh of relief when she saw two empty parking spaces in front of the emergency entrance.

Screeching to a halt, she threw on the handbrake, turned off the ignition and pulled out the key, then flew around to the other side and helped her dad, still clutching Beth close to his chest, out of the car. He looked unsure of what to do again, so she pushed him in front of her and through the sliding doors. Once inside, she ran ahead, frantic, calling for a doctor.

The duty nurse took one look at her dad's face, and the bundle in his arms, and paged someone. Then she grabbed a wheelchair herself, wrestled Beth out of his arms and into it, and wheeled her down the corridor. Mike stared after her, the look of helpless terror still on his face, until the nurse turned back and gestured impatiently at him to follow them.

Rhiannon watched as they moved through another set of doors and disappeared from view. The burst of adrenaline that had given her the strength to take charge and get her parents to the hospital ebbed away, and she shivered, her lip trembling and her eyes starting to well as she slid down the wall onto the floor, all the nervous energy that had animated her through the morning's crisis leaving her as fast as it had arrived. Dropping her head onto her knees, she wrapped her arms tightly around her legs and finally let the tears fall. Sobs shook her body as she cried as silently as possible.

She cried for her mum, and the pain she was so clearly in.

She cried for her dad, who was struggling so hard to keep it together, but who seemed to be retreating further and further away from them, as though his fate was linked to his wife's.

She cried for her little brother Brodie, who couldn't understand what was happening, but was reacting to the fear everyone around him was feeling.

And she cried for herself. Right now she needed her mum more than ever. How could Beth be planning to leave her all alone? Didn't she know how much the family needed her? How on earth were they going to cope without her?

Time stopped and started and stopped again, until finally one of the nurses came out to the corridor, and Rhiannon gazed up at her, desperation in her eyes, fear in every sharp angle of her body. Part of her wanted to know what the white-clad woman standing over her was going to tell her, because maybe it was good news. Another part of her was sure it could only be bad though, and quailed in terror at knowing with certainty. Yet the not-knowing was crushing her.

"You can go to school now," the nurse said brusquely. "Your mother has stabilised, so she will be fine."

Her face paled as Rhiannon gasped, and she looked regretful and suitably uncomfortable over her choice of words. "Well, she'll recover from this setback," she clarified. "And then she'll continue her battle to overcome the greater issue."

The "greater issue". Wasn't that a handy euphemism. Rhiannon's face was blank, but her eyes were pools of hurt. "But what caused this?" she begged, even though she didn't really want the answer. Not if it was what she suspected.

Was it her fault her mum was even worse today, after having to go out into the storm and rescue her last night? Because if that was the case, she knew the guilt would destroy her.

"She's just pushed herself a bit too hard," the nurse said. "We're going to keep her in today so she can rest, and we'll observe her overnight too, just to be sure. But she'll be okay."

As Rhiannon trembled on the floor, she didn't look like she was okay, or that she thought her mum would be okay, or that she believed anything would ever be okay again, but she smiled grimly at the nurse, even as her heart broke within her chest.

"It's my fault," she whispered.

The nurse shook her head, clearly impatient to get back to the ward. "It's no one's fault, it's just part of your mother's illness," she said, voice coolly professional, briskly reassuring. "Now, you head off to school, and make your parents proud of you. You can come back this afternoon, okay?"

The young girl nodded absently, but continued to sit where she was on the floor, shoulders hunched, unable to convince her legs to lift her to her feet.

"Do you need me to get someone to drive you?" the nurse asked, her suddenly clipped tone revealing her exasperation.

Although all Rhiannon wanted to do was curl up on the floor right there and fall into oblivion, she finally managed to stand up and haul her bag onto her shoulder. Feeling something sharp in her pocket, she fished out the keys to the family car.

"Could you give these back to Dad for me?" she asked, and the nurse smiled at her.

"Of course dear. And are you sure you're okay to walk to school? I'm sorry if I seemed pushy, it's been a busy morning…"

Rhiannon stared at her blankly for a moment, then forced herself to speak as calmly as she could. "It's fine, I'm just struggling to focus on anything else but Mum right now, so I guess a walk will do me good," she replied, and reluctantly made her way outside. It was cold in the shade, but she liked the numbing effect of the wind on her face, on her ears, on her hands. It matched the feeling of her heart, frozen inside her, incapable of thought or action or care.

"Happy Birthday Mum," she whispered as she gazed back at the hospital, then slowly, sadly, turned away.

Dragging her feet up the front steps to school was even more difficult than she'd imagined. It felt as though she was wearing concrete boots, which got heavier with each foot fall.

She didn't know how she was going to face her class, let alone Debbie. And speak of the devil…

"Hey, did you see my brother last night?" she demanded, eyebrows raised and voice a strange mix of anger and approval.

"Wait Deb," Sue interrupted, noticing Rhiannon's pale face. "Are you okay? How's your mum?"

Tears filled Rhiannon's eyes, and she scrubbed at them impatiently, annoyed at her weakness. "We had to rush her back to hospital this morning," she whispered. Sighing, she tried to convince herself as well as her friends that it was only her mum's ill health that was upsetting her, but there were tears of fear and shame and self-loathing too. Her face reddened as she felt Debbie's brother's hands on her shoulders again, felt them moving lower, felt his horrible hot mouth running over her body.

When a hand closed on her arm, she jumped and cried out, spinning around to face her attacker.

"Rhiannon, hey, it's just me," her teacher Ms Henderson said quickly, apology in her tone, kindness in her eyes. "Are you all right? Your dad called, and told me Beth had a bad turn this morning. If you need to go home…" she offered, her words hanging in the air between them.

Shaking her head as she tried to shake off the feeling of revulsion creeping over her, she somehow choked out enough words to let them know she would rather be at school, with her mind on other things, while the doctors did what they could. Her two friends switched to sympathy mode, and she was grateful for their concern – and for the change in topic their teacher had wrought. What on earth was she going to say to Debbie next time the conversation turned to her brother?

Relief filled her as her friends headed off to history while she got ready for English, and she somehow managed to sleepwalk through the first half of the day. But as she grabbed her books from her locker after lunch, a guy from the year above her pushed his way over to her and looked her up and down in a way that made her skin crawl.

"So, did you have fun last night?" he asked, loudly, as he leered at her. "Evan said you had a late night rendezvous planned, and I bet you were a fire cracker in the sack. What do they say about witches – easy and slutty? How about meeting *me* in the woods tonight?"

Shock froze Rhiannon in place, even as every instinct in her demanded she run far away. Icy fear clutched at her stomach, and she felt her head spinning and her cheeks burning, even as all colour drained away. Bile rose in her throat, and she knew she was about to throw up. Not that even *that* could make her feel any more mortified than she already was.

Horror rolled over her in waves – horror that anyone else could know what had happened to her in the woods, horror that Debbie and Sue would soon find out, horror that this one incident would become what she was known for and defined by for the rest of her high school days.

But even worse than the horror was the shame. She wanted the floor to open up and swallow her whole. How could she face her fellow students, face her friends, face her family? Her mum had promised she would tell no one about it, and she hadn't – yet it seemed as though the whole town would soon know anyway. She felt the shame spiralling around her, hot and heavy, felt his hands holding her down and his breath on her face. Stars spun above her as blackness closed in around her, and she was dimly aware of the rolling crash of thunder overhead as she slid to the floor.

When she floated back to awareness, she was sitting on the ground – again – propped up against her locker, and Ms Henderson was standing over her, lines of worry etched deeply in her forehead and around her mouth. "Rhiannon, please, are you okay?" she repeated, voice urgent. "What happened?"

Rory stood behind her, wide-eyed and nervous.

"Um, I'm okay," she whispered, then laughed inwardly. *Yeah, real okay.* "I'm sorry."

"There's nothing to be sorry about, I just want to know if you're all right. Are you sick? Has this happened before? What do you need? What can I do?"

Rhiannon shrugged. "I was just a bit dizzy, but I'm okay now, I promise. I guess I've been too stressed to eat properly or something, worrying about Mum," she muttered. *Dear god, could this day get* any *worse*? She'd wanted no attention, no detection, but somehow everyone seemed to be focusing on her, seemed to know she was having a terrible time.

"Rory, go to the vending machine, get her a chocolate biscuit," their teacher barked, pulling some money out of the bag she had slung over her shoulder. "Hurry up."

He scurried off to do as she'd asked, then fled the moment he handed it over. There was a fleeting sense of satisfaction for Rhiannon that he looked so regretful of the chain reaction he'd set off. Ms Henderson waited with her, making sure that she ate every bite of the cookie. Only when she'd finished the whole thing did some of the panic leave her face, and her expression soften. "Are you sure you're okay?" she finally asked.

Rhiannon nodded miserably. *Okay.* What did that even mean? And why did people keep asking her if she was, when she so clearly wasn't? But she wasn't going to throw up the biscuit she'd been made to eat, so she guessed that could pass as okay in this world where no one knew she was dying of shame.

"Why don't you go back to the hospital and see your mum," her teacher suggested, snapping her back to the present. The present where she wanted to disappear from the world. "You can make up this afternoon's classes tomorrow."

"But Brodie —" she began. How hard would it be for him to cope with seeing their mum looking as frail as she had that morning? It was scary enough for her to see it.

Ms Henderson held out her hand and gently hauled her to her feet. "I'll call Ben's mother — I'm sure Brodie can go home with him this afternoon, and stay there until you and your dad are ready to pick him up. Now go, and please give my love to Beth," she said, and Rhiannon remembered belatedly that her teacher was a close friend of her mum's. She wasn't the only one who was hurting.

Running all the way to the hospital left her with a bad stitch, so she paused for a moment, leaning against the low entrance wall as she gathered her thoughts and tried to control her gasps for air. She'd been so desperate to get here — but now that she'd arrived, all she wanted to do was run away. To bolt for home, fly up the stairs to her bedroom, bury herself under her huge quilt and hide away from the cruelty of the world.

But she owed her mother more than that. First she had to apologise again about last night, for dragging her out into the cold woodland to save her, then adding insult to injury by taking her coat. And then... well, she really needed a hug, and for her mum to hold her and comfort her and reassure her that it wasn't her fault. Then tell her how to recover from it and move on. *Surely that wasn't too much to ask, was it?*

With a great effort she pulled herself together, mentally and physically, hoisted her backpack over her shoulder, and walked through the hospital gate. Electricity started to crackle in the air around her...

Chapter 6

Beth... Twenty years ago...

From her bedroom window upstairs, Beth gazed down at the path to their front door, and smiled as she saw Violet walking slowly along it. It filled her heart with joy to know that this girl liked her, that she wanted to be friends with her. She'd been shocked when Rose's daughter had called her last week to invite her to an upcoming ritual, then suggested meeting up for a coffee that very afternoon. And today she'd come to pick her up so they could go to the movies with Mike, since for some reason she still hadn't figured out, they both seemed to like her, and want to spend time with her.

But now she sighed as she watched the dark-haired girl standing at the door of their huge house. Violet looked nervous, as though the obvious wealth made her feel out of her depth, slightly less-than – which unfortunately was her mother's intention. Money had never meant anything to Beth, and she'd always hated that her parents used theirs to intimidate people, and intimidate *her* friends, especially as they had no plans to share it with her. Which was fine, since she didn't want it. It just hurt when people judged her on it.

As Violet stared down at her clothes then looked even more nervous, Beth felt butterflies in her stomach. She knew that right at this moment Violet was wondering what she was doing here, and why Beth would want to be friends with her. It had happened so many times growing up, and she'd become used to people making excuses not to play with her, or visit.

But before Violet could change her mind and go back home – leaving her to spend another day alone in this cold, empty house – Beth's haughty, condescending mother opened the front door and stared imperiously at her friend.

"Can I help you?" she asked, in a tone that suggested that was the last thing she would want to do.

"Hello Mrs Bishop, I hope you are well. I just came over to pick up Beth, because we're going to the movies today," Violet stammered anxiously.

The woman continued to glare at her, giving nothing away. "And *you are?*" The sneer in her voice was pronounced.

Beth cringed. As if she didn't know exactly who she was – everyone knew everyone in this village, a fact that had suffocated Beth when she was growing up. This was just another ploy of her mother's to ensure people knew that she was more important than them – in her own mind at least.

"I'm so sorry, my name's Violet, Violet Tyler. I'm a friend of Beth's, and Mike's," she explained, her voice still a little shaky. No doubt she was starting to realise just why Beth wanted to escape her family and spend time with her and Mike, anywhere but here.

At the mention of Mike's name, the stiffness in Patricia's face softened a little, and she thawed a degree or two. "Oh yes, Michael is a lovely young man. I must invite him, and his parents too, back over for another cosy dinner," she said, and there was a note of triumph in her voice when she saw Violet's expression.

"You know, he's the first man Elizabeth has been interested in that I've approved of," she added, now clearly starting to enjoy herself at Violet's expense.

Beth screamed inwardly. How could her mother tell this girl that she was interested in her boyfriend? For her part, Violet was looking vulnerable, overwhelmed and confused, trying to understand what the woman was referring to. The expression on Patricia's face made it clear she was insulting her guest, but Violet wouldn't understand why a stranger would want to do that to her. God, what Beth wouldn't give to swap parents. She adored Rose, and even Violet's dad sounded lovely.

Still, at least Violet would really believe the stories about her mother now. Sometimes as she recounted them they sounded outlandish, even to her, but her friend was experiencing first-hand the haughty woman who lived to upset others, for no other reason than her own amusement.

She never worried who the hurt was aimed at – family, friend, associate, stranger – as long as she derived the pleasure of inflicting pain on someone. She was a psychic vampire, draining the life force from people, draining their confidence, making them doubt themselves, making *her* doubt herself.

It was time for her to intervene, and save sweet Violet from the discomfort of being in her mother's presence. Picking up her bag, she clattered down the stairs, to let her friend know she was on her way, and cut her mother off mid-sentence.

"Why didn't you tell me Violet was here?" she asked, keeping her voice level with a supreme act of will, and wondering how long Patricia would have grilled her friend before she allowed her inside, or at least let her daughter know she'd arrived. "I'm so sorry," she said, turning away from her mother and smiling at Violet. "Do you want to come in, or should we head out now?"

"I guess we should go," she replied, trying not to sound relieved. She was always so unfailingly polite, even when the person didn't deserve it. "Mike will be getting there any minute."

Beth turned to the hall table, grabbed her keys, then pushed past the ogre in the doorway to freedom. "I shouldn't be late home Mother, so I'll see you then," she said flatly, then fled down the path to the street. Violet watched as the weight her friend had been carrying on her shoulders lifted from her with every step they took away from the house, and within a few blocks she looked like her normal self again.

"I'm sorry," Beth offered finally, embarrassment colouring her voice and her cheeks. "I should have just met you both in town."

"It's okay," Violet said softly. "I just, wow, I'm so sorry you have to tiptoe around her so much. I know I'd always be so scared of offending her – too scared to do anything at all."

Beth nodded sadly. "Yeah, I'd forgotten just how claustrophobic it is to be in the same house with her. She just breathes disgust and contempt, and I can't win – if I appear too cheerful and happy she complains, if I'm supposedly too miserable she complains. If I do nothing I'm lazy, if I do something I'm criticised for it not being perfect," she sighed.

"But enough of that, this is our time, so we shouldn't dwell on my pesky home life. Soon enough I'll be back in London or Paris and can put all this behind me."

"So you'll leave once the wedding is over?" Violet asked, and Beth felt a warm glow when she realised there was a layer of disappointment in the other girl's voice.

Smiling, she inhaled the beautiful sunshiny aroma of the blossoms as they walked around the edge of an apple orchard. "I can't stay, even if I wanted to. Mother and I bring out the absolute worst in each other – we shouldn't live in the same village, let alone the same house. But I'll really miss you and Mike," she said. And as she spoke she realised that she actually would miss them, and she'd miss both of them, not just Mike.

They lapsed into silence for a few blocks, but it was a comfortable one, where they both thought about the growing friendship between them. For her part, Violet was overjoyed to have found a friend, especially one who was open to coming to rituals with her. Most of her classmates at school thought she was weird on a good day, and working with the devil on the bad ones.

She did have a black cat, Shadow, and her mother was considered a witch by some because she ran ceremonies to celebrate the seasons and honour the phases of the moon. But there was nothing evil about that, they were just attuning themselves to the energy of the earth, an energy anyone could tap in to.

And Beth was equally grateful that Mike and Violet had welcomed her into their lives, and into their relationship. That they cared for her because of who *she* was, not which family she came from, and encouraged her to be herself. Not like her parents, who wanted to turn her into something *they* thought she should be. It was sad – her mother had no idea what she wanted to do or be, and zero interest in finding out.

So maybe the three of them really would stay in touch when she left, not just mouth the platitudes then forget. Maybe they would write letters to each other, or send postcards at least. Maybe they'd invite her to their wedding. And perhaps Violet would even visit her in France, and she could take her to the sacred places of the west coast she knew she longed to see.

Excited at the possibilities, Beth wrenched her attention back to her friend, just as they reached the cafe where they were meeting Mike after his morning delivery job. Her heart sped up when she caught sight of him. He'd snagged their favourite booth table, and as Violet opened the door and they walked over to him, he gazed at her with such love and welcome on his face.

Beth was embarrassed to admit that she was jealous of the way Mike looked at Violet, and of all the little moments they shared without even being conscious of them.

The way they leaned in to kiss every time they paused before crossing a road. The way Mike shielded her from wind, rain and rowdy revellers with his body. The way they both deferred to each other and never made a decision without checking with the other, in a way that was considerate rather than co-dependent. The way Violet could soothe Mike when he was upset with just a touch of her hand or a flicker of warmth in her eyes. The way they were each so hyper-aware of where the other one was, even when they were away from each other in a crowd, speaking to other people.

It was so beautiful – and it made her sad and envious. She yearned for someone to love her the way Mike loved Violet, but she swallowed it down and tried not to reveal her resentment, because spending time with them, even when it filled her with longing, was so much better than being stuck at home.

She was still surprised they wanted to hang out with her though. If she had a boyfriend like Mike, she wouldn't be letting a pretty girl tag along on their dates – but they were both so sweet that their compassion for her overcame their desire to be alone together. When she'd pressed Violet about this she'd just laughed, and told her that she and Mike had forever to be alone together, and they liked her and enjoyed spending time with her. In another time, another place, she and Violet might have become life-long friends.

Beth's relationship with her sister was also improving, as they made an effort to spend time together away from their parents. She had always been a little jealous and a lot in awe of Jenny, who was just that bit too much older than her to have been a friend or confidant, and who seemed to have such a great relationship with their mother. But her older sister laughed uproariously when Beth mentioned that.

"Oh sweetie, I spent every day of my life desperate to leave home, to get away from her and her condescension, her expectations, her casual cruelty. Why do you think I studied so desperately in my final two years? I knew which university I wanted to go to – perhaps not coincidentally, the furthest one from here – and I knew that I'd need a full scholarship, because she'd already told me they would pay for me to go to the local college but nowhere else, so they could keep an eye on me I suppose, keep controlling me."

She smiled fondly at her sister. "Did you think you were the only one she tried to manipulate? I wanted to study science, which she never approved of, and so I had to make it happen for myself. When I decided to major in renewable energy, I kept it a secret so she couldn't pressure me to change it. She still thinks I studied business, so I could go into the family firm, and I've done nothing to dissuade her from that belief."

Beth stared at her sister, mouth open in shock. She'd always thought Jenny was the perfect daughter, always doing exactly what their parents wanted and expected. But it seemed she was just a much better liar than her. "No way!"

Jenny laughed at the expression on her face. "Absolutely. And when I fell in love with Josh my first year at uni, I never told her about him. I knew she planned to set me up with one of Father's business cronies, to try to marry me off for their own advantage – just like she's going to try to force you to marry Mike, so our family's business can merge with his."

Fortunately she didn't notice Beth's hiss of indrawn breath, or the flush that stained her cheeks.

"I'd actually planned to elope, so she couldn't do anything to stop me, but Josh convinced me otherwise. Although he would also prefer to get married back home, on a windswept beach in the Orkneys with only seals for witnesses, he convinced me that fighting her on this just wouldn't be worth the grief, not long term. It's one day, one small thing, and if she feels like she's won on this issue, she may be less inclined to anger on other things."

"But shouldn't your wedding day be just the way you want it? Be special?" Beth asked.

"Neither of us are that fussed about the wedding, we just want to be married, to be husband and wife. The ceremony is for others, it's only the vows we make to each other that are important – and whether I say them barefoot on a beach in Scotland or wearing stupid shoes in a church here in front of a cast of thousands of people I don't know, none of that changes the magic of what we are committing to. And if it helps smooth the way for me to finally admit to Mother the job I'm actually taking, it will have been worth every torturous moment."

"Wow!" Beth breathed, amazed. "I had no idea."

"Of course it will be much easier confessing to my degree and my new employer from a safe distance," Jenny said with a laugh, before turning serious. "But I am sorry that I left you with them, and that I wasn't strong enough to stay," she continued sadly.

"You have no idea how happy I was when I heard you were going to London to study, and even more so when you moved to France. I figured you would be far enough away from her to be able to live your own life. I really had to search my conscience before I invited you to the wedding, because I know how weak I become in her presence, how much easier it is to bend to her will than to fight her, and I didn't want you to feel that you had to come home for it just for me. But I'm glad you did," she said suddenly. "I've really missed you Beth."

Beth smiled, incredibly touched. Underneath the resentment, she'd always adored her sister, and to know that she cared about her too made the suffering of her trip home worth it.

"Besides, I hoped that together we could be strong enough to stand up to her, and to shift the power in our dealings with her, and I think we have. I feel braver because you're here, and I hope you feel the same way. That's why I was so determined to let you have the bridesmaid dress you wanted – it became a representation of us making the decisions we wanted despite her," Jenny said with a grin.

"I know it sounds silly, to feel that a simple dress is worth fighting a battle for, but it seemed symbolic somehow, like the tide started to turn when she capitulated on that."

Hugging her sister, Beth nodded eagerly. "That meant the world to me. And I know it's just a dress, but it was you standing up for me that was so important, even more than the dress itself. I always figured that you agreed with her, that you thought I wasn't good enough, that I didn't live up to our supposedly *honourable family name*," she said sarcastically. "I thought you would think I was stupid too, wanting a black dress, so you defending me against *her* was really touching."

Jenny took her hand. "Oh sweetie, I'd never think that. She's always driven me crazy, but I was so desperate to get away myself, I tried to seem as though I was going along with her ideas until I had the strength and the means to escape."

Beth sighed. "Well, I could definitely learn from that, because you fooled me. I guess I need to swallow my pride and pretend I agree with her a little more often." She laughed, trying to make it sound like she was joking, but she vowed that she would start that very night.

A sharp, panicked knock on her door a few days later woke Beth from a surreal dream, and she sat up in bed and rubbed her bleary eyes as she tried to shake it off.

"Yes?" she called out.

Her sister burst into the room. "Quick, get up! There's a spiritual fair on today, a few villages away, and if we can leave before Mother gets back from the hairdresser, she won't be able to stop us from going."

"What?" Beth asked, staring at her through sleep-dull eyes.

Jenny grinned. "Come on, you said you wanted more magic in your life! Isn't that why you like that Violet girl?"

"Well, partly, I guess," Beth admitted, wondering if that was true, and suddenly feeling bad about it.

"So come on, let's go! There are psychics and healers and tarot demonstrations and fire eaters and clothes stalls and all kinds of things. It will be fun!"

Smothering a yawn, Beth tried to think. She'd never been a morning person, and part of her wanted to curl back up under the covers and sleep a bit longer. But escaping her mother's plans for the day was definitely tempting, and Jenny looked so excited. She'd never taken her sister for the new age type, but it seemed there was a lot she didn't know about her.

"Okay, just give me a minute and I'll get dressed," she finally said. "Do I have time for breakfast though?"

Jenny jumped up and skipped to the door. "Nope, no time. We have to leave fast, but I'll toast you a bagel while you put some clothes on and you can eat it in the car. And there will be coffee once we get there, I promise."

Laughing at her sister's enthusiasm, Beth dragged herself out of bed and threw on her most colourful dress, hoping to somehow match Jenny's early morning energy. Then she brushed her teeth and ran downstairs, the thought of their mother coming home early and stopping their adventure adding speed to her steps. Soon they were heading off down sunshine-dappled laneways, music turned up and laughter bubbling between them. Beth couldn't remember the last time she'd spent any real time with her sister, and she was grateful for these precious moments.

The fair was busier than they'd expected, and filled with colour and sound. Stalls selling everything from crystal bowls and Tibetan bells to velvet dresses, silver jewellery and herbs dotted the field, and vivid-hued tents advertising gypsy fortune tellers and psychic mediums already had lines outside their doors. And over it all, the smell of frying food, baking treats and freshly brewed coffee hovered, drawing them in.

Jenny raced over to the drinks cart, and quickly handed Beth a steaming mug of coffee. "Is all right with your world now?" she said, mock-serious, and her sister laughed.

"Yes," she admitted sheepishly. "And, um, I'm sorry I was so grumpy before. Thank you for dragging me along despite that – this looks like it will be fun. And it's so nice to be doing something together, just the two of us."

For the first hour they simply wandered around, checking out all the stalls, admiring the beautiful items for sale, trying on clothes they wouldn't usually wear, pausing to observe artists at work, and being amazed by all the different people.

Beth smiled as she watched her sister watching a juggler, her face radiant. "Are you happy Jenny?" she asked wistfully, when she finally caught her eye.

"Well, I've been pretty stressed while I've been here – being around Mother always does that to me – but yes, I really am. Josh and I have a wonderful life up there, and I loved my studies, and can't wait to start working in the field. There are so many amazing renewables projects in northern Scotland, and I've already accepted a job with my mentor, who I did work experience with, and I'll start there as soon as I get back home. Of course Mother still thinks I graduated with a degree in business, and I won't correct her. I just don't have the energy for another one of her arguments," she said, rolling her eyes.

"And I'm glad you're happier now Beth. I was worried when you arrived. You seemed really sad, but you've been looking so much stronger the last few days. Are *you* happy?"

Taking a big sip of her second coffee, Beth gazed around the field, trying to gather her thoughts and decide how much she should share with her sister.

"Hey, you don't have to tell me anything," Jenny said, touching her shoulder and peering more closely at her.

Beth smiled. "No, it's fine, I want to, I'm just not sure where to start. I was really happy in London – it was amazing to discover who I actually was, once I didn't make every decision based on how Mother would react. And France was beautiful. I travelled around the countryside for a while, spending lots of time submerging myself in the sacred places there, which whispered to me of freedom and faith and my own self-development." Her face glowed as she spoke, and Jenny smiled with relief.

"And I fell in love with Paris, and with the family I was working for – I felt like I'd come home. I was looking after children, educating them, which is what I've always wanted to do. I even investigated part-time courses I could do there to get my qualifications while still enjoying my job with them."

Throwing her arms around her sister, Jenny hugged her tight. "I'm so glad," she whispered. "And you will be an amazing teacher. You're so kind and empathetic." When Beth froze, she released her hold on her and peered into her eyes. "But?"

"God, I don't know," Beth groaned, casting her eyes skyward. "I met a guy, the usual story. We fell in love, at least I thought we did, but then just after he'd convinced me to move in with him, he suddenly announced that he couldn't be with me any more and disappeared back to England. So now I'm torn between going back to Paris, to my life there, or setting up in London again and trying to get in touch with him. Ah, sucks to be me I guess," she said, then shrugged.

"But enough about that, this is your time. The countdown to your wedding, to the start of your new life. I really am so happy for you sis," she grinned, the term of endearment she'd never used before not feeling as strange as she'd expected.

"Thank you sweetie," Jenny replied. "And your time is coming. How about we go have a psychic reading, hmm? Ask the gypsy woman to tell you when your tall, dark and handsome new man will sweep you off your feet."

Beth's cheeks reddened as an image of Mike popped unbidden into her head, and she quickly agreed in order to shift Jenny's focus off her, even though she wasn't sure she really wanted to know her future. But if someone could give her hope that one day she'd meet a guy like Mike, it might stop her obsessing over him and then feeling guilty about Violet.

Arm in arm, they wandered over to the row of rainbow-coloured tents, and gazed at the small signs pinned to each entrance. A woman with a clipboard approached them, and asked what kind of reading they were looking for.

"I'd like a general reading please, and my sister would like a future love reading," Jenny replied, handing over the money for both of them and shaking off Beth's offer of cash. The woman indicated the nearest tent, a bright green one, and Jenny ducked inside, then she led Beth further down the row and pointed to a red tent, with a sign announcing Mirella the fortune teller.

"Thank you," she murmured, then nervously went inside. She had no idea what to expect, but the sweet smell of the incense reminded her of Violet's mum Rose, which put her at ease, and she gazed around with great interest. An elderly woman with long black curls streaked with silver sat at a small round table, wearing a bright scarlet dress and illuminated by candles.

"Come child," she said in a raspy voice. "Take a seat here."

Her voice sent a thrill of fear through Beth. For a moment she was scared by the strangeness of the woman, the oddness of the charms around her neck and the mystery of the darkened space, and wanted to flee back outside into the sunshine. It felt dank inside, but more than that, it was uncanny, with an Otherworldly chill to the air.

"Sweet child, there's nothing to be frightened of," the woman said, voice more soothing this time, and Beth was reassured by her tone, and impressed that she'd picked up on her nervousness. Then again, it probably didn't take a psychic to realise she was feeling uncomfortable.

Pushing away her anxiety, she walked slowly over to the fortune teller and sat down opposite her. The woman gestured for her hand, and she reluctantly held it out to her. Mirella's hands were clammy but her fingers were soft, and a shiver ran up Beth's arm as the woman traced the lines on her palm.

"You're a restless soul," she began. "Couldn't wait to leave home, spread your wings, eh?"

Beth nodded.

"And you've been across the seas, and were happy there," she added, looking up at her quizzically.

Beth nodded again. Was she supposed to be agreeing though? Was this woman just reading her reactions, garnering clues from how she responded to what she was told?

Mirella laughed. "Some people do give it all away, which can influence the divination, and then they only hear what they want to hear anyway. You're right though, it's good to be a little bit sceptical in a reading, and in life. And you shouldn't take everything I say as gospel – this reading will be true for today, but your future can change from day to day, hour to hour, depending on the decision you make, the path you take, the person you pursue, or don't."

Beth stared at her, suspicious now. What did this woman know about her?

"What do you know about yourself?" Mirella shot back, and smiled as Beth squirmed a little. "What do you *want*?"

Conflicted, she racked her brain. How much did she want to reveal of herself? Yet what was the point in holding back? She'd never see this woman again, and she was wasting her own time, and Jenny's money, if she asked anything other than what she actually wanted to know, deep down. She could ask about her relationship with her mother, but that was no use – she was past the point of no return with her, and somewhat surprisingly, she realised she was actually okay with that.

So, taking a deep breath, for calm and for courage, she opened her heart. "I want the love that Violet has. I want a guy who looks at me the way Mike looks at her. Who cares about me, no matter what. Who is kind and considerate, and patient, and who will make a great dad one day."

"Done!" the woman cackled. "But be careful what you wish for dearie." And she stood up abruptly and left through a gap at the back of the tent. Surprised, Beth sat for a while, wondering if she would return, and growing increasingly anxious. Had she just made some kind of deal with the devil? What did the woman mean, "done"? She was just supposed to reveal what would occur in the future, not make it happen. *Right?*

Desperately she tried to remember her exact words. She'd told the woman she wanted a love like Violet had, hadn't she? A chill ran up her spine as she recalled her answer. She'd said she wanted the love that Violet has, not *like* Violet has.

Feeling deeply unsettled, she made herself wait another five minutes, just in case Mirella came back and she could ask her to undo whatever she'd apparently done. But the fortune teller didn't return, so slowly, hesitantly, she made her way back outside to find her sister.

Chapter 7

Darkness Falls

Rhiannon... Today...

The closer Rhiannon got to the hospital entrance, the more her pace slowed and her feet dragged. She wasn't sure she had the energy, or the strength required, to see her mum looking so sick, and her dad looking so scared. Their little family would implode if Beth died, and the fear of that possibility paralysed her.

For long moments she stood out the front of the building, staring up at the second floor windows, unable to walk through the doors. Again she found herself in limbo, in that liminal state between knowing and not knowing, where fear for her mother was still balanced equally with hope, and she could pretend for a second that all was well, or would be. But she couldn't stand out here forever – at some point she had to go inside and face the doctor, and the prognosis, and discover whether her world would ever feel right again.

Steeling herself, she forced herself to march up to the door and slipped inside, trying to ignore the hospital stench – antiseptic mixed with the aroma of boiled vegies, sweat and fear – that sought to strangle her. A nurse she hadn't seen before smiled and asked if she could help her, but Rhiannon shook her head and headed for the stairs. Her heart lifted though. The smile had given her hope – yet it evaporated the minute she stepped onto her mum's floor, and the nurse she'd seen that morning stared at her with red-rimmed eyes and a look of quiet panic.

Time. Sound. Life. Everything halted around her, and she felt as though she was wading through thigh-deep mud, so achingly slow was her progress down the corridor to the room at the very end. Every instinct inside her was urging her to turn around and flee, to run as fast as she could in the opposite direction, to get as far away as possible from this place, from this life, from this looming death.

Her stomach clenched in fear, and a cold sweat broke out all over her body. She couldn't do this. She couldn't know such an awful truth. She didn't have the strength.

Just as she was about to give in to her basest urge and escape from this building that suddenly felt like a tomb, her father poked his head out from around the furthest door, and the broken look on his face froze her where she stood.

"Dad?" she whispered, voice ragged.

Mike tried to speak, but his mouth just opened and closed, unable to form words, and she saw in his eyes that he couldn't think a coherent thought either.

She rushed into his arms, but there was no warmth, no comfort there, as her father's body shook and his unfocused gaze took her in without comprehension of who she even was. His blank expression chilled Rhiannon to the core, and she feared the worst, while not able to get any real confirmation out of him either way.

Dread clutched at her heart, and her blood ran ice-cold with fear, but she had to know. Gently disentangling herself from her dad, she took one tiny step after another until she stood in the doorway to her mother's room. Hope flared again as she gazed at the figure in the bed, face relaxed and peaceful, body less thin, less fragile, than it had seemed in Mike's arms that morning. Her mum looked like she was sleeping, and Rhiannon walked quickly towards her, hand stretched out to touch her cheek, to hold her in her arms.

But as she got closer, terror seized her, and she jerked backwards when she noticed the grey pallor and unnatural stillness of the body. This couldn't be her mother, couldn't be the vivacious and energetic woman who never stopped moving, whose face was always rosy with excitement, or passion, or the simple joy of being alive.

A strangled sound came from the doorway behind her, and she sensed someone approaching her, reaching out for her.

"No!" she screamed, as she turned away from the bed. "This can't be right! Do something!"

The nurse took her arm, but she shrugged it off.

"She can't be dead, okay? She's not dead, she's just under the anaesthetic still, right? She'll wake up any minute and talk to me, won't she?" she demanded, but her voice came out sounding far less certain than she'd been hoping for.

"Rhiannon," the nurse whispered, gently, calmly. "Come outside, come and be with your dad."

Horror washed over her, the answer clear though the nurse hadn't actually replied to any of her questions. Wildly she gazed around the room, drowning in panic, in denial, in anger. Distantly she heard the sound of thunder from outside, while the silence of the room she stood in slammed into her.

There was no sound. That fact alone made her understand the awful truth. Every other time her mum had been in hospital the room had hummed, with machines, with people, with breathing. Her mum wasn't breathing. She wasn't even being helped to breathe. This was it. This was final.

A numbness descended around her, and she felt herself sink to the floor for the third time that day. Everything slowed, then stopped altogether, as she sat where she'd fallen, body crumpled, mind stilled, heart broken. She waited for the blackness to take her.

A hand on her arm and a gentle murmur of voices eventually pierced her consciousness and brought her back, and she became aware that she was sitting on a cold hard plastic chair in the hospital corridor. Her dad knelt in front of her, clutching her shoulder. Dimly she realised he was talking, and she tried to focus on his words, but a fresh shock of fear slammed into her.

"Brodie?" she asked, panicked, but her dad smiled – or grimaced, she wasn't sure which. "It's okay, he's with his friend," he replied, voice hoarse with pain. "Laura left a message for me, that Ben's mum picked him up, and he can stay there until we're ready to get him."

Rhiannon nodded, remembering what her teacher had said, what felt like a lifetime ago, and grateful for that small mercy.

Awkwardly her dad took her hand. "Did you want to see your mum, and say goodbye properly? The doctor suggested –" he began, then trailed off and stared into space again.

A shiver of revulsion passed through her, and she stared at him with eyes full of pain and fear before shaking her head. But the nurse bustled over then, cool, calm and collected.

"I can take you in," she offered, gently yet firmly grabbing Rhiannon's arm as she spoke and hauling her to her feet. Too numb to protest, she allowed herself to be led back inside the darkened room and deposited by the side of her mother's bed.

Her mother. Was this eerily still figure really her? Had it ever been her? Slowly, achingly, she lifted her eyes until she was peering at the body, then reluctantly, gradually, her gaze swept upwards to the face.

It looked like her mum, yet it didn't. The features were the same – the hollowed cheeks, the high forehead, the delicate nose – yet the lips gave it away. They were still full, yet the colour was no hue Rhiannon had ever seen, the blueish tinge as confronting as the chilling stillness of the demeanour.

Haltingly she reached out a hand to stroke her mother's face, and was confused when she noticed how much it was trembling. Some part of her had an irrational fear that the body would suddenly be reanimated, would lash out at her in some way. Which was stupid, because she'd love nothing more than for her mum to come back from the dead. Well, to not be dead in the first place. With a great effort, her mind shied away from the image of zombies that had entered her head, distracting her from her task.

As her fingers hovered over her mother's cheek, she forced herself to really look at the body before her, and realised with sudden clarity that Beth was not in the room with her. She was no longer housed in the pile of flesh and bones laid out on the bed beside her, and that awareness made it easier for her to reach out and gently touch her mother's face. The cold, clammy skin didn't repel her as much as she'd imagined it would, and on some level she understood the nurse's wisdom in forcing her to come back inside and see the body.

At least now she knew that it wouldn't be her mum that they buried, wouldn't be her mum trapped underground, desperate to escape. Beth had found a release from the pain and sickness of the last six months. She was free, no longer tied to this mundane physical body that had been so racked with illness and agony. Which meant she wasn't here anymore to haunt her daughter – or to help her.

That was when Rhiannon's tears started, when the feelings of loss became real, and she sank down onto the bed, holding her mother's hand, no longer overwhelmed by the eeriness of the situation or repulsed by the cool flesh that she clutched.

"Oh Mum, I need you. I know I should be grateful that your pain has ended, but I'm not. I want you back! It's selfish of me, I know, but I can't do this without you. I can't live without you. None of us can. What about Brodie? What about Dad?" she demanded, voice tortured, and her head and heart just as angry as they were devastatingly sad.

"It's not fair!" she cried. "How could this happen to you? How could this happen to *me*?" Her sobbing became louder, her shoulders shook harder, and for a while she didn't know if she would ever be able to stop crying.

A gentle hand on her arm eventually broke her reverie, and she turned to see Rose standing before her. The older woman drew her into a warm hug, and Rhiannon tried to get her tears under control, to hold it together in her presence. The priestess was the most composed person she'd ever known, and she was shocked to see just how distraught she was.

"Oh sweet girl, I'm so sorry for your loss," Rose said, as she held her tight, one hand gently stroking her back. Rhiannon felt warmth flowing into her, and wondered if she was trying to calm her with a spell. Then she realised how sad Rose would be too.

For Beth, who'd had such a painful relationship with her own parents, Rose had been a mother figure, a mentor and a friend, the two women weaving magic together in their small, close-knit circle, as well as spending time together over cups of tea, sharing their lives, their hopes, their dreams.

And the priestess, who had no children of her own, had been like a grandmother to her and Brodie, joining their family for festive holidays and birthdays for as long as she could remember, babysitting them when they were younger, always there to support them in any way she could. For Rose, losing Beth would be like losing her own daughter, so this was a deep and terrible blow for her too.

"I'm so sorry for your loss Mrs Tyler," she managed to reply, voice a whisper. "I just... I can't get my head around it. How can she suddenly not be here? What are we going to do without her?"

Rose didn't answer, perhaps loath to utter any of the ridiculous cliches people expressed at times like this.

"*She's in a better place.*"

"*It was her time.*"

"*Everything happens for a reason.*"

Instead she just held Rhiannon's shaking body close and was present with her pain, supporting her physically as well as emotionally as she cried, honouring rather than trying to diminish her grief.

And eventually the young girl ran out of tears. She took a deep, gasping breath, making an effort to get herself back under control, then rubbed a hand across her face, trying to wipe her eyes dry, before disentangling herself from Rose's embrace.

"Thank you." She sighed as she turned red-rimmed eyes to the corridor, then back to the hospital bed, and the body that was no longer her mother's. "I guess I should see how Dad is," she added apologetically, and Rose tried to smile in return.

"I'm here if you need me sweet girl, if any of you need me. I love you all very much, and I am so sorry that you have lost your beautiful mum. There are no words that will make it easier. Just know that I am here for you, whenever, however and whatever you need."

Nodding, Rhiannon felt her eyes start to well again at the older woman's kindness, and impatiently brushed the tears aside as she made her way out to where Mike still stood, leaning brokenly against the wall.

"Dad," she said softly, touching his arm. She repeated herself twice before he finally came back to the present, and her heart broke all over again at the pain and desolation writ so large across his face.

"Come on, we need to pick Brodie up, and try to explain it to him, and go home," she said, but her voice caught on the final word. *Home.* Would their house ever be that again?

Her dad was still dazed, still not really in his body, or his head, and certainly not with her in this sterile hospital corridor. Gently she took his hand and led him outside to the street. Someone had moved their car further down the road during the day, away from the emergency entrance, so she headed there, then fished around in her dad's jacket pocket for the keys and unlocked the doors.

Quickly she pushed him into the passenger seat and wrapped the seatbelt around him, then buckled herself in on the driver's side and slowly, cautiously, pulled away and moved out into the traffic, grateful that Brodie's friend's house wasn't too far away. Driving in her current state wasn't a great idea, but she was more present than her father right now.

Glancing over at him as she paused at a stop sign, she saw the raw agony etched into his face, and the frozen stiffness of his body made her chest feel as though it would explode with pain. As broken as she felt by her mother's death, it was hitting her dad even harder. Fear gripped her insides as she wondered whether she'd be able to reach him. She couldn't lose him too.

Struggling to catch her breath, she turned into the street where Brodie's friend lived, and pulled up haphazardly out the front of the house. She told her dad that she'd only be a minute, but if he heard her, he didn't bother to respond.

Steeling herself, she walked up and knocked on the door, head spinning as she tried to work out what to say to whoever answered. And, far more importantly, what she should tell her brother. He was only five years old. Would he even be able to grasp the truth of what it meant that their mother was dead?

Dead. The word had lost all sense of meaning to her – it was too big, too complex, too tiny, too not-enough to even begin to explain the concept they were going to have to work out how to live with.

Could they do it? Could she?

The opening of the door broke into her reverie, and she tried to paste a calm, reassuring smile on her face for Ben's mum. "Rhiannon, hello," the woman said nervously. "Would you like to come in?"

"Thanks Mrs Pearson, but Dad's waiting in the car. Is Brodie ready to come home?" she asked, trying to keep her voice steady. The woman peered at her searchingly.

"Ben! Brodie! Come down here, it's time for Brodie to go home now," she called out, as Rhiannon tried to understand the woman's response to her.

"So, um, is your mum, well, is she…" Mrs Pearson began, but broke off, relieved, as the two boys hurtled down the stairs.

Rhiannon nearly broke down, right there on this woman's doorstep, when she saw the happiness on her brother's face as he raced his friend to the door. Was she going to have to be the one to turn his life upside down? To wipe the joy from his eyes, and his heart? A wave of anger rushed through her, and a boom of thunder rumbled overhead as the sky darkened.

Ben's mum shivered. "Looks like we're in for a cool change," she said, as she put her hands on her son's shoulders and drew him closer to her, as though she could shield him from physical storms, as well as the emotional turbulence of loss. Sadly, Rhiannon was now painfully aware that she couldn't. No one could.

Finally she mustered a shaky smile. "Brodie's always welcome to stay with us, if things are… well, if you need that, okay?" she offered, her words as they tumbled out betraying just how awkward she felt.

"Thank you, that means a lot to us," Rhiannon replied. "I'll let Dad know." Hearing the tremor in her voice, she quickly took Brodie's hand and turned towards the car, desperate to get away from the woman's pity-filled eyes. She felt uncomfortable enough, without having to try to make things easier for other people.

Sighing with exhaustion, she wondered if this was how everyone would look at her now – sympathy mixed with terror, and a desperate worry that it could happen to them too. Almost as though death was contagious, and if they got too close to her they would lose someone they loved as well.

She'd never felt so alone, so alien, so not-herself.

Buckling Brodie into the back of the car, she returned to the driver's seat and turned the key in the ignition.

"Hi Dad," Brodie said in his achingly innocent little voice.

Mike didn't answer, and Rhiannon turned fiery eyes on him.

"Dad," she hissed, trying to pierce his daze. "Brodie's here."

He turned empty eyes to him, and gave a half-hearted wave. "Hey buddy," he said softly, vaguely, vacantly. "How was school?"

Rhiannon headed home, relieved that Brodie kept up a running commentary of his day, and his adventures with Ben, and didn't seem to notice that their father had checked out emotionally. Uncertain of how to reach him, she turned in to their driveway, bundled Brodie out of the car and stomped into the kitchen.

While her brother played outside, ignoring the gathering storm, and her dad sat shell-shocked on the couch, she picked up her broken dish from that morning – had it really only been twelve hours ago? – then started pulling things out of the pantry, banging pots and pans, rattling cutlery and attacking the vegetables with a fury she couldn't contain.

Then, as dinner bubbled on the stove, she went through the house like a whirlwind, tidying away books and toys, picking up discarded clothes in her and Brodie's rooms and throwing them in the washing machine, vacuuming the hallway and mopping the bathroom floor, all so she didn't have to think.

When there was nothing left to clean, she stood at the top of the stairs, looking over at the door to her parents' room, paralysed. Her thoughts slipped back to that morning, when she'd rushed up to check on her mum, brain clouded with fear. Now it was swimming in dread and depression, and fear seemed so much more preferable.

The door still stood ajar from their hurried departure, and she walked slowly towards it, as if being drawn in. Then on the threshold she froze, the scent of her mother's jasmine perfume drifting out, and clouding her mind and her heart.

Just before she stepped inside, the aroma of the curry she'd been cooking snaked up the stairs to her, and she raced back down to the kitchen, lowering the flame and stirring the saucepan full of vegies and chickpeas just before it boiled over, and burning her mouth as she checked the rice that was cooking in the pot next to it.

Swearing, she turned the burner off and poured the rice into a strainer, then went to check on her dad. He was sitting in the same position he'd collapsed into when they got home, and he didn't even look up when she walked into the room.

"Dad," she said softly, but he didn't respond. Kneeling down in front of him, she placed a hand on his arm, yet he remained oblivious.

"Dad," she repeated, a little louder this time, a little less patient, and he finally gazed up at her, with eyes that didn't even seem to recognise her.

"Yes?" he muttered.

"Dad, dinner's ready."

"I'm not hungry," he sighed.

"You have to eat. Brodie has to eat," she retorted firmly.

"Brodie?"

"Dad! Your *son* Brodie," she said. "He needs to eat. And you need to tell him –"

This time it was her voice that cracked, her voice that couldn't get the words out. How would they tell her baby brother that he'd lost his mother?

"Anyway, dinner is ready, so could you go and get Brodie from out the back, so we can eat together?"

He stared at her blankly for a moment, but eventually he stood up and headed outside, returning with his son while Rhiannon set the table. Sheepishly he took a seat, and smiled wanly at his daughter as she served out the dinner. Without waiting to say grace, he picked up his spoon and dug it into the fragrant bowl of curry and rice, but he stopped abruptly, food halfway between bowl and mouth, when Brodie spoke.

"Where's Mumma?" he asked, then popped a spoonful of curry into his mouth while he waited for the answer.

Rhiannon gasped, and for a moment Mike's eyes took on that faraway look, but then he put his spoon down and reached across the table to take his son's hand. "Remember what we were talking about last week buddy?" he began carefully.

"That Mumma was going away for a while?" Brodie asked, his sweet, child-like voice ripping at Rhiannon's heart.

She stared at their dad in consternation. Going away?

Mike glanced at her as though he could read her thoughts, and grimaced, but he forced a smile onto his face as he looked back at Brodie. "That's right. She's gone to stay with the angels," he whispered, voice tortured.

"Okay," Brodie said calmly. "Can I go to Ben's tomorrow after school?" His matter-of-fact tone chilled Rhiannon.

"Sure," Mike replied shakily. "I'll call his mum after dinner."

Brodie smiled, not picking up on the tension in the room, and started telling them about the fort they were going to build in Ben's backyard. Then he abruptly changed the subject.

"Dad, can I get a pet?" he asked. His voice was plaintive, but not whiny, and Rhiannon wondered suddenly how much he did understand of their current situation.

The phone rang then, breaking her out of her whirling thoughts, and they listened in growing horror as Beth's voice boomed out, filling the room as she greeted whoever had rung and thanked them for their call, before instructing them to leave a message. Mike and Rhiannon sat frozen, while Brodie grinned and said "Mumma".

"Hi Mike, hi kids, it's Rose. I'm terribly sorry for your loss. I just, well... I just can't believe that Beth is gone," she said, sniffing tearfully. "But I wanted to make sure you know that if you need anything, you only have to ask. I'll bring around some dinner for you tomorrow night, so you don't have to worry about that at least, but anything else, please give me a call. I'm thinking of you all, and sending so much love," she added, compassion in her voice.

"Oh, and I called the restaurant, to let them know we won't be in tonight, and they're fine with that. Talk soon..."

The restaurant. Tonight was meant to be a big celebration for Beth's fortieth birthday. Instead they were sitting at home without her, and the only thing left to plan was her funeral. As the answering machine clicked off, Rhiannon glanced at her father. Face deathly pale, he pushed away from the table and left the room, his bowl still full, muttering something about curses.

Rhiannon grimaced and pushed her own food away, unable to stomach it either, but she waited patiently for Brodie to finish his dinner, then got him ready for bed. After she switched off his light, she went back downstairs and cleaned up the kitchen, then looked through the fridge so she could write a shopping list. But when she grabbed the notepad out of the drawer and saw her mum's large, distinctive scrawl at the top – tomatoes, lentils, pumpkin, herbs, soap – grief slammed into her and knocked her off her feet.

As she slid to the floor, tears started to fall, and she sobbed until she could barely breathe. It still seemed so surreal, so hard to grasp. Her mum, always so vibrant, was never coming home. The woman who wrote out the weekly shopping list. Who listened patiently to their troubles and soothed their fears. Who dropped them off to and picked them up from all their after-school activities. *Who was her best friend.*

She would never see her again.

Anger shot through Rhiannon then, and she felt like raging to god, or her mother's goddess, at the injustice of it all. As her emotions built to an agonising crescendo, the storm that had been brewing all afternoon hit, and a sense of satisfaction grew within her as it shook the house just as she was shaking her fist at the heavens.

For a moment she felt separate from her body, felt like she was part of the storm. She had a sudden flash of the fear she'd felt the night before when she'd been transported outside into the rain. But that didn't make any sense – she couldn't have just beamed down into the garden like someone in a Star Trek movie – so she dismissed the crazy notion and went back to enjoying the violence and power of the storm raging outside, as it raged within her just as fiercely.

It felt right, that the whole world was crying for her mother.

Chapter 8

After the Storm

Bang. Bang. Bang.

Groaning, Rhiannon pulled the pillow over her head and tried to block out the sound of the howling wind and the insistent banging, but it continued to hammer at her skull, driving her even crazier than she already felt. Untangling her limbs from the quilt, she staggered out of bed and tried to figure out the direction of the noise.

It was the top shutter above her window seat, which must have come loose in the storm that had been raging for the last three nights. She hoisted herself up and slammed it shut, then collapsed down onto the cushions.

Pulling her legs up, she wrapped her arms around her knees and fell back against the window pane. It shot icy shivers up her back as her skin made contact with the frozen glass, but she welcomed the sensation of pain, and the chill that soaked into her bones, and into her heart. Gloomily she lifted her head and gazed outward through the bleakness of the pre-dawn haze, eyes skimming over the dull green of the grass in their backyard, the muted hues of the flowers she could just make out beneath her window, and the gentle beauty of the tor in the distance.

Unseeing.

Uncomprehending.

Uncaring.

Unbalanced, she might add. Since her mum had died three days ago, she'd lost the ability to cope, to function, to do anything more than hide in her room in a daze. She'd been okay the first night, fired up with adrenaline and the need to protect her brother. But after cooking and cleaning and coping through dinner, she had returned to her room and slowly fallen apart.

Leaning down, she picked up a woollen jumper from the mess on her floor and pulled it over her head, then wrapped the quilt around her shivering form. Nothing helped though, because the ice in her heart had spread outward, had infected her whole self, and she had no idea how to thaw it out.

It was autumn, a time of crisp blue skies, pale sunshine and vivid flame-coloured leaves, yet in this room, in this body, in this mind, it was the deepest and darkest midwinter. She was frozen, numb, and so tired of crying, so tired of feeling disconnected from herself, from the world, from her father and her brother. She knew she should be downstairs comforting Brodie, trying to help him understand the immensity of their loss, and yet she wondered if there was any point drumming into him just how much had been taken from him.

Wasn't ignorance bliss? Mike had told him Beth had died, explaining that Mumma had been taken to heaven to help the angels, and while he wouldn't be able to see her again, she would always be with him, always watching out for him, always holding his hand and caring about him.

Her soul ached to tell him the truth, to rip away the sugar coating, yet another part of her just wanted to stroke his forehead and soothe away his pain, his confusion, his attempts to grapple with the well-intentioned words of well-meaning adults. To soothe away the horrifying fact that their mother was dead, and turn back time to make things turn out differently.

The anger was torturing her, consuming her, but she couldn't stop herself feeling it, or turn it off – it just kept burning and shaking through her, in time with the storm raging outside her window.

Just last week Beth had convinced them all that she was improving, that her will to live and her obvious need and determination to be back with her family was enough to heal her, to save her, to transform her.

Yet despite all assurances to the contrary, she had been torn away from them. Her death was real, and it broke Rhiannon's heart moment after moment after moment to be reminded of it.

The sound of a teardrop splashing onto paper shook her back to the present, and she stared down, bleary eyed, at the notebook in her lap, puzzled to see words scratched across the page in an angry red scrawl. She hadn't even realised that she'd picked up the pen, but it was definitely her handwriting.

The storm.
The maze.
The fear.
The guilt.
The pain.
The horror.
The scream.
The echo.
The silence.
The agony.
The fire.
The burn.
The cracks.
The devastation.
The breaking down.
The breaking open.
The dissolution.
The dissolving into nothingness.

Her mouth opened in a silent scream, and she felt herself falling, until the world went black around her.

A few hours later she awoke to silence, dead silence, which was just as unnerving as the storm had been. Her room was achingly, devastatingly, lacking in any noise whatsoever. There was no restless wind howling around the corner of the house, no shifting of the floorboards as they creaked and cracked. It was eerily still, and for a brief moment she hoped that death had come for her too.

Yet she had no such luck. Heralded by a crash of thunder, sound washed over her again. She heard the flapping of birds flying past the house, imagined she could feel the beat of a butterfly's wings outside the glass, pricked up her ears as she tried to listen to her father and Brodie downstairs in the kitchen. Desperately she wished she could fly away on feathered wings, but she couldn't. Her anchors were here in this house, and she knew she couldn't leave either one of them behind, couldn't indulge her fantasies of leaving this world, not when the only two people she cared about needed her to remain.

Not that she was much use to them right now, sitting up here, yet she couldn't bring herself to move, couldn't face the thought of tackling the stairs – or seeing their sad faces and disappointment. She supposed she was meant to step up now, to fill her mother's shoes and keep the family together, but she was too busy breaking down to hold anything together.

The next morning she woke earlier than she had been, surprised to feel the sun on her face, and for the first time since her mum had died, she felt hungry enough to drag herself out of bed and traipse downstairs. Relief flooded her when she realised she had the house to herself, and she stood in the kitchen and ate yoghurt straight from the container as she wondered what on earth to do with herself. For a while she paced, thinking of chores she should be doing, but she had no will to start.

When it struck her, just how cooped up she felt, she grabbed her keys and walked out through the back garden into the laneway that ran behind their house. The blue sky began to turn grey, and she grinned as angry black clouds formed above her. It was like they had waited for her, had followed her. Like she had her own personal bad weather system to command.

Energised, she raced to the top of the tor, and threw her head back and her arms to the sky as the rain began to fall, pouring down over her, soaking her to the skin, and washing away the tears that spilled over and traced a path down her cheeks. As she screamed her pain and rage to the heavens, lightning split the sky, and she laughed, a slightly hysterical note to it, as she embraced the power of her storm.

She screamed for the thing that had happened to her, for the loss of her mother, for the look on her little brother's face that tore her heart to ribbons every time she pictured it. She screamed because she didn't know what to do, or how to move forward, and because she couldn't see any way through this emotional devastation.

There was a lull in the chaos of the weather as she paused to draw breath, then it roared again when she did. Fear vibrated through her as she wondered if she was controlling the storm. Had she called it? Did she fuel it? Then laughter bubbled out of her again, and she wondered if she had finally snapped, imagining that she could control the weather. *Who was she, god?* If that was true, her mother would still be alive.

Time passed slowly, then sped up, as her mind spun and she tried so hard to shut out the chaos of memories beating at her brain. But after what felt like hours, the ache in her bones from the cold outweighed the ache in her heart, and she staggered back down the hill.

Mike and Brodie were at home when she returned, and tried their best to entice her into the kitchen with them, where they were drinking hot chocolate and making cinnamon cookies. Turning away from their sad, hopeful eyes, she traipsed upstairs, slamming her bedroom door as she went in. Shrugging off her wet clothes, she wrapped herself in a dressing gown and piled her dripping hair up on her head in a towel, then went back to the window seat and curled up on the cushions.

Though the weather had let up while she was walking home, now a flash downpour began, and she could hear each individual drop as it hit the glass, could sense its pathway along the cold pane of the glass, could see the tiniest movement as it made its way downwards.

It was hypnotic, and she felt herself falling into the depths of that one drop – before she was suddenly outside again. Staring around herself in panic, she wiped the rain from her eyes and tried to focus. She was in the woods, although she had no idea how she'd gotten there, or how she would get home.

A flash of lightning lit up the dripping trees, and she gasped as she saw Evan standing there, just metres away. How the hell did he get there? What was he going to do to her?

Yet the chill of the rain lent her strength, and she felt her terror giving way to anger – and the angrier she got, the louder the thunder crashed above them, and the more frequently the lightning struck the clearing where they stood. And as she peered through the relentless downpour, she saw that he was quaking in fear, shrinking in on himself, his once-swaggering demeanour crumbling in the face of the wind and the rain and the rolling thunder.

How strange, that he was afraid of a storm. That in the face of nature's fury, his confidence suddenly deserted him, like the schoolyard bully shaking with fear when confronted by someone even crueller than them.

But as she stared harder, a strange smile crossed her face, as she realised that he wasn't just scared of the worsening storm – he was scared of *her*.

"What are you doing?" he asked, voice strangled with dread, and she almost laughed. The threatening tone from their last meeting had disappeared, and his voice shook with apprehension.

"Me?" she said, genuinely puzzled. "I'm not doing anything, other than admiring the power of this beautiful storm. A storm you seem a little nervous about."

"Stop it, witch," he hissed, and she noticed the whites of his eyes glowing when the lightning illuminated the forest again, and the thunder seemed to shake the ground beneath them.

This time she did laugh. "Witch? You're the one with the magical powers, remember? I'm just a young girl in need of teaching, right?"

His eyes slid from hers and moved down her body, but it wasn't the sleazy sizing up of her supposed charms that he'd subjected her to last time, so she followed his eyes, curious – then jumped in fright. Sparks were shooting from her fingertips, and the leaves on the ground around her feet were smouldering despite the rain. There were even small flames burning in a circle around her, and she felt them protecting her with their warmth, and an energy she sensed herself pushing outwards, at him.

He seemed to feel it too, because he paled even further, and if she wasn't so scared herself she would have laughed. For a moment she almost gave in to the panic, afraid of what was happening to her, what she was capable of doing. But the rain around her eased in answer, soothing her now with a gentle caress, while it continued to pelt down on him as he stood cowering before her.

Closing her eyes and taking a deep breath, she tried to centre herself – and felt the palms of her hands tingling, then a crackle of electricity zinging through her long, wild hair. She felt strong, and powerful, and strangely in control of a situation that should have been sending her crazy.

"I'm sorry," he said shakily, and her eyes snapped open, alighting on him again and noticing this time his misery, and his shame. She glared at him, about to unleash a torrent of words on top of the rain he was drowning in, words of anger and scorn, words he needed to hear, and deserved to be lashed by.

But abruptly she was thrown off balance as she felt something pulling her away from him, away from herself. In an instant she was back in her bedroom, crouched on the floor, the window open and rain pouring in on her. Shivering with cold, she staggered to her feet to close it, then collapsed back onto the window seat.

Strange images swirled through her mind, and she stared down at her hands. They were no longer tingling, no longer sparking. And she was dry. The fear that she was losing her mind was interrupted by a knock on the door, then her dad poked his head into her room.

"Sorry darling, I've been knocking, but I wasn't sure you could hear me," he said, voice full of apology, eyes full of apprehension. *Was it his knock that had brought her back from… wherever she'd been?*

She looked at him quizzically, and he slowly entered her room, a steaming cup in his hand, which he nervously offered to her.

"It's lemon balm tea with mint leaves," he explained hesitantly. "Rose brought it over, and said it would be good for you. Apparently it supports those who are grieving emotionally, and it helps them to sleep better too." He broke off, worried she would be offended. "You should see how big the bag she brought us is – she said I need to drink it every night too."

Rhiannon stared up at him. At last she was present enough to see his pain and his nerves around her. God, the poor man. He was trying so hard – he had to, because she'd deserted him – but he was just as lost as she was.

"Thanks Dad," she said finally, reaching out for the cup, and he smiled with relief. She was relieved too, that she'd managed to calm her mind enough to take it, because her first instinct had been to smash it out of his hand, or hurl it across the room. But it wasn't his fault she was hurting.

She knew that her mother had wanted her to tell her dad about… the thing that had happened to her… when she was ready, but how could she do that to him? It was painfully obvious that he wasn't coping very well as it was, the devastation of his beloved wife's death coming close to destroying him, and the burden of caring for their two children far more than he could handle right now.

Already he was uncomfortable around her – he'd looked plain scared when he'd seen her wrapped in a towel after her shower the other night. She felt for him, the awkward man who'd always left the girlie teenage stuff to his wife, preferring to see Rhiannon as his young daughter still. Even hinting to him about what had happened to her would send him over the edge, and so she knew what she had to do.

Not that she'd spared much thought for that night anyway – it had been submerged by her grief and pain, drowned beneath her guilt and anger and loss. Compared to her mother's death, well, what did anything else matter?

And so she swallowed it down and buried it deep within…

Chapter 9

Healing Her Heart

Beth... Twenty years ago...

After another bitter argument with her mother over her supposedly inconsiderate behaviour – because daring to have her own opinion of her own life was clearly frowned upon by her parents – Beth slammed the front door and stormed off towards the village, not caring where she walked or where she ended up, just knowing that she had to get away from the house, and the toxic relationships within it.

She didn't want to be angry all the time, or bitter, but as soon as she'd walked into her childhood abode a week ago, she had reverted to her childhood self. Angry, resentful... hell, she'd probably regressed back a few years in age too, because dealing with her mother made her want to contradict everything she said, whether she agreed with it or not, and deny even the vaguest of similarities between them.

Leaving town the day high school finished had been her one successful act of defiance. Living in London for a year, she'd felt like herself for the first time, free to think how she wanted to think, live how she wanted to live – god, even eat what she wanted to eat. It was even better, and more freeing, when she'd moved to France for a year, thus avoiding even the occasional visits home she'd suffered through while still in England.

Admittedly it had been weird at first, having people ask her opinion, let alone value it, because she'd been so used to deferring to, or being over-ruled by, her parents in every aspect of life. But she'd thrived in her new circumstances, and had blossomed into a happy, confident and independent young woman, loving her job, and her life.

The moment she'd come back here though she'd become her miserable old self again, giving in to her parents because it was easier than arguing with them, and feeling once more that her opinions were of no consequence and her dreams were stupid, petty, unrealistic and unachievable. Standing up for herself just wasn't worth it – she was already worn down, exhausted from her few minor and ill-fated attempts at rebellion. How was she going to survive another month?

Tripping on the sidewalk, she finally lifted her eyes to her surroundings, and was surprised to find herself outside Rose's shop. As she gazed at the beautiful shiny crystals, colourful clothes and books in the window, she smiled. There were magical novels, spell books, tomes on shamanism, druidry and witchcraft, and even one on how to create rituals that would change your life. She could sure use one of those!

Next her eyes alighted on a sign listing all the healing modalities offered, and she realised it wasn't just a shop and a place of ceremony, it was a healing centre as well. Maybe that was what she needed, but she was too scared to go inside.

As she turned to walk away, the door opened, and Rose poked her head out. "Hi Beth," she said, voice gentle and loving, and full of acceptance. "I was hoping you'd come by. I just had a cancellation, and I thought you might like to take it – learn about the so-called oogeldy-boogeldy that your mother so despises." And she grinned a cheeky grin.

An expression of deep longing lit up Beth's face, but it was quickly replaced with a look part fear, part suspicion. Responding to the first, most honest response, Rose guided her inside.

"Sweet girl, there's no charge, and no expectation of anything in return. The room's already set up, and it would be a shame to let it go to waste," she insisted.

"It's an energy healing, so there's no physical contact. You just have to lie there, fully clothed, and relax. Worst case scenario, you leave feeling a little more peaceful than you do right now. And who knows, maybe it will help you in more ways than you can imagine. Would you like to?"

Beth wrestled a little longer between fear and hope, but the latter finally won out, and she nodded shyly.

Smiling, Rose led her up the stairs, and Beth tried to focus on the sense of peace and wellbeing she'd experienced at the ceremony the other night. When they reached the landing, they turned away from the street side of the building where the ritual space was, and entered the small, cosy room opposite.

A candle was burning on the table, while an oil vaporiser infused the room with a soothing blend of lavender, chamomile and another herb she couldn't identify.

As Beth stood uncertainly on the threshold, Rose beckoned her inside. "If you'd just like to take your shoes off and lie down on the massage table, you can let me know if you'd like another blanket, or need some more pillows. Then just close your eyes and relax," the priestess instructed her.

"I'll be doing reconnective healing, which is hands-off, and will be working my way around the table, so don't panic if you sense movement around you. You may experience a warmth or even a tingling in your limbs, or it may feel like my hands are on you, although they won't be. Or you might not feel anything physical – there's no wrong or right way, so don't stress over the outcome," she continued, voice gentle and reassuring.

"Some people feel teary, while others laugh – it's nothing to worry about, just emotions being dealt with and released."

The healer paused for a moment, and it seemed she was wrestling with whether or not to continue. "Sometimes I receive messages while I'm working, from my guides or yours, so if I do, would you like me to tell you afterwards, or would you prefer not to know? Some people aren't interested in that side of it, which is absolutely fine," Rose offered.

Beth nodded uncertainly. "I guess that would be okay," she replied, although she was feeling even more nervous now, and starting to have second thoughts.

"You might hear a voice or get messages yourself, so feel free to speak them aloud if you want to, so I can help you remember them afterwards, or just take them in on your own. And if you have any questions at any point just ask me. There's no standing on ceremony here, so if you feel uncomfortable in any way, just tell me to stop – there's no pressure at all, okay?"

Beth nodded again, still nervous, but no longer looking quite so apprehensive. Slipping her shoes off, she lay down on the table, positioned the pillow under her head and lifted the blanket up over her body. Motioning to Rose that she was ready, she closed her eyes, and the older woman gently began, holding her hands near her patient's temples, a few inches above her physical body.

At first Beth was wary, feeling vulnerable with her eyes closed, in a small dark room with a virtual stranger, but gradually she relaxed into it, and exhaled the breath she'd been holding. A beautiful warmth enveloped her, and she smiled, loving the feeling of floating free. She imagined she saw a great web of golden strands above her, stretching out through a universe of stars and sparkling, shiny hearts.

For a moment she felt dizzy, as though she was flying above the planet, too high and too fast for her fragile human body to keep up with. But then that settled too, and she was floating again, at one with the world and at peace with herself at last. Tears leaked out of her eyes and trickled down onto the table, but she let them fall, understanding on some level that they were releasing toxic emotions and fears she'd been holding on to for so long.

As she had that thought, she felt a soothing touch on her forehead, and the warmth and peace crept down into her mind, into her heart, into her very bones. Thinking it was Rose's hand on her brow, she opened her eyes for a moment to thank her – and saw that the healer was standing at the other end of the table, arms held out over the tops of her feet.

Surprised, she quickly closed her eyes, and her mind filled with a vision of a much older woman, with long and wild silver hair flowing loose around her shoulders, and a face of such wisdom and beauty it took her breath away. Deep lines were etched into her face, but they were lines of character and strength and kindness, lines that only added to her beauty.

The woman smiled at her, and Beth was suffused in a cloud of warmth and protection. "Arm yourself with this feeling beloved," the woman said, and Beth strained to work out whether she was speaking aloud or if it was mind to mind. "Wear it like a cloak, and hold it tightly around yourself, to be reminded of your own strength and beauty and wisdom."

The scent of the candles reached Beth then, and she inhaled deeply, feeling a calmness flow into her. But she was sad when she realised that her focus on that had driven the vision away. For a moment she felt bereft, as though she'd lost a dear friend, but then she heard the echo of laughter, and a voice whispering to her that she could connect with her at any time she needed to.

For a while Beth concentrated on her breathing, just inhaling and exhaling, enjoying the freedom from stress, from thought, from the battle she seemed to be constantly engaged in – between liking herself and despising herself, between seeing herself as the person she wanted to be, who was at war with the person she became around her mother.

Suddenly she felt tingling on her legs, like tiny bubbles, as though she was sitting in a bath filled with champagne, sparkling with light and energy. She giggled, then clapped her hands over her mouth. "Sorry," she whispered, opening her eyes for a split second and glancing down to the end of the table where she assumed Rose was still standing – and was surprised again when she saw that the healer wasn't holding her hands over her legs, but was now at her left shoulder.

"It's okay sweet girl, it's all okay," she crooned soothingly, and Beth felt her eyes closing again, without her even being aware she was doing it.

The silver-haired woman from her vision returned, and handed her a red rose, a yellow rose and a pink rose. "Flowers of forgiveness, of joy and of love," she said. "Forgive yourself beloved, and try to let go. Your mother sees the world differently to you, for her own reasons, and her actions and reactions are not a reflection on you. She will not change, she is as unyielding as stone, but you can change the way you respond to her, and the way you see the world. Choose to let go of your angst towards her. Choose love."

Drifting for a while, Beth lost track of time, but eventually the sensations in her body died down, the silver-haired woman bade her farewell, and Rose put a gentle hand on her shoulder and softly told her she could open her eyes when she was ready. Blinking in the soft golden light of the candle flame, she slowly sat up, her hand brushing against her forehead curiously. Rose raised an eyebrow at her in question.

"I didn't realise you were going to use essential oils," she said, and Rose looked even more puzzled.

"On my forehead, when you dropped the scented jasmine oil between my brows – all I could think was that I would have to wash my hair as soon as I got home, so Mother doesn't roll her eyes at me again and tell me that I'm not respecting her, or whatever today's complaint is. Because obviously the way I dress and how I wear my hair has nothing to do with my own preferences, it's all carefully orchestrated just to annoy her," she said, and sighed a heavy sigh.

"I didn't use any oils," Rose replied.

"Yes you did, there were four drops of what smelled like jasmine oil, on my forehead," Beth said firmly, touching her brow again and wondering why it didn't seem at all oily. "Just five minutes ago."

Shaking her head, Rose motioned to the table, which was bereft of any small potion or oil bottles. "I was standing at your feet for the final twenty minutes, I promise. But that's fascinating, that you felt that sensation. It's nothing bad."

"I smelled it too," Beth said, a touch of anxiety in her voice.

The priestess smiled reassuringly. "People do experience all kinds of sensations in a healing like this, from tingling bubbles that seem as though you're in a spa bath, to changes in temperature, and even the feeling of hands on your body. But it's nothing to worry about," she assured the shaken girl. "What were you thinking about when you felt the oil drops?"

Beth cast her mind back. "When I giggled, it was because I felt like I was in a bath tub full of champagne, and all the bubbles were touching my skin and popping on impact, which was all pretty tickly – and also a bit nerve-racking, since I opened my eyes for a moment, expecting to see you with your hands above my legs, but you were at my shoulder."

She paused, and looked scared for a moment, but then she continued anyway. "And with the oil, aside from the conscious thought that Mother would be furious if I didn't wash my hair right away, when I let that go I felt like I was floating. And... um, well... I know this will sound crazy, but I saw a woman with long silver hair, and she talked to me for a while, then handed me three roses, and told me what they represent, and how I could maybe deal with Mother better."

Rose smiled at her. "I saw her too," she admitted, hoping Beth wouldn't be too freaked out by that idea. "She was such a gentle soul, and she loves you very much. She told me a little about your struggles with your mother, and offered a few insights, if you would like to hear them?"

Seeking comfort, Beth drew up her knees and wrapped her arms around her legs, then sat pensively, doubt flickering over her face, her emotions flashing through her eyes. Clearly she wanted to know, yet part of her was afraid. And another, smaller part, still thought it was all a load of rubbish.

"I should go," she finally said, voice wavering, and got up from the table. "Thank you for today, it was very... interesting. And are you sure I can't pay you for your time?" she asked.

Rose stared at her sadly. "Yes, I'm sure, it was my pleasure," she insisted. "But before you go, I understand if you don't want to talk about your mum. My mother and I, well, we didn't see eye to eye on anything either, and it was truly the best day of my life when she moved to America. Distance can certainly neutralise the pain and angst, and I heard today that your father has expanded his company, and they'll have to move to the city, if that helps you to decide what you want to do from here."

A smile lit up Beth's face, and relief flooded through her. "They're really leaving town?"

"Apparently they're going to announce it after your sister's wedding," the priestess replied.

Hope ignited in Beth's heart. If her parents were leaving, she no longer had to flee the village, and for a moment she dared to dream that she could stay here, be friends with Violet and Mike, and pursue her passion to be a teacher – a vocation her mother had told her in no uncertain terms was beneath her, and definitely not an option.

A great weight lifted from her shoulders, and she felt the same sense of freedom she'd discovered when she left home two years ago flare back to life.

"You will be a wonderful teacher," Rose said, ignoring Beth's nervousness. "But that's not what I wanted to talk about," she continued, her voice gentle and non-judgemental. "Sweet girl, your guide told me that a man has hurt you."

"Oh... well, he didn't really mean it," Beth replied, shame washing over her. How could this woman know that? "And he apologised afterwards, and made up for it."

"But it wasn't a one-off occurrence," Rose stated, and this time there was a touch of sternness in her tone.

"Um, okay, yeah, it did happen twice, but it was nothing. It's not like he really hurt me – there were no broken bones, or skin, and no bruises," she finally admitted. "But it's over. I'll probably never see him again."

She blinked in surprise as she heard the words coming out of her mouth. Something had definitely shifted in her. Her plan had been to go back to London after the wedding, track Andrew down and do anything and everything she could to repair their relationship, to try to win him back.

But spending time with Mike and Violet had shown her what real love looked like. And now, sitting here in this candlelit room with the lavender and chamomile in the oil vaporiser soothing her heart and her mind, she realised that for the first time since she'd met Andrew, her yearning for him had dulled, and the thought of never seeing him again no longer filled her with anxiety, as it usually did, but relief.

And if she didn't need to find him, she could go back to Paris, and resume her job with the family she loved so much.

Suddenly she grinned. Maybe this healing really had worked on her in some strange way.

"Darling Beth, you deserve so much better than that," Rose said, breaking into her thoughts. "You deserve a man who respects you, who treats you well, and who loves and encourages and supports you. Promise me you won't go back to him. That you will only be with a man who is worthy of you."

Trying to banish the image of Mike that came into her mind at Rose's words, she nodded, feeling the truth of the sentiment, then asked her again if she could pay her.

Suddenly Rose couldn't bear it any more. Standing abruptly, she moved over to the shy young woman and cautiously embraced her. Although Beth was stiff at first, she finally relaxed into the embrace, and once that happened the floodgates opened and tears streamed down her face.

"Oh sweet girl, it's my pleasure to have been able to offer this to you, as a gift, so of course I don't want payment. You deserve a healing, and you are worthy of receiving gifts, no matter what their form. And I hope it wasn't *too* personal. Please know that everything we shared today is completely confidential, okay?"

Beth nodded.

"Now, be gentle with yourself for the next few days, and pay attention to any messages you get or dreams you have. You are stronger and wiser than you comprehend Beth, so listen to your inner guidance, and trust yourself."

Her tears came even harder in response to the love and kindness she felt from the healer, and so did her embarrassment at being so vulnerable. She shuddered as she fought down her desire to flee. This woman, practically a stranger, had gone out of her way to help her, had given her a free healing, and most importantly had listened to her.

That's what cut her up the most about her parents – they didn't even acknowledge she was there most of the time, and even if they were drawn into a discussion, they dismissed her comments outright or just ignored them, which was what really hurt. She wanted to be seen, and heard.

That was the most important gift Rose had given her – she'd listened to her, and she'd *seen* her.

And Mike and Violet had reminded her that she was worthy of being a friend, which meant that there were other people out there who would value her thoughts and opinions too, value *her*, and who would think she was worth having a conversation with. *Worth having a relationship with even?*

Chapter 10

Rhiannon... Today...

The screeching of her alarm clock ripped Rhiannon from another nightmare, and she groaned as she rolled over to hit the off button. Sleep tried to draw her back under, dreams tried to pull her back in, but her brother's high-pitched voice from his room next to hers dragged her back to awareness. She didn't know what was worse, the terror of her dreamscapes each night, of storm, fire and flood, or the brutal reality of her waking hours. There was a gaping hole in her heart, an agony that she could feel physically, and a web of despair surrounding her and weighing her down, like her own personal black cloud, always ready to pound her to the ground with its thundering presence.

The last week had passed in a blur of shock and pain and grief, and she was grateful that her dad hadn't made her go to school. It would have been pointless her even trying – she couldn't think straight, let alone speak coherently to anyone. For his part, their dad had managed to get Brodie ready and drop him off at his primary school every morning, but then he returned to the house and locked himself in his office all day, keeping his distance from her, giving her space – or protecting his own, she wasn't sure which.

Fortunately Rose had been as good as her word, coming over each night with dinner for the three of them – a vegie lasagne the first time, a pot of chilli beans the next, a tray of spinach filos after that. Patiently she washed the dishes piled up in the sink, served Mike dinner and poured him a glass of wine, took a plate of food up to Rhiannon and left it at her door, then crawled around on the floor with Brodie. It was the most attention he got, because his sister and his father were too shattered to do more than stagger zombie-like through their days. Rhiannon knew she had to get over this crushing grief and help her little brother, but she just couldn't. Not yet.

A knock on her door jolted her from her reverie, and she glanced at the clock to realise she'd just lost fifteen minutes.

"Hey love, we need to leave soon for the church," her dad called out, and the blackness she felt within was answered with a rolling crash of thunder that seemed to be right above their house. Forcing herself out of bed, she walked across to the window and peered out from behind her thick blood-red velvet curtains. Although the forecast had said there would be blue skies today, it looked like a huge storm was about to unleash itself, and Rhiannon felt a strange stab of satisfaction.

They shouldn't be farewelling her mother under calm, clear skies – the world *should* weep for Beth, it *should* express its outrage at her being taken from them far too soon. Rhiannon desperately wanted the rain to fall and the storm to rage – she needed the physical world to match her tumultuous inner world, even if just for a moment.

Hurrying over to her closet, she pulled the long black dress off the hanger, but as her hand touched the fabric, she jumped back as though she'd been burnt, the electricity crackling through the fabric from her fingertips. Glaring down at her hands, she backed away from the dress and threw herself onto the bed, giving herself over to her sobbing grief. She couldn't believe that the dress she'd bought to wear to her mum's fortieth birthday party was instead going to be worn to her funeral. And although she was trying not to think about it, it was freaking her out that her fingers seemed to be shooting sparks of electricity.

"Rhiannon!"

Sighing, she pushed herself off the bed, gingerly picked up the dress and slipped it over her head. It fit perfectly, and when she'd tried it on in a store in the city on a recent day out with her mum, she'd felt really good in it. It was the most grown-up and sophisticated outfit she had, and she'd really been looking forward to wearing it to Beth's birthday dinner. But now, instead, she was going to wear it as she watched her mother being buried. If this was what being a grown-up meant, she didn't want it.

Mirrors still terrified her, because she was sure the brokenness of her soul would be reflected back to her there, so she picked up her brush from the dressing table without looking into the glass, and scraped her hair back into a severe ponytail. No ribbons, not even black ones, and no make-up. She wanted to be invisible in her grief, wanted to blend in to the sidelines. She didn't want anyone to notice her, or look at her, and she certainly didn't want anyone to think she was trying to look even remotely attractive.

Downstairs she greeted her dad with a half-smile, touched her little brother on the shoulder in greeting, then spooned some muesli into a bowl. Her appetite was non-existent, but she'd tried not eating in the first few days after Beth died – accidentally, not on purpose, just too upset to even try – and it had made her grief and anger even harder to cope with when she added grumpiness to the mix.

Shovelling the cereal into her mouth, she forced herself to chew it then swallow, despite it tasting like cardboard. What could she expect though? All of the sweetness had been sucked out of her life, all the goodness, and she'd been left a broken shell, trying to get through each day as best she could.

"I hope this storm clears up soon," her dad said, voice distracted as he peered out the window. "Although I guess there's something poetic about even god crying for Beth."

A shiver snaked up Rhiannon's spine. There was nothing poetic about death. Nothing poetic about her losing her mum, or her dad losing his wife and best friend. And there was certainly nothing poetic about her little brother growing up without a mother, or even the memory of one. It broke her heart to know that he would soon forget their brave and beautiful mum.

Glancing over at him now, her eyes filled with tears. He didn't understand what Beth's death meant – part of him just thought she was still in hospital, and would soon be all better, and hurrying home to them so life could go back to normal. But she knew nothing would ever be normal again.

A sharp rapping on the front door startled her out of her pondering, and she looked at her dad in panic.

"It's just your grandma, kids," he began. "Not that one!" he added hastily. "Nanna Anne offered to pop down and stay with us for a few days, to make sure we're doing okay…" He looked as though he wanted to get up and invite her in, but just didn't have the will or the strength to get out of his chair. Rhiannon glanced at him as she stood up, noticing for the first time that his tie was knotted all wrong, and his jacket was inside out. Yes, they could definitely all benefit from a little TLC.

As she stumbled down the hallway and wrenched open the door, she suddenly wondered if she looked just as unkempt as her dad. But before she could glance down at herself, her grandma had pulled her into her arms, and she could feel tears falling onto her head. Oh god, no more tears. She couldn't cope. They would only set her off again, and she wasn't sure there was any moisture left in her body.

Fortunately she was saved by her dad coming towards them with Brodie in tow. He hugged his mum, thanked her for coming, and shepherded them all out to the car, although not before Rhiannon caught the look of naked pain that he was trying to hide. Clearly he was handling this as well as she was – that is, not at all.

It was stifling hot in the church, and Rhiannon found herself longing for the cooling, cleansing rain that seemed to have been following her around lately. She was still out of sorts, and she thought it might soothe her fury a little. When her dad had announced they'd be having a funeral at the huge cathedral over in Smithfield to farewell her mum, she'd been angry, disappointed and annoyed. Surely Beth would prefer a ritual at Rose's healing centre, or if it had to be religious, for it to be held in the small local church where she had attended services from time to time.

Mike had agreed with her, but he'd shrugged helplessly. Beth's parents had swooped in and taken over the arrangements, and no amount of explaining what their daughter had actually wanted had swayed them from planning a society funeral for all their friends and business associates, who were coming down from London for the day. *Like vultures.*

"But they didn't even come and visit her the whole time she was sick. Why do they get to take control now?" she'd whined.

Smiling a tired smile, Mike had leaned over and ruffled her hair, which had disconcerted her. She was sixteen, not a kid!

"I agree with you love, but this was the only way they'd let us bury your mum at home, where we can spend time with her. They have no interest in that, they just want to put on a grand show, to pretend they care. And your mum won't mind – she's not here now, she's *here,*" he'd said, pointing to her heart.

"I'm sure she's laughing and rolling her eyes that we have to endure this," he'd continued. "And Rose is facilitating a ceremony tomorrow, a proper memorial, and we'll bring your mum back home and bury her close to us. So we'll do it right, I promise, the way she wanted, we just have to compromise a little by doing this too. Don't let it get to you love – funerals are for the living, not the dead."

Reluctantly she'd agreed, but her resentment swirled around her now as she watched her grandmother walk down the aisle towards her, string of pearls around her neck, hair perfectly coiffed and as stiff as the elegant, obviously expensive black dress she was wearing, and a fake smile plastered across her perfectly made-up yet insincere face. How this woman had given birth to her kind, creative, free-spirited mother she had no idea.

Beside her she heard her father take a deep breath as he spotted Patricia too, and she sensed him pull back his shoulders and stand a little straighter, braced for confrontation with his cruel mother-in-law. It made her smile secretly, to know that her dad was on her side, and that she wasn't the only one who dreaded having to speak to her battle-axe grandmother.

A sour expression flitted across the older woman's face when she caught sight of Rhiannon, and she tried to swallow down her hurt. But as her grandmother reached out to shake hands with her – there were no fond kisses hello in *this* branch of the family – a clap of thunder boomed out directly above the cathedral, and Rhiannon almost laughed at how perfect the timing was, and how rattled the perfect Patricia was by it.

Fear touched the woman's eyes as the sound reverberated through the great stone cathedral, quickly followed by a look of distaste.

"Hello Grandmother," Rhiannon said, voice demure and deferential, even as her heart recoiled at the sad charade. "I'm so sorry for your loss."

"Rhiannon," she replied curtly, and for a moment it looked as though she'd forgotten why she was actually there, and what loss she was referring to.

"And Michael," she added, voice clipped, emotionless, as she extended her hand just as coolly to her son-in-law. If her performance today was any indication, it didn't look like Patricia would be keeping up the in-law appearances for much longer, which Rhiannon couldn't bring herself to feel sad about. The woman had been cruel to Beth, as a child and as an adult, which was reason enough to not want to spend time with her or build a relationship. But on top of that she'd also been nasty to Mike for years, and distant, cold and occasionally downright mean to her and Brodie.

A small hand on her leg brought her attention back to the present. Her little brother was hiding behind her skirts, eyes scared as he gazed up at the imposing figure of his grandmother and saw the hostility in her eyes.

Rhiannon tried to shield him, pushing energy outwards from her core, as Rose had explained at one of the rituals she'd attended with her mum. And the more she concentrated, the louder the thunder crashing above the church spires became. She felt all the fury of the storm, felt herself becoming stronger, more powerful, as it grew, and a smile spread across her face.

It slipped the moment Brodie opened his mouth though. "Where's Mumma?" he asked her, and Rhiannon felt sparks coming from her fingertips as her heart split in two. More insanity, she thought, as she peered down at her hands. Why did she keep imagining fire and electricity, thunder and lightning? There was no way she could be controlling the weather.

Was this increasing delusion part of her grief, this strange desire to be in control of something? Trying to shake it off, she clenched her hands into fists, knelt down at her brother's side and put her arm around him, realising in that moment just how fortunate she was, that she had sixteen years of memories with her mother.

"Hey sweetie, we've talked about this, remember? Mumma is with the angels now, but she'll always be with us, in our hearts, and watching over us, loving us always. She's very sorry that she had to leave us, but we're still all together, you, me and Dad, and Mum will be with us too, as long as we remember her and honour her."

It hurt her heart to see her brother's little face scrunched up in concentration, trying so hard to understand that the safety and security he'd taken for granted no longer existed. How could a five-year-old comprehend death? How could she? But she continued her efforts to reassure him.

"Why are we here?" he persisted, his sweet face looking pained as he tried to understand what was going on.

"Today we're saying goodbye to her in this huge cathedral, so Grandmother and Grandfather can wish her well, but tomorrow we'll have a ceremony with Rose, and lay Mum to rest in our cemetery, so we can talk to her whenever we want to, take her flowers, pick her favourite ones, maybe even plant a jasmine vine for her, so the scent reminds her of us, and we can spend time near her..." she said gently.

"For god's sake Rhiannon, how can you live with these lies?" her grandmother snapped. "I know it's not entirely your fault," she added, glaring pointedly at Mike. "But Elizabeth is dead, there's no romanticising that, and filling your brother's head full of rubbish is just cruel. She won't be with you, and she's not watching over you. It's all nonsense."

"Excuse me Patricia, but don't you ever speak to my children that way again," Mike interrupted, voice sterner than Rhiannon had ever heard it, and far colder and more firm.

"You have no idea what Beth is doing now. You made her life miserable when she was young, you were stone-hearted when we got married, and you didn't visit her once while she was sick. We've allowed you to run this farce of a funeral so you can look like you have some compassion in front of the society associates you clearly care for far more than your actual family, but I will not let you destroy our children's memories of their mother, or make them more upset than they already are, just because you're so heartless and cruel."

Mouth open in shock, Patricia stood speechless in front of him. Rhiannon was equally stunned, and totally amazed, that her usually quiet and unassuming father, who she'd thought was spineless when it came to his mother-in-law, had found the courage to stand up to her.

"Go and join your poor, long-suffering husband in the front row, and try to manufacture a few fake tears for your dead daughter. I know that Beth will be relieved that our children won't have to see you again after today."

"But, their inheritance…" she stammered.

"Oh Patricia, please," he scoffed. "You've made it perfectly clear on several occasions that you aren't going to leave any money to Rhiannon and Brodie, and that's fine, we never expected you to. You've also made it plain that you don't want to spend any time with them, or see them again, so while I feel sad for you and Frank that you'll miss out on so much, I can't say it's any great loss for us that you want no contact with our family," he said sternly.

"Now go, please. This is an incredibly difficult time for us, mourning the loss of the most precious person in our lives. Your disrespect is an insult to Beth's memory, and I won't hear another word," he added. Then, leaning down, he picked up Brodie, winked at Rhiannon over the young boy's shoulder, and led them to the pew across the aisle from his in-laws.

Flabbergasted, Rhiannon stared at her father, shocked and impressed in equal measure. But he held up his hand to stop her when she opened her mouth to speak.

"I took no pleasure in it darling, and it makes me sad that you were about to compliment me for being so harsh. But I won't have her being cruel to either of you, especially today. To be honest, I feel sorry for her. She's a cold, lonely woman, and I can't even begin to understand how she could not want to have a relationship with both of you. But it's her loss," he said firmly. "Now, let's not waste another moment thinking about her, all right?"

She nodded. "I love you Dad."

"And I love you," he replied, smiling a smile that didn't quite reach his eyes, before gently pulling Brodie onto his lap.

Rhiannon's heart bled for him. He was too young to be a widow, too inexperienced and ill-equipped to be a sole parent. And he looked so lost without his beloved wife. Her mum had been the outgoing one, the social one, the strong one. And yet her dad had displayed a steeliness and power of his own over the last week, keeping things together for Brodie when she knew he would have been happy to check out and join his wife, and now standing up to his ogre of a mother-in-law.

It struck her finally, that there were different kinds of strength. Some would consider Mike a pushover, because he was happy to let others choose the car, or the restaurant, or the holiday destination, to let them take the lead. Yet when it really mattered, like today, he dug deep to find his voice and speak his truth, standing up for himself, his children and his wife.

"Oh love, you have to pick your battles," he said, as though reading her mind. *Hmm, he was also more intuitive than she'd given him credit for.* "If something doesn't matter to me either way, I'm happy for others to choose. It's the time together that I loved about our family holidays, so the places we went never mattered to me, it just made me happy knowing we could go where your mum longed to visit. But the big things, the important things? That's different. I will always fight for you and Brodie. With my last breath I will protect you both."

Tears welled in Rhiannon's eyes, but no sparks flew from her fingers and no thunder crashed overhead. She felt sad and a little bereft that she'd underestimated her dad for so long.

"Bravery isn't about bossing people around or fighting against everything in life just for the sake of it," Mike continued. "If I'm happy with either option, why would I insist on choosing when it means something to the other person? But I will not stand by and watch you two being hurt, no matter how uncomfortable it makes me feel," he insisted.

"And yes, of course I'm terrified of Patricia, I have been since the day I met her, and she thrives on that. I don't care for me, but it used to break my heart that she hurt your mother so deeply. Beth knew it was nothing personal though, and she let go of trying to impress her, or convincing her to love her, a long time ago. Our family, the four of us, was always enough for your mum, and don't you ever forget that."

Rhiannon smiled sadly. "And your parents loved her like a daughter. That must have helped."

Leaning forward, Mike kissed the top of Brodie's head and smiled at his growing-up-too-fast daughter.

"Yes they did. And so did Rose," he said, but his words were twisted with some emotion she couldn't identify. A sharp spear of pain shot through Rhiannon's heart, and she stared at him, panicked. Why did it hurt him to say that? What made him so devastated by the mention of Rose loving Beth like a daughter that she could feel his emotions and his struggle?

"Why didn't Rose ever have kids?" she asked, surprised she'd never wondered before. "I know she lost her husband quite young, at least I think she did, but she never remarried?"

Mike's face paled, and it looked like he was going to pass out. "Rose and Louis did have a child, a daughter," he whispered, and Rhiannon stared at him in shock.

"What?"

"Violet. We went to school together. But she left home when she was seventeen, and Rose never heard from her again. No one knows whether she died, or just disappeared," he said, sadness in his voice, and… *was it regret?*

"It would have destroyed most people, and in some ways it did break Rose, and defeat her, but it also made her even kinder, even more compassionate. And Beth's death is really hurting her, although she's trying to be strong for us. But she cares about you love, so if you ever need her help, or advice, or anything at all, know that you can go to her. If something is too hard for you to discuss with me, Rose will be there for you."

Before she could make sense of Mike's revelation, or ask any more questions, the priest strode out of the side room. Beth's coffin was raised on the platform, and from that moment on everything passed in a blur. Rhiannon was aware that her grandmother spoke, her words chilling in their insincerity, and that the priest preached and hymns were sung, but she didn't feel fully present.

And all the while, the violence of the storm outside raged on above the old stone cathedral.

Chapter 11

The Final Farewell

Blue skies greeted Rhiannon when she peeked out of her bedroom window the next morning, and for the briefest of moments she forgot just how black her world had become. But then, abruptly, it all came flooding back, and the grief poured through her limbs, clouding her mind and piercing her heart all over again. She wanted to crawl back into bed, hide under the quilt and stay there forever. She didn't want to speak to anyone, listen to anyone, or see anyone. She wanted to disappear from the world.

Yet she couldn't, not today at least. Today was Rose's memorial ritual for her mum, and learning that the priestess had lost her own daughter twenty years ago made Rhiannon even more grateful to her for the love she'd always had for Beth, and her determination to honour her as she deserved.

It was a small mercy to know that at least it couldn't be any worse than yesterday's funeral service, and a fleeting smile crossed her face as she recalled her dad standing up to her grandmother for the first time. And it seemed that she wouldn't have to worry about seeing the woman who had been so cruel to her own daughter, so disdainful of her son-in-law, and so cold towards her and Brodie, again. She couldn't understand why people like that even had children, but she supposed she should be grateful, because her mum had been the sweetest, kindest, smartest person she'd ever known.

Steeling herself for the ordeal ahead, she threw on some clothes and made her way downstairs. Her nice grandma Anne was in the kitchen with Brodie, making pancakes and chatting with him about the bike he'd been learning to ride, the fort he was building at Ben's place, and what he'd like for lunch.

"Sweetie," Anne cried, moving over to the doorway where Rhiannon lurked and hugging her. It felt so nice to be held, yet it also reminded her that she would never have one of her mum's cuddles again, and that thought almost made her lose what little composure she had. Taking a deep breath to calm herself, she walked over to her brother and kissed him hello.

"Are you feeling better now Rhi-Rhi?" he asked, his innocence breaking her heart. "Nan said that you haven't been feeling well, so I shouldn't go and wake you up."

Her grandma grimaced, and mouthed "sorry", but Rhiannon smiled gratefully at her. "Thank you," she whispered.

"I'll be okay buddy," she said to Brodie with forced cheer, and sat down next to him. "So, can I eat all your pancakes?" she asked, hovering a fork over his plate, and he squealed and shook his head, his worry forgotten as he protected his breakfast.

Anne brought Rhiannon her own towering plate of pancakes drizzled with maple syrup, and told her that Mike had gone to the cemetery to finalise preparations, but would be home in plenty of time. Rhiannon tried to lose herself in her interaction with her brother, tried to be brave for him at least, and shut off her emotions, but it was tough, and she was relieved when her grandmother finally told her to go and get ready, while she took Brodie down to the park.

That afternoon, her legs felt like lead as she reluctantly climbed the stairs of the healing centre and braced herself for the ritual to come. It had seemed a nice idea when Rose had offered – Rhiannon had been so mad at her dad for letting her mean grandmother take over the funeral service, so a ceremony of remembrance with her mum's real friends sounded perfect. But now she didn't know if she could face any more public grief, any more sympathy, any more compassion, any more sad eyes levelled at her, bringing out her guilt. Just as she decided to turn around and flee, she heard the door above her open, and froze where she stood.

"Rhiannon, sweet girl, I'm so glad you've come," Rose called out from the landing, and she cursed her timing as she glanced up to the top of the staircase. There was no going back now, no escaping the heart-rending, heart-breaking, ritual to come. The priestess looked formidable, her long silver hair floating loose and wild around her face, her expression reminding her of an ancient power brought forth into their world, with the wisdom of the ages residing within her heart and mind.

A glimmer of fear shot through Rhiannon as she felt the strength contained within the woman facing her, but she shook it off. For as long as she could remember, Rose had been like another grandmother to her, a real grandmother, caring for her and Brodie, sharing holidays and special moments with their family, teaching her things, encouraging her, championing her.

There was no rational need to be afraid of her, and yet she was. She was scared that this wise old crone would see within her heart, see the broken parts of her, see the shame snaking through her veins and blackening her soul. See that it was her fault that Beth was dead and her family was shattered.

A crack of thunder shook the building, and the flash of lightning seconds later sent a ghostly illumination into the upstairs room, which spilled out onto the landing and lit up Rose's face. From her position halfway up the stairs, Rhiannon paled, but the priestess smiled.

"Come sweet girl, you can help me prepare," she offered calmly, holding her hand out to her.

"I'm not sure I can do this. I don't think I should be here."

Rose's face clouded over, and for a moment she looked angry. Rhiannon trembled, nervous again, but the expression passed, and the older woman extended her hand a second time.

"You need to do this," she said, voice stern but eyes now kind. "You will regret it for the rest of your days if you don't. Now, did you bring the objects I asked for?"

With a sigh of defeat she nodded, then forced herself up the remaining stairs and handed the black velvet bag over. Closing her eyes, she whispered a prayer to the heavens to help her get through this afternoon, then jumped, shocked, when another rumble of thunder crashed above their heads.

Rose stared at her with narrowed eyes as the lightning flashed through the windows, and Rhiannon was terrified that the wise woman knew she was causing the storm. But maybe she'd imagined her expression. Maybe it was simply a trick of the light in this gloomy space. She hoped so.

"Perhaps you could light the candles," Rose suggested, and Rhiannon shivered again at the way she was watching her, scared that every thought she'd ever had, and every thing she'd ever done, would be revealed. Yet she made herself move forward, made herself pick up the box of matches then walk over to the candelabra in the corner, the one furthest away from the all-seeing, all-knowing priestess.

"Sorry Mum," Rhiannon whispered as she slowly began to ignite the wicks. "It's not that I don't want to be here honouring you, grieving you, loving you. It's just that I don't know how I will keep it together amongst all these people who were so close to you. Or, to be honest, with Rose. I know she's going to see right through me, she's going to know, the minute the ritual begins, that it's my fault you're dead. And I don't want to disappoint her, not after all that she's done for us, all that she's been to us," she added with a sigh.

"It wasn't too hard to rein in my emotions at the church, because I knew you weren't really there. There was no sense of you in that coldly austere building, in those words picked out by the mother you loathed, witnessed by her friends and associates. People who didn't even know you, who had no idea who Dad, Brodie and I were, who had no sense of you as a person. Yesterday you were just a cold reflection of your mother, a chance for her to pretend her grief in front of those she seeks to impress, the demonstration of her lie that she is caring, and motherly. So her service meant nothing to us." She tried to control her trembling.

"But here? Today? I know you will be with us. I know you will be drawn close by our grief and love for you, by the magic you wove with these people, the healing they gave you when you were sick, and the care and comfort they offer us now."

Swaying unsteadily on her feet, Rhiannon worried for a moment that she was about to collapse, too emotionally drained to continue, but she took a deep breath and forced her shoulders back and her spine to straighten.

"Today is the real farewell, the final farewell, and I'm not ready for that," she said, her voice croaky with emotion. "I can't let you go. You're my mother, you should be here. I need you. Brodie needs you. God knows Dad needs you. How will he cope without you? How will he be able to go on? You were always the strong one. The capable one. Even when you were sick you kept us together as a family, kept us sane, and centred."

Hearing soft footfalls behind her, Rhiannon spun around, not realising that tears were pouring down her cheeks until she saw one fly off her face. As Rose gathered her into a hug, the sobs she'd been trying to keep under control finally escaped, racking her body with violent shudders.

The priestess held her tight, soothing her, comforting her, letting her cry for as long as she needed to. Not making her stop, or trying to shush her. Honouring her, and her grief, and honouring Beth and her impact on all of their lives.

"Let it out sweet girl. No one is arriving for another hour, so you take all the time you need."

Momentarily shocked into silence, Rhiannon peered up at her. "But you said two o'clock."

Eyes twinkling with mischief, Rose smiled at her. "Yes, and I told everyone else three o'clock. Allow yourself this time Rhiannon. You've been so strong over the last week, holding it together for your dad and for Brodie, but you need to mourn too. You need to give yourself permission to grieve."

Shaking her head fiercely, Rhiannon glared at the white-clad woman before her. "I'm not strong," she muttered. "And I'm not holding anything together. Our family is falling apart, and I can't do a single thing to stop it. The only reason we eat is because you bring us dinner every night, and make Brodie's lunch for the next day. I feel so broken, so lost. And you'd be horrified by just how weak I am, just how useless."

Choking down another sob, she hiccupped, then almost laughed at how morbid and depressing she sounded. Still, this was a funeral, right? Surely that was allowed.

Taking Rhiannon's hands, Rose led her over to a bench along the wall and sat down with her. "Of course you're allowed to feel sad, and to grieve, sweet girl. The death of a loved one is the perfect time to break apart, to break down, to break open. You have lost a part of yourself, a part of your family, and you will always feel the loss, always feel that a part of you is missing, because it is. And that's okay. That's good!" the priestess said passionately.

"You don't ever want to feel normal without them, to feel totally fine and wholly moved on. You *should* be sad! And the hole in your heart that you feel will be there forever? It will be, yes, but over time you will fill it with new memories, new moments, new people. Not to replace your mother, never that, but you, Brodie and Mike have a new bond now, a new commitment to each other, to keep your mum alive in your hearts."

"But I'm no good to them," Rhiannon argued. "And god, it's my fault she's dead!" She tried to stand up, to get away, but Rose held her hand in a vice-like grip, deceptively strong.

"Sweet girl, it's no one's fault. Beth was very sick, much sicker than she let on to you. She fought desperately to overcome it, because she didn't want to abandon you, and miss out on so many precious moments of your life – your first dance, your first kiss, your graduation, your career, your wedding and children, if you choose that," Rose said, voice soothing.

Her well-meaning words just made Rhiannon more agitated though. Because her mother *did* know about her first kiss – had found her in the woods right after it – and the feeling of shame rose up around her again, hot and red and angry. A furious crash of thunder roared overhead, and another flash of lightning lit up the suddenly dark sky outside, piercing through the windows and illuminating the altar in the middle of the room. *Oh god oh god oh god, don't let me be causing these freak weather disturbances.*

"Rhiannon," Rose said sharply, and the frightened girl focused back on the priestess. "Your mother loved you so much, and she was very proud of you. Proud of how you had been looking after the family when she couldn't, and proud of the wonderful young woman you are becoming. She felt bad that you had to shoulder so much extra responsibility, and immense guilt that her deserting you now will make things even harder for you. But she had no doubts at all that you would handle all of it with your customary grace."

A shiver ran up Rhiannon's spine. Her mother was wrong. She had no grace, and all she'd felt for months now was weak, and not good enough. Her horrible night out in the woods had only exacerbated that and made her feel even weaker, so she knew there wasn't a strong bone in her body.

A heavy sigh brought her attention back to the room, back to this moment, back to the look of frustration on the wise woman's face. "Your mum told me that you've been shouldering more than your fair share of the chores since she first became sick, and looking after Brodie too. You are older than your years sweet girl, and I feel honoured to know you, to have seen you grow up. And I know just how proud your parents have always been of you. That's why you're taking part in today's ritual," she continued firmly.

New terror clutched at Rhiannon. "I can't," she whispered. "You can't expect me to do that. I wouldn't know what to say."

An amused expression crossed Rose's face. "So it's lucky that you got here early, right? I have to pop home now to gather some more things for the ceremony, so you've got lots of time to think of what you want to express while you weave together the wreath for the altar and prepare the herbal blend that we'll use for smudging the room and the guests."

Jaw dropping, Rhiannon stared at her in shock. "What?"

Laughter filled the room. "I've placed a selection of herbs on the altar, so choose the ones we'll use in the ceremony, then put together the smudge stick so you can perform the ritual of purification," the priestess instructed. "You have almost an hour before people will start arriving, but I'll be back in half that time, and then we can discuss what you'd like to say and when."

And she was gone, floating out of the room and down the stairs, the bell over the front door tinkling as she made her way onto the street. Rhiannon gazed around the gloomy room, trying to gather her thoughts. She supposed she could point blank refuse to take part, but that would be terribly embarrassing, as well as an insult to her mother's memory. There was no choice.

She wondered suddenly if Rose had been able to honour the loss of her own daughter, but if she didn't even know whether she was still alive, she guessed not. How terrible to not know. To not have closure. No wonder the priestess was insisting that she take part in honouring her mother, so she wouldn't be left to wonder, or regret her shyness.

And so, despite feeling she'd been bullied into it, she strode over to the doorway and flipped on the light, then, cursing loudly, made her way to the altar in the middle of the room.

"Okay Mum, I'm here," she said, trying to soften her voice as well as her emotions. "And I want to be here, I promise, I just feel like a fraud. But if I can't have you back, and I can't get out of this public performance, I may as well try my hardest, right?"

The windows rattled as a vicious wind beat against the building, and she tried to shut it out and focus only on the plants in front of her, and her vague recall of Rose's lesson on herbal healing that she and her mother had attended together last month. God, just one more thing she wouldn't be able to do with her mum – go to rituals and explore magic with her.

Cautiously she ran a finger over the bay laurel leaves, remembering that they were good for communicating with the dead, and that in the past they'd been used as a base for funeral wreaths. Clearing a space in the centre of the altar, she arranged them in a circular pattern, then sought out the next herbs to add.

Mistletoe for protection. Mugwort for inner sight. Holly for renewal and resurrection. Not that there was any chance of that, sadly, but she wanted to believe that her mum would have a new existence somewhere, somehow. Sighing, she touched the next herbs. Rosemary for remembrance. Marjoram for comfort and consolation. Ivy for rebirth and celebration.

Lovingly she wove the flowers and leaves into the wreath, tucked smaller sprigs amongst them, then bound it together with green ribbon. She smiled wanly. Despite her doubts about her ability to do it, she'd created a funeral wreath steeped in magic, and in memories.

Tears blurred her eyes as she recalled the look on her mum's face last Christmas, when she'd hung mistletoe over the doorway to the kitchen, and then swooped down and grabbed their dad the moment he got home, covering him in kisses, much to her and Brodie's amusement.

The ivy leaves sent her back to the leaf-clad cottage they'd stayed in up in Scotland last year, when they'd been rained in for the whole week, but had still managed to have an amazing holiday, the four of them easily keeping each other entertained.

And she smiled sadly as she remembered some of her cooking lessons with her mum, as Beth had taught her which dishes went best with rosemary, marjoram, basil or sage.

Next she had to create a smudge stick, and she racked her brain to remember which herbs would work. Beginning with a bunch of sage, she added cedar leaves for cleansing and purification, lemon balm for spiritual clearing, and pine needles for their beautiful scent as well as their grounding energy. Then she wove lavender flowers into the herbal bundle as well as the wreath, to induce peace, encourage memories, soothe the spirits and calm all those left behind. Those left to suffer and grieve, and try to pick up the broken pieces of their lives and continue as though everything was normal.

Finally she bound the bundle of smudging herbs tightly together with cotton thread, and placed it in the ceramic dish to her right, ready to be lit in order to cleanse the room and all those who entered with its pungent, potent smoke.

As time passed Rhiannon grew increasingly anxious that Rose still hadn't returned, but she kept working, since she had no other option. She unwrapped a wrought iron incense dish and opened three small cloth bags of resins, and carefully poured them into the shallow dish. Frankincense, for purification and spiritual transformation. Myrrh, for protection, healing for those left behind, and purifying the departed soul for the next journey. And sandalwood, for its sweet smell and purification properties.

Then she gathered up twigs from the sacred woods to be burned in the small cauldron – cypress for endings and letting go, elder for transformation, yew for protecting the bodies of the dead, oak for renewal of the soul, and birch for rebirth and renewal. Once that was done, however, she was at a loss. While her hands had been busy and her mind occupied, she'd managed to keep the worrying at bay, but now her thoughts started wandering again and her fears returned.

Just as she thought she might pass out from the panic engulfing her, Rose swept back into the room, a huge basket of flowers in her arms, and smiled at her reassuringly.

"I thought you should select the flowers that will be on the altar too," she said, laying them down on one of the benches along the wall, next to a huge vase shaped like a chalice.

"No, you choose, you know so much more about all of this than I do," Rhiannon protested, but the healer shook her head.

"Sweet girl, this is something for you to do, to honour your mother and celebrate the magic you created together. Beth worked closely with nature – she wove spells with it and took strength from it, and it's to nature that she returns now. You have no idea how much it meant to her, that you came to a few of the seasonal rites with her, that your hearts beat together to the rhythms of the earth and the moon," she explained.

"So choose the pieces of nature that we will farewell her with, communing with the plant spirits that brought her so much joy. And choose them for yourself as well – funeral flowers don't only honour the departed, they also honour and provide solace for the broken-hearted ones left behind."

A single tear fell from Rhiannon's eye, but she smiled. "Okay, I can do that," she offered reluctantly. "I'll call on the nature that she loved so much, to send her on her next journey, and to hopefully give me the strength to get through today."

Rose embraced her, then returned to the altar to prepare, while Rhiannon gazed down at the lush floral pile. Reaching a finger out to touch the delicate petals, she marvelled at their beauty. What witchery had the priestess worked to entice them all to bloom at this time of year? To survive the storms that had plagued the village all this week?

Carefully she lifted the white lilies and placed them in the vase – lilies for love and resurrection, for purity and sympathy, and for the innocence of the lost soul as it is reborn. It amazed her that she recalled the flower meanings, but she was glad. Unless it was her mum who was somehow guiding her? The thought made her smile, even as she rejected the possibility.

Around the lilies she arranged the beautiful white roses her mother had loved so much – roses for love, protection and purification – along with white poppies for restfulness and remembrance; white carnations for pure love and their sweet scent; and white chrysanthemums, symbolic of death, lamentation and grief.

For the smaller vases she chose pretty blue forget-me-nots, as a promise to her mother that she would be remembered always; and pink xeranthemums to represent love, eternity and immortality.

As Rhiannon placed the large vase on the altar then arranged the smaller ones on the windowsills, she heard a bell tinkling downstairs, and realised that the first guests were arriving. Turning in panic, she stared imploringly at Rose, but the wise woman simply smiled at her, and beckoned her over to the altar.

"The smudge stick is perfect," she assured her. "And it would be wonderful if you could stand at the door, smudging people as they enter and welcoming them to the ritual."

While Rhiannon was annoyed by the task, and wanted to run, to avoid having to see anyone, and talk to them, and face their pitying eyes, she soon became glad of it. People took her hand in sympathy or hugged her, but then they had to move on, because she had a job to do. Rose was a crafty, clever witch, knowing how grateful she would be to have something practical to do, an excuse not to engage too much with the other mourners.

But when her teacher climbed the stairs and held her close, she almost broke down again. Laura, also known as Ms Henderson, had been a close friend of Beth's. She was a fellow teacher at their school, and another member of Rose's ritual circle, and Rhiannon suddenly realised how deeply she must be reeling as well. She'd been so focused on her own grief that she hadn't even thought about anyone else's, but the warmth and sadness in the room today reminded her how profoundly loved her mum had been, and how much a part of the community she was... or had been.

So many people were grieving, which made her feel even sadder in some ways – that so many others were suffering Beth's loss too – but also comforted and relieved, especially for her brother. Brodie would grow up surrounded by people who remembered his mum, who would care for him on her behalf. Although she'd often wished she lived in a big city, because Summer Hill could be boring at times, for once she was glad she'd grown up in a village, with such a strong sense of camaraderie and community.

When everyone had entered the ritual space and been smudged with the potent smoke, Rose stubbed out the sage stick and left it near the door, then took Rhiannon's hand in her left, and raised the wand she held in her right. Slowly they walked around the outside of the circle that had formed around the altar, moving deosil, with the sun, and Rose began to speak, her voice deep and strong.

By our will a circle formed,
Between the worlds where love is born.
Contain the energy raised within,
As the borders between the worlds do thin.
Hold us safe throughout this rite,
As we farewell our loved one to the light.
The circle is cast, so mote it be.

Rhiannon could barely breathe, but she felt the power of Rose's words embrace her, felt the energy of the community gathered there with her, and felt the anxiety of the moment as the priestess turned to her and indicated that she should begin.

For a moment she was paralysed by her fear, but slowly the terror melted away. This was not about her, it was about her mum. If she stumbled over her words or said the wrong thing, no one would care, or judge her harshly. It was only her intent that mattered.

Moving slowly, while her heart raced wildly, she made her way to the far corner of the room and raised her hands to the sky. She'd never done this before, and wondered if she could. If the words would come out, or get stuck in her throat, strangled by grief and pain. Yet here she was, no choice but to open her mouth and speak, regardless of how much her voice trembled and her body sweated with fear.

I call forth the guardians of the west to please bless us today, and to cleanse, consecrate and protect this space during our rite of farewell. And I ask the waters of the oceans, the rivers and the sacred springs to soothe our breaking hearts, and wash away Beth's pain, wherever she is now. Thank you, element of water, and welcome.

A sudden downpour outside startled her, and elicited a collective gasp from around the room. Rhiannon smiled. It was comforting to think that the elements were working with them, responding to her call, even if it was just her imagination. It gave her a little more confidence as she moved around the circle.

I call forth the guardians of the north to please bless us today, and to cleanse, consecrate and protect this space during our rite of love. And I ask the stones, the crystals and the very earth that we walk upon to ground and strengthen us, and to hold Beth safe within its womb. Thank you, element of earth, and welcome.

Her voice remained low, little more than a whisper, but slowly she felt herself strengthen, felt the awe in the room, not for her, but for the magical process that was unfolding. She sensed Rose's energy too, reaching out to her, enveloping her, holding her up, supporting her as she moved to the next quarter. And she wanted to believe that her mum was there, watching her as she summoned the courage to speak.

I call forth the guardians of the east to please bless us today, and to cleanse, consecrate and protect this space during our rite of sadness. And I ask the winds of the planet, both stormy gale and gentle breeze, and the very air itself, to inspire and uplift us, and transport our messages of love and loss to Beth. Thank you, element of air, and welcome.

A whoosh of wind rattled the windows, and Rhiannon thought she felt a breeze race in the door from the staircase as she turned in that direction. Dismissing it once more as wishful thinking, or her imagination, she raised her arms skyward one final time.

I call forth the guardians of the south to please bless us today, and to cleanse, consecrate and protect this space during our rite. And I ask the flames of light and heat, and fire itself, to burn away our fears and grief, and keep Beth warm on the cold journey ahead of her. Thank you, element of fire, and welcome.

A flash of lightning split the sky, and illuminated the altar once more. There was another sharp intake of breath from those gathered, but as Rhiannon returned to her place in the circle, it was only Rose's attention and approval she sought, and the priestess nodded to her, pride in her eyes.

"Thank you, sweet girl," she whispered, her words filled with gratitude and respect, before she lifted her own arms back up to the heavens. Her voice boomed out of her, deep, dark and powerful, and connected so solidly to the earth.

Great Mother, divine goddess of wisdom and light,
Shine your blessings on us so bright.
Lord of the woods, of nature and might,
Shine your blessings on our sacred rite.
Hekate, deity of the crossroads, goddess of death and of balance, I invoke you.
Please illuminate the darkness as we say goodbye to our friend, mother, wife and loved one, and set her free.
And Ceridwen, goddess of death and rebirth, in your aspect of wise crone and elder, I call on you.
Please lend us your wisdom and strength, and guide our beloved Beth on her final journey.

Lowering her arms, Rose brought her awareness back into the room, into the circle, and looked around at each person.

"Today we gather to say goodbye to our beloved friend Beth," she began, voice heavy with the gravity of the occasion. "Death is but a doorway, it's said, a portal to a new life, a new adventure. So we have come together today to farewell dear Beth, and send her on this journey surrounded by our love and well wishes. We are here to celebrate her life too, and the profound impact she had on all of us. She was like a daughter to me, and I am more grateful to her than she could ever know that she allowed me to be a small part of her family."

Rhiannon's eyes filled with tears, but this time they were not for herself but for Rose, who had lost her own daughter, but become a de facto mother to Beth, who'd been so badly treated by her own parents. Rose had bestowed all the love she had on someone else's family, and Rhiannon was so grateful to her, while also being devastated that she'd never known, or thought to ask, about her lost child. But she could ponder all of this later, tell Rose how sad she was for her loss another day. Right now she had to focus on the present, and on her own loss, and pay attention to these rites.

"Beth was an important part of our magical circle, always so welcoming, so supportive, and so filled with magic and wonder. She was a vital part of the local school too, a favourite of every pupil who had the good fortune to be in her class, and she adored being a teacher," Rose continued.

"Dearest to her heart though was her role as wife to Mike and mother to Rhiannon and Brodie, and it devastated her that she had to leave them now, that she wouldn't get to see her children grow up. That she was letting them down, or so she thought. But knowing Beth, even for a short time, was to be transformed, and so each of us here today knows the magnitude of this loss, and shares the pain as we face life without her."

Gazing around the circle, Rhiannon was awestruck by the tears as well as the smiles being drawn out as Rose eulogised her mum, before she dragged her attention back to the priestess.

"Beth faced her illness with incredible courage, drawing strength from her family, even as she tried to be strong for them. She never complained about the treatment or the pain, although it viciously attacked her frail body towards the end. She never moaned about the weakness that overwhelmed her, and she never wanted sympathy. She hid the worst of what she suffered, and she would have endured much more for even one additional moment with her loved ones."

As Rose paused, Rhiannon realised that even the usually unflappable wise woman's composure was slipping now. Sadly she watched as the priestess took a few deep, steadying breaths before she was able to continue.

"I spent a lot of time with Beth over the past few weeks, and indeed over the past twenty years," Rose shared. "And she was adamant that she didn't want people to mourn her when she left us. Instead she wanted us to celebrate her life, and to be grateful for the time we *did* have with her. And I vow that I will try my best to do that for her, no matter how difficult."

Mike was crying, great heaving sobs, and Laura had an arm around his shoulders in comfort. Rhiannon had tears pouring down her face too, but Rose's beautiful words filled her with pride as well as sadness. It wasn't just that the priestess had seen the beauty and kindness and strength in her mother, it was that everyone else here saw it too. It wasn't much, weighed against the loss of her, but it gladdened her heart to know it.

"Now Beth's daughter would like to offer a few words," Rose said, and extended her hand to Rhiannon. She froze. How on earth could she do this? How could she vocalise the depth of her grief in front of these people? How could she do justice to her mother, her kind, selfless mother, in mere words? Her brain had turned to mush – so maybe she could start there.

Slowly she walked to the centre of the room and stood there, shaking slightly, her gaze darting anxiously from face to face. All of them she knew. These were the people who had spent time with her mother, who her mother had cared about. The people who *should* be honouring Beth's life, unlike the farce at the cathedral yesterday, filled with people who'd never met her.

The ghost of a smile lifted the corners of her mouth, although her eyes remained sad. "Thank you for coming today, and honouring Mum as you pay your respects to her. She would be so happy to know that you are all here, and also a little surprised by the massive outpouring of grief. Not that she should be surprised, because she touched so many people's hearts, but she was too modest to understand how deeply she affected us all," she said, then paused, battling her nerves, her fears, her pain.

"I'm not surprised though, because the grief at her loss has smashed into me like a truck, like a head-on collision, with a violence that has totally flattened me. So I apologise that I'm not making much sense. I can't get my head around the idea of a world without her in it, and I'm not sure I ever will. Nothing makes sense to me right now," she sighed.

"Grief is such a strange thing, so intangible, so elusive, so hard to explain and describe, and so sadly real. It's so chaotic that I can't think straight, or see straight, or talk straight. It's a creeping pain that has hollowed out my chest, and a shuddering, throbbing vibration like a monster, which rampages through my body and eats away at me – at my mind, at my heart, at my soul..."

Gazing around the room, she saw the stricken looks of all those who had loved Beth. And then she saw the awful pain on her dad's face, which made her realise they hadn't actually talked about how the grief was affecting them, infecting them, crippling them. She could express herself here, where it felt somehow less personal, but she wasn't ready to talk to her dad about how deeply she was hurting yet. Perhaps it was because she knew he was hurting just as badly.

"It feels like my whole world has collapsed, or blown up, and nothing will ever be the same – yet in some ways nothing has changed. And it makes me so angry that the world hasn't stopped. That life is continuing on regardless. But mostly it makes me sad," she reflected.

"Of course over the last few months I tried to bargain with god, or the universe, or whatever it is that controls these things. 'Take me instead of Mum.' She had so much to live for, so much still to do, so much still to give. She was the kindest person I know, and I think

I will live all my life in her shadow, trying to live up to her, trying to make her proud of me."

She stopped, the tears in her throat making it hard to speak, but finally she managed to swallow hard and go on.

"And I wonder, did I appreciate Mum enough when she was alive? Did I tell her often enough just how much I loved her, just how important she was to me? If I've learned anything this week, it is to cherish the people who are here, while they are here. To tell them that you love them while you still can. Right now. Celebrate those you love while they are alive – don't wait until they die, please," she whispered, voice ragged with pain. That was enough. She couldn't go on.

Rose walked over to her and hugged her, then moved back to the altar. And her dad, pain so clear on his face, put his arms around her and led her back into the circle, where they watched the priestess thank everyone on their behalf.

Exhaustion hit Rhiannon, and she watched, numb, as Rose continued the ritual. But finally she farewelled the quarters and the deities and closed the circle, then instructed everyone to have a biscuit to ground themselves after the magic they'd all woven together. When people came over to express their condolences to her and her dad, the weight of her grief pressed down on her, and she felt her legs buckle. But the wise woman was there to catch her.

"You spoke beautifully sweet girl," Rose said, holding her close, and Rhiannon felt strength flowing into her, the strength to stand up, and the strength to keep going, for now at least, even though all she wanted to do was go and hide in her bedroom, and never come out.

"I was in a total panic," she admitted. "The whole time. I thought I would pass out from the fear, and the lack of preparation, and the pressure of all those people staring at me. The pressure to do right by Mum, and do justice to her with my words," she grimaced.

"And yet you didn't," Rose assured her. "Why do you think I left you here alone to make the wreath and the smudge stick, and blend the incense? It was so you'd be too busy trying to work out which herbs to use to worry about what you were going to say, or to prepare excuses to avoid speaking, or to worry about what people would think of you."

Rhiannon mustered up a half smile, part of her impressed with Rose's plotting, another part a little put out by her manipulation. But she was glad that she'd spoken for her mum, because the priestess was right, she would have regretted not being brave enough to do it.

For a moment she wondered if they should have allowed Brodie to come, but she thought her dad had made the right call. At the funeral in the cathedral yesterday her little brother had been so confused, and so frightened when he'd seen their grandmother. Even worse, he'd picked up on the distress and pain of everyone there, without understanding its cause.

As much as Mike had wanted his son to be with them today, in the end he'd asked his mum to look after him while he and Rhiannon were at the memorial service, then burying Beth in the local cemetery. Anne had been reluctant to miss the ceremony herself, but she'd agreed that it would be too much for Brodie, so she had kept him company at home.

As Rhiannon joined the flow of people making their way to the cemetery, she began to wish she'd invited her best friends Debbie and Sue, to have some support of her own. She'd been worried they would find the magic too weird though – she'd never told them her mum was a regular at Rose's magical circles, that she was what some people in the village would call a witch.

And after her recent spellworking in the woods, and its disastrous outcome, she wasn't even sure how she felt about magic anymore. But she'd really enjoyed the couple of rituals she'd been to with her mother, and the sense of possibility, friendship and support that the participants all shared, so she knew she should try not to let her one bad experience colour her feelings.

Rose had told her that she was welcome to come to their rituals on her own now, but she didn't think she'd have the guts to turn up without her mum by her side for moral support. She longed for a friend to share all of this with, someone who understood the beauty of Rose's magic, someone who wouldn't find her, or it, weird. Even more importantly, she yearned for someone who comprehended the depth of her grief. She felt so totally alone in her loss and bereavement, cut off from the flow of life and normality.

When they had all finally assembled in the cemetery, the burial itself passed in a blur, Rose and the local priest respectfully hurrying the ceremony because of the grey skies and threat of another storm looming over them. Tears for her mum, which made Rhiannon smile.

Soon enough her dad was surrounded by friends and well wishers leading him to the pub for a small wake. The bar manager told her she could join them, but she shook her head. Her mood was darkening along with the sky, and all of a sudden she really had to get out of there, to hide away and be alone with her pain.

As Rhiannon headed home, the heavens opened and rain poured down on her, and she laughed.

Chapter 12

Love and Friendship

Beth... Twenty years ago...

When Violet had invited Beth to the upcoming new moon ritual, she'd politely made an excuse not to go. She was grateful to Rose for the healing, and had felt a lot better, and a lot more patient, ever since, but she was mortified that the priestess knew so much about her now, and embarrassed that she'd cried in front of her. She just couldn't face her.

And what if Rose had told her daughter Violet about her, about what she'd discovered? She'd think she was an idiot, surely, that she'd been with a guy who hit her. *She* certainly thought she was. And no doubt she would think less of her too, that she hated her parents, since her own were so great.

But after another long and challenging night at home, Beth had reconsidered. Rose probably would have kept her confidence, even from her daughter. And no doubt Violet wouldn't really think any less of her – she was so damn sweet and non-judgemental, which would be annoying in anyone else, but in her was endearing. So when Mike called the afternoon of the ritual just in case she'd changed her mind, she thanked him gratefully and borrowed one of Jennifer's long golden dresses to wear.

She'd been nervous as she climbed the stairs, but Violet met her at the door, hugged her and led her inside. And the magic had crept over her again as soon as she entered the beautifully decorated room, thrilling her to the core. Part of her had worried that she'd just imagined the sense of Otherworldliness of the first ritual she'd taken part in, her rational mind being unable to explain just how full her heart had been, how inspired and lost in enchantment she'd felt.

But now, as Rose welcomed the elements and the deities, relief swept over Beth as she felt the tingle on her skin, the goosebumps racing up her arms, and the swelling of emotion deep within her. It hadn't been a one-off, that first time. This was something real, something she could be part of, something that made her feel stronger, made her feel more than she was, or thought she was. More than her mother allowed her to be.

Violet squeezed her hand, as though she knew exactly what she was feeling, and Beth's face lit up with joy. Grinning, she squeezed her friend's hand in return, then focused her attention back on the ritual before her, following it more closely now that she was a little more familiar with it.

The knowledge that the priestess hadn't betrayed her confidence to her daughter warmed her heart – then a flash of jealousy slammed into her. If only Rose was *her* mother. She was such an amazing woman, such an inspiring role model, such a beautiful soul. It hurt her so deeply that she had to contend with her own cold, cruel, uncaring parents. But quickly, consciously, she reined in her bitterness. She was so grateful that the wise woman seemed to like her at least, even to care about her. It felt so nice. So unusual and yet so welcome.

During the ritual Rose explained about the power of the new moon, and its ability to inspire and fuel new goals. Then she handed them each a candle so they could craft their intentions for the coming month, and send it out to the universe.

"A spell is like a prayer, the vocalisation of your wishes and desires, the distilling into its essence of what you want to grow in your life," she explained, voice rich and deep and quivering with power.

"Once you know what it is you desire, you can send your intention out into the world." She paused, and gazed around the circle. "But isn't that the trick, actually knowing what it is that you want?"

Her words were serious, but there was love and a hint of mischief in her voice. "Tonight we will each light a candle to represent our new moon wish, but first we will meditate on exactly what it is that we plan to do or achieve this coming lunar cycle, what it is that will bring us happiness and joy."

Beth's head spun, and for a moment she panicked, scared that she would mess it up and embarrass herself. But she followed those around her, and by the time the gods and goddesses were farewelled, the circle had been closed and everyone was heading home, she could feel the possibility and potential of new love, life and hope igniting within her.

As she wandered slowly home along her street, hoping that her parents were already in bed, movement up ahead of her snapped her out of her daydreaming. A thick white blanket of mist had descended over the entire town, and she peered cautiously into it, trying to work out what it was that had caught her eye and jolted her from her wishing. Was that a figure lurking under the street lamp up ahead?

She felt rather than heard laughter echoing around her, and it made her feel unsettled and extremely vulnerable. Was someone following her? Slowly she took another step forward, then another. Not sensing anything further, her mind and her muscles relaxed – so that she jumped even more when a pale presence in what looked like a long dark cloak loomed out of the fog and materialised right in front of her.

"Hello?" Beth whispered nervously, voice thin and ethereal as a wisp in the now eerily quiet night. "Um, are you okay?"

A small smile flickered across the woman's face. "I am well beloved, thank you for asking," she said graciously. "But it is you I have come to help."

Beth stared at her, struggling to process what it was about the figure that was making her so uncomfortable, while also wondering what on earth her words meant. How did this stranger know anything about her? What did she want to help her with? Why would she make the effort? And calling her beloved? What did that mean? It sounded like something from an old-fashioned romance novel, or something very old. Was she a friend of Rose's?

Confused, she tried to focus on the vision before her. The woman had long, fiery red hair and was wrapped in a dark blue robe. She was standing so still, smiling at her, and seeming to hold the mists within her and around her like a cloak. Yet the more she focused, the more muddled she became. And while she'd heard the voice, she realised the figure's lips hadn't moved. Was this some kind of weird trick? Or was she hallucinating? Was the woman even real?

The laughter echoed around her again, and she tried to pinpoint the direction of the sound, but it swirled around her in the mist she was falling into. It stuck to her skin, and she felt it with every breath she took – a crisp, cool wetness in the air, and within her now, inhaled deeply into her lungs, and her very being. Should she be alarmed that she was breathing in the cold? That it was becoming part of her, its icy fingers spreading through her veins, through her heart?

And yet, she wasn't scared. Somehow she felt comfort as the thick mist weaving around her became part of her, or she became part of it. Which way did it go? Was she gaining something new, or losing a part of herself to this fog? There was something soothing about giving up control, of letting the magical substance guide her hands, guide her feet.

"There is so much possibility within you darling Beth," the woman finally said, gliding closer to her. "So much potential. You just need to see it, to believe it."

For a moment her heart lifted and swelled with joy – until reality crashed back around her. "You don't know me," she grumbled, as the black mood that came from thinking about her mother descended on her again. "I'm not deserving of such worthiness."

"Oh Beth, of course you are. Everyone is. And I know that you have had challenges, I know your upbringing has been difficult. You cannot lose what you have never had, yet I know that you were robbed of a proper maternal figure, and I do understand how hard that has been, and how unfair. But you are kind and empathetic despite that, no matter how harshly you judge yourself. And now you have found one anyway, a mother figure who will nurture you and care for you and inspire you to be far more than you can imagine," she said, her voice a whisper, a smile, a promise.

Puzzled, Beth stared at her. Why did this woman speak to her in riddles? Was she even from this century? And what did she mean, that she'd met a mother figure? She was enjoying her new friendship with Mike and Violet, but they were her age, or a couple of years younger, so that made no sense.

The tinkling laughter echoed around her again.

"Rose, your priestess friend," the blue-clad woman explained softly, although that made Beth more confused than ever. How and why would Violet's amazing mother ever take her in? Take her on? She already had a much-loved daughter, not to mention a ritual room full of inspiring, kind, magical people who were already close to her, in awe of her, keen for her approval and her love. Why would she spend any more time on a not-altogether-content-with-her-life young woman without a shred of enchantment or skill, who was leaving town soon anyway?

Turning questioning eyes on the mist-wreathed figure, she shook her head, regret stabbing at her heart as she risked another fleeting moment of contemplation of how wonderful it would be to be Rose's daughter, to live here, close to her – and close to Mike – to be surrounded by people who were caring and compassionate.

"Have faith Beth. You will be very important to Rose, and you'll become very close to her. And despite what you think now, you will be most worthy of the relationship that bonds you together. I know you doubt yourself right now, and you doubt magic, but dare to take a leap of faith, I implore you," the woman said gently.

"Tonight is the new moon, and you know what to do. Focus on what it is that you really desire, and feel that intention filling you, enveloping you, spilling out of you and off into the world. And believe that you are worthy of having it."

Beth shook her head again. "That sounds so lovely, and I'd give anything for Rose to have been my mother, I promise you. But I'm not planning on staying here – I just came back for Jenny's wedding, and then I'll be gone again, back to my life in Paris. Which is a good thing, believe me," she insisted.

"I try to be a good person, I really do, but being around my mother turns me into the worst version of myself, makes me feel petty and mean, and lower myself to her expectations just to spite her. Which I know makes absolutely no sense, and that I'm only hurting myself with such childishness, but I can't help it. Spending time with her is definitely not good for my soul – or for the people I interact with afterwards."

A blush stained her cheeks, and her hand flew to her mouth. She'd said too much, revealed too much, and whoever this woman was, she'd turn her back on her any second now and leave her in her misery.

At least, that's how she'd thought it would pan out. But instead the mysterious woman surprised her by taking her hand and drawing her to the side of the path, under the street lamp, where her vivid green eyes sparkled and danced in the golden light, and her translucent white skin shone with an inner glow. It was almost enough to distract Beth from her embarrassment and her confusion. Almost. Her mind was unsettled again, but just before she drowned in her panic, a sense of peace and comfort washed over her.

Suspiciously she eyed the figure before her, sure that she must be doing something to her, manipulating her emotions and feelings in some way, controlling her mind. Was that even possible? Who the hell was this woman?

"Beloved, calm your mind. How can you hope to think straight when you are so consumed with stress and paranoia? Breathe," she instructed.

Beth tried to do as she said, but it was difficult. Being told to relax usually had the opposite effect on her, but she smiled gamely and continued trying to slow her breathing and focus on the present moment.

When the mist-wreathed woman was finally satisfied with her, she began to speak again, voice low and confident, despite her lips still not moving.

"You have a wonderful opportunity here to grow and learn and develop the magic that is within you, as well as to overcome the bitterness you feel about your family. There comes a point where you can no longer blame others for your unhappiness – you have to choose to leave all the bitterness and the blame behind, and take responsibility for your own happiness, your own actions, your own emotional health."

For a moment Beth felt as though she'd been slapped, then that sweet, soothing sensation wrapped around her again, and she smiled. The woman – *was she a woman though?* – was right. Her parents were hopefully leaving the village soon, and she was a grown-up. She couldn't ruin all these amazing opportunities with her anger. If she did, she'd regret it forever.

Glancing up to thank the woman, she was surprised to find herself alone on the dark street. She gazed around, confused. Had she just imagined it all? Was she hallucinating?

Before she could get too stressed, the mists cleared, and she realised she was almost home. Filled with new positivity and purpose, she strode up to the front door then tiptoed upstairs to her room, where she fell into bed and drifted off to sleep, illuminated by the golden glow of her new moon candle.

Chapter 13

The Rain In Her Heart

Rhiannon... Today...

It was an hour before dawn when Rhiannon finally gave up on sleep, after tossing and turning all night. As the tiniest hint of light crept between the gap in her curtains, she felt an overwhelming need to be outside. Out in nature, out in the wild of the storm she could feel in her bones. Pain ripped at her heart, and a restlessness shuddered through her body until she dragged herself out of bed. Quietly she dressed and slipped on her boots, then crept down the stairs and out the back door.

The air was wet and cold as it soaked through her clothes and into her skin, and the wind battered against her, trying to force her back home. But she pushed onwards, refusing to give in, until she reached the top of the sacred tor. Gazing out over the misty fields below her, she raised her arms, then turned her face to the sky.

The sweet scent of the approaching rain lifted her mood for a moment, and she smiled as she felt the sharp decrease in temperature right before the first drop fell. Each splash of water felt soothing as it landed on her eyelids, on her cheeks, on the tip of her nose. And she laughed as she sensed the power of the storm starting to build just as she allowed her own grief to swamp her.

It was like a switch flipping inside her, and as the brief moment of peace she'd felt within twisted into a whirlpool of anger, the gentle rain became a violent storm. Fury blinded her, echoed in the flashes of lightning that made her squeeze her eyes shut, before she finally turned her gaze back upwards and raged at the heavens.

"Why me?" she screamed up at the gloomy, threatening sky. "Why my mother?"

Silence greeted her question, but she continued her railing. "It's not fair! Mum was so young, and so loved, and so needed," she cried. "And she was so good…" She trailed off, her voice cracking before it disappeared altogether.

Broken, she fell to her knees in the wet grass, the wild rain pummelling her body as her mind was flooded with the memory of an afternoon not long after Beth's relapse, when they'd been at home together, just the two of them, cooking up a feast for a dinner party that night.

Beth had appeared so full of positivity that day. She'd been determinedly trying every alternative treatment she could find, and had convinced them all that she would beat this second bout of cancer as easily as she had the first. So when she laid down her knife and turned serious eyes on Rhiannon, her daughter was shocked to the core by her words.

"Darling, I won't be here for much longer," Beth said in a calm, matter-of-fact tone.

Denial slammed into Rhiannon at her words though, and she laughed them off. "Oh Mum, don't be silly. You're the strongest person I know. You'll get better, I just know it," she replied cheerfully. "You're already halfway there."

A shadow crossed her mother's face, and for a moment she slumped against the bench in despair. But then she straightened her shoulders and took a deep breath, steeling herself.

"My darling, being positive is admirable, and I don't ever want you to lose that quality, but unfortunately we have to face the facts. This is a battle that I'm not going to win."

Rhiannon trembled, her face pale with fear and panic. "But –"

Her mum smiled at her, but it was a tired smile. "We have some time, but when that moment comes, I want you to be grateful for all that we've shared together, for all the time we have had. Not many families are blessed with the amount of love we feel for each other, and the closeness we're so privileged to possess. We are so lucky."

"How is this lucky, you talking of leaving us?" Rhiannon demanded, voice defiant.

"I know it's hard to see it that way now, but there aren't many mothers who are fortunate enough to have such a wonderful daughter, to have such a wonderful relationship. Some of my friends say their kids are embarrassed to be seen with them, but we've always been so close, and I appreciate that more than you will probably ever know."

Something in Beth's voice alerted her daughter to the truth of her words, and tears started to spill down her cheeks, chasing angry rivers along her reddening skin, while violent sobs racked her body. She tried to keep them in and push them down, tried to hide her fear and her grief, but it was all too much for her, and soon all that she'd been holding in was unleashed. Her face scrunched up, her shoulders shook, and she gasped desperately for breath.

"It's not fair!" she shouted. "Why you? Why us? You're too good, too loved, for this to happen to you. Why can't it be someone else, someone no one cares about, someone who is mean and bitter, who's wasting their life? You can't be taken away, we need you! Brodie needs you, Dad needs you – and I need you," she wailed, and threw herself into her mother's arms, arms that shocked her with their fragility even as they clung to her.

How had she not noticed how frail her mum had become? When had it happened, this collapse into acceptance of her impending death? It seemed like only yesterday that Beth had been strong and healthy, the indomitable centre and spirit of their family, the warrior woman who supported her husband emotionally, who took on every challenge they faced, who worked full-time yet was still always there for her kids with their schooling and activities, who was a member of  both the parents and the teachers committees, who was such a vital part of the community, and of Rose's circle. So busy, so bold, so alive.

Yet here she was now, in the blink of an eye, or so it seemed, suddenly so thin and so weak, so dependent on others. So frail and apparently close to death.

As Rhiannon felt her mum's arms around her, she leaned in to her body to test its strength, and realised that Beth now weighed less than her teenage daughter. And as she peered more closely at her face, she saw a shadow of the pain she was in and wondered how she'd missed it. How had she been so selfish? Or had her mother worked incredibly hard to conceal it from her, from all of them? That thought made her devastatingly sad, as well as furiously mad.

"My god, stop being so bloody calm and accepting," she shouted, face reddening with anger and frustration. "How can you be so mature about it all, so okay with what's happening? Why aren't you fighting this tooth and nail?" More tears threatened, but she brushed them away impatiently.

"Darling," Beth began, voice a whisper.

"Don't darling me," Rhiannon snapped. "It's not fair. How can this happen to us? Why me? Why you?" she repeated, voice breaking.

Her mum put her knife down gently and took her daughter's hands, guiding her around the kitchen bench to the barstools on the other side. Falling onto one of them, she gestured for Rhiannon to take a seat too.

"Listen to me my darling," she said, squeezing her daughter's hands with the little strength she still had. "I'm so sorry that you have to go through this, especially now, when you should be concentrating on boys and school and having fun with your friends. More than anything in the world I wish I could spare you this pain, wish I could spare all of you," she whispered, voice raw and naked with regret.

"And I know how helpless you all must feel, and that hurts me deeply, knowing the pain you and your dad are in because of me. I think in many ways it's easier to be the person who is sick, rather than the loved one looking on, feeling so useless," she continued.

"But there's no point upsetting yourself with 'what if's and 'why me's. Of course I thought that too at first. Why me? But that just tips you over into a downward spiral of helplessness and victimhood, makes you blame everyone and everything else, and focus on the negative. It's not productive or useful, especially when I need to be focusing on fighting to get well. Besides, the more I thought 'Why me?', the more I realised, 'Why not me?' What makes me more – or less – special than anyone else? Who would I wish to take my illness, my fate? Who deserves it more than I do?

"No one does," she said firmly, before her daughter could interrupt. "Why me isn't the question darling, it's why not me."

Rhiannon stared at her mother, impressed by her reasoning, but still unconvinced. She was sure there were plenty of people who deserved it more than her. Sighing, Beth reached up a hand and cupped her daughter's cheek in her hand.

"Oh darling, one day you'll understand this. Besides, in many ways I'm really glad that I have this forewarning. I imagine it would be devastating to die suddenly, to have not had any time to get my affairs in order, to say my goodbyes. No time to prepare myself, and all of you, for what is to come.

"I am determined to beat this, I promise you, but even if I don't, I cherish this time with you, which is made more precious because it is finite. We've had so many special moments together because of this illness, because it has given every second we have more weight, and I don't take a single bit of that time for granted." Her voice was cracked with pain, but deep, and passionate.

"Some of my friends barely see their kids, because they're off living their own life, off with their friends instead of their family. I know you're missing out on a lot of those things because I'm sick – school events, social things, friendships – but I am so grateful that we've had all this time together, and I hope you don't feel like you're sacrificing too much because of it."

Tears blinded Rhiannon as she shook her head, and try as she might, she couldn't control the sobs that shuddered through her body. But Beth hadn't finished.

"I don't want you to be sad – I want you to be happy," her mother entreated her. "I want you to celebrate all that we've had, all that we still have. I want the rest of our time to be joyous, and to create happy memories. And afterwards, when I'm gone, I want you to be happy too. Happy that we chose each other, and happy that we made the most of our time together.

"Remember the good times – the festive gatherings, the birthday celebrations, the holidays, and all of the beautifully ordinary days in between. Remember the way we made every moment precious, whether it was travelling overseas or just staying in, cooking together, like today, or watching a movie. Sitting around the kitchen table just talking, and catching up on our days – all the tiny golden moments that make up a life," Beth said, her voice trembling with emotion.

"It's those ordinary moments that have meant the most to me, and I want you to remember them – I need you to remember them – and to honour me by continuing to value those things with your dad and your brother, making new memories together, living your lives. Because I will always be with you my darling, as long as you keep me in your heart. So please don't be sad for my loss, just be happy that we loved each other, and loved so well – and know that I will carry a piece of each of you with me for the rest of my journey."

Rhiannon's tears increased, and she tried to get her mum to stop, because each word she said broke her heart a little more. But Beth just patted her hand and continued.

"You have to be brave my darling. Promise me you will. I know how much of a burden this has been for you, and I'm so sorry for that. Brodie is too young to understand, so it will be easier for him, easier to let go, to move on, to move forward. And your dad is stronger than you think – he will be okay. It's you that I fear most for, and you that I feel the worst about leaving."

"Then don't go Mum," she cried.

"Oh my sweet Rhiannon, I need you to accept this. I need you to let me go. And swear to me, that when your dad finds love again, you will support him, encourage him even."

"Mum!"

"I mean it honey. Too many grieving people are made to suffer, to feel they must be alone for the rest of their life just to prove how much they cared. But you will all honour me by continuing to open your hearts, not by closing them off. Be strong my darling, and be kind, to yourself as well as everyone else."

Rhiannon had pretended to accept it that day, but she'd crossed her fingers as she promised she would do as her mother pleaded with her to do. And it had been in that moment that she had decided to go ahead with her own spell, in the woods late one night with Evan. Of course her mother had soon convinced her, convinced them all, that she was getting better – helped by the glamour spell she'd been casting, which Rhiannon discovered too late.

Now, as she felt the wet grass soak through her jeans and chill her legs, she stood up and screamed again at the heavens. Her mum had overestimated her. She wasn't strong, she wasn't kind – she was bitter and she was angry. Yet she couldn't bring herself to regret that, since it was only the anger that was keeping her upright, keeping her here.

The thought of her grandmother's cold face flashed into her mind, and she felt hatred coursing through her. Her palms got suddenly hot, and when she glanced down, she saw sparks crackling from her fingertips, right as a crash of thunder rumbled overhead and lightning pierced the grey sky.

Terrified, she ran down the hill and back along the laneway, heart thumping and breath coming in ragged gasps. Her hands were still sparking, and she wondered if it was the electric power of the storm fuelling it – or was she causing the storm?

Fear thrummed through her veins. Once she made it inside the house, she raced up the stairs to her room and staggered over to the window to draw the heavy drapes closed, trying to keep the storm away from her. But as she reached her hand to the glass, a spark fell from her finger onto her teddy bear, the one her mum had given her when she was a kid.

Horrified, she tried to smother the tiny flame, then wrapped the bear up in a towel and threw it across the room, away from her, before crawling into bed and burying herself under the covers, mortified by what she'd wrought and desperate to disappear.

What the hell had just happened? Surely she hadn't created that storm – it had been heading their way anyway. *Right?*

She didn't have magical powers, no one did, and she couldn't influence the weather or call a storm into being – that was crazy! And she couldn't be the cause of the flame either. That was insane, to think that she was shooting sparks from her fingertips, that she'd started a fire.

But what if somehow she had? What if it just kept getting worse? What if next time she hurt a person, not a plush toy? What if she harmed her little brother? Scared and shaking, she waited anxiously for the blackness of sleep to claim her…

Chapter 14

The Twist Inside

A sense of impending doom clutched at Rhiannon's heart the moment she woke up, and fear coursed through her veins. She'd thought she was crazy in the church when she imagined that she was calling the storms, creating havoc overhead as her emotions burned through her. Yet this morning up on the tor the storm had broken above her as soon as she'd become angry, and sparks had flickered from her fingertips in time with the lightning splitting the sky.

Horror slammed through her as she remembered running home, trying to close her bedroom window to keep the pouring rain and crashing thunder out – then seeing the sparks fall from her fingers and ignite into a tiny flame as they dropped onto her teddy bear. *Dear god, she couldn't handle this.*

She took deep breaths, trying to reorientate herself in her body and figure out what time it was. The clock said one o'clock in the afternoon, which explained her hunger, so she dragged herself out of bed, eyes averted from the bear in the corner. Keeping the still-damp jeans she'd fallen asleep in on, she pulled on a dry jumper then headed downstairs to see if there was any food.

She didn't know anyone else was home until she opened the kitchen door, and Brodie called out an excited greeting. Exasperation slammed into her, and she sighed. She wasn't ready to face anyone, let alone her little brother, but she couldn't run back upstairs to hide in her room now. It made her angry, but with a great effort she managed to push the emotion down and keep a lid on it, so the whole world didn't turn black again, or lightning bolts fall from the sky.

Pasting on a bright smile, she tried to keep her tone pleasant, non-committal, but it was tough. Especially when she saw the pain etched across Brodie's face, and the hurt in his eyes, when he asked when they could spend some time together, and the disbelief when she muttered "soon".

Every day she seemed to be letting him down in some way, but she couldn't help it. She felt so sorry for him – until that sympathy inevitably turned to anger, like all her emotions did at the moment, when she felt the pressure weighing so heavily on her. She knew she should be trying harder to help her brother through this loss, one he couldn't even really comprehend, yet part of her was furious that she had to be there for him, that she had to be the mature one. Where was the person who was supposed to help her through this?

The boiling anger began to rise inside her again – she felt it searching for a way to get out of her and find expression, seeking a target to unload upon. Closing her eyes, she took a deep breath to try to calm and centre herself, then smiled at her little brother. It was time to get over herself and be present for him, to work out a way to somehow help him – and who knows, maybe she'd get something out of it too, perhaps find something to help them both pick up the pieces, or at least a few of them.

For a while they sat at the table together and chatted, munching on sugary cereal because their dad wasn't there to stop them, and skirting around their pain. Then she helped him with one of his homework projects, a rare gift of her time it seemed, judging by how overwhelmingly grateful he was that she was there. And she had to admit, it wasn't the worst thing in the world to be with him, to stop obsessing over her own fears for a while, and the obvious joy it made him feel warmed her stony heart a little.

It was all going so well, until her brother nervously asked her when she would start walking him to school again.

Later she couldn't understand why his innocent question had made her snap, yet it had. For a moment her gaze had flickered strangely, and she saw through hazy, blurry eyes. Then her anger clarified, and congealed, and she felt her hands getting hot. Panic raced through her veins, but before she could turn away, or channel this strange sensation elsewhere, she was standing up, facing her brother across the table, hands outstretched like some kind of demented superhero, with none of their healing powers.

This was her, raw and uncensored, out of control – and not able to rein in her fury, or stop the sparks shooting towards Brodie. Mortified, she stood frozen as everything ground down into slow motion, and watched in shock and disbelief as his exercise book caught fire, then a few sparks landed on his jumper – and then he clutched his face and howled in fear.

She knew she should stay with him, knew she should do something – check he was okay, make sure the flames were out – but instead she turned around and ran out the back door, fleeing the scene of her crime, trying to flee herself. But no matter how fast she ran or how far she got, she could never outrun the sheer horror of that moment.

Her heart pounded with exertion and her breath caught in her throat and burned her as she raced back up the steep slope of the tor, careless about where her feet were landing. There were rabbit burrows dotting the slopes, but she deserved a broken ankle, at the very least. Her greatest fear about these strange – *powers?* – had been that she might hurt her brother, and now she had.

Now she really had become the monster she'd suspected was inside her, and a twisted part of her was relieved. She'd been right. Now maybe her dad would believe her, and make sure she could never do it again. Send her away perhaps. That's what she deserved. That's what was necessary.

But what was wrong with her? She wasn't a character in a movie, with special effects at her disposal. People didn't just start shooting sparks from their fingertips. Her life, already a total nightmare, had somehow become even worse than she'd dared imagine. Wasn't it enough that her mother had been torn away from her? That she'd been such a let down to her father and brother? That she felt so alienated from her friends?

She felt as though she'd slipped through the cracks into another dimension, a horrifying place of towering flames and scorching pain. Was it hell? Had she somehow entered the devil's domain, to do penance for her sins?

Her muscles ached and her legs were burning as she kept climbing, but a restless wind forced her up the hill, while a stinging rain pelted down on her, battering her heart, battering her soul, battering her sight. She sensed the summit before she could see it, and as lightning flashed across the suddenly black sky, she fell to her knees, arms raised in supplication as she screamed her fury to the universe.

Words flashed around her brain, searing deep into her heart, into her very being.

An accusation: *"Storm Caller."*
A denunciation: *"Storm Witch."*
A truth: *"Destroyer."*

What did it all mean? What had she done? It felt like she'd harnessed the power of the storm to bring destruction to those around her, those she loved, but how? How could she and the storm be one? How could it feed off her? Or was she feeding off it? Was their tempestuous melding somehow evolving, growing, making them both stronger, making them both worse? Making her dangerous?

As she crawled the last few steps to the top of the tor, she collapsed onto the wet ground, and let the drenching rain pummel her body into the earth. She felt feverish, and delirious, and the voices were close, darting around her head like minions of the devil, taunting her.

Storm Caller.
Storm Witch.
Destroyer.

Storm Caller? That was crazy. She didn't call the storms, or control them. *Did she?*

Storm Witch? Could she be a witch? But that was silly – they weren't real. People said Rose was one, said her mother had been one too, but they were both sweet and kind, not cruel. They didn't harm people, like she did.

Destroyer? That felt right. The word echoed in her mind, becoming louder and louder, so loud that she didn't hear anyone approaching her – she just all of a sudden became aware that there was a presence looming over her.

"You are no destroyer," said a voice from above her, and she stared upwards in alarm. A woman stood there, pale faced, with vivid red lips and eyes that looked black to match her hair. A red cloak swamped her body, and it moved around her like flames, swirling then settling then swirling again, insubstantial as air, and yet Rhiannon could feel heat emanating from her, even in this rain.

A shiver of fear snaked up her spine, yet she felt excitement too. This woman looked dangerous, looked destructive, looked like everything she wanted to be – or already was.

"You are not dangerous, or destructive," the being insisted, then sank down onto the wet ground next to her.

Stroking Rhiannon's dripping hair back from her forehead, the stranger crooned at her, a kind of unintelligible yet soothing sound that wrapped around her like a warm and comforting hug. She resisted it though, no matter how much she longed for it. Her mind was fractured, her heart shredded, and she felt as though anyone who saw her would know of the damage she caused and steer clear of her. So why was this woman staying at her side?

"Oh Rhiannon, you are not evil. You are not dangerous."

The words cut at her, disappointing her. She was both of those things, and if this woman didn't see it, she could provide no comfort to her. Not that she deserved any. Dismayed, her tears renewed, and she was grateful to the icy rain for washing them away, and for being so cold that her body had become numb. Perhaps she could just dissolve into the earth and disappear forever. Surely that would be best for everyone.

"No beloved," the stranger said, voice insistent. "You are loved, and you are needed. Your father needs you, and so does your brother." Her voice was so sweet, so calm, and she wanted to believe her. But she couldn't.

"No! I hurt my brother! I have to stay away," she cried, on the edge of hysteria. "It was one thing to cause a storm that got people wet, or even burn the side of a teddy bear, but I hurt Brodie. I heard his scream, smelled the burning on his face! There's no way to come back from that!" she screamed.

"How can I face him, face Dad? I'm supposed to be looking after them, soothing their hurt, not damaging them even more. Dad will have to send me away now, to keep Brodie safe."

Her voice rose, and she almost choked on the violence of her hiccups. She wanted to let the warm dry hand on her forehead soothe her heart, but she couldn't. She didn't deserve comfort or reassurance, didn't deserve to feel okay.

Yet the woman didn't leave her, no matter how much she raged at her to go, and eventually she cried herself out of tears, out of anger, out of any emotion at all. She was totally numb – body, mind, soul and spirit.

A low-pitched sound – *a spell?* – swelled around her. She couldn't hear the words, but she felt their soothing power, and in her exhausted state, she could no longer resist them. They danced over her body, and knitted themselves into her mind, into her bones, while her eyelids finally began to grow heavy, until they closed altogether in defeat, and she felt her consciousness slipping away.

Fervently she hoped that it was permanent, that she would never wake up again, yet still she felt the stranger's warm hand on her forehead, heard her hypnotising voice. Until she was no longer aware of a single thing.

When Rhiannon opened her eyes hours later, she felt confused, discombobulated. Somehow she was back in her own bed, and her clothes were dry, although she could feel the knots in her damp hair, and her hand closed around a torn leaf when she tried to detangle the mess with her fingers. Its touch brought back all the horror of hurting her brother, and running out on him, and she screamed in fear.

Dear god, she'd hurt Brodie, hurt him badly. There was no coming back from that.

Her dad burst into the room, alerted by her scream, and she flinched and drew back, scrunching her body as far away from him, and as far into the corner, as she could.

"Are you okay darling?" he asked desperately, his face white as he stared at her. "It's getting late to still be in bed, even for you, and I didn't want to barge in on you or invade your privacy, but I heard you scream, and…"

"Get away from me Dad, I'm dangerous!" she choked out, eyes wide with fear and shame.

"Darling, what's wrong? You're not dangerous," he said, voice soothing, but puzzled. "Have you had a nightmare?"

"I wish! But seriously, get out before I hurt you too."

Mike smiled. "Sweetheart, you wouldn't hurt a fly," he began, but Rhiannon became more and more agitated.

"Get out! Get out! Get out!" she screamed, voice rising, eyes widening in distress.

Her dad tried to comfort her, tried to put his arms around her, but she just got more and more worked up, and finally he nodded, defeated, and backed out of the room…

Chapter 15

I'll Be Your Magic

Beth... Twenty years ago...

As the bell over the door tinkled cheerfully to announce her arrival, Beth had second thoughts. Or was it third? Violet had invited her to a workshop at her mum's healing centre – it had a fancy name, something about spirituality, divination and self-development, but all Beth remembered was that it had sounded like some kind of Witchcraft 101 class.

Of course she'd been interested, because she loved being part of Rose's rituals, and wanted to know more, and be able to do more, but now she was scared. She wasn't magical. She couldn't channel energy, change her fate or implore the gods for favours. What was she thinking, that she could ever be anything like the priestess she had come to admire so much, or even like her daughter, who seemed wise beyond her years, and kinder and sweeter than anyone she'd ever known?

Of course Violet had tried to reassure her, and make her feel better about herself – she had a knack for encouraging people to see the potential within themselves – but now she just felt awkward and stupid all over again, and totally out of her depth. It was becoming a common sensation.

Smoothing her long black velvet dress down around her hips, she tried to dredge up some confidence, but she felt uncomfortable, like she was playing dress-ups, pretending to be someone or something she wasn't. Someone magical, and mysterious, someone enchanting and full of the possibility of creating the life she wanted.

Deciding again that she should flee, Beth turned back towards the door – and ran smack bang into Rose. *Damn.*

The priestess smiled as though she'd heard her cursing, and folded her into her arms for a hug. "It's lovely to see you again Beth, and I'm so glad you came today," she said, leading her to the stairs.

The black-clad younger woman resigned herself to having to attend, and was relieved to find a small flicker of excitement hiding beneath her fears. The whole trip back for Jenny's wedding had been about facing her fears and doing it anyway – facing her mother, forging a relationship with the sister she'd always felt hadn't liked her, making friends with Mike and Violet, and, perhaps strangest of all, taking part in magical moon rituals, which was a whole world away from her comfort zone. So this class was just one more thing she had to get through to become a stronger, better version of herself, right?

She thought she'd convinced herself, yet when she walked into the room with Rose, who was resplendent in an amethyst dress, and saw that everyone else was also clothed in bright jewel colours, she blushed. Of *course* she was the only one who looked like a stereotypical try-hard witch. Why hadn't Violet told her to dress in vivid hues? Why hadn't she thought to ask her if there was a dress code? And where was her friend anyway? Cheeks flaming, she thought again about leaving, but Rose took her hand.

"It's all fine Beth, and you look beautiful," she said gently, drawing her into the room. "Violet sends her apologies – she's been throwing up all night, so I ordered her to stay in bed – but you'll feel right at home here with us."

Quickly she introduced Beth to the other women who had assembled, but everything was a blur, and panic washed over her as she realised she wasn't taking in any of the names. When Rose stared into her eyes though, a sensation of peace and calm enveloped her. It made her worries disappear, yet that in itself made her nervous. How *had* they disappeared? Perhaps when people described Rose Tyler as a witch, they really were being literal.

The priestess laughed, and Beth felt a shiver of fear. Had she read her mind? Was that even possible? Reluctantly she joined the other women as they all sat down on soft cushions arranged in a circle, and took out notebooks and pens.

Once they were all settled, Rose carved out the magical space between the worlds that they would work within, then welcomed the deities and the elements to their learning circle. Already the words were becoming familiar to her, from the two rituals she'd been to already, and she felt comforted as they enveloped her in warmth and wonder.

And as soon as Rose began the teachings, Beth forgot her anxiety and her self-consciousness, and allowed herself to fall into the reassuring swirl of the magic the priestess wove.

"Some of you have come today out of curiosity, some because a friend recommended it, some because you've been to a few of our rituals and want to know more about it all, and one or two remain sceptical – which is a good place to be," she said, and smiled at Beth when she blushed.

"Please know that whatever your reason for being here today, you have come at the right time for you, and will learn whatever it is you need to know. I understand that there is still some fear around the word 'witch', in this room and within the community, but I want to set your mind at ease. Witchcraft is simply an earth-honouring spiritual path, which encourages your own self-development, self-determination and self-awareness, and which most importantly sees nature as sacred, and our connection to it as vital. There is no worshipping of evil forces, no doing harm, no brainwashing."

A glint of amusement sparkled in Rose's eyes as she heard the sigh of relief that echoed around the circle, and Beth was surprised to realise she'd been holding her breath waiting for that reassurance too. She smiled as she slowly exhaled.

"The funny thing is, we all practise magic, even those who denounce me as a witch. Whether it's making a wish as we blow out the candles on our birthday cake or drinking a toast to the new year, magic is a part of life, a part of our world, it's just that many people close their eyes to it and turn away from all the enchantment we can taste and feel and touch, if we only let ourselves."

Beth wondered why not everyone embraced it then, if it was so lovely, so natural, so simple, and was rewarded with another smile. Yep, Rose was definitely reading her mind.

"Good question Beth," she announced with a cheeky grin. "It *is* simple, but it isn't easy. It involves a lifetime of study, of hard work and hard-won experience. But having said that, you can begin right now, today, because the most important thing is your will and your intent, your connection to the earth and to your own inner wisdom."

Rose gazed around the circle, making everyone there feel as though she was speaking only to them, her voice intimate, her meaning clear. "Witchcraft is an internal thing, not external – you are responsible for your own ethics, and your own choices. There aren't any strict rules or prescribed beliefs, there's no single book or 'one true way', there's no hierarchy of power, or of people telling you what to do," she explained.

"It's about taking responsibility for yourself and your actions, being aware of consequences, and seeking your own faith, developing your own creed. Others are happy to teach you things, to help, to share, to inspire, but you're also encouraged to do your own study, and discover your own beliefs and morals, because no single person on earth will be on the exact same path that you are on. They won't have the same experiences, interests, dreams, skills, questions, powers."

Alarmed, Beth stared at the priestess. Powers? That totally freaked her out. She'd only gone to the first ritual because she wanted to get to know Mike better, and if she was honest, she'd thought that Violet's belief in magic was a little strange. And now there were powers? Then again, she definitely had felt something during the two rituals she'd taken part in, and in the healing session with Rose – but she'd just assumed it was Rose who had the power.

"Oh Beth, all of us have magic within us. *You* have magic within you. Witchcraft is not hierarchical, it's not about a powerful person, or a supernatural being, holding something over you, dictating wisdom, knowing more, controlling the outcome – *every* person has the ability to create their own life, and weave together all the magic and potential of the universe. But you have to know that for yourself, believe it, and feel it deep within you. I hope that today's workshop will help you begin to achieve that," she said.

"Now I'm just going to run through a few brief cliff notes, to give you all the basics, then we'll start exploring and creating our own spells and rituals. But please feel free to interrupt me at any time, and to ask any questions you have. Today will be tailored for all of you, so I need to know your interests."

Intrigued, Beth picked up her purple pen, and started furiously scribbling down notes.

Do witches cast spells?

This is usually the first thing I'm asked, and yes, we do. But they're not the movie-style spells of enchantment and greed and corrupting someone's will. We don't work magic or cast spells to turn someone into a toad, or make a person love us, or force anyone to do anything at all against their will. Spells are like prayers, they are a sending out of our intention into the world, which is then backed up with action and belief. They can involve chants, invocations, herbs, flowers, crystals, colours, sacred days – or be as simple as focusing your will and speaking your intent.

What do witches do?

We work with the cycles of the moon, the earth and the sun, connecting with the turning of the seasons, celebrating the eight sabbats, or festivals, of the Wheel of the Year, attuning to the energy of the earth as it swells with growth and abundance in spring, comes to fruition in summer, starts to wane in autumn, then goes within, conserving energy, during winter. We work with nature, with energy, with plants and crystals, and with the elements and directions. We help and we heal, and we divine the future as well as the past, looking within our own hearts to discover our inner truths, as much as we look for others. Most of all we work with intent, aware of the consequences of our words, our thoughts and our actions, and I can't stress strongly enough just how important that is.

Is there one correct way or belief?
There are many different pagan paths, and different blends of spirituality and wisdom, from druidry and shamanism to witchcraft, goddess worship and vodou. And over time you may be drawn to one of these paths more than others, or you might prefer to combine the aspects of several of them that resonate with you into your own eclectic practice. There are many different deities too. Some people work with just one god or goddess, as a single being, while others build a relationship with a whole pantheon, perhaps Greek, Roman, Egyptian or Celtic, and see them all as aspects of the divine. Others reject all deities and simply revere the natural world. Some practitioners work in a coven, others walk the path alone. All are valid – there is no single truth, or "proper" way to work magic.

Are there limits, or can we do whatever we like?
Yes, there are limits. This is a path of self-responsibility, of changing ourselves rather than others. We follow the three-fold law, that what we direct outward returns to us three times stronger, thus pain and negativity are never part of our spellworkings because we know it will harm us more than anyone else. Not that we would wish harm on anyone though, regardless of that rule! And we never bind anyone to us or impinge on another person's free will – so no making someone love you, or changing someone else's life, or casting on behalf of anyone without their permission. There are consequences to any magic you wield, and you are responsible for them. Responsible for yourself, and every action you take, or don't take.

Rose paused for a moment, as a gasp of surprise rippled around the circle, and one of the women giggled nervously. Beth wondered if she'd cast a love spell on someone, and was now suddenly worried that the priestess would find out – which seemed likely, given that she'd read every thought Beth had had since walking into the room.

"Admittedly there is no way we can police this," Rose said, sounding sad yet stern. "There are a few unscrupulous people who have embraced witchcraft in order to take advantage of those who seek to learn, who have no qualms in abusing free will, in creating power imbalances and declaring themselves gurus. So please be discerning with who you learn from or take part in rituals with. *Never do anything you feel uncomfortable about.*"

A shiver of recognition raced up Beth's spine, and her thoughts flew to Andrew, to his insistence on her doing what he wanted, when he wanted, and his belief that he was better than her, more "enlightened", and she should follow him. She wondered why she hadn't seen it that way at the time, why she'd felt so flattered that he was interested in her.

A softly-worded query by one of the women about working skyclad broke into her thoughts, and she returned her attention to the class and to their teacher.

"That's a great question," Rose said, approval in her voice. "Part of the answer is related to my last comment, that you should never do anything that makes you uncomfortable. Working naked is something that should be reserved for a circle in which you trust every member. And even if you've done it once, it doesn't mean you have to do it every time – you must decide who and what you feel at ease with, and that could change day-to-day depending on all kinds of things. If you ever get a bad vibe from someone, or feel pressured in any way, just politely excuse yourself and leave."

The woman opposite Beth looked relieved, but the original questioner seemed disappointed, at least until Rose continued.

"Of course this goes both ways, because witchcraft embraces all parts of us, our minds and our bodies, and encourages us to feel comfortable in our skin, to shake off the feelings of shame that some religious paths inflict, particularly on women. So don't do anything you feel uncomfortable about – but equally, don't ever let anyone make you feel ashamed. You are perfect just the way you are, and working skyclad with a circle in which you love and trust every person can be an incredibly healing experience. There is no shame in it. No shame in being you."

Her words struck a chord deep within Beth, and she felt a warmth spreading through her mind and her heart. A light was being shone into the darkest recesses of her mind, bringing up all the cruel taunts that her mother had thrown at her over the years – shaming her about her body, her appearance, her personality, her boyfriends, her attitude, her very being, which had held her hostage in so many ways – and gently burning them away.

Throughout the day she kept taking notes, scribbling in great detail about how to cast a circle and carve out your own protected space in which to make magic. How to welcome the guardians and the directions, and the gods and goddesses, and build a relationship with them based on respect and reciprocity. How to work with the elements in a practical yet enchanted way. And as she wrote, a small part of her was watching, astonished, as the light within her grew, and blossomed, and marvelling as she felt a huge weight lift from her shoulders and melt away to nothing.

As they paused for a cup of tea and a slice of Rose's homemade lemon cake in the afternoon, the priestess broke into Beth's reverie and drew her back into the room.

"If anyone is interested, our Year and a Day course starts soon. We'll gather every week to explore all of these topics, and to celebrate the seasonal festivals, honour the moon phases, study healing and divination, cast spells for ourselves and others – learn and grow and become stronger together. It will be a small, intimate group, and it will require a great deal of work on your part, and a willingness to be fearless as you examine your life and your spiritual practice," she warned.

"But it will be rewarding beyond measure, so I hope that you will give yourself this opportunity to share and to grow, and to find the magic that is already within you."

Beth felt herself starting to awaken, to come alive, and a great yearning built within her, a longing to be part of this circle, to feel this sense of connection with the priestess, and with the rest of the group, and most importantly with her own true self, which she felt had been hidden all these years, even from her.

As evening approached and the sky outside began to darken, Rose closed the circle, and everyone slowly disbanded. After Beth had gathered her belongings, the priestess came over and invited her home to see how Violet was. And so the two women walked together through the gloaming, a soft sparkle of enchantment still dancing just outside of Beth's vision.

"So, do you think you'll join us for our Year and a Day of study?" Rose asked, and Beth felt a whole world of possibility unfolding within her. Yet her fear remained.

"I'm not sure I should – I don't want to slow the group down, or be in the way," she muttered.

"Oh Beth, you won't slow anyone down. No prior knowledge is necessary – that's the point of it, everyone will be learning together, growing together, tapping in to their own wisdom together. You'll teach as much as you learn, that's the beauty of such a circle. I will learn things from all of you too," she insisted.

"The lessons will evolve depending on the interests of each of the participants, and everyone will have a chance to choose a topic, plan a ritual, run one – if they'd like to – or just take part if they'd prefer to be less vocal. It's a wonderful way to push through your limitations and work through your fears, and we'll all help each other become stronger in all aspects of our lives, not just the magical side."

Beth's eyes shone as she allowed herself to imagine a future with the enchantment of a weekly ritual circle underpinning it, and finally she nodded.

"I'd really like that," she said softly, shyly. "But I don't know how long I'll be staying here."

Rose smiled knowingly, then bent down to pat the black cat that had emerged onto the pavement to weave around her ankles.

"This is Shadow," she said, voice full of love. "And Shadow, this is Beth," she added. As Rose opened the gate and turned in towards the front door, the cat looked up at Beth with wise green eyes, and the small white star on her forehead seemed to glow in the soft light of the street lamp.

"Hello Shadow," she whispered, and leaned down to stroke her soft, fuzzy head. When the cat started to purr, Beth felt a wave of peace and joy wash over her, and she followed her new friend up the steps and into the cottage.

Violet was out in the kitchen, stirring a pot of delicious smelling soup, and her face lit up as she saw Beth. "I won't kiss you hello, just in case, but I'm feeling okay now, so don't worry. Would you like some vegie soup?" she asked, her voice so bubbly and welcoming.

For a moment Beth wondered again why Violet was so nice to her, then she decided to ignore her insecurities, for now at least, and let herself be swept up in the love and positivity of this sweet family. She adored the casual manner of their meal, and was so grateful she wasn't at home, enduring another frosty three-course dinner where no one spoke, and she was almost too afraid to eat, in case her mother criticised her supposed lack of etiquette.

An hour later, Violet's dad Louis came home, and he cheerfully pulled up a chair and sat with them, knocking back two bowls of soup and several pieces of toast, and listening to his wife and daughter speak with the most contented look on his face. When the last crumbs had been eaten, Rose made a big pot of tea and retired to the lounge room with Louis, while the girls washed the dishes, then sat down again at the kitchen table and drank their tea.

Violet told her friend she wanted to study to be a social worker after she left school, and for a moment Beth feared that was why she was being so nice to her – she was practising for her future career. But she managed to talk herself out of that particular thread of insecurity, and finally confided her own long-held dream.

"I've always wanted to teach, but Mother said it was beneath me, and so I felt I had to escape this village, to run as far away from my parents as possible so they wouldn't have any power over me, and wouldn't be able to control me or my decisions. And yet, in doing that, they had the power anyway. They *did* influence all of my decisions, from where I lived to what I did," she confessed.

Violet smiled at her as she lifted her mug of tea. "You can stop running now Beth," she said, eyes friendly, and sure. "You're home."

Chapter 16

Rhiannon... Today...

Her face flushed red and her body sweated from the heat, before she suddenly switched to icy cold, then started burning up again... And so the cycle went. Restless and feverish, Rhiannon tossed and turned, limbs twisting her sheets as she thrashed around in panic. Reality and nightmare blurred, and she couldn't work out what was true and what was imagined, what was real and what was dream. Some part of her was aware she'd forced her father out of her bedroom, and it pierced her heart when she recalled the look on his face as he'd backed away from her – there was love, as always, but also confusion, and fear. He must think she was breaking down, so strange would her behaviour seem.

Then the knowledge that she'd hurt her brother sliced through her, and all concern about her father spun off into the background. She broke out in a cold sweat as the memory of Brodie's face, contorted with pain, flashed before her eyes. Was he okay? What must he think of her? *What had she done?*

She was too scared to find out, yet the more she worried about it, the more frantic she became. Her dad had said her brother was fine, and had seemed puzzled by her declaration that she was dangerous, yet her palms tingled as she remembered the flood of hatred and the intensity of the anger that had swamped her just before the sparks had flown from her fingertips across the table towards Brodie, igniting on his homework, then landing on his face.

Desperately she sorted through her memories, in an attempt to discover what was true. After she'd fled from the house, from her brother, there was the flight up the tor, panicked and terrified, and a woman in a long red cloak who sat up there with her, comforting her, and doing her best to convince her that she wasn't dangerous, that she hadn't hurt anyone.

Was the woman real? She hoped so, because if she was, maybe that meant Brodie was okay. But when she tried to picture the woman's face as she'd spoken to her, she couldn't – she just drew a blank. And when she made an effort to recall the sensation of the woman's hand on her forehead, it seemed it had been warm and dry, untouched by the pouring rain, which was impossible. Anyone up there on the summit with her would have been as drenched by the storm as she was.

Blocking her fear from her mind with an extreme act of will, she buried her head under her pillow again, wanting to disappear from this house, from this village, from this world. Should she run away? What if she set the whole kitchen on fire next time? Wouldn't Brodie be safer without her in the house? Wouldn't *everyone* be better off without her?

A soft knock on her door startled her, and she sighed. Why couldn't she be left alone? Didn't they understand how traitorous her body and her mind had become? Didn't they know that she was influencing the weather, and the elements? What other explanation was there for the black clouds that formed instantly overhead whenever she thought about her mother? How else had she ignited a childhood toy – and shot sparks at her brother's face? She was a danger to people, and they should all just leave her alone.

"I'm busy," she called out. "I'll be down later." She wouldn't, of course. A few hours from now she would cautiously open her door, and discover the plate of sandwiches or bowl of salad that her dad had left for her so she wouldn't starve. She had to admit that he was pretty good about not hassling her – so she was shocked when she heard the door handle turning. Instantly she felt the fury building in her chest, and the tingling in her fingers beginning to increase. *Oh god, not again.*

"Dad!" she exploded. "I don't want to talk! Don't come in!" she screamed. She could hear the anger in her voice, feel it thickening and growing in power, but she couldn't bring herself to care enough to soften it. She was losing control, and she didn't know how to stop it. Or didn't want to know, she couldn't tell which.

"That's okay Rhiannon, you can just listen," said a gentle voice. The door cracked open, and Rose walked in.

"What are you doing here?" she demanded, panicked, as she quickly sat up in her bed and wedged her hands under her legs. Grimacing and anxious, she hoped she wouldn't burn a hole in her pyjama pants or the mattress.

"You know how worried your dad is about you, so I won't bore you with that," Rose began, her tone less judgemental than Rhiannon had expected. She was relieved – until the older woman continued. "But he sensed that you're going through something you don't understand, something he can't help you with. So he's hoping that I can, if you'll trust me enough to tell me, and let me try."

Suspicion flashed through her eyes as she gazed at the priestess, then she shrugged. "I don't know what you mean."

"Your dad said you've been having terrible nightmares," Rose began, voice patient, soothing. "That you're worried you'll hurt your brother, inflict some kind of pain on him."

"I already did."

"You did what sweet girl?"

"I hurt Brodie."

Electricity fizzed through the room, and Rhiannon's hair started crackling, while outside the house, thunder rumbled overhead. Her face flamed red with embarrassment.

"What is it?" she implored, terror clutching at her heart. No longer could she pretend it had nothing to do with her. Panic and dread were swallowing her whole. She felt as though she was drowning in it, but she wasn't sure she wanted to be rescued. That she *should* be rescued.

Rose sat down next to her on the bed, moving slowly, as if to let the scared young girl know that she could stop her at any moment. That she still had some control. The priestess smiled at her and pulled one of her hands out from under her thigh, squeezing it reassuringly.

"There's no need to fear, sweet girl. You didn't hurt Brodie."

"So it was all just a dream?" she croaked. Of course she hoped that was the case, prayed with all her heart, but it just didn't make sense. It had been so vivid, so real, such a tangible sensation. First the teddy bear, then her brother's sweet but horror-struck face. Even as she recalled it she felt her skin growing hot, and her palms start to burn. She stared down at them, expecting to see flames leaping upward, leaping at Rose, yet there was nothing there.

"Your feelings were real, and powerful, even if the flames were not," Rose said, and leaned forward to stroke her cheek, to show her she wasn't afraid. But Rhiannon jumped in fright, and worry, scared that she would set her alight.

"Oh my dear, you are not dangerous, or destructive," the priestess added, echoing the words of that red-clad woman on the tor. "You are simply hurting, and devastated by loss. And you are allowed to be. It would be strange if you were not."

"But what's happening to me?" she cried. "My anger is destroying me, destroying those around me. It's causing chaos in the heavens, shooting sparks from my fingers, bringing down rain and thunder, and causing lightning to tear the world apart. And I burned my bear, even if I didn't hurt Brodie," she insisted, eyes glancing to where she'd thrown him after she'd extinguished the tiny flame.

"You are tuning in to the power of the storms, like all pagans, or witches, or whatever you want to call us, and amplifying them with your energetic disturbance," Rose explained. "But you are not starting fires or burning things. And you will not hurt your brother, or anyone else."

Rhiannon felt her body hunch over, slump down, in relief, she assumed, or exhaustion. Yet she wasn't totally convinced. What was Rose not saying?

"Breathe child, breathe, and try to relax. The most violent of your memories – the burning of your bear, the scalding of your brother – surely they were just dreams," she suggested. "Well, nightmares," she conceded, at a black look from the girl on the bed.

"Perhaps they are a key of sorts, a way for you to express your anger safely, to lash out in the way you feel you need to, without harming anyone. And maybe you're not causing the storms, they're just reflecting your turmoil back to you so you can see it and become aware of your emotions."

Rhiannon stared at her, uncomprehending.

"Your dreams can be a powerful way to vent your anger and express yourself without danger or consequence. It's your subconscious clearing your conscious mind, discarding what doesn't serve you. So you could be dreaming of fire to purge away all you can't process in your waking hours, playing it out as a way to manifest your fury into a safe way of expression."

A jumble of thoughts ran through Rhiannon's mind – denial, confusion, a sense of futility. It still didn't explain how she'd managed to transport herself outside into the storm the night before her mum died, or out into the woods to confront Evan, and nor did it shed any light on the strange red-robed woman she'd spoken to atop the tor. But if she hadn't hurt Brodie, and Rose still had faith in her and thought she was a good person, could there be a rational explanation for all the craziness?

She was very grateful her brother was unharmed, yet she still felt unsettled. She couldn't wrap her head around what had been happening to her, or what hadn't. "So I'm just some power-mad fool, imagining I can control the weather and create storms, who dreams of hurting her brother, and was deluded into thinking I have super powers?"

Rose took her hand again. "Sweet girl, you are grieving. And you are trying to make sense of a world in which you feel powerless. Of course your dreams have been disturbed, have been violent and fearful, and have felt completely real to you as your whole world has turned upside down."

"I feel so stupid," Rhiannon whispered. "What do I tell Dad, that I'm an ego-maniac on some kind of power trip?"

Rose laughed, but there was kindness in it. "Not at all. In a reality where you have no control, it makes perfect sense that you would dream that you do."

"But if I was going to dream up a power, surely it wouldn't be as a Storm Witch," she complained, then shivered as she recalled those voices up on the tor, baiting her, accusing her.

Storm Caller. Storm Witch. Destroyer.

"Surely I would imagine myself more like you, a healer who does energy work and ritual and makes people better? Who grows things, and makes things, and heals things. That sounds like a much preferable power to me," she grumbled. "Yours actually helps people. Mine just destroys them. I'm like Carrie in that horror movie."

Trying hard to hide her smile, Rose reached out her hand to the vulnerable girl and lifted her chin.

"Now you listen to me Rhiannon Stark. There is nothing wrong with you – no reason to be scared, and no reason for anyone to fear you. It can be dangerous to start thinking that you're more powerful than you are – but that goes both ways. Don't you dare ever think you are *less* powerful than you truly are either. Don't doubt yourself or your ability to make a difference," she said, voice serious, insistent.

"You have the power to heal within you too – the power to help your brother get through this, and to help your dad. And in doing that, you will help yourself too. Got it?"

Reluctantly she nodded, and made an effort to smile, to look like she agreed with the priestess. But she was mortified. It was very humbling, to discover that the control she'd thought she had, the control she'd secretly liked, was a lie. And there were still so many unexplained things, feelings, actions – things she was too scared to ask about, or even ponder. God, maybe all this solitude was making her crazy, was making her hallucinate, yet she wasn't sure she could face anyone again. Certainly not right now.

Rose hadn't finished with her though. "Why don't you come to our rituals, and learn all about this? You could study like your mum did, take your place in our circle, and start to understand the magic you have access to, that we *all* have access to, and start to unlock all the potential within you."

Rather than being a calming option though, she recoiled at the thought. She didn't want to unlock anything, didn't want to develop even more that she could lose control of.

"You can work with the element of fire to banish your fear," the priestess said softly, and Rhiannon winced that she'd read her thoughts, even as the woman in red flashed into her mind. Was she someone from Rose's magical circle?

"We can help you to focus, to purge, to cleanse – to let go of what does not serve you. And later, when you have dealt with all of this, you can use the passion and heat of fire to reignite your self-belief, and your self-love."

Rhiannon must have looked overwhelmed, because Rose stopped, and smiled self-consciously. "I'm sorry, we can talk about this later, when you're ready. There is no rush."

She nodded, but suddenly she was so desperate to be out from under the shrewd gaze of the priestess, that she could barely stay civil. She mumbled non-committally, knowing she would never go to a ritual, but not wanting to explain how she felt. Gratitude swept over her when her visitor picked up on her cues, hugged her goodbye, and left her to her own miserable company.

Chapter 17

And Life Goes On

If her dad had expected Rose's visit to return her to normal, whatever that was, and make her want to rejoin their family, he was sorely disappointed. While Rhiannon was relieved to know she hadn't hurt her brother, Rose's revelations hadn't magically cured her misery. She was still angry, still wanting to be alone, and still feeling she *should* be ostracised.

She was also still unwilling to return to school. Her dad had been fine with her not going for the first week after her mum's death, unable as he was to cope with his own job and responsibilities, and sort of okay with a second week. But he thought that was long enough, so he brought in reinforcements.

After another broken-hearted phone call, his mother Anne became so concerned for the bereaved family's welfare that she drove back down and moved in with them, taking over the guest room, and the whole house, and trying to keep some semblance of normality alive for her son and grandchildren.

For the month of October she stayed, cooking and cleaning, comforting her son as best she could, and spending lots of time with Brodie, who was still bewildered by the sudden change to his formerly so reliable family unit. When Rhiannon tearfully said she still couldn't face school, Anne let her stay home for a third week – then informed her that she was going back, no discussion. Surprised, she appealed to her dad, but his mother had forced him back to work, so while he sympathised with his daughter, he told her he believed it would help her, and insisted she do as her gran had instructed.

And so every morning Rhiannon dragged herself out of bed and threw on some clothes, wrapping herself in long black skirts and thick black woollen jumpers, and walked off in the direction of school. She did try a few times to force her feet up the front steps, but she hadn't been able to do it.

Instead she'd taken to wandering around the countryside, spending hours at a time meandering down country lanes, revelling in the bleakness of the landscape as the earth circled from the colours of autumn to the cold chill of winter, and feeling deep satisfaction when the weather turned and the heavens poured down on her, which usually happened when she was spiralling back down into her own pit of despair. The storms still broke in time with her bursts of anger, but she forced herself to see it as a coincidence and nothing more.

Other days she headed off towards school but jumped on the bus to the nearby town of Smithfield instead, losing herself in the cobbled streets and green leafy parks where no one knew her, or wondered what she was doing when she raised her arms to the sky as thunder rumbled overhead. She didn't even really know what she was doing herself, except trying to out-walk her pain, out-walk her grief.

And always she would get home at the right time, mutter that she had homework to do, and hurry upstairs and collapse onto her bed. Some afternoons she would cry herself to sleep, others she would wear herself out with wondering what she was going to do with herself, with her life, with her pain. And as often as possible she skipped dinner with her family, not wanting to talk to anyone, even them. Especially them.

It was getting awkward though, because Anne was asking more and more questions about school, and Rhiannon was starting to worry that her continued truancy would be discovered. She was also getting tired of being lectured by her gran about her black clothes. It was all she felt comfortable in – they made her feel invisible, and safe in some way, while the sight of brighter, cheerier clothes made her feel even worse than she already did. And that was saying something.

A few days after her mum had died, Rhiannon had gone through her wardrobe and snatched out every yellow, orange or blue dress, every red, purple or green top, every white or multi-coloured skirt or vivid pair of tights, leaving only the black clothes, and a few dark navy things that she still hadn't worn, but wasn't too offended by.

She'd dragged the huge bag of discarded items down the stairs and left them in the hall, asking her dad to take them to the charity bin when he had a chance. Then she'd scoured the op shops in Smithfield on the days she spent there, buying black clothes to replace what she'd thrown away.

Her grandma also complained about her black bedroom, but Rhiannon loved that it so perfectly suited her mood. It was dark and gloomy, with black wallpaper, black furnishings and black bedding, and thick blood-red velvet curtains blocking out the light.

It reflected her frame of mind and articulated what she could not – that she was drowning in gloom and doom and bleak, black depression. She didn't even mind when her dad teased her about being the lonely goth, after a song she liked, because she couldn't bring herself to care about anything.

But at the end of October, five weeks after Beth had died, Anne packed up and went home to her husband, worried that he needed her attention too, and convinced now that her son and grandchildren would survive their grief. Mike had been going to work every day, but that was more to escape the memories at home than because he was coping. Yet he thanked his mother and made a vow to his kids that they would be okay. Rhiannon doubted that very much, but thought it was nice that he believed it.

On the afternoon following Anne's departure, Mike was sitting at the dining room table when Rhiannon got home. "How was school today?" he asked carefully.

Rhiannon shrugged. "Okay I guess."

"Come and talk to me darling," her dad said, indicating the chair opposite him.

"I've got homework," she replied dismissively, and headed towards the stairs.

"Sit down Rhiannon," he insisted, voice louder, and firmer. "It's not a request."

Startled out of her apathy for a moment, she peered at her father closely, for the first time in a long time. He was gaunter than she remembered, and his face now was stern.

"Okay," she sighed, pulling out a chair and collapsing down into it. The air crackled with electricity, and she crossed her arms in front of her chest and tucked her hands into her armpits, just in case there were sparks, then waited impatiently for whatever her dad was going to say so she could go upstairs and hide in her room again.

"I know you haven't been going to school," he began, and she gasped. Horror crossed her face, and panic, and she suddenly felt a lot more uncomfortable.

"How do you know?" she demanded, face defiant, surly.

"Darling, Laura's a friend, of course she was going to tell me. And even if she didn't, one of the other teachers would have called to ask about your long, unexplained absence. Not to mention the bus driver, who asked me if you were going to school in Smithfield now."

She sighed theatrically, but stayed silent. What could she say to that? The funny thing was, she didn't actually care any more. What was he going to do? Send her to her room? Ground her? She'd been pretty much grounded for the last month anyway, spending as much time as possible hiding in her room, avoiding people, places, even her family. She'd really *like* to be officially grounded.

"Besides, you might have fooled your grandmother with your daily excursions, but I've known for a while," her dad said, and she stared at him, surprised.

"I decided to let you have some time, to see if that helped. I was hoping you would eventually feel strong enough and return of your own accord, but it's been more than a month since your mum died," he continued, and she could tell he was struggling to keep from crying. A pang of remorse swept through her. This was just what her dad needed while grieving his beloved wife – a troubled teenager causing problems.

"You may have checked out of our family Rhiannon, and I'm trying really hard to be patient about that, but you can't abandon your schooling. Your mother would be so disappointed in you."

"Well, she's not here, is she?" she said spitefully. "She checked out of the family long before I ever did."

Her father looked as shocked as if she'd slapped him, and for a split second she felt guilty. But the sensation passed.

"Rhiannon!"

"Fine, I'm sorry," she snapped, and she did seem contrite, for a moment at least. But soon enough her expression slipped back to surly and defiant.

"There's a week-long school holiday starting on Monday, so I guess you can have these last two days, then the week, but you have to go back when term starts," he said, and his tone let her know that his decision was final. Part of her was impressed by his take-charge attitude, which she'd only ever seen before at the church with Patricia, yet she still wanted to rebel.

"Everything just seems so pointless," she moaned, and this time when her mask of surliness dropped she just sounded sad. "It doesn't seem like there's any reason to do anything without her."

"I know darling, believe me," he said, voice low, and still devastated. "But this is for you. I don't want you to throw away your chance of future happiness, of being able to pursue your dreams, because I let you give up on yourself."

"What future happiness? What dreams?"

"It's not always going to be quite this painful, I promise. We will learn to live with our loss, and we will create a new life together, a new future," he replied, although she wasn't sure if he was trying to convince her, or himself.

"Besides, going back to work actually helped me – it gave me something to focus on, to take my mind off my grief."

Rhiannon glared at him. "But you still cry yourself to sleep every night," she said bluntly.

Her dad shrugged, and she could tell he was losing patience with her, although he tried to hide it. "Yes I do, and who knows when that will end," he conceded. "But my days are a tiny bit easier when my mind is occupied, I promise. You have to let us in darling, let us help you. Reconnect with your friends and your family."

The accusation put her on the defensive, even though she knew he was right, and she angrily stomped off upstairs.

And so she finally returned to school. Six weeks had passed since the death of her mum, yet the fog of anger and guilt that hovered like a red haze in front of her eyes, no matter what she was doing, hadn't come close to dispersing.

She hated being back in the classroom, hated having to deal with teachers, with students, with fake-sympathetic eyes and talk that died down whenever she entered the room. She hated being behind in her classes, and unable to concentrate enough to catch up. It was a nightmare she walked through like a zombie, taking nothing in, giving nothing out, but somehow managing to fake her way through well enough that people thought she was okay.

It had been almost impossible to compose herself when she saw her two best friends for the first time, on that first day back. Debbie and Sue had shrieked when they saw her, and raced over to drag her up the steps and off to their first class, speaking over each other in their attempts to apologise.

"We've missed you so bad," Debbie said, regret in her voice.

"And we've been thinking of you so much. I'm so sorry we were too scared to visit you. We just didn't want to intrude, or annoy you with our presence," Sue added, sounding as though she was on the verge of tears. "Can you forgive us?"

Rhiannon pasted an attempt at a smile on her face. "Of course," she shrugged. Deep down she wasn't sure she would be able to forgive them, but that was something to think about later. Today – and every day back in the hell that was school – she just had to somehow keep it together long enough to make it to home time without bursting into tears.

It was hard though, because the absence of her mother loomed over everything. Each time she bumped into the teacher who'd taken over Beth's classes, or came face-to-face with the photos of her mum with the debate team or the netball squad that were still proudly displayed in the gym, her heart broke. She wondered if it was ever going to get easier to bear, with the constant reminders.

People were pretty good about giving her a wide berth though, and letting her sulk through her days without too much pressure put on her. But she still couldn't face their kind eyes or their well-meaning advice. She didn't want to learn how to cope, or hear another positive pep talk, or get another condescending prescription for how to heal. And she could sense how uncomfortable they all were around her, which made her feel awkward all over again. Worst of all were the cloyingly sympathetic "I know how you feel" moments. No they didn't. How could anyone understand what she was feeling?

Each week she could feel the pressure building, feel the people around her losing patience with her, deciding that her time of mourning and all the "allowances" they'd been giving her should end soon. Was there an unwritten rule she hadn't been informed of, about the acceptable length of mourning? An official day on which people automatically stopped dropping off dinners, or hugging you in sympathy? When they stopped being careful not to ask how you were, because they thought you must be fine by now, must be over the pain?

There was no way she was ready though, and she didn't know if she ever would be. It still destroyed her to see the hurt in her little brother's eyes when she fobbed him off again. To see the disappointment and fear in her father's eyes. But even if she wanted to, she didn't know how to claw her way out of this hole she was burying herself in.

When the two-month anniversary of her loss rolled around, she was still struggling to cope. Still struggling to get through the days, to not push everyone away. Loneliness surrounded her, and while she wouldn't admit it, it hurt her deeply that even Debbie and Sue avoided her when they could, and were so obviously uncomfortable whenever they were around her. The few times they had tried to reach out to her, she'd been so grateful that she cried, which hadn't helped matters.

It tortured her, that people had cared about them for a few weeks after Beth died, had brought them casseroles and flowers, and offered to shop for them, babysit Brodie, collect homework for her, clean their house even. But then the sympathy had dried up and the visits had stopped, and everyone went back to their normal lives, with their normal families, and seemed to forget their tragedy – and want them to forget it too. They all acted as though she should be over it by now, moving on, happily accepting the new status quo and not needing any extra consideration. One of her classmates had actually told her that her sadness was "getting old", and she should hurry up and get over it already. Gritting her teeth, she silently prayed for the term to end, so she could hole up in her room again, and spend her days avoiding everyone.

Weekends brought at least some respite, because she could hide away, pretending she had homework. But one Saturday morning she woke up with a great sense of foreboding. Frantically she racked her brain, then groaned when she remembered that her dad expected her to visit her mother's grave with him that day.

She still hadn't been able to face visiting her mum's final resting place in the local cemetery. She wasn't even sure why. It wasn't denial, because she was very well aware that Beth was gone. Perhaps she was just a coward, without the courage to do what she knew needed to be done, for her own sake if nothing else.

Fortunately her dad was called in to work, which took the pressure off a bit, but finally she dragged herself out of the house and down the road leading out of town, towards the old cemetery. The last of the autumn leaves crunched under her feet, but she was immune to their beauty. All she saw was grey, despite the blue sky, vivid leaves and weak sunshine. All she felt was the chill of the coming frost, and the drabness of the grey headstones stretching out across the hill.

Nervously she opened the gate, jumping when it squeaked, then quickly stepped inside. It looked even more gothic than she remembered from the times she'd wandered through it in the past, back before she'd had a loved one there and wanted to avoid it at all costs. Ivy wound around the wrought iron fence, and along the base of some of the graves. Peering from under the big old oak tree, she took in the whole of the grassy space. At the back, where the ground sloped upwards, were the oldest memorials, and she headed there first, not yet ready to visit her mum.

One of the ancient headstones had fallen over and lay on its side now, the gaping hole in the earth where it had been making her feel sad, and a little freaked out. But other granite memorials and statues were beautiful, and filled her with a sense of longing and wonder.

Who were these people who had died so long ago? Did anyone still remember them? One of the graves had fresh flowers lying in the shadow of its tombstone, despite the person having died more than a hundred and fifty years ago. An ancestor, she supposed, but someone who would never have met the deceased person. How did it feel, to revere someone so far removed? Was it a family obligation, handed down through the generations? And had the other long-gone people in neighbouring graves been forgotten over time, or not long after they'd been buried here?

Some of the headstones were cracked, and most of them were too faded to read the inscriptions. But the ones that were still legible filled her with pain. Little Alice had died aged five, and her brother Johnny at eighteen. Henrietta had been just fifteen. Mother-of-three Agnes was taken from her family aged twenty-two. In contrast though, others had lived long existences, especially for their time, with at least three of the oldest graves being home to people who had survived until their late nineties.

The wording of their memorials also struck a chord deep within her. Some hadn't died, they'd "fallen asleep". Others had been "taken home", one to "a far better place", which made her sad. Had their life on earth been so much worse than the nothingness that faced them after death?

Many of the older graves featured round silver cylinders with holes in the top. A few had flowers wedged into them, but others remained empty and bare, filling her head with visions of air holes for the dead, which made no sense at all.

Shivering as a brisk wind lifted her long wavy hair from her neck, she breathed in the scent of herbs and wildflowers, and smiled when she recognised the sharpness of the rosemary and the sweetness of the lavender that grew wild throughout the space. She shivered too at the reality of all the deaths spread out before her.

In the past, she would walk by the graveyard without giving it a single moment of contemplation, yet all that had changed now. She'd been avoiding it since her mum's death, taking the long way to school so she didn't have to see it, but it was time she faced her fears.

A gate behind the oldest graves caught her eye, distracting her, and she wandered over, intrigued. A small sign announced that it marked the entrance to the green burial site, where people could be buried without grave or tombstone, as a part of nature. Gazing over the small hill, she noticed the indentation of grave-sized dips in the grass, and realised people were buried here, but in a non-permanent fashion – as time passed, they would literally return to the earth.

Something about it touched her deeply. There were herbs on a few of the mounds, and wildflowers on others, and earthen paths meandered beside the spaces then curved around and disappeared under a stand of trees. A few wooden benches were placed there too, with small brass plaques on them, and she thought it was a wonderful idea, to rest in peace in such tranquil surroundings, in a place where your loved ones could come to sit with you in tranquillity, remembering you with the sound of bird song and the scent of flowers.

She tried to imagine how many people were buried there, and whether it would become really popular over time. It was certainly practical, since cemeteries were filling up fast, but it was also a really beautiful idea. Idly she wondered if Rose had performed any ceremonies there, and whether it was what she would choose for herself. It seemed an incredibly pagan and priestessy kind of way to be laid to rest.

Curious, she read the information on the back of the sign. Any kind of service was allowed, be it religious or secular, and you could have an officiant run it, or do it yourself. But there were restrictions. The only coffin materials allowed were quickly biodegradable ones, such as softwood, cardboard or wicker, and there could be no hardwood, metal or manmade materials included. Small native wildflowers could be planted on the grave, and cut flowers could be left, as long as they were cleared away after they wilted.

The idea appealed to her, and she wondered if her nature-loving mum had known about it. Then again, graves were for those left behind, and there was a certain romance to having a place where you could "visit" your lost loved ones. The graves of people she didn't even know had moved her deeply, and she was glad that her mum had one too. Which didn't explain why she was still avoiding going to it.

Taking a deep breath to calm and steady herself, she turned back to the cemetery, and slowly made her way down the hill, noticing the change in tombstone styles, and the dates of birth and death of those in this newer section.

As the graves became more modern, the lettering got clearer, and the weathering less dramatic. And finally, her feet dragging, she found herself at her mother's burial site. Grey stone outlined the rectangle of her grassy green plot, a small marble angel statue stood in one corner, and the black inscription stood out starkly against the pale grey headstone.

> *In loving memory of Beth Stark,*
> *Adored mother, wife, friend and teacher.*
> *Off to unpathed waters and undreamed shores,*
> *and forever in our hearts.*
> *Blessed be...*

Tears welled as she read the engraved letters, and remembered Rose's beautiful ceremony for Beth. The priestess's kind words played over and over in her mind, bringing her a measure of comfort, and some of the tears that streaked down her face were happy, or at least grateful ones, for the knowledge that she had been so blessed to have such an amazing mother.

But the rest of her tears were sad, and angry, and she grimaced, then almost laughed, as she saw dark clouds form in the distance before racing towards her. Carefully she tried to breathe calm back into her body, into her mind, to still the frantic racing of her heart and soothe the fury that seemed to be fuelling the storm clouds overhead.

Bowing her head, she focused her attention on the grave. It was covered in grass, like the surrounding ones, but a small rosemary seedling was rooted in the dirt in the centre, with a narrow gold ribbon tied in a bow to one of the sprigs. A wish, a talisman, a sign post for the journey ahead? She guessed that Rose had threaded it through the tiny spiky leaves, or perhaps it had been Laura, her own teacher, but much longer her mum's close friend, confidante and fellow seeker of magic.

For a moment she felt dizzy, and her instinct to flee got even stronger, but she forced herself to focus, and so she gazed down at the vase of pretty flowers her dad must have left there recently. Shoots of ivy were starting to take hold around the headstone too, and she smiled despite herself. Nature couldn't be slowed, or contained, let alone withheld, and that thought gave her a strange sense of comfort.

At the funeral, the priest had announced that her mum was free now, that her spirit had ascended to a better place, but all Rhiannon had cared about was that she was free of pain. Beth had fought so hard to disguise her agony in her final weeks, so they hadn't known just how bad her illness was, or how much suffering she'd endured yet hidden from them to spare their feelings, until it was too late.

Only her mum would waste precious energy to fuel a glamour spell so her family didn't know the extent of the cancer spreading through her body, rather than focusing on making her last weeks as least-difficult as possible. Beth had been strong and brave and selfless to the very end, and her daughter imagined she was still just as strong and brave as she had been in life, wherever she was now.

Sinking to the slightly muddy ground, she pulled her knees up close and wrapped her arms around them, seeking comfort of some kind. Comfort she was afraid she would never experience again. "Life goes on" seemed to be everyone's go-to mantra, and she hated it. Her life had been irretrievably cracked open, pulled apart and broken down.

A line of a poem came to her. *Step softly, a dream lies buried here.* Smiling, she breathed in the softness of the moment, and measured the depth of her immense grief, then the size of her love for her mother. Most days the grief and anger outweighed all else, but today she was determined to let love win.

Chapter 18

A Sacred Heart

Beth... Twenty years ago...

As Beth walked slowly home from Violet's place through the clear dark night after Rose's witchcraft course, her friend's words echoed in her mind. "You're home."

A growing sense of excitement warmed her belly, a sensation of rightness settled around her shoulders, and she felt the truth of it, deep within her. *Home.* But how could that be? She'd spent her whole life waiting to escape this village. Her desperation to leave had defined her. Always she had known that there was nothing here for her, that her destiny lay elsewhere, lay far away. That it was only in leaving that she would be able to find herself, to be herself.

When she moved to London the day after graduating from high school, she had been ecstatic. She found a summer job in a cafe in Chelsea, where she could spend her lunchtimes wandering in the footsteps of much-loved artists and writers, or sitting under a tree in the gorgeous Chelsea Physic Garden, where she breathed in the scent of lush herbs and pretty flowering plants before catching the train back to her cramped house-share several suburbs away.

But she didn't mind the commute, or the close living quarters and rotating roster of flatmates, because she came alive as she sat up drinking wine with them until the early hours, or brewing coffee and making pancakes in the mornings for the more hungover amongst them. She adored meeting so many new people, going on dates, seeing bands, watching movies and experimenting with new cuisines with her friend Priya, who she'd shared a room with since she'd arrived.

Even when her course began, she stayed in the huge, tumbledown house on the outskirts of London, not caring about the noise and the constant interruptions while studying, because she found such great joy in the camaraderie and closeness there, after feeling so isolated and alone in her childhood home. Surrounded by almost-strangers, she managed to find herself.

On completion of her first year, she travelled to France on a whim, piling into an old kombi van with Priya and three of their most recent housemates. The guys planned to go to music festivals and live out of the van for as long as they could afford it, Priya was keen to spend one last summer with friends before she settled down with her betrothed, and Beth just wanted to see some of the world between semesters.

She fell in love with France though, and the bohemian heart it opened within her, so when the others went back to London, she stayed, putting her studies on hold and joining some colourful new friends to hitchhike around the countryside.

Enchanted, she meandered through mysterious faery forests and past mirrored lakes, and crawled into dark and ancient megalithic tombs. Captivated, she swam in the ocean believed to hold a lost civilisation beneath its surface, and danced on golden beaches under the full moon. Truly happy, she worked on farms or picked fruit in order to earn enough money to eat, or a place in a barnyard to sleep when the rains fell.

Each day she woke when she wanted to, did what she wanted to, and celebrated her freedom from her family. During late nights gathered around campfires she argued history, politics and philosophy with a shifting cast of fascinating characters, and started to define the things she believed, and the things that mattered to her.

For six months she revelled in the gypsy life she'd become so enamoured of, before the winds changed, and she headed to Paris to see La Ville-Lumière, the City of Light, and enlightenment, and look for work. And the romance and magic of the sprawling metropolis caught her up and drew her in from the moment she stepped off the train from Brittany into the midst of the leafy green city.

Despite a grey sky threatening rain, she set off on the long walk to the historic artist neighbourhood of Montmartre. Every street offered something new and exciting to see, and her brisk stride warmed her body as effectively as the woollen gloves she'd knitted while camping warmed her hands. She felt virtuous too, not paying for the fare, since one less metro ride meant one more coffee or crepe on her limited budget.

After wandering through the red light district and gaping at its iconic Moulin Rouge, she finally reached the merry-go-round at the base of Montmartre Hill, and was mesmerised by its bright lights and tinkling music, and enraptured by the shining faces of the children riding the white horses. Her gaze rose to the grassy summit above her, and with a light heart she began climbing the steep steps, smiling at the old-fashioned street lamps whose warm glow illuminated the grey day, and the ghostly dark tree branches that pierced through the swirling fog.

Her imagination fired up as she wandered the crooked cobblestoned streets of Montmartre, admiring the street artists as they painted in front of her, gazing in wonder at the galleries and museums, and drinking coffee in a tiny cafe.

Later, as the winter sun came out, she sat on the grassy hill with a baguette and stared up at the shining white domes of the Basilica Sacre-Coeur, built on the site where the druids of ancient Gaul had worshipped, where the Romans constructed temples to Mars and Mercury, and where a succession of Christian churches had risen and fallen and risen again.

Then she turned and looked back over Paris, thrilled by the amazing view of old stone buildings, parks, cemeteries, the shining thread of the River Seine, and the Eiffel Tower in the distance. For a moment it felt surreal, that she was here in this beautiful city, the whole of it laid out before her, ready to embrace her. The new her. The her she was becoming.

Swinging her backpack onto her shoulders, she headed down the hill, suddenly nervous that she had nowhere to sleep that night. It was the middle of winter after all, and she picked up her pace, skipping down the stairs with new purpose.

Just before she reached the merry-go-round, she heard an exasperated shout, and saw a young mum pushing a stroller and holding another child's hand as she watched a festive red scarf being lifted on the breeze and blown away, a sense of hopelessness in her eyes. Beth dropped her backpack and ran after it, then returned it with a smile. The stressed-out mother looked at her with relief and gratitude and a strange sense of longing.

"Merci beaucoup, Mademoiselle, je suis tellement reconnaissant," she said, her voice strained.

"Ce n'est rien," Beth replied with a shrug. It had been no effort on her part, no big deal. Picking up her backpack, she was about to walk away, to try to find a place to stay for a night, or a week, or something, when the woman laid a hand on her arm.

"Excusez-moi, mais êtes-vous anglais?"

Beth smiled and nodded. It seemed her schoolgirl French and bad accent made it pretty obvious to everyone that she was English.

"Oh, thank god," the woman said, switching languages, but still looking stressed.

"I'm Beth," she told the stranger, holding out her hand. "Um, can I help you with something?"

For a moment, wild possibilities ran through her head, and she wondered if she should have kept quiet. What on earth could an elegant Parisian woman want with a foreign backpacker? Yet when her situation was revealed, Beth was torn between wondering if it was a con – or the answer to all her prayers. Could destiny have placed her on this hill, in this moment, for a reason?

The woman, Melisande, was stressed because her husband had left the day before on a two-week business trip to Vienna. His semi-regular travel for work usually caused no problems, but last night their nanny had needed to rush back to Nice to look after her suddenly hospitalised mother. At any other time, the busy mum could have taken a few days off work, but tomorrow she was to begin facilitating a four-day conference that she couldn't get out of, and she didn't know what to do.

"Last night I dreamed that I would meet a young English girl in this park, who would be able to come and stay with us for a few weeks, to look after the girls, and teach them a little English. Could it be you? Is there any chance you have worked with children before? And are you available?"

Melisande looked so hopeful, and so desperate, that Beth really wanted to help her. Was she qualified though? Or at least capable? She *had* begun her training to be a teacher, before she'd given it up to travel around France, but she wasn't a nanny. And yet, she really needed a place to sleep, and here was someone practically begging her to come and stay in the family home. And be paid for it. Would it be wrong for her to accept?

"The girls are both really good, very well behaved, I promise," the woman said, mistaking her hesitation. "And look, Joceline already likes you."

Gazing down, she saw that the girl in the stroller, who was probably around two, was smiling up at her, with the most adorable expression on her face. Beth smiled back, and felt herself falling under the toddler's spell. She had a mischievous sparkle in her eyes, but seemed calm and centred too.

"And this is Aveline," the mother added, nudging the older girl forward. "She'll be five next week, and it would be so good to have some help for that too. My husband had hoped to be home in time for the party, but alas, his work had complications."

"Bon jour, Mademoiselle. C'est très agréable de vous rencontrer," Aveline said, so polite, so sweet, and with such a charming accent.

"Bon jour, Aveline. Vous aussi," Beth replied, and she really was happy to meet her too.

For a moment doubt clouded her mind though. Could it all be a ruse, to invite her to their home and then rob her, or worse? But if that was the case, they could surely have found a wealthier-looking and far more suitable target. She had no doubt that she, and her travel-worn backpack, looked dusty and tired, and she knew her clothes could do with a good wash – as could she. She grimaced, even while recognising that she loved that her backpack was so battered from experience, and contained everything she owned, which wasn't much at all. It gave her the amazing freedom to pick up and move on at a moment's notice. Or, potentially, to stay.

Not understanding her silence, Melisande's face fell. "I'm sorry, you must be busy. I cannot expect you to drop everything at a moment's notice to come and save a stranger."

This was true – they were complete strangers. Yet as weird as it sounded, this sweet woman seemed familiar to Beth. It felt as though she'd met her before, or dreamed of her at least. Was it a sign, that Melisande had dreamed of *her*? Every day of her French adventure had been about using her intuition, taking chances, letting her life and her self emerge from being placed in unlikely situations and by following the signs of destiny she came across.

No matter her qualms regarding her qualifications, or lack there of, this was a job she was born to do, a job she could do. And here was her chance. Could she really turn it down? Melisande was desperate, and the thought of being able to help her – as well as having a hot shower and sleeping in a warm bed tonight – was beyond enticing. So into the fire she leaped, grabbing the opportunity with both hands.

It was a brilliant decision. She and Melisande became great friends, and Beth adored her two young charges, who filled her days with joy, and inspired her with their curiosity about her, and the world, and life. When their dad returned, he was lovely too, and she felt really welcomed into their family. So when their nanny called to nervously ask if she could take more time off to look after her mother, Beth agreed to stay for as long as she was needed.

And she was surprised by just how easily she slipped into her new career, her new family, her new home, her new skin. How effortlessly she realised that she really was a carer, a teacher, a nurturer. Out of the shadow of her own family, she was discovering who she was, and developing confidence in her abilities, her strengths and her worthiness.

A month after she moved in, Melisande and Julius took the girls to visit their grandmother for a long weekend, and encouraged Beth to go to the music festival she'd bought a ticket for some time ago. And it was there she met Andrew, and began her grand romance. It was there, within the circle of his arms, that she found another home, another part of herself, another piece of the puzzle that was her.

Without the job she loved in Paris, without Andrew, could she really find a home here? Could Violet be right? Until that moment tonight, sitting in Rose's kitchen drinking tea with her friend while the priestess and her husband chatted together in the lounge room, Beth had considered herself a gypsy. Travelling around France, she'd finally felt like herself. There was a freedom she loved, freedom from her parents definitely, but also freedom from their view of her. She'd always seen herself through their eyes – small, shallow, inferior, a failure.

In a new country though, with new friends, she could reinvent herself, or reveal herself, as the person she truly was. With no one's perceptions or misconceptions projected onto her. It was just her, cracked open and laid bare, truly herself.

But now Violet spoke of freedom right here, as she was, at home in the place she'd been born and then spent so long trying to escape from. Was it possible?

Up ahead, out of the corner of her eye, she saw something move in the shadows, and she snapped her head up, towards it, and peered into the inky blackness. A trickle of fear ran up her spine – but then a sense of calm suddenly enveloped her. Puzzled, she stared harder, remembering the strange blue-robed woman that she'd met once before, on the walk home from her second ritual, who had somehow managed to suffuse her with peace and wellbeing. Had she returned to soothe her heartache with magic? Or to dish out more cryptic advice?

Laughter echoed around her, and as the moon came out from behind a cloud, Beth could just discern a figure coalescing out of the swirling mists. But this woman was draped in gold, not dark blue, with a gown that could have been fashioned from fireflies or lunar beams. A golden light radiated from her, and Beth felt a wonderful warmth, and a languid air of comfort and support that weaved around her and through her.

"Beloved, of course your home is here, if you want it to be," the woman began, and she seemed more light-hearted than that other being. There was a sweetness to her voice, to her manner, even to her glittering eyes.

"Home is wherever you are able to be truly yourself. It is not a place you escape to, an adventure on foreign shores, or defining yourself through being with someone else. It is a journey to your self, a journey within. Home is where your heart is."

Beth stared at her blankly. When Andrew wasn't calling her ma cherie, my darling, he was referring to her as his rambling girl. He loved that she had travelled so much, that she had no ties that bound her, that her gypsy soul had found such freedom as she camped out under the stars, as she followed the old druid pathways, as she drank from sacred wells and let go of the things that weighed her down.

"Oh Beth, it was not the travelling that gave you the freedom and your new wisdom, it was your decision to stop seeing yourself through your mother's eyes. There is no need to be the rambling girl to impress anyone else, or yourself."

Shock spiralled through her as the gold-clad woman used Andrew's term of affection, which was met by a laugh that swirled around her, holding her safe, keeping her warm.

"But I became more myself because I travelled," she argued. "I could not have changed if I'd stayed here, in the shadow of my parents. I could not have been here for Jenny now if I hadn't become a better person through my new experiences in a different city, a different country."

The woman in gold shook her head sadly, then reached out her hand to Beth.

"Beloved, this is not about becoming someone better, someone different. It is about allowing yourself to become who you already are, who you have always been. Just beneath the warped view of yourself that you held, through your mother's eyes, you have always been you, you have always been this so-called 'better' person. You have just been afraid to show your true self to others, to yourself even. You have allowed your mother to diminish you, but now it is time to stop. To take control. To be yourself, wherever you are."

Beth's head was spinning. Part of her wanted to keep arguing, because what was the point of everything she'd done over the last two years, if not that? And yet, the possibilities excited her, if this was true. She'd thought she couldn't wait to return to Paris, or to Andrew at least, to be seen again the way she wanted to be perceived, to be who she wanted to be.

And yet, Mike and Violet had befriended her anyway, right here. Rose had been so kind to her, in the heart of this village, with no pretence. Maybe they could see her true self too, regardless of her being back here, where she thought she couldn't be, couldn't live, couldn't thrive.

"Do not flee this town for anyone, your mother included. Do not wander aimlessly for anyone else, unless *you* want to," the woman said softly. "Travelling can help you see yourself more clearly – but you can achieve all of that without leaving home too. Dear girl, you were already worthy of love, worthy of friendship, worthy of respect, long before you left this village."

It reminded Beth of what the blue-clad being had told her, that she would become very close to Rose, and that she would be worthy of her trust and friendship. But how could she be worthy of a relationship with the healer?

"Oh Beth." The words were a sigh, were a sadness, were an expression of frustration, but still the mysterious being took her hands and gazed deeply into her eyes. Beth stopped feeling scared, stopped feeling anything, and fell into the swirling gold flecks in the vivid green of the woman's eyes. A vision hung there, suspended, of herself in a long white dress, with a diamond ring on her finger, her hand in the hand of a man she couldn't see, and her face radiantly happy as she climbed the tor.

Another one shimmered into life, of herself holding a baby in her arms as she drank coffee with a faceless friend in one of the local cafes. Then she saw herself in a red dress, arms raised to the sky as she stood with Rose in the centre of a circle in the priestess's ritual room, magic spinning around them as they shaped the healing energy they'd raised and sent it outwards.

Each vision was of herself living so happily in this village – joyously married, a radiant mother, a powerful witch using her magic to help and to heal.

Then her face fell. That last image had given away that they were false images. "I have no magic," Beth said, defeated, and the disappointment that she wouldn't have that life pierced her heart. Now that she'd seen it, she wanted it desperately.

The woman in gold drew her into her arms, and she felt the soothing energy flowing into her again, strengthening her.

"Oh beloved, of course you have magic. You already feel it when you take part in Rose's rituals, when you walk through the countryside, both here and in France. You feel it in your connection with Violet, your friendship with Mike, and your bonding with your sister after all this time." The woman's voice was still soft, still kind, but she was becoming frustrated with her.

"The magic is not external, it is within you, and it has always been there, I promise you."

Beth shrugged, not convinced.

"This is for you," the woman finally said, handing her a small package wrapped in gold velvet. Slowly, carefully, she opened it, and gasped. It was a beautiful necklace, strung with small rose quartz crystals, and with a huge rose quartz heart in the centre, nestled in a delicate silver setting and with ivy leaves, hearts and butterflies surrounding the crystal.

"It will remind you that you are loved. That you need to trust. That you must open yourself to the love being offered. And when you doubt, it will reassure you that you are indeed filled with magic." Beth's eyes welled with tears, but she blinked them away, focusing on the beauty of the crystal she held in her hands.

The woman hadn't finished though. "It will also remind you that you are a part of this land, of this countryside, of this village, and that you are able to access the magic right here."

She placed her hand over Beth's heart, and she felt the warmth seeping into her, the love wrapping around her.

"We are here, those who love you are here, and you will find the magic within you, right here, right at home. You are *home* Beth," she said, voice a whisper, a caress, a promise.

"I don't know what to say. It's so beautiful."

The woman smiled, and moved around behind her, slipping the pendant and its string of crystals around her neck, then lifting her long hair to do up the clasp. A moment later Beth spun around to thank the gold-clad stranger, but no one was there.

The street was empty, and silent. The shadows up ahead were pools of inky blackness, but there was no movement within them. Sadness overwhelmed her as she wondered if she had hallucinated the meeting. And yet she felt the weight of the pink heart on her chest, and when she hesitantly raised her hand to her neck, the necklace was there, sitting against her collarbones, so beautiful, so heavy, so present.

And the woman was right. It felt like home.

Chapter 19

A Yuletide Miracle

Rhiannon... Today...

The wintry grey sky perfectly reflected Rhiannon's mood, as she sat hunched in the window seat of her room. Once again she was pretending to read, yet was mostly just staring outside at the bleakness that seemed to call to her. A knock on the door dragged her from her reverie, and she sighed as she called out to her dad to come in.

It could only be him. Brodie had given up trying to entice her out to play with him long ago, and she hadn't seen her friends since school had finished for the term four days ago. Not that she blamed any of them, or even spared them a thought. In her case, misery did *not* love company.

"Hello darling," Mike began cautiously, and she rolled her eyes at him. Yep, she was so mature, but did he have to be wearing a silly Christmas jumper? And why was he? She thought about figuring out what day it was, but couldn't find it within herself to actually care.

Her dad edged into her room, studiously avoiding glancing at the mess on the floor, not wanting to antagonise her in any way. "I was hoping you could watch Brodie for an hour or so. He's not feeling well, and I have to go out for a while. It would mean a lot to both of us if you could pop down and spend a bit of time with him."

Guilt. Just what she needed. "Fine," she said, sighing dramatically, but she pushed herself up from her cosy little sanctuary and followed him downstairs. Her brother was lying on the couch under a blanket, listlessly staring at the TV but not taking anything in.

"Rhi-Rhi," he cried when he saw her, and a smile lit up his face. "Will you read me a story?" he asked, then quickly looked away. But not before she saw the pain and anxiety on his face, and – *fear?*

"What's wrong?" she asked, as she picked up one of his books from the floor and sat down on the couch next to him.

"I'm sorry, don't worry about reading," he said softly. "I know you don't like me any more."

A wave of guilt swamped her, and she looked at him, really looked at him, for the first time in… god, could it have been almost three months since she'd spent any real time with her brother? She'd held him as he cried in the church during their mum's funeral, but seeing his face now, and his quiet acceptance of her neglect, she realised that she'd pretty much checked out emotionally the following day, when she'd buried her pain about the thing that had happened and drowned herself in grief about her mother instead.

"I'm so sorry Brodie," she said now, heartsore as she noticed the changes in his face – the hollowed out cheeks, the furrow between his brows, the nervousness as he watched her.

"Are you going to die too?" he asked, voice small and scared. "Will you leave me all alone?"

Shocked, she threw her arms around him and drew him close. "No buddy, I won't ever leave you, I promise," she whispered, trying not to sob on his small shoulders. "I'm so sorry I've been… well, that I haven't been myself. But I never stopped caring about you. I love you so much."

"Really?" he asked, and the tremor in his voice cut Rhiannon to the core. She pulled back so she could look him in the eyes. So he could see that she meant it.

"Oh Brodie, of course I love you. And Dad loves you too. I'm so sorry that I've neglected you. I've just been so sad, about, well…"

He smiled at her bravely. "About Mumma, I know. Dad said you didn't mean to ignore me, you were just trying to work out how to cope. I miss her too," he added, and she broke down at that. When he patted her on the shoulder, trying to comfort her, she castigated herself even further. God, she'd left her five-year-old brother to deal with the loss of their mother on his own, and now he was trying to make her feel better. How heartless could she be?

When Mike got home, both his kids were sitting on the couch together, sharing a blanket and drinking hot chocolate as Rhiannon read her brother a third story. For the first time since his precious wife had died, he felt a kernel of hope that somehow their family would be able to go on.

"Hi Dad, I hope it went well on your mission," Rhiannon said, with a genuine smile, rather than the sarcastic grimace she'd been doling out for the last few months. "Do you want to take over here with Brodie and I'll make dinner?"

"That would be amazing," he said, hugging her as she passed him, then perching on the couch with his son.

"Did you get the stuff for Rhi-Rhi?" Brodie asked, and his dad nodded. "Want me to help you wrap it?"

Mike laughed, and walked upstairs with Brodie, the two of them giggling together, thick as thieves. When Rhiannon called them down two hours later, they both gasped. She'd set the table in the dining room with their best china, and had assembled Beth's small Christmas tree, draped it in festive baubles and tinsel and placed it on the sideboard with candles lit on either side of it. And on the table was a lentil and vegie loaf filled with fresh herbs and smothered in thick mushroom gravy, a serving dish overflowing with baked pumpkins, potatoes, carrots, parsnips and beets, and a bowl of steamed zucchini, broccoli and peas.

Brodie squealed and ran over and pulled up a chair, reaching out a small hand for a piece of roasted pumpkin. "I've missed your baked vegies so much," he said with a happy sigh, and Rhiannon almost cried with shame and regret.

"I'm so sorry I've been so… well, so absent," she said quietly. "For both of you."

Mike walked over and hugged her again, his eyes shining with relief and hope as he took in the warmth of the candles, the look of joy on Brodie's face, and the wonderfully festive Christmas feast.

"How did you manage all of this?" he asked. "Not that I'm complaining, it's amazing! Did you plan it?"

Rhiannon laughed as she took a seat opposite her brother. "No, I'm embarrassed to admit that, despite your kooky jumper Dad, I didn't even register it was Christmas Eve until Brodie mentioned it. So I had to cheat. The lentils are from a can, and the roast vegetables are in such small pieces so they would cook more quickly. And I'm afraid there was nothing in the kitchen I could turn into a dessert."

For a moment Brodie looked crestfallen, but then he shrugged and started spooning more vegies onto his plate.

"It's lucky I picked up a chocolate Yule log while I was out then," Mike said, and Brodie's face lit up like the proverbial Christmas tree. Rhiannon felt even worse, that she'd neglected her family for so long, but her dad shook his head.

"Darling, it's okay. I understand that you had to pull away from us to be able to start healing. I did that too," he said gently.

"It's not that," she admitted reluctantly. "I've been so selfish. And totally unfair to you, and to Brodie. Mum would be devastated if she knew I'd let you all down like this, and for so long." For a moment she wanted to run back upstairs, pull the pillow over her head and hide again, but she forced herself to stay.

"Your mother was, and is, incredibly proud of you," her dad said sternly. "And all that matters is that you've returned to us now. There's no point dwelling on the past, or beating yourself up with regret, we just need to move forward, together. I've missed you so much darling, and Brodie has too."

Blushing, she tried to raise a smile as her little brother looked at her across the table, his face so open and joyous, while she was consumed with guilt. He didn't have it in him to be mad at her, he was just glad to have her back.

"Merry Christmas," she said softly, and took both their hands to say grace.

Over dinner Rhiannon was astounded to discover how mature her little brother had become while she'd been hiding in her room, not just in his language and increased vocabulary, but in his attitude to school, and his friendships, and all the things he'd been doing around the house. Was this how parents felt, that they turned around for a minute and suddenly their kids had grown up?

When they'd all finished eating, Brodie hopped straight up and cleared the table, without being asked, and Mike smiled over at his daughter. "Not such a little kid any more, is he?" he asked her, and there was pride in his voice.

"I'm so sorry Dad," she said again, wondering how many times she would have to say it before she felt even the tiniest bit of atonement had been made.

"Say no more," he insisted. "Love means never having to say you're sorry, right?"

Rhiannon frowned at him. "God no Dad, that's an awful thing to say. Love absolutely means apologising when you're in the wrong. I feel terrible because I care so much about you both, yet I behaved so badly, right when you needed me most. I have a lot to be sorry for, and I will keep apologising for all of it. I'll also be doing all I can to make up for it," she insisted.

Her father sighed and smiled all at once. "Wow, it's not just Brodie who's growing up," he replied, reaching over to squeeze her hand, and Rhiannon was touched, and a little surprised, to hear pride for her in his voice.

"Clearly I've never actually thought about what that quote could mean, other than at face value, but you're right."

The intensity of the moment ended when Brodie came back out from the kitchen, three plates and a cardboard box in his hands, and his eyes alight with joy. "Can we eat it now?" he begged, and their dad laughed.

"Of course buddy," Mike replied. "Or would you rather open your presents first?"

"Presents!" Brodie cried, dumping the cake on the table and jumping up and down with excitement. Panic engulfed Rhiannon, and she felt mortified. She hadn't even thought about Christmas, let alone gifts, until tonight. She was a failure all over again. About to apologise for the thirty-fifth time that night, she looked over at her dad, shame turning her cheeks red, but he shook his head at her and rose, picking up a large box wrapped in red paper and tied with blue ribbons that had been sitting in the corner of the room.

"This one's for you Brodie, from your sister," he said, handing over the gift.

"Thanks Rhi-Rhi!" her brother said, voice high with anticipation as he reached for the package and tugged at the ribbons. Inside was another set of boxes, all separately wrapped, and Brodie swooped on the biggest one and tore the paper off. His high-pitched squeal of excitement almost deafened Rhiannon, and she stared at the present, eager to see what "she" had bought him. Inside the first box was a Spider-Man suit, complete with mask and boots, as well as a pair of winter pyjamas emblazoned with the wall crawler's face and webs. She hadn't seen her brother look so happy for… well, months… and his joy was contagious.

"I don't know whether to put it on now, or open the next present," he gasped, and Rhiannon laughed, while their dad pushed the next box over to him. Nestled inside were two web shooters with several canisters of web-making fluid, and the other boxes each revealed an array of matching toys and figures. Brodie ran around the table to hug his sister, then stripped off all his clothes and stepped into the superhero suit.

"Maybe we should wait for the morning to start shooting webs though, right buddy? And only outside?" their father suggested, as it looked as though the excited five-year-old was going to wreak havoc on the room. Reluctantly Brodie sat back down, but in mere seconds he had opened one of the action figure sets and was happily playing with that instead.

"Thank you Dad," Rhiannon whispered, and he smiled at her before turning back to the superhero in their midst.

"Did you want to give Rhiannon your present?" he said, and Brodie carefully sat the figures down and nodded enthusiastically. Mike handed her a box as big as the one Brodie had just opened, which was surprisingly heavy.

"For me?" she asked, surprised, and he nodded and told her it was from Brodie.

"Thanks buddy," she said, then asked him to help her open it. He was by her side in an instant, ripping at the paper as enthusiastically as he had been when he opened his own gift. He really didn't have a selfish bone in his body, unlike her. But while she knew she didn't deserve a present, she was curious about what it could be.

And as the paper came away, she wasn't sure whether to laugh, cry or be offended. On top was a gorgeous deep amethyst patterned quilt cover, and beneath that were two pale purple curtains, matching sheets and pillow cases, and plush lavender cushions for her window seat. It was all so light and airy and soft, and a million miles from the dark and gloomy way her bedroom looked right now. And the thing that had made the box so heavy? Tubs of paint in the palest yellow, called lemon blossom, and three paintbrushes.

Turning wary eyes on her dad and her brother, she waited for an explanation.

"We wanted to cheer you up Rhi-Rhi. Your room is so dark and gloomy, and it's making you be like that too."

One part of her started to get angry, out of habit, but a surprisingly large part of her was touched by their gesture, and as she stared at the paint tubs, she felt the tiniest bit of hope worm its way into her heart, along with the promise of lemon blossoms and spring sunshine.

"You don't have to change a thing if you don't want to," her dad said, picking up on her unease.

Shaking her head, she tore her gaze away from the paint tins and smiled. "No, it's all good. I should make over my room."

"Only if you're sure," he offered gently.

"I am," she replied, knowing there was no turning back once she started, but surprisingly eager to dive in. "Thank you both, really. Will you help me?" she said, turning to her brother, and it warmed her heart when his face lit up with delight, and the joy of being included.

"Can we start now Dad?" he asked eagerly, hopefully, and Mike laughed.

"It's going to be a very big job buddy, so we might have to wait until we have a whole day to dedicate to it, okay?"

Brodie's face crumpled for a moment, then he shook off his disappointment and went back to his action figures. Rhiannon turned to her dad with an embarrassed frown. "I, um, haven't had a chance to get you anything yet," she admitted, blushing.

But he took her hand, and Brodie's, and smiled, the first genuine smile his kids had seen on him for more than three months. "This is all the present I need," he said softly, and she could tell he meant it.

"So, time for the Yule log?" Brodie asked, his voice trembling with a mixture of exhaustion and excitement. Laughing, Mike picked up the knife and did the honours, and Brodie sighed with happiness as he tucked in to the dessert. Their mum used to bake a Yule Log each festive season, to match the wooden one she burned with Rose at their solstice ritual. This would have been Rhiannon's first time accompanying her mum to the midwinter celebration, but although Rose had reminded her that she was welcome to take part on her own, she'd missed it in her self-imposed exile. Maybe next year.

Bringing her attention back to the present, she asked her dad what he had planned for them for the next day. Their family had always loved Christmas, but she'd been oblivious that it was upon them, and she still struggled to imagine there was any way it could still bring her joy now that her mum was gone.

"Well, Nanna Anne and Grandpa William are staying in a cottage in the Lake District for two weeks, and they said we're welcome to go up and join them tomorrow, or at any time, if we'd like to. But we don't have to do that," he added quickly, trying not to scare his daughter with too much too soon. "We could just hang out here together, watch some movies or something, or we could visit Rose…"

Rhiannon gazed at her brother, who'd been pale and listless on the couch just a few hours ago, and marvelled at the colour in his cheeks, the change in his energy and the joy in his eyes from just this tiny amount of family time. As much as she really didn't want to leave the house, she had to admit she was just being lazy – and scared. These grandparents loved her and Brodie, and she knew how much it would mean to her dad to be able to spend Christmas with his parents. And Anne and William would love to see them all too. She was aware of how worried her grandma had been about them.

Forcing a smile, she shook her head. "What the hell, it's about time we had a road trip, right?"

Her brother squealed, looking thrilled again, and Mike gazed over at her with pride. "Thank you darling, for tonight, and for tomorrow. And for coming back to us."

"I'm just sorry it took me so long," she sighed.

She was saved from having to say more by Brodie, who had cut another piece of the chocolatey dessert and was digging in with a look of pure happiness on his face. After just a few bites his eyelids started to droop though, and Mike carried him upstairs and put him to bed while Rhiannon washed the dishes and tidied away their gifts. As she gazed again at the strange box of curtains and quilts and paint, she was surprised to acknowledge that she was actually looking forward to making her room over. It was time for new energy to come into her life. For a little sunshine to pierce her darkness.

When her dad came back downstairs, she'd made him a cup of his favourite tea, and he sighed with pleasure as he took a sip. "We'll have to leave really early tomorrow, is that okay?" he asked nervously.

Nodding, Rhiannon headed upstairs to pack. She knew she'd be too much of a zombie in the morning to do it properly, so she opened her wardrobe and looked inside, then groaned. All her clothes were black, except for one navy top and a dark blue pair of jeans. In her initial grief and anger over her mum's death she really had thrown out every piece of colourful clothing she'd owned.

Grabbing a few dresses, some jumpers and thick tights, she stuffed them into a bag with underwear and a toothbrush, then collapsed into bed. Smiling inwardly, she thought perhaps it was a Christmas miracle that she was beginning to emerge back into the world...

A knock on her door early the next morning roused her from sleep, and she dragged herself out of bed, groaning that it was still dark outside. Quickly pulling on her jeans and the navy top – she remembered how bitterly her gran had complained about her all-black clothes when she'd stayed with them after Beth died – she headed downstairs for a quick breakfast, before she and Brodie piled into the car with their dad and hit the road.

When they merged onto the motorway north, Rhiannon turned around to ask her brother something, but he was fast asleep, still in his Spider-Man suit, a look of peaceful contentment on his face.

"He only let me take it off him last night because he could get straight into the Spidey pyjamas," Mike grinned. "And he was still curled up with the web slinger plush when I woke him up this morning. Good choice of gifts," he teased.

"I'll pay you back, I swear," she said quickly. "And thank you again, so much, for saving my butt with that one – it would have destroyed me if I'd had nothing to give him. But I don't have anything for Nan and Pop either," she groaned. "Is there somewhere we could stop on the way?"

"It's all covered darling, please don't worry."

"Thanks Dad."

As the sky started to lighten, Rhiannon gazed out the window and vowed to make an effort from now on, to be there for her brother, and to stop being so grumpy, angry and closed off. She wasn't the only person who had lost so much, and she'd been absent for long enough. As devastated as she still was, the constant ache in her heart hurt a tiny bit less now, and while she knew she'd probably never be totally over the pain of her loss, she was coming to realise that life did go on, and her selfishness had to stop.

And she kept her promise. Brodie was overjoyed to have his sister back, and they spent long hours roaming along the lakeside when the weather was clear, returning with rosy cheeks and freezing noses, more than ready for another mug of hot chocolate. When it rained they curled up on the massive couches under warm blankets and watched cartoons together, or played board games with their dad and their grandparents in front of the roaring log fire.

The absence of Beth cast a pall over all of them, and Brodie wasn't the only one who woke crying in the middle of the night. But Rhiannon was overwhelmed to realise that her pain was lessened a little by the love and support of her family, and her father pulled her aside a few times to thank her again for being there for Brodie.

And on a personal level, she was making progress. After Christmas lunch, her grandma handed her a large soft package, and she let

Brodie help her unwrap it. Just a day ago she would have been furious at its contents, and lashed out, but today tears welled in her eyes — tears of gratitude, embarrassment, dare she say pleasure? — as she pulled out a riot of rainbow-coloured dresses, skirts and tops, each of them in a vivid, cheerful hue or bright mix. Rhiannon threw her arms around her grandparents in turn, then rushed into her room, tore off her black clothes, and slid into one of the multi-coloured dresses and a long purple jacket. It shocked her, just how different, and how much brighter, she felt out of her gloomy black uniform.

After seeing how dramatically the new clothes lifted her mood, her dad nervously confessed that he'd never gotten around to taking all her colourful clothes to the charity store when she'd wanted to throw them away, so they were all still waiting for her at home, neatly bagged in the attic. While a momentary stab of anger ran through her, that he hadn't respected her wishes, mostly she was happy, and relieved, and she hugged him and thanked him for knowing her mind better than she had in the turmoil of her grief.

For six days the three of them stayed in the lakeside cottage with Anne and William, and Rhiannon was glad to see her dad starting to laugh a little more readily. There was still great sadness though, and twice she came upon her dad and his mother crying together in the kitchen as they tried to comfort each other. With a shock she remembered that Anne's first husband had died when Mike was young, just after he'd married Beth. Perhaps her son's distress at losing his wife was bringing back sad memories for her too.

Yet as Rhiannon watched Anne and her second husband William together, she smiled. He was such a loving, supportive spouse, and had always been a wonderful grandfather to her and Brodie. And as he and his wife banded together to ease Mike's sorrow, her mum's words came back to her, imploring her to encourage her dad if he found love again.

As hard as it was for her to imagine it, her grandparents made her realise that it might be possible to have two great loves in a lifetime.

Chapter 20

Mist rolled in over the lake and black clouds loomed low across the sky as Rhiannon shared a pre-dawn breakfast with her grandparents. Her dad joined them as she was brewing a second pot of coffee, then they packed themselves and Brodie into the car, with many more bags than they'd arrived with, farewelled Anne and William and headed home.

Sprawled out in the back seat, her little brother slept again, physically worn out from all their nature walks, and mentally exhausted from the constant attention and excitement of the festive break. Rhiannon was awake though – really awake, for what felt like the first time in ages – and in a reflective mood.

"One holiday down and a new one to get through," she said sarcastically, rolling her eyes. Then she consciously adjusted her tone. "I don't mean that. I'm sorry I almost missed Christmas, but I know it's New Year's Eve today. What do we have planned?"

Her dad smiled across at her, but his voice was tentative. "Well, Rose invited us all over for dinner tonight, but we'll both totally understand if you'd rather just chill out at home and have a quiet night in. I really appreciate the effort you've made all this week, and how difficult it must have been for you, so I promise you, there will be no hard feelings on anyone's part if you don't feel up to socialising again tonight."

Rhiannon sighed, her default response of late, then shrugged off the habitual gloom. "It's okay Dad, I'm not quite as delicate as you think. That sounds really lovely."

When they pulled up at home a few hours later, Brodie woke up, brimming with energy, and eyes alert. "It's time to change your room Rhi-Rhi!" he shrieked, and sprang out of the car and ran to the front door, presents forgotten in his excitement.

Her first instinct was to refuse, to delay, to put things off, but it was New Year's Eve. What better way to usher in a new year than with a makeover, of her room and her self? Her father raised an eyebrow at her in question, trying to determine whether she needed a way out, but she just shrugged and followed her brother inside, then raced him up the stairs.

After three hours of hard work, the curtains were hung, her bed was made over, and all her walls were painted. One wasn't quite as professional looking as the others, since Brodie insisted on painting his wall all by himself, but Rhiannon loved it because of that.

By the time they finished, their arms were aching, the fumes were starting to get to them, and they suddenly realised how hungry they were. Packing up their brushes and paint tins, they headed downstairs for a very late lunch. When Brodie collapsed on the couch and fell asleep as soon as he'd finished the last bite, Rhiannon put the kettle on, and her dad dashed upstairs, returning with a silver-wrapped parcel tied with purple ribbons. With a sad smile, he handed it to her.

"What's this? Seriously, I got more than enough presents for Christmas, I don't need anything else!"

Mike took a deep breath, suddenly nervous. "This one is from your mum," he explained gently. "I wanted to wait until you could open it in private."

Stumbling backwards, Rhiannon clutched at the sink behind her and tried to steady herself. She felt like she'd been punched in the stomach, and she didn't know whether she wanted to flee from the room, from the house, from the world – or tear at the ribbons and open it right away.

It took a moment for her breathing to return to normal, then slowly she reached out and took the parcel. Offering her another sad smile, her dad walked out into the lounge room to give her some privacy, scooping Brodie from the couch and carrying him upstairs to his room to continue his nap.

Sinking to the floor, Rhiannon clutched the parcel to her heart, until she finally worked up the nerve to open it. Nestled in the shiny paper was a gorgeous white dress, with layers of different fabrics creating texture and swirl in the long, floaty skirt. It was the complete opposite of everything she'd worn since her mum died, and she wasn't sure she'd have the courage to put it on, let alone go out in it.

This dress said hope. It said peace.

Yet she was so without hope, and so lacking in peace.

As she spread the material over her lap, a card fell out, and her name on the envelope, in her mum's distinctive handwriting, made her gasp. Her hands were shaking as she tried to open it, but eventually she managed to slip the card out. It was pretty, like the dress, with a sweet white bird on the front, and the word hope emblazoned on a banner beneath it. It was the perfect card for this dress. For this moment.

Smiling through her tears, she read the words inside.

My darling Rhiannon,

If you are reading this card, it means I am no longer with you, and I am more sorry about that than I can ever express. I know Christmas will be difficult for you, for all of you, but I trust that you will be the light within our family, the sweet and gentle warrior who keeps your dad and Brodie together, and the warmth at the centre of our home now that I am gone.

As the new year rolls around, I wish you the strength to deal with my loss, and the ability to grow from it, rather than being diminished. I know you will be kinder and more open-hearted, not less, as a result, because you have always been my strength. You are the strongest, bravest and kindest person I know, and I implore you to remember that.

As the years pass, I wish you the confidence to always know your true worth, and just how much you deserve to be loved. I wish you the passion to follow your dreams, and the dedication to work

*to make them come true. And I wish you all the blessings of love
and contentment. I know you will face the world without fear,
that you will forge your own path with courage and authenticity,
and I only wish I was privileged enough to be able to see it happen.*

*It devastates me that I won't get to see you grow up, that
I won't be there as you graduate from uni, travel the world, get
married, start your own family, progress in your dream career.
Whatever you choose to do with your life, or not do, I want you to
know always that I am so very proud of you. That I trust you,
and always will. That I have such faith in you, and the choices
you will make and the paths you will journey along. It makes me
so happy to know that you will grow and blossom and learn and
dream and shine your light for the whole world to see.*

*My darling girl, I fell in love with you long before you were
born. I adored you every single moment that I was alive. And I
will continue to cherish you every second of every day, wherever
I am now. You are the best thing that ever happened to me, the
light of my life, the reason for my existence, and I hope you know
how truly and deeply loved you are, and that I will hold you in
my heart for eternity. And I want you to know that, wherever
I am, you will be my love, and my light, and my hope forever.*

All my love, always. Mum xx

The tears flowed faster, until Rhiannon couldn't bear to be inside a
moment longer, contained within these four walls that were closing
in around her. Shaking with misery, she pushed herself to her feet
and fled out the back door.

Without making any conscious decision, she found herself
climbing the tor. As the hill got steeper, her breath came in
short gasps and her cheeks reddened, but she pushed herself onwards,
wanting to feel the stitch in her side, the difficulty breathing, the
burn in her throat, the deep flush of the heat in her cheeks.

When she reached the summit she collapsed onto the damp grass,
and let her long hair fall around her face like a curtain, hiding
her away from the world. Hot, fat tears ran down her cheeks, and her

shoulders shook as great sobs racked her body. She'd been holding in her pain, still scared that it would overflow and hurt someone, or upset her father, but now it was like a dam close to bursting, and she knew that her control was about to slip and tear her apart.

She wept for her mother, and the life she'd been cheated out of. She wailed for herself, for her dad and for her brother. She sobbed for the loss of her friends, their inability to understand her grief, and her reluctance to pull them into her despair.

And she cried for her guilt. Guilt at the stress she'd caused her mum, guilt at not being enough for her dad or for Brodie. Guilt for burdening her friends with her pain. Guilt at not being able to handle her loss and despair in the more mature way her mother had expected she would.

As the ferocity of her thoughts and tears finally slowed, she became aware of a presence next to her, and she froze, mortified that someone had been a witness to the violence and rawness of her pain. She tried to get her crying under control, to rein in her ragged breathing, even as she cursed whoever it was for invading her space, and prayed they would leave.

Instead she felt an arm go around her shoulder – but rather than making her leap to her feet or cry out in fear, which would seem a normal reaction, an inexplicable sensation of calm and comfort washed over her. What was going on? Why hadn't she run screaming down the hill the moment she'd felt the stranger's touch? Why did she feel so peaceful, and so loved, and so safe, so protected? Her body felt languid, and dreamy, as though she was wrapped in a soothing cloud, and nothing and no one could hurt her. Even her heart felt a little lighter, a little less burdened by grief and loss.

Peering nervously to the side, she saw a beautiful woman with flowing red hair, draped in a long blue dress and wreathed in mist and fog. A gentle smile gave warmth to her features, and her kind eyes were deep pools of calm strength that Rhiannon wanted to dive into and submerge herself within.

"Who are you?" she asked in wonder, but the stranger was silent, her eyes never leaving hers. Reaching out a pale hand, she placed it over Rhiannon's heart, which made her suck in her breath in fear, before she felt a wonderful warmth seep into her skin, into her bones, into her soul.

Then the tears came again, even more violent than before, as the woman folded her into a close embrace. But while they flowed for the longest time, these ones were different. These ones were cleansing and soothing and clearing. *Final.*

"Sweet Rhiannon," she heard, in the kindest voice imaginable. "You are a survivor, a warrior, a healer."

She drew back from the arms that were holding her and looked up. The mists were swirling around the blue-clad figure, and around her. She couldn't work out what was going on, but it felt so reassuring that she finally let her defences fall, and gave herself over to the sensation of peace she was being surrounded with.

Time stretched out and snapped back, weaving itself around the two of them, and while they sat there, no one else climbed the hill. There was blessed silence. She didn't even hear the sound of birds soaring above them.

Finally, as the sun began its slow descent to the western horizon, Rhiannon sensed movement over her head once more. Pulling back from the shoulder of the mysterious woman, she gazed upwards, and felt her heart lift as she saw white birds wheeling above them, where she had only ever seen black ones before. They looked like tiny white angels, their wings spread wide as they soared so effortlessly through the calm skies.

"Angel terns," the woman in blue whispered. "Some call them faery terns. They represent peace, and hope. And they have come to whisper to you of magic and of healing. Sweet Rhiannon of the birds, of healing and inspiration, they are a part of you, a reminder that you hold all that you need within you. That you are stronger than you think you are."

The sunlight reflecting off their wings dazzled her, and she smiled as she watched them, so playful with each other, so swift and graceful. And their song was beautiful – she felt it within her, stirring her soul, soothing her heart, lifting her spirits higher.

Dropping her gaze for a moment, she turned to the blue-robed woman to share her joy, but there was no one there, just a swirl of mist and a hint of colour that faded away into nothingness. She looked back to the sky, but the birds had gone too. For a moment she felt bereft, as though she'd lost a friend, but then she smiled with recognition as she sensed something change within her. Suddenly she felt so loved, so understood, as though she had a layer of protection – or the blue-clad woman's cloak of mist – wrapped around her. A strength she didn't recognise took root in her heart, peace filled her, and the first fluttering of hope stirred within her.

As she slowly walked back down the hill, she thought of the white bird on her mother's card, and the white birds that had wheeled above her. When she got home she picked up the white dress from the kitchen floor and went upstairs, pinning the card from her mum to her mirror frame, and slipping the white dress over her head.

It sounded crazy, but whatever it was – some combination of her mother's gift and the touching card, the beauty of the birds who had appeared to her, or the comfort and kind words from the mysterious stranger – somehow the little things that had been hurting her so deeply stopped hurting quite as much. And after months of feeling as though her mother had left her, she began to sense that Beth was still with her in some way.

Smoothing the dress over her hips, she twirled around in a circle, and smiled as the white fabrics floated softly around her. When her dad knocked on her door and asked if she was ready to go to Rose's, she nodded, and his heart filled with hope as he saw the light in his daughter's eyes, which had been dulled for so long, reignite.

"Thank you my darling," he whispered to Beth, and for a moment he felt his wife around him too.

Later that night, curled up in bed in her newly pale, light-filled room, Rhiannon reached out for the first of her beautiful new gifts. Dinner at Rose's had been lovely, from the food, the candlelight and the conversation, to the vases of white roses, jasmine and gardenias on the table and throughout the cottage, which smelled so much like her mother, and made her happy and sad at the same time.

After the main course, Rose had asked her to go to the kitchen with her to help serve the dessert, but it was just a ploy to get her alone.

"I wanted to give you this," the priestess said, handing her a parcel wrapped in purple satin. "You can open it now," she added, when Rhiannon hesitated.

Carefully she unwrapped the colourful cloth, and smiled when she saw the pretty journal. It was a deep dark purple colour – the same shade as her new quilt cover – with swirling silver filigree embossed over the top. Book of Shadows was written on a small plaque in the middle of the cover.

"It's beautiful," she said, slightly awestruck by the gift. "But I'm not sure what I would write in it..."

Rose took her hand. "In your own time sweet girl. You might want to start tonight, or you might want to wait until next year, or a few years from now. I just want you to know that you are welcome within our magic circle, and at our rituals, as well as within the inner coven – if and when you feel ready," she offered.

Then the priestess picked up another parcel, this one wrapped in green satin, and handed it over. "I wanted you to have this too, and so did your mum."

Rhiannon raised her eyebrows. "I don't deserve so many presents," she insisted, but Rose just smiled.

"It's not like that."

Gently untying the ribbon, she had stared, stunned, when the fabric slid to the floor to reveal an old leather book, with hundreds of pages within it. The cover was embossed in swirling leaves and ivy, and it was bound together with silver clasps. Rhiannon ran her finger over the cover in awe. It looked ancient, and it felt powerful.

"It was your mum's Book of Shadows, which she'd been adding to for more than twenty years, since her very first ritual," Rose explained.

Rhiannon's heart felt as though it might overflow with all the emotions warring within her – sadness, regret, loss, fear, angst, love – but there was a growing sense of connection too. "Thank you. It's perfect," she whispered.

Rose had hugged her, given her a pretty fabric bag to put the books in, then picked up the apple pie and warm pot of custard from the bench and led her back to the table.

Now, Rhiannon opened her mum's Book of Shadows, running her fingers lovingly over the pages, over words familiar and not-so-familiar. It was fascinating to see her writing style change as the years passed, so intriguing to skim over amazing rituals Beth had done, that she couldn't even begin to understand. It seemed her mother had been far more of a witch than she'd ever known, and she longed to explore her world of wisdom.

After a while though, she gently put it down on the bed beside her and reached for the other book, her book. It was gorgeous, so much her style, and her colour even. She was touched by the beauty of the gift, and the meaning and care Rose had obviously taken in choosing it for her.

And it was so perfect for this night. It was New Year's Eve — ushering in a new year, a new page, a new chapter, a new beginning. A new hope. Slowly she opened to the first page, picked up her purple pen, and started to write.

> *I am Rhiannon. Motherless, and grandmotherless too on my mum's side (by her choice, not her death), but I am just beginning to realise how much I am loved.*

As she carefully wrote down the words, she realised how deeply true they were.

> *I have a wonderful father, who is so much stronger and more complex than I had ever known. I have a brother who I adore, and it seems I have Rose, the best mentor anyone could ask for, the best substitute gran, the best friend even…*

Her eyelids were starting to droop as sleep circled around her, so she gently placed the books on her bedside table and reached out to turn off her lamp, just as the clock struck midnight.

"Happy New Year," she whispered, and was surprised to find herself hopeful. Then she laughed. It certainly couldn't be any worse than the one just gone…

Chapter 21

Written In the Stars

Beth... Twenty years ago...

As sunlight poured through her window, Beth woke up with a smile on her face. Today she was spending the day with Mike and Violet, doing a divination course with some apparently awesome teacher/guru, and she couldn't wait. Since attending Rose's rituals, doing the witchcraft course and having the healing, plus her psychic reading at the fair with Jenny, she'd become intrigued with the potential for magic and spirituality.

It also touched her deeply that Violet and Mike had invited her to go with them. Travelling was wonderful, and she'd met some amazing people and done so many incredible things, but it was tough to make lasting connections when you were constantly moving on. And while her employers in Paris were lovely, she wasn't quite as fluent in French as she would have liked, and the language barrier on their part too precluded any really deep sharing. She'd missed having close friends, and now that she was thinking she might stay here, it meant even more to her that they'd included her.

Although Mike and Violet were a few years younger than her, and had barely left their village, they were both so wise – and in some ways she felt they were more mature than her. She giggled.

Perhaps she needed to step up and stop being so immature. Take responsibility for her life and her choices.

It still surprised her that they had both welcomed her so genuinely, and invited her to be part of their magical world. And it made her feel ashamed, because she knew that if it had been her going out with Mike, she wouldn't have let Violet tag along. She'd be guarding him, and their time together, jealously, and zealously. God, that was a terrible rhyme!

Laughing as she threw the covers back, she quickly got ready, then ran downstairs, her mother's goading as she ate breakfast not even penetrating the cloud of joy she held tightly around herself. When she heard Mike beep the car horn, she raced outside and piled into the back seat. Even the drive over to the town half an hour away was fun with her new friends, and she admired the easy camaraderie they drew her into, and longed for the love they had for each other.

While one part of her, the mean, jealous part, wanted to dislike Violet, she just couldn't. The girl was so kind and sweet, and so together. She'd already decided she was going to be a social worker, and help people, and she saw learning divination and other psychic and alternative healing modalities as an extra way to assist them, offering spiritual insight and reassurance in addition to traditional therapeutic methods.

On top of that she was really funny, and the three of them were still laughing as they found the building the course was being held in and walked into the classroom.

But when the teacher turned towards them, they all froze, their laughter dying off into silence. Beth felt suddenly hot, then freezing cold, and her stomach clenched in shock. The teacher was Andrew. Her Andrew. The guy she'd been dating in Paris, who'd sworn his love to her then mysteriously disappeared from her life. What the hell was he doing here?

Once she finally managed to breathe again, she glanced over at Mike, and saw him staring at the guy with unusual hostility. Puzzled, she looked at Violet, then back to Andrew, and was perturbed to see their gazes locked on each other, with an intensity that was disturbing, and so clearly oblivious to everyone else in the room. Silence cloaked them for long moments, until finally, thankfully, someone else walked in behind them and slipped into a seat in the back row, breaking the teacher's concentration.

"Good to see you again Shelley," he said to the girl who'd just come in, then he moved over to Beth and her friends.

"Hi, I'm Andre," he said, sticking out his hand to Mike. As Violet's boyfriend reluctantly introduced himself, Beth stared, confused. *Andre?* This was Andrew.

"I'm Beth," she said, challenge in her voice.

He shook her hand too, and grinned. "Andre," he insisted.

For a moment she doubted herself. Could she be so mistaken? Could he have a twin? But she'd seen him just a few weeks ago. Had been *kissing* him just a few weeks ago. And assuming they would be reunited as soon as she could get back to London. Of course it was him.

She watched, numb, as he turned his full attention to Violet, holding her hand far longer than was necessary, and his gaze as he looked her up and down all too familiar. And filled with lust. No wonder Mike looked so uncomfortable.

Seating them in the front row, with Violet closest to his desk and Beth positioned between her and Mike, Andrew began the class. But right away Beth vagued out, blushing with embarrassment that she'd dated the teacher. She was terrified that Violet and Mike would think less of her if they found out, and worried that Andrew would say something about it, single her out and make fun of her in some way, in front of the whole class.

Mike seemed as on edge as she was, and she felt bad for him. It must be awful to see someone else so obviously fawning over your girlfriend. Especially when that someone technically had his own girlfriend – *her!* Then she noticed that inbetween gazing up at Andrew with adoration, Violet was furiously scribbling notes. She couldn't bring herself to concentrate enough for that though, no matter how interesting the topic.

When the class took a break mid-morning, Mike went off to grab coffees, and Violet turned to Beth with shining eyes.

"Isn't he amazing?" she gushed.

"He's lovely," she replied. "And he loves you so much."

Violet gasped. "What? I just met him!"

"Oh, I thought you meant Mike. Your *boyfriend* Mike."

"No silly, Andre! He's just so wise, isn't he, and so magical, and so gorgeous! I could listen to him talk for days!"

Or talk about him for days, it seemed, as she continued raving about how great he was, everything from his teaching methods and wisdom to his long, apparently beautiful hair and chiselled cheekbones. So enamoured of him was Violet that she didn't notice her friend hadn't said a word.

Beth was relieved when Mike returned with their coffees, assuming Violet would change the subject, but she didn't, and the poor guy looked more devastated by the minute. When Violet pushed him to agree with her admiration, he muttered that sure, he was impressed so far, then he asked her a question about one of the exercises they'd done. And off she went again, gushing about the class – and the teacher – and oblivious to the discomfort of her companions.

Throughout the next session, Beth tried to figure out how she felt. And what it meant, that her boyfriend had turned up with a new name, was pretending he'd never met her before, and was hitting so hard and so obviously on Mike's girlfriend.

During the lunch break she was quiet, preoccupied, but Violet kept up an endless stream of conversation about how brilliant "Andre" was, and didn't notice her silence. And Mike was too busy brooding, and struggling with his own misery, to be aware of anything else.

In the next session, Beth started feeling angry. She and the so-called spiritual teacher had been declaring their love for each other just a few weeks ago. The only reason they'd ended their relationship, or so he'd claimed, was that he had to go back to England – hence her acceptance of her sister's wedding invitation, so she could move back to London and move in with Andrew. Yet it was abundantly clear that he didn't have the same expectations of their relationship, if his behaviour today was any indication.

Seeing him had shaken her to the core, and being in the same room with him all day, listening to his smooth voice, was bringing back every moment of their time together, every line he'd spoken about his love for her – which seemed now to have been a lie, and yet she still so wanted to believe him.

When she'd walked into class that morning she'd been speechless with shock at seeing him, unable to find her voice when he asked the class questions, and barely able to mutter "I don't know" in answer to the one he'd directed at her.

His smirk at her inability to speak made her furious, but mostly she was sad. Quite separate to her plans to return to London to be with him, she'd wanted to share this course with Violet and Mike, and had been so looking forward to the three of them spending this time together, laughing and learning and sharing as they developed their divination skills.

Violet had raved about the teacher, who she'd read about in a few spiritual magazines, so she'd hoped she might find some insight about her situation with Andrew in whatever they learned in class. And it seemed that she *had* found answers – just not in the manner she'd expected.

It hurt her head to wonder at his motive, to try to understand his actions. Why tell her he loved her if he didn't? She'd never pushed for commitment – he'd been the first to say it, to claim his love for her, and she'd only considered how deep her feelings for him ran *after* he'd confessed that he loved her.

When they broke briefly for afternoon tea, Violet continued gushing about how wonderful he was, how inspiring, how charming, how charismatic. In contrast, her boyfriend seemed even less impressed with the teacher than he had been earlier, and increasingly put out by Violet's over-the-top enthusiasm.

And when class resumed, Andrew – sorry, *Andre* – was paying even more attention to Violet, playing up to her, telling her how wonderful she was, how enlightened. Even worse was that Violet was lapping it all up, and the anguish on Mike's face when he saw her gazing up at their teacher with puppy dog eyes nearly broke Beth's heart, quite aside from how devastated she felt that her supposed boyfriend was taking such delight in flirting so dramatically right in front of her.

Towards the end of the day, Andre offered to do a reading on someone in the class as a demonstration of his skills and methods, and of course he chose Violet. As she stood up from her desk and walked towards him, overjoyed to have been picked, Mike gritted his teeth. And when Andre took Violet's hands then began the reading by saying that new love was coming into her life, it looked like Mike was going to throw up, or punch the guy in the face. Just quietly, she voted for punching him in his sanctimonious mouth.

"Violet, can I call you that?" the teacher began, voice smooth as honey and saccharine sweet. "You are such a wonderful person, already so far advanced along your spiritual path, and so much wiser than your years. I sense you've been in a relationship for some time, but it is not fulfilling you," he continued, with a sly sideways glance at Mike.

"But I see a grand love coming into your life – you may have just met him – and he will challenge you and inspire you and teach you, and push you to open your heart in new ways. You are too special to settle for *ordinary*, in life or in love. This new man will be older than you, mature, wise, and he is the only one who can love you the way you deserve to be loved."

Now Beth thought *she* would throw up, and she could tell Mike was getting more upset by the minute.

"And once you meet this man, your relationship up until this point will seem a poor and pale imitation in comparison, consigned to the scrap heap of childhood friendships and entanglements. He is not worthy of you – you need someone *special*, someone amazing, someone who can see your true essence, as a being of pure love and light, and allow you to reveal all of your magnificent potential."

Mike's face was red and angry, and Beth longed to comfort him, while also feeling hurt herself. Andrew had said all of this to her in France, almost word for word. Not the comments so clearly directed at Mike, dismissing Violet's actual relationship, but the whole "you're so advanced spiritually" thing, and the "you're too special for ordinary, you need someone – like me – who'll love you the way you deserve to be loved" line. She felt so stupid that she'd fallen for it, and was horrified to see that Violet was succumbing too.

Of course all of that was true – but it was true for every single person. Everyone deserves love, and everyone is special. But how could he lie to Violet like that about Mike? And, even more ethically and morally wrong, make it sound like *he* was the new love? Twist everything around under the guise of a psychic reading, so Violet would believe that what he said was true, and inevitable.

Before today, Violet would have proudly told anyone who asked just how much she loved Mike, and how much she was looking forward to starting her life with him as soon as they left school. That was all true, and real. Yet now it seemed like she'd forgotten it, and was lost in an alternate reality, staring up at Andre with love-sick eyes, basking in his attention in a way that turned Beth's stomach.

God, had she been like that when she'd met him? Had she looked so pathetic? Somehow she had to convince Violet to tone down her obvious admiration, because Mike looked heartbroken. And that was the saddest thing of all.

It was quiet in the car on the way home, each of them lost in thought. Mike's silence was prickly, as he seethed in the driver's seat, while Violet was happily looking out her window, daydreaming about the reading she'd been given and totally oblivious to his anger and fear. Beth sat in the back, trying to be unobtrusive, but she could sense the strain, and felt so uncomfortable – not just because of the undercurrent between her two friends, but because seeing Andrew had really thrown her. All her feelings of unworthiness and confusion were flooding back. He'd helped her work through some of her insecurities, made her feel worthy after years of emotional abuse at her mother's hands. But if their relationship hadn't been real, where did that leave her?

She felt herself diminishing under the weight of the memories, under the weight of how he'd made her feel before – and the dangerous path that learning his love had been a lie was sending her down now. Bitterness rose in her, and she coughed, almost choking on it. They were stopped at a give way sign, and Mike turned to her, concern in his eyes.

"Are you all right Beth?" His voice was gentle, and tender, and his sweetness soothed her heart a little.

"Sorry, I'll be fine," she said, embarrassed to be breaking into his thoughts, and hoping they would soon be back in the village so she could escape this tension-filled car.

"What did you think of today?" he asked.

"It was okay," she replied reluctantly. "He got a few things wrong though, and he seemed to rely only on what he claimed he could see of the future – which no one can verify yet – rather than revealing anything from our pasts that we could have judged him on. But I guess it will get more detailed as the course progresses. Why, what did you think?"

Mike shrugged, and seemed hesitant to speak too. "I guess you're right. I wasn't overly impressed to be honest, although I wasn't sure why. But the no verification thing was probably a big part of it," he said, grasping at the excuse she'd given him.

"He was *amazing!*" Violet burst out, and they stared at her in consternation. "His reading for me was incredible, and so accurate. How awesome, that he could see all that about me!"

Beth paled. Was she referring to that whole "you'll meet your great love soon" bit? The bit that totally ignored Mike's presence in her life, and made it sound like she was happily single right now? And if she didn't mean that, what was she focusing on? The old "you're the most spiritually advanced person in the room" line? *The very same line she'd fallen for when Andrew had said it to her.*

In an instant she was transported back to the festival in the French countryside where she'd met him. She'd been watching a band, dancing in the weak winter sunshine, then someone had dragged her into a tent for a workshop. A man was sitting in the centre of a small circle of people, teaching them methods to centre themselves and go within, then set off on a shamanic healing journey.

Each time he caught her eye, it felt like he was staring into her soul, reaching inside her and holding her heart in his hands – which she wasn't sure she liked. Yet when he started winding up the talk and gestured to her to stay behind, she did. Nervously she waited until everyone else had left, half terrified, half excited, by the thought of speaking to him alone.

He took her hand and drew her over to the corner of the now-empty tent, then settled on a pile of cushions, pulling her down with him. Without saying a word, he took both her hands in his and gazed into her eyes, and deep inside her. Blushing, she tried to figure out why he was staring at her so intently, tried to understand what he wanted from her, and why he'd chosen her.

"Ma cherie, vous êtes si belle," he whispered, and although her French still wasn't great, she knew it was a compliment from the way he was looking at her, and the way his hold on her hands tightened, his thumbs stroking the palms of her hands, his eyes greedily drinking her in. She blushed again, then whispered her thanks, and he reached out his hand to her, holding her chin and lifting her face until she was falling into the depths of his eyes too.

"You are so beautiful bella," he repeated, in English this time, hand stroking her cheek, then moving down to caress her neck, then her shoulder. "And so spiritual, so illuminated. You have no idea how many people I meet at these things – doubters, sceptics, and those who think they know everything after listening to a two-hour presentation," he said with a sigh.

"But you, I can see deep into your soul, and it is luminous. Your heart beats in time with mine, and I can feel your hand inside me, holding it safe," he continued, taking her left hand and holding it to his chest, positioning it so that she felt his heart beating, felt his chest muscles rippling, felt the heat of his skin as it pulsed beneath her palm.

With his other hand he reached over and touched her heart, and it sped up instantly – part nerves, part anticipation, part hope. For a moment she thought he was going to kiss her, and she almost groaned with the desire building in her for him to do just that. Then she shook her head. Why would this amazing healer, this acclaimed teacher, want to kiss her? She had to get a grip.

But then he shocked her by leaning in towards her, his eyes flashing with something she couldn't quite place, before all thought was driven from her head by the sensation of his lips on hers. Suddenly she was falling, dangerously fast, but she didn't want to stop, didn't want to land. She had no idea why he was kissing her, but she didn't care. In that moment she felt desired, she felt wanted, she felt special, and it soothed the part of her that still yearned for her mother's acceptance, and her father's attention, and her sister's friendship.

They kissed for what felt like hours, and each time someone came in to try to speak to him, he told them in no uncertain terms to leave. Later he asked if she was hungry, and when she sheepishly nodded, he opened a basket and fed her strawberries, and cheese, and glasses and glasses of wine. And the whole time he kept up his flattery, kept telling her how special she was, before starting to kiss her all over again.

Finally a surly woman came in, and refused to leave. After a scathing look in Beth's direction, she told Andrew he had a performance on the main stage he couldn't skip, then an interview with a TV show that would screen nationally. Regretfully he stood up, then he leaned back down and whispered in her ear. "Ma cherie, please don't leave me. I will be back soon, I promise, and I have big plans for you." Then he kissed her, more passionately than she'd ever been kissed, and hurried away.

For a while she floated, ecstatic, her mind drifting over all the things he'd said to her, over the way his lips had felt on hers. But when she realised that every button of her shirt was undone, she was horrified. Desperately she tried to remember him doing that, but it was all a little hazy. No wonder that woman had given her such a filthy look. What was she doing here, with a man she didn't know, a man who hadn't even asked her what her name was?

Yet the thought of leaving filled her with sadness and regret. She felt bereft at the idea of not seeing him again. Then she recalled the sensation of his lips on her lips, on her neck, on her shoulder, then slowly moving further down... And again she heard his voice in her ear, telling her she was beautiful, she was desirable, she was smart and spiritual and special. And so she stayed, and eventually drifted off to sleep.

When she woke up it was dark, and she was wrapped in his arms, their breathing in sync, their skin warm against each other's where they touched. Her shirt was off, which startled her, but her worry about that dissolved under his kisses, dissolved into nothing as he held her close and whispered sweet everythings in her ear. She shivered when he took her hand and placed it on his bare chest, and blushed, but then she gave herself over to the feeling of being in his arms. And when he placed his hand on her bare chest, she moaned with lust and longing.

The next morning, an icy chill on her naked flesh woke her from a dream filled with raw passion, heat, and sexual abandon – which made it even worse when she realised that not only was she freezing cold, but she was alone. Tears of humiliation welled in her eyes, and she clasped the blanket they'd been lying on around herself as she desperately searched for her clothes. She was buttoning up her shirt when she saw movement at the doorway, and she froze, mortified that someone would see her here like this, witness her shame.

And yet... it was him. He'd returned, and he had a bowl of fruit salad in one hand and two mugs of coffee in the other.

"Ma cherie, what are you doing?"

Shrugging and squirming with embarrassment, she finished doing up her shirt then ran her fingers through her hair, trying to look presentable. But it wasn't necessary. He walked straight over, handed her a coffee, stroked her hair – then ripped off her shirt and pulled her into his arms again. It was hours before they got around to eating any of the fruit or drinking the now icy coffee, and another day until he let her get dressed, in one of his shirts, since every button on hers was now missing.

And once they discovered they both lived in Paris, their passionate romance began. Two weeks after they'd met he finally asked what her name was, although he continued calling her ma cherie, which she secretly liked. And while the memories of how much of their time together she'd spent naked made her squirm now, she had to admit that he'd helped her deal with her relationship with her parents, and even heal a little from the pain. It was this process that had given her the courage to accept her sister's wedding invitation, and believe she could cope with being back home for more than a month.

He had been so sympathetic when he'd finally coaxed her story out of her. "Oh, ma cherie, you've been so terribly misunderstood by those who should see you the best and most clearly, who should see your true self and appreciate all of your amazing qualities. I'm so sorry that you have suffered this, but you have to know how wrong they are. And how sorry I feel for them, because they have lost you. That would be an unbearable loss for me, I promise you."

"**B**eth!" The voice sounded worried, and she turned towards it. Oops! She was in the car with Mike and Violet, and now they were both peering at her, concern in their eyes. "Are you okay?" Mike asked, voice soft. He was such a kind man, it hurt her heart to look at him. Why did he have to be in love with Violet, who right now looked like she'd run off with Andrew if given half a chance?

"Sorry guys, I'll be fine, I guess the course just brought up some bad memories." She tried to laugh at the irony. It certainly had, but it wasn't the subject matter that had upset her, it was the supposedly wonderful teacher and the mystery of his disappearance from her life, and the reappearance here now, with what seemed to be intentions towards Violet.

She just couldn't get her head around it all. He'd seemed to genuinely care about her – had professed his love, and asked her to move in with him – although clearly that was no longer the case. But if he didn't feel that, why had he come back that first morning? Why had he pursued her when she returned to Paris? Why had he worked so hard to help her with her mother issues? Why had he spent so long convincing her that he loved her?

Memories and questions swirled in her mind, and it took her a moment to notice they'd pulled up outside her house. When Mike opened the car door for her she jumped, startled, then took his hand gratefully as he helped her out.

He gave her a hug. "Thanks so much for coming with us today, and I hope you'll be okay," he said, voice so kind and genuine that she almost cried. "And Beth, if you ever want to talk, or whatever, just let me know, okay?"

Smiling, she nodded at him, then leaned in to say goodnight to Violet. Her friend still had a silly grin on her face, but she waved to her and called out a farewell. Mike walked her up to her front door – he was so polite! – kissed her on the cheek, then hurried back to the car and drove off.

The verandah light switched on as she put her key in the lock, and she noticed the front room curtains twitch, before the door was pulled open to reveal her mother standing there in the harshness of the hall light. Oddly though, she looked happy.

"So, I see you are making an effort to impress Michael," she crowed, and there was a strange pride in her voice. "When will you see him again? Are you dating him yet?"

Shoulders slumping with frustration and exhaustion, Beth followed her mother inside and closed the door, trapping herself under the same roof as the monster for another night.

"We're not dating Mother. I told you, he's with Violet. But we are friends, and we have been spending lots of time together, the three of us, and will continue to do so. They're both really lovely, and I value their friendship."

"Oh Elizabeth," Patricia spat, disappointment mingling with anger in her voice. "When will you learn? You have to go after what you want. You have to make things happen. Violet is just his high school girlfriend, but she's a flighty one that girl. She won't be content to stick around here with him, she'll leave the minute she can, and go off and see the world."

Her tone was disparaging, and Beth wanted to defend her friend, and convince her mother that she was wrong about her. And yet, was she so wrong? Until tonight, she would have defended Mike and Violet's love to anyone – it was the exact kind of relationship she so badly wanted for herself. And she would have put money on the wedding vows, which they planned to make once school finished, lasting forever.

But now she wasn't so sure. Seeing Violet's head being turned by Andrew tonight had introduced a sliver of doubt to her mind, and made her worried for Mike and the love he clearly had for her. A memory came back to her, of the night she'd met Violet at her first ritual, and the way her face had lit up whenever she spoke of Mike. Would it still do that now?

Not that she would reveal any of these doubts to her mother, or admit that there could be any truth to her nasty assumptions. Patricia traded in misery and innuendo, and she would not be a party to that, especially not when it involved her friends.

"Goodnight Mother," she sighed, and hurried upstairs. But as she lay in bed, her mind whirled with possibility. She wanted someone to look at her the way Mike looked at Violet, to love, respect and care for her the way he so obviously did for his beloved.

God, it was tempting to encourage her friend to focus on the teacher who'd so enchanted her, so that she could have Mike for herself, yet she knew that was crazy. She couldn't make someone who loved someone else fall for her, and even if she could, she wouldn't want to. Mike loved Violet, and if she was as much their friend as she'd just said she was – as she hoped she was, as she wanted to be – she would convince Violet not to be swept off her feet by the mysterious, and to appreciate the wonderful that was already right by her side...

Her decision and her resolve were tested the very next morning though, when Violet knocked on her door, hours before she was supposed to see her. The three of them had planned to meet at Violet's place that afternoon to practise their tarot reading, since Rose had so many different decks they could work with, yet here she was, eyes sparkling and skin flushed with excitement, imploring her to sit down and chat with her before Mike joined them. She was so buoyant and excited that she didn't notice Beth's reticence, or her discomfort. She didn't even notice Patricia hovering in the background with her ready air of disapproval.

As Beth made them coffee and tried to look non-committal and non-judgemental, her friend started talking a mile a minute, words spilling out all over themselves in her eagerness to talk about Andrew. Well, Andre.

"Oh Beth, isn't he amazing? And he's so gorgeous! Really distinguished, and really attractive, and oh my god, he's so sexy."

"Hmm," she muttered, praying Violet wasn't paying any attention to her, since she'd gone bright red at her words. Yes, she did know how sexy he was. And how his bare chest felt under her hands. How his lips felt on her naked body. But enough of that – she was not going there ever again.

"He's just so worldly, and so accomplished, isn't he? And so spiritual, and intuitive, and just so accurate, right?"

"Well, we don't know how accurate he is, because he didn't say anything we could verify, nothing that had already taken place. It was all just predictions of the future, things which may never happen, or might happen only because he said they would, and so you create it into reality," Beth stammered, worried every word she spoke would give away that she knew him, that she had been in love with him herself.

Violet was staring at her, shocked by her words, yet thankfully oblivious to her inner turmoil. "Do you think that about all psychics?" she asked sharply. "About my mum?"

Shaking her head emphatically no, Beth tried to reassure her friend. "Your mother is amazing, you know I think that. She had incredible insight into my past – perhaps a little too much – and she knew so many things that had happened to me, both as a kid and right now. She knew things no one else could know, not even my sister," she revealed, voice conciliatory.

"But the guy yesterday, the teacher, nothing he said was past tense and thus verifiable. Which isn't necessarily a bad thing – for all we know he is amazingly accurate, and it will all come true eventually – but I'm just not willing to trust in his accuracy or speak for him until he reveals it in some way."

Violet took a deep breath, then a big slurp of coffee, and finally nodded. "Okay, you're right about that, and Mum would agree with you. So I'll reserve judgement on that score. But can you at least agree that he's amazingly hot?"

A shiver ran up Beth's spine, and she squeezed her eyes shut against the memories that threatened to swallow her. Not the passionate memories, or the healing memories, or the loving memories – and there had been a lot of them, she had to admit – but the ones trying to drown her in the kitchen right now were the later ones, the ones she'd glossed over at the time, explained away because she was so in love with him.

The night he'd hit her because he thought she'd been flirting with someone else, although she hadn't been. Then a second time because he was angry and drunk and frustrated with his manager. She'd overlooked it then, but now she was mortified that she'd put up with it, that through her inaction she'd seemed to accept it, seemed to feel herself deserving of that, and even worse, allowed him to think it was okay with her.

And his verbal assaults had been as painful as his blows, and cut her even more deeply. She shuddered now, as she recalled him cruelly using the things she'd confided in him earlier against her. She'd buried these memories after he'd apologised, and convinced herself that he hadn't meant what he said, that it didn't hurt her, but now it hit her with the force of a sledgehammer.

The time she'd been too sick to have sex, and he'd turned on her, all of a sudden trying to convince her that her cruel mother was not a woman who'd treated her badly all her life, as he'd once told her, had once believed, but a loving, strict parent who had simply had enough of her selfish behaviour. And that her distant, angry father was loving to everyone else – it was just her that he despised.

Every little secret she'd confided in him, he'd whipped out and twisted up and thrown back in her face, using her own words against her, using them to trap and destroy her. The betrayal was doubly painful because he'd helped her to heal those insecurities, helped her to let go of that pain – before he turned around and pulled the rug out from under her and made it even worse.

It shocked her, that a so-called healer could reverse any good he'd done, undo all the progress she'd made, in a matter of moments. Wasn't his motto supposed to be to heal and to help – and do no harm?

"Beth?"

Her mind was drawn back into her body, back into the room, and she stared at her friend blankly.

"Are you okay?" Violet asked her. But she was saved from replying when her mother walked back into the room, glared at the two of them, then stormed out again. The interruption gave her time to pull herself together.

"I'm fine. It's just a little challenging to be here. But we were talking about you, sorry. What were you saying?"

Her friend started babbling again, about how great Andrew – Andre – was, and Beth withdrew emotionally once more, worried now how much she should reveal. Did she have a responsibility to disclose that she knew him, and how well? Wasn't that the friendship code, to look out for each other? Or had she already left it too late, by not mentioning it yesterday? And would Violet just assume it was sour grapes on her part, that she was jealous of her, and the attention she was getting?

God, she'd never known that friendships could be so stressful! Should she be supportive of whatever Violet wanted to do, and just listen to her waxing lyrical about the guy? Or was she supposed to tell her friend that he could be manipulative and cruel beneath the layers of charm and sophistication? That he had hit her a couple of times? Had emotionally healed her, then harmed her even more?

And yet, maybe he wouldn't do that to Violet. Maybe it was something only she deserved, as he'd tried to convince her. Did she bring out the worst in him, and make him angry enough to do that to her? Or was she just blaming herself again for someone else's bad behaviour?

But... what if he really was Violet's soul mate, as she seemed to think? It wouldn't surprise her – she was an amazing girl, so smart and kind and sensitive, so open to the magic of the earth, and the possibilities of the world and so full of knowledge of the spiritual and esoteric, thanks to her priestess mum...

She didn't know what to do.

Chapter 22

Wake Me Up Inside

Rhiannon... Today...

Still buoyed by the comfort of Rose, Brodie and her dad, and the energy of her newly-made-over room, Rhiannon didn't feel the same dread as she headed back to school for the first day of the new term. She wasn't thrilled by the idea, but it wasn't as traumatic as the last return had been. And this time she was determined to make up for all the time she'd lost, so she got to each class a few minutes early to request extra homework and enquire about the possibility of additional assignments she could do for extra credit. It was boring, but it was what she needed right now – a steady routine and a sense of purpose to keep her going, a way to focus on the future and avoid wallowing in her own misery.

Her dad had been right, when he'd said she couldn't put her life on hold forever, or give up on her dreams for the future because of her mum's death. She'd been drowning in grief, self-pity and anger for three months, and now it was time to get back on track, and try to find reasons to go on after being so shattered by her loss. She still had no idea what she wanted to do with her life, what she wanted to be, but getting her grades back up so she had options when she finally figured it out was a good enough goal for now.

School was hard though. Her mother's death had changed her, she knew that, and although she was trying to go back to how she'd been, to re-find her spark, she just couldn't. She did her best, getting up every morning to put on her brave face along with her uniform, forcing joy when she saw her friends, pasting a smile on for every teacher who expressed concern.

It wasn't working too well, not like she wanted it to, but all the extra study was making it easier for her to deal with the knowledge that Debbie and Sue still weren't comfortable around her. Although they'd waited for her out on the snow-covered front steps the first morning back, and let her hang out with them at lunchtime, their old closeness had gone, and they often made up excuses to avoid her.

It hurt her deeply, even as she understood why they were doing it. They hadn't lost anyone close to them, and so it was hard for them to know what she was feeling, to empathise with her, and to be themselves when they were with her. It was as though they were tiptoeing on eggshells all the time – they were cautious around her, and so afraid to upset her, which wasn't much fun for her or for them. She desperately longed to meet someone who comprehended the depth of her grief, as well as her need to try to forget it when she could.

But it was okay. She wanted to focus on her grades, and having extra work to do gave her the excuse she needed to avoid awkward situations. She still wasn't ready to socialise, so there were times that she was actually glad Debbie and Sue planned outings without her.

As the weeks passed, and the bitter cold of midwinter loosened its grip, she found herself spending a lot of time looking after Brodie, as her dad began to rejoin the land of the living. He still missed his wife terribly, and still cried himself to sleep at times, but he finally went to a few work events, and was surprised that he could function okay. Not great, but okay.

He even signed up for a weekend course in the city, after Rose insisted he go as a way to get out of his comfort zone, for the sake of himself as well as his kids. He'd been reluctant, since often just getting through his day remained a challenge, but he finally acquiesced. And he had to agree, on his return, that it had been a positive step.

So Rhiannon spent every non-studying moment looking after her little brother, and cooking and cleaning, but she didn't mind. Well, not too much. And she genuinely enjoyed spending time with Brodie, helping him with his homework, and reading books to, and increasingly with, him. Because while she and their dad were still diminished by grief, her brother was growing in leaps and bounds, mentally, emotionally and physically. He stayed over at his friend Ben's place once a week, and she was grateful to Ben's family for taking him in, and giving him some time to socialise outside of their still-not-quite-back-to-normal home.

There were times she envied Brodie his innocence and resilience. He never cried, he never asked awkward questions, and after a couple of initial enquiries just after Beth died, he seemed to be coping with her absence pretty well.

Of course he didn't have all the amazing memories of their mum that she did, but he wasn't suffering from the pain that still woke her up in the night either. The pain that still crushed her with the weight of her loss, which sneaked up on her at the most unexpected times, ripping the breath from her chest and leaving her flattened and gasping for air.

But even these moments slowly became further apart, and there were times she could go whole days without being brought to her knees by her grief.

And after understandably terrible class results the previous term, Rhiannon had been convinced by her maths teacher to take on an extra class, since all her added studying and bonus assignments had revealed a hither-to unknown aptitude for numbers, equations and problem solving.

Quite possibly it was the cold, unyielding, emotionless nature of the subject that appealed to her – numbers were what they were, no emotional investment necessary, no piece of herself laid open and bare, like she was struggling with in literature and even history. Numbers were unchanging, and didn't care at all how she was feeling at any given time.

Perhaps her hazy state of mind appreciated the clarity of the equations and the beauty of the sense of control she had over them too. Maths was black and white, right or wrong, and she liked that. She'd taken up an offer of extra tutoring each week, and all of a sudden concepts she'd struggled with became clear, and she began to top the class. Her teacher suggested she look into careers in the field, and she shocked herself when she began to seriously consider it, rather than dismissing it as foolish or boring.

While everything else in her life seemed difficult and so drenched in emotion, she came to love maths and science because they allowed her to bring order to the chaos on the page, and in her mind. She could solve problems and control outcomes. Previously she'd pondered being a children's book author, or an English teacher like her mum, but now they seemed too arbitrary, too weighted with emotion, with vulnerability, with having to expose herself in some way. She loved the impersonal nature of maths and science, the coldness and correctness, so she started looking into the sciences rather than the humanities, and scoping out subjects for her final year of study that would set her on this new career path.

When the half-term holiday arrived, just as spring was sending out its first tentative shoots, Rhiannon was happy to stay at home for the week, loving the respite from the constant crush of people around her at school, the constant noise and talk and interaction.

It was also a chance to work even harder on her assignments, and research the extra-credit papers she'd committed to in algebra and calculus. And when Laura, Ms Henderson, told her how impressed all the teachers were with her progress, and her dad told her how proud he was of her for catching up on all her classes, she was surprised by how happy it made her feel.

Part of it still struck her as a betrayal, that she was moving on, and learning how to live without her mum, yet she also felt immense satisfaction, that despite checking out of school – and life – for so long, she was almost back to where she had been before their shock loss, with a new career path set out before her, and a new appreciation for study and achievement.

In between assignments, she went for long walks, and was overjoyed to feel her mum around her as she watched the countryside start to come back to life. It had been such a bleak winter, physically as well as emotionally, externally as well as within. She'd felt so hopeless, so bereft, while it snowed outside and turned dark so early, and the constant storms had ravaged her mind and heart.

But now the growing signs of spring filled her with the possibility of hope and new beginnings. She wasn't quite at the feeling positive stage, but she could feel her grief shifting a little. Not disappearing or even lessening in any way, but changing form. It was always present, yet it wasn't quite as strong or all-consuming now, it didn't control her every waking moment or haunt her every dream. It had simply become part of her, as natural to her as breathing.

And she was getting used to their diminished family, and the extra responsibilities on her shoulders, growing up faster so her dad wasn't burdened by two kids to look after. Without considering that she could replace her mother in any way, she started picking up the slack at home, cooking dinner when she could, cleaning the house, even packing her dad's lunch as he picked up extra shifts to bring a little more money into the household coffers. They weren't totally struggling without her mum's pay cheque, but she was very aware of their expenses, including the medical bills that were still trickling in from Beth's treatment and hospital stays.

So she lived as frugally as she could, making more of their meals than usual so they didn't have to eat out, taking her own lunch to school, and being as savvy as she could. It made her laugh when she ended up topping the class in home economics as well as maths and science. She didn't do any extra work for that one, it was simply because she was already living the concept of budgeting that they were learning at school.

Just as things were getting… not easier, but a little less difficult… the six-month anniversary of Beth's death arrived, and hit Rhiannon and Mike like an avalanche. Neither could believe how much time had passed – and how different yet still the same things were. And the blow was even deeper because this year the anniversary fell on Mother's Day.

On the Friday before Mothering Sunday, Brodie came home from school confused and upset. Some of the kids in his class had teased him when he'd asked what he should do, since he didn't have a mum to make a card for. While his teacher had been sympathetic, and helped him create something artistic for his grandma Anne instead, he'd been puzzled by the behaviour of his classmates, then panicky that he wasn't as sad as they thought he should be.

It broke Rhiannon's heart that he was suffering so much for something beyond his understanding, and also that he was already forgetting his mum, forgetting what she looked like, what she sounded like. So she vowed to help him remember.

On Saturday they made their own Mother's Day cards, safe at home where no one could laugh at them for acting as though their mum was still alive. They left them on the mantelpiece, next to a photo of the family from the Christmas before Beth had died. Brodie drew a picture on the front of his card of the four of them as they had been, all holding hands and smiling widely, and dressed in matching clothes, which made Rhiannon smile.

For her part, she poured out her heart over all that she missed about her mother…

Dear Mum,

I can't believe it's been six months since you left us. In some ways it feels like forever, and I fear that I'll forget the smallest things about you. At other times it feels as though it was only yesterday, that you've just popped out to the shops, and will be walking back in through the front door any minute. It just doesn't make sense that you're gone.

I miss you so much, every second really, yet I am trying to move forward with my life. Trying to make you proud of me, and to emerge from the heap I fell into when you died, and become something more than I was, in order to honour your memory.

So, on this Mother's Day, a day that will always hit me in the heart with the pain of your loss as well as the gratitude of having been blessed with your presence in my life, I thank you for choosing me as your daughter. I thank you for being the best mum ever, and I will try to remind myself it is quality, not quantity, that matters.

You were right. We had more special mother-daughter moments in our sixteen years than most people will have in a whole lifetime, and while I will always wish we'd had more, I will do as you implored me and try to focus on what we had rather than what we won't have, and to make an effort to celebrate your life rather than regretting your death.

I will love you always xx

Later that night she tiptoed downstairs to get a glass of water, and found her dad standing by the fireplace, clutching their cards in one hand and his head in the other, shoulders shaking from his sobs. The pain he was suffering radiated out from him, stabbing at her heart and leaving her feeling so helpless, and so desperately sad for him.

She still had one parent, but he had lost his dearest love, his partner in life, the other half of himself. How daunting it would be, to suddenly be left alone to cope with two children, and she was mortified by how much extra suffering she'd put him through in the aftermath of their loss.

When she woke up the next morning, sadness shrouded her as she remembered the previous year's Mother's Day, when she and Brodie had made breakfast in bed for their mum, then taken her out for the day, travelling a few counties over with her for a flower festival celebrating spring, then digging in the garden with her that afternoon to plant all her new herbs and other seedlings.

That evening their radiant mother had gone to Rose's Ostara ritual, and Rhiannon had been struck by how beautiful she'd looked, and how full of life and love and vigour. It was only a couple of months before she'd discovered how sick she was, and Rhiannon could still picture so perfectly the glow of health and energy she'd exuded that day, which had made her diagnosis so shocking.

Despite the forecasted spring sunshine, this Mother's Day dawned cold and grey, which seemed appropriate. Their dad made breakfast for the three of them, trying to pretend nothing was wrong for Brodie's sake, but having a miserable time of it. Rose had invited them to her new moon healing ritual that night, but they'd turned down her offer, preferring to wallow on their own in their sadness, and scared they would depress everyone with their pain if they turned up. While the priestess had denied that would happen and pressed them to come, they'd thanked her profusely yet stuck to their guns.

Rhiannon wasn't sure she would ever want to be part of a ritual again, because it reminded her too much of all she had lost. The memorial at the healing centre had been wonderful – terrifying and devastatingly sad, but wonderful – yet that hadn't been about her. If she became part of Rose's magical circle though it would be, and it would require a vulnerability and an opening up of herself and her heart that she wasn't sure she could handle.

Chapter 23

Looking Forward

As her seventeenth birthday approached at the end of May, Rhiannon was relieved that it would fall in their week-long half-term holiday, and glad they were going to spend it with their grandparents – the good ones – in a little seaside village in Wales that they'd visited together a year ago. She couldn't face a party, or being the centre of attention or, even worse, feeling rejected if people forgot, or didn't want to celebrate with her.

She was relieved too when the last of her teachers announced that she was more than caught up – her extra study and optional extra credit assignments meant she was actually ahead of where she'd been academically when her mum was still alive. Her maths teacher even recommended an advanced program she could take part in over the summer holidays, and was pressuring her to sign up for it, but she wasn't sure how she felt about that.

She was still pondering whether or not to attend as she walked home from school on the last day of term. Bird song filled the air, and she was excitedly picking the first blackberries of the season from the wild hedgerows. They were still a little tart, and that brought back bittersweet memories – she and her mum had gone berry foraging last summer, and had returned with tongues and fingertips stained purple, and a basket of fruit they'd turned into hot pies and crumbles.

A sharp pain hit her as she reached out for another berry, and she cursed as a thorn pierced her thumb, then watched the drop of crimson blood rush to the surface. Sucking on the wound, she was too distracted to hear that someone was approaching her – until all of a sudden she glanced up and saw there was a woman standing right next to her.

The hairs on the back of her neck stood up as she recognised the blue-clad figure she'd met up on the tor on New Year's Eve, the one she hadn't been sure was really there, had really existed. Was she a flesh-and-blood person, or an Otherworldly being? Goosebumps covered her arms as she felt a sudden drop in temperature, and noticed grey clouds gathering overhead, and a thick white mist closing in around them. Okay, so her money was on the latter...

"Good evening Rhiannon," the woman said, voice terribly formal yet filled with warmth, an unexpected pairing.

Nodding hesitantly, she gazed at her cautiously, unsure what to make of the sudden appearance and the dramatic shift in weather conditions, since her own seeming effect on the air around her had eased after the new year, if it had even been her causing all those storms in the first place.

Desperately she tried to recall what they'd spoken of the last time they met. She'd been heartbroken then, inconsolable, and hardly paying the attention she should have been, but she did remember the reassurance the woman had provided, so she offered her a shy smile, before feeling guilty that she'd managed to move on from that all-consuming grief.

"Oh beloved, you have no reason at all to feel guilty," the blue-clad figure crooned. "It is a good thing, a healthy thing, that you have been able to find a way to move forward. It does not mean you love your mother any less."

Blushing, Rhiannon nodded in acknowledgement, yet she still felt bad. It wasn't like you could turn off a feeling just because someone told you to. The ghost of a smile crossed her companion's face, then she turned serious again.

"I know you are feeling lost, and wondering what to do with your life, but do not give up on yourself, and your beautiful heart, just because something seems easier right now, and appeals to you for that reason."

Puzzled, Rhiannon stared at her, unsure of what she was talking about. There was no easy option for her to take – if there was, perhaps she would have taken it, but she didn't know of any. Her brow crinkled in consternation.

A mirthless, impatient chuckle echoed through Rhiannon's mind. "You have been rewarded for your new aptitude in mathematics, and told you should consider a more scientific career path," the woman in blue explained bluntly.

"Well, it's something to think about," she replied, suddenly defensive. "The idea of calculations and equations and things being black and white, right or wrong, does hold a lot of appeal. It's certainly not easy though! But I'm not sure that I have much emotion left to give to a more creative or caring field. Besides, what's wrong with science? My aunty is a scientist, and she's changing the world for the better."

Wow, she hadn't thought about her mum's sister Jenny since the funeral, yet she'd always liked her, and admired her single-minded focus on succeeding in her field and proving her horrible mother wrong. Beth had told her a few stories about when she and her sister were growing up in that cold, emotionless household, ruled over by their cruel mother.

Patricia had been furious when she'd discovered that her oldest daughter Jenny – the supposed "good" girl – had lied to her from her very first day of university, pretending she was studying business, as "suggested" by her parents, but in fact undertaking a rigorous double major science degree, topping her year, and landing a well-respected – to all but her family – position as the head of a research team studying renewable energy off the coast of Scotland.

Beth had been astounded by and overwhelmed with admiration for her sister, partly because of her academic achievements, and partly because she'd managed to thwart their parents. She'd grown up thinking that Jenny was doing everything their mother wanted of her, obeying her in all things – but it turned out she was just smarter than her, and realised that complaining and rebelling were pointless. To get what she wanted and pursue her own dreams, she'd flat-out lied to their mother's face until it was a fait accompli.

As she'd recounted the story to her daughter, Beth had laughed, thinking of all the pain she could have saved herself if she'd done the same thing, rather than wasting so much time, energy and hatred on fighting pointless battles with her mother at every turn.

A further drop in temperature brought Rhiannon back to her surroundings, back to the cold and swirling mists, back to the mysterious blue-robed woman before her.

"Oh beloved, there is absolutely nothing wrong with science, and your aunt Jennifer is making incredible contributions to the protection of the earth. But it is her passion. Since she was a child she burned with curiosity about how to create things, and change things, and she loved every moment of dedicating herself to her scientific cause. At school she loved science and mathematics, at university she did electives in engineering just because it fascinated her, and extra physics and chemistry classes because she found them fun. That is how her brain works – to fulfil her heart's desires, and her mission in life, she must use her mind in that way," she explained.

"But you are so very different to her, more like your mother, which is wonderful. Your contribution to the world will come from your heart, not your mind. You thrive on feeling and emotion, and will feel restricted by the structure of what you are contemplating."

Rhiannon almost laughed – she hadn't even realised she was contemplating anything. And yet, when she thought about it, her head had been turned by the praise she was receiving in her extra maths classes, and by talk of careers in that field. Surprisingly, the woman in blue was right. If she was honest with herself, she had to admit that she didn't actually enjoy the subjects, she just appreciated them for the structure they contained, and the black and white nature of the answers. The way she didn't have to use her heart, just her mind. Would she be miserable if she pursued a career based on that?

It only took a moment of soul searching to realise that yes, she would hate it. The thought of four years at university in the cold, clinical fields of maths and science made her throat tighten, and without even being aware of it, she started moving her shoulders, trying to unclench them from the strict rigidity they'd taken on when she foresaw that path.

Sighing, she lifted her head to admit the truth, but the woman was gone again, disappeared in a cloud of mist and the sweet scent of honeysuckle. Slowly she began to walk home, feeling a little more soothed. She still had no idea what she wanted to do with her life – and the mist-wreathed woman hadn't been very forthcoming on what she *should* do, only what she shouldn't. But perhaps it was up to her to figure that out – would she really want to have her career, her life, dictated to her in the way her mum and aunt had suffered?

And she didn't need to decide now anyway, she had another whole year at school ahead of her. But at least she knew now what she didn't want to do, so she decided to see the school counsellor the minute they got home from Wales and change her electives back. She didn't need to do the advanced double maths classes – just because she was capable of it, that didn't mean it would be useful to her. There were other classes she found more interesting, which might make more sense for her still-unknown career path. Perhaps she'd do a unit on politics, or history, or geography, or something…

Either way, the strange woman was right. Life was too short to waste time on things that didn't interest her, or wouldn't contribute to her ultimate plans. And while she still didn't know what she wanted to be when she grew up, it was a relief that she'd realised what she *didn't* want to be.

On the morning of her birthday, Rhiannon woke up early, remembered the date and groaned, clutching the pillow over her head, and wanting to burrow down under the covers and hide away forever. With her mum gone, it was tough to celebrate anything, but there was no way she could escape it. No sooner had she moved a muscle, than Brodie leapt out of bed and flung himself at her, laughing his high-pitched laugh.

"Happy Birthday Rhi-Rhi!" he cried. "I've been waiting for *hours* for you to wake up."

"Thanks buddy," she said, teeth gritted but smile pasted firmly on. Of course they'd be away and sharing a bedroom on the day she most wanted to be left alone. Sighing, she made a concerted effort to feign enthusiasm as she peeled back the quilt and sat up. Her heart ached that her mum wasn't here for this milestone, but for her brother's sake she tried to push that out of her mind and look like she was excited.

At least they were away from the familiar, away from the memories, in this cute slate cottage in a sunny seaside village in Wales. Not that it helped much, since all she could think about was her mum's birthday pancakes, which she used to make for them each year, and the red velvet cake they would have celebrated with at lunch time.

A clanking from the kitchen downstairs interrupted her reverie, then their father called out to them to come down for breakfast. Sighing theatrically, she dragged herself out of bed, pulled a cardigan on over her pyjamas and shepherded Brodie out of their small, narrow room.

"Happy Birthday darling," her dad said, kissing her on the cheek as he handed her a parcel, then going back to the stove. A sizzling sound erupted as he flipped whatever was in the frypan over, and her heart lurched as she smelled the familiar scent of cinnamon and butter. He was making her their mum's special birthday pancakes.

"Thanks Dad," she whispered.

"Open mine first!" Brodie shrieked, running over to the bench and picking up a messily wrapped gift. Rhiannon untied the bow, but was clearly going too slowly, because her brother leaned over and ripped the paper off for her. It was a jewellery box, strong yet delicate, wrought in silver, with ivy engraved into the lid. Inside it was velvet lined, with a large tray that pulled out, plus several compartments of various sizes. It was gorgeous. Hugging Brodie tight, and making him blush from her profuse thanks, she ran her finger over the soft interior.

Reading her dad's card was tough – words of pride for how she was coping, words of thanks for what she was doing to help him and Brodie cope – but she managed a slightly teary smile before turning to his presents.

The first one was a journal, different to the Book of Shadows Rose had given her, but still pretty, and she figured it would be perfect for recording her thoughts and her day-to-day life. Not that it was really worth recording right now, but when she'd spoken to the school counsellor recently, he'd encouraged her to start writing down her feelings as a way to reveal them to herself, and eventually move forward. An uncharitable thought ran through her head, as she wondered if he'd mentioned the idea to her dad. Would the counsellor betray her by passing on what she'd said in their sessions?

When she opened the second gift though, her breath caught in her throat, and all thoughts of annoyance left her. Nestled in a pouch of midnight blue velvet were her mum's engagement and wedding rings, understated yet beautiful.

Turning tear-stained eyes to her dad, she whispered her thanks, and smiled as she noticed him trying to hide his own tears. She wasn't sure she had the courage or strength to wear these rings, which had meant so much to her mum, but it moved her deeply to have them. She'd thought her dad would want to keep them, to hold them close to his own heart, yet perhaps it was too painful for him. She opened her mouth to ask, then closed it when he quickly interrupted.

"They're for you," he said, taking her hand. "Your mum wanted you to have them, and for me to choose the right time to pass them on to you. I don't need them, and I can't wear them, so it will mean more to me that you have them. And whether you choose to wear them or not, whether you want to store them in your new jewellery box or place them on a necklace, that's totally up to you – please don't do anything either way on my behalf."

A key in the lock of the front door interrupted them, and her dad squeezed her shoulder and went to help his parents with the bags of groceries they'd popped out to get.

"Happy Birthday darling," her grandma said, coming around the table to hug her, and hand over a card and a gift.

"Thank you Nan and Pop, but you didn't have to get me anything," she protested.

"Oooh, what is it?" Brodie asked, then fell on it and started tearing the paper off, too impatient to wait again.

Anne laughed, and swooped in to kiss her grandson on the forehead. He giggled, then noticed the cake box his grandpa was holding. Squealing, he leapt off his chair to have a peek inside, then nodded approvingly at William.

Left in peace for a moment, Rhiannon lifted out her gift – a gorgeous bright blue dress with matching blue topaz earrings, plus the new novel from her favourite author – and thanked her grandparents for their thoughtfulness. Then she was finally able to tuck in to the towering stack of maple syrup-drenched pancakes her dad placed in front of her, and savour the latte her grandma had picked up from the cafe down the road.

After a blissfully lazy morning curled up in a dark and cosy corner reading her new book, she caught up with her family for lunch. And when her gran lit the candles on her red velvet birthday cake and they all sang Happy Birthday, she smiled with genuine pleasure, glad to be with them – even when Brodie swooped in to blow out her candles and hijack her wish.

Being with this set of grandparents reminded her to be grateful. For the last few days she'd been focused on how negative and soul destroying her other set were, and the pain Beth's mother in particular had caused them all, and she'd forgotten just how thankful she was for Anne and William. They weren't showy or pushy or even especially outgoing or vocal, but their calm acceptance of her, and their gentle missing of Beth, was a great comfort to her now that she was starting to come to terms with her loss. She'd definitely underestimated them and their capacity for feeling, and caring.

"Can I help you with dinner Nan?" she asked later, after she'd returned from a walk through the crooked cobblestone streets. Her dad and William had taken Brodie out fishing in the small bay below the village, and Rhiannon was surprised to acknowledge that she was happy, rather than reluctant, about being alone with her gran.

"That's not necessary love," Anne replied, but she looked pleased by the offer, so Rhiannon picked up a vegie peeler and got to work on the pile of potatoes on the bench.

"Coffee?" her grandmother asked, putting the kettle on.

"Thanks Nan."

The two pottered around the kitchen together in comfortable silence for a while, but once they each had a steaming mug of coffee in hand, they took a break, sitting down at the small table and eyeing each other a little nervously.

"I'm really sorry for your loss love," Anne began. "I can't even begin to imagine how you feel, and I know your father is so proud of how you're handling yourself, and how much help you're giving him at this awful time."

Rhiannon blushed. "Well, I wasn't much help at first, but I'm trying to be better. And I want to thank you, for being so patient and sweet at Christmas. I'm sure Dad told you I was a bit, well, *angry*, at first, but spending the week with you at the lake was really healing – and it sure improved my wardrobe," she added, trying to lighten the mood a little.

"I know I've never told you how much I appreciate your quiet support – and I guess I've never really acknowledged it myself. Grandmother can be so mean, so disapproving and distant, but you're the perfect grandma. And being with you and Pop at Christmas was a turning point for me. So, well, thank you for that, and for everything."

"Oh sweetheart, thank you. That means the world to me," Anne said, wiping a tear from her eye. "And give yourself a break, please. You've only just turned seventeen. No one expects you to be perfect, and there is no right or wrong way to react to such a tragedy. You've done the best you can, and continue to try to be better, and that's all any of us can do. And I'm very sorry that your other grandmother has cut off all contact with you, but that is *her* problem, not yours, and her loss. Foolish woman!"

Rhiannon tried not to laugh. She's never heard her grandma criticise anyone. "You're right, it's certainly no loss to me – but that's because of you and Pop, and Rose too, because you all care about me so much. Thank you."

Anne leaned over and hugged her, then they drank the last of their coffee and got back to work, chatting more casually after their brief heart-to-heart. By the time twilight had fallen and the men had returned, the whole cottage smelled enticingly of baked vegies, spinach filos for Rhiannon, and roast lamb for the rest of them.

When they returned home after their week of coastal walks, prehistoric monument visits and a churchyard filled with ancient yew trees that allegedly cried blood, Rhiannon felt stronger and more at peace, wrapped in the love of her family, and an increasing connection with nature.

Summer had set in, and the warmth of the season was making her a little less morose. Being outside, feeling the sun warming her face and inhaling the scent of wildflowers from the hedgerows, somehow made her more hopeful. The longer days helped. Even before she'd lost her mum, winter had been depressing – getting up in the dark, then coming home from school in the dark too. But the soft golden light of summer mornings and the glow of long golden evenings made her feel more alive, and more cheerful too.

After a winter of extreme storms that had so well reflected her inner turmoil, these balmy, mellow summer days were encouraging a new sense of calm. Now she felt attuned to the earth and the energy of the gently sloping meadows around their village. Connected to the warm breezes that enveloped her, the soft gentle rain that occasionally fell to wash the world clean, and the soothing splash of water in the meandering stream by her house – a stream that had grown angry and uncharacteristically agitated when it flooded over its banks more than a few times during the cruel winter she'd just suffered through.

But the time of dramatic thunder, flashing lightning, furious downpours and roiling storms seemed almost dream-like now, and Rhiannon found it hard to comprehend just how struck with grief and anger, and delusions of fury-filled power, she'd been for the first three months after her mum's death.

Rose had asked her again if she wanted to come along to a ritual – her circle would soon be celebrating Litha, the summer solstice, which marked the midpoint of the season and the longest day and shortest night of the year. For a moment it tempted her, but then she chickened out again. She couldn't face it, couldn't go and do something that had been her mother's. Maybe one day she would find the strength to take part, but it wouldn't be any time soon.

Visions of the rituals had been invading her dreams though, always with Rose as the high priestess in the centre of it all, beckoning her forward and drawing her in to the middle of the circle, surrounded by velvet-robed women with faces full of love. Perhaps she thought the reality would be less welcoming and nurturing than her dreams were, that the real-life version would disappoint her and leave her feeling even more bereft. Or perhaps she just craved solitude still, and the idea of being swept up in the social side of the circle was too much to face.

Rose was disappointed, she knew that, every time she turned her down, and she wondered how long she would keep trying, keep inviting her in. Because although she didn't want to go now, she was scared of the day Rose would stop imploring her to join them. Which was silly, to be so contrary as to crave an invitation to something she didn't want to attend.

A thought struck her then, that perhaps Rose was insisting she come and take part because she'd made a promise to Beth to welcome her daughter into the magic circle she had loved so much. To let her follow in her footsteps, and feel just how much love and nurturing and self-discovery she had gained from it. Her mum had adored her time in the healing and ritual space above Rose's shop, had loved the camaraderie and the support of her magical sisters, and the confidence it gave her to bring back into her own life, to make her a better mother, a better wife, a better teacher, a better friend.

God, she missed her still! And yet the pain was less dramatic now, less constant. Perhaps she was growing up after all. Her mum would always be a part of her, but she knew she had to be brave enough to move forward. She was seventeen now. Soon she'd be starting her final year at school, and trying to figure out what she wanted to do with her life.

It worried her a little that she still had no idea, but when she thought of her conversation with the woman in blue, she was relieved that she'd talked her out of going down the mathematical route. She wished the mist-wreathed figure had been a little more specific, but even though she didn't know what she wanted, it was good to know what she didn't.

Chapter 24

True Love's Kiss

Beth... Twenty years ago...

Beth woke up with a smile on her face, and leaped out of bed, the early morning sunshine peeking through her window filling her with joy and energy. Today was Jennifer's wedding, and she was taking Mike as her date.

Glancing over at the gorgeous black dress she'd be wearing for her bridesmaid duties, she bubbled over with excitement. Now that she knew Mike would see her in it, she was even more grateful to her sister for standing up to their mother and letting her choose her own outfit for the ceremony. Walking up the aisle with him while weighed down in some dowdy pale apricot taffeta confection would have been hard to bear.

Elated, she raced into the room next to hers and yanked the door open. "Come on Jenny, get up! Today is the day!" she cried, jumping on her sister's bed. She gasped, as a really old memory hit her, of doing the same thing. There had been a time, when they were both really young, that they were close, before their cruel mother had pitched them into competition with each other for her miserly affection. Smiling at the memory, she shook it off as she shook Jenny's shoulder.

The bride-to-be opened her eyes slowly and stretched, then yawned leisurely before she grinned up at Beth.

"It really is," she said, joy suffusing her features. "I can't believe that Mother will have to let me go now, since in just a few hours I will finally be 'grown-up' and 'respectable' – according to her, anyway – since I'll be married," she continued, rolling her eyes at the old-fashioned notion and grinning sarcastically.

Then she looked more closely at Beth. "How come you're so happy? And up so early?"

"My beautiful sister is getting married to her true love today, and running away to her dream life far from our pesky parents, so what's not to celebrate?" she asked, raising one eyebrow in mock hurt.

Jennifer laughed. "True, but there's something else. You seemed so sad when you got here, but now you're just radiating joy and contentment. Excitement even."

Blushing, Beth tried to school her face, not wanting to give away just how happy she was. "Well, it's been really nice becoming friends with Violet, and weaving magic with her and her mum Rose. And it's been eye-opening, to say the least, to discover what it would have been like to have a mother who actually cared about me. What I wouldn't give to be able to swap parents with Violet," she sighed.

Jenny squeezed her sister's hand. "It doesn't matter now. We don't need to put ourselves through it any more. I'm going back to Scotland with Josh, and you're free too. Free to stay here, or return to Paris, or go to London, or New York, or Sydney – wherever you want to go! The world is your oyster. You're free to let go of all the drama and let your beautiful heart shine."

Beth smiled, her heart overflowing with emotion. "Becoming closer to you has been the best thing about coming home," she said, and it was true. "I really regret that we were both in too much pain to be friends when we were younger."

Her sister nodded. "I totally agree, and I really look forward to you visiting us soon, so we can spend more time together. But there's something else to your happiness, isn't there," Jenny stated, and it wasn't a question. "Something that's making you glow. It's gotta be a guy, right?"

"Well, it has been amazing getting to know Mike a bit better too," she finally admitted. "He's so kind, so considerate. Between him and Josh, it kind of gives me hope that there are nice guys out there..." she trailed off.

No matter how close she'd grown to her sister over the past few weeks, there was no way she could reveal just how much she liked Mike, and how often he filled not just her dreams, but her waking moments too.

"He's coming today, isn't he?" her sister asked, with a glint of mischief, and Beth was worried that she would reveal her feelings in her voice or expression if she said any more. So she just nodded, feeling her blush returning, and wondered how to change the subject before she incriminated herself.

It wasn't quite the escape she'd hoped for, but at that moment their mother rushed into the room to castigate them both and order them downstairs for breakfast before the hair and make-up artists arrived. Patricia was like a whirlwind as she bossed them both around, fired off orders to the caterers, then collapsed into a chair opposite her daughters.

Disapproval radiated off her as she criticised their food choices, their manners, the apparently massive black circles under their eyes – because it was clearly an affront to her, that they hadn't been able to sleep much the previous night thanks to their excitement. The bride-to-be rolled her eyes at her sister, earning a giggle that was quickly frowned upon, and when their mother started harping on about the unsuitability of Beth's bridesmaid dress, for the fourth time that week, they quickly stood up and made their excuses to run back upstairs and get ready.

As annoying as the time with her mother had been though, nothing could pierce Beth's bubble of joy at knowing that Mike would soon arrive to accompany her to the church, and stand by her side during the ceremony. It was like a real date, and as much as she knew she should feel guilty about her intentions towards Violet's boyfriend, she couldn't bring herself to care. Besides, her friend was currently obsessing over Andrew, so surely she could dream a little?

knock on the front door made Beth's stomach flip with nerves, and when her father called up the stairs moments later to let her know that Mike had arrived, she suddenly felt light-headed. It was stupid that she felt more nervous than her sister, who was about to walk down the aisle and vow to love a man forever, yet Jenny looked the picture of calm and contentment, while she was shaking like a leaf.

Touching a hand to the mysteriously gifted rose quartz heart pendant around her neck for strength, she hugged her sister and told her she'd meet her at the church, then made her way down to the lounge room. She gasped as she caught sight of Mike, who looked even more handsome and grown up than usual as he leaned casually against the mantelpiece in a black suit. And when his eyes met hers, she'd swear she saw admiration as he looked her up and down, from the sleek black stilettos to the sophisticated yet sexy long black dress, her smoky-eyed make-up and the wave of blonde curls spilling down her back.

"Mike, thank you so much for coming with me today," she said, voice a little unsteady. But his wide grin instantly set her at ease, and she remembered there was no need to be scared or nervous. This was her friend Mike, who she'd done everything from eating hamburgers to performing magical ceremonies with over the past month, who'd seen her dressed up for a ritual and looking pretty, as well as rain-soaked and bleary eyed, with tomato sauce dripping down her chin, at a recent lunch with Violet. Her breathing returned to normal, and she decided to just enjoy the day, and get to know Mike even better than she already did.

When a car horn tooted outside, he took her arm and guided her down the front steps and out to the waiting black limo. Jenny's best friend Katie and her boyfriend Eric, and Josh's brother Brandon and his wife Phoebe, were already inside, and opened the door for them and ushered them in.

"You look gorgeous Beth," Katie said, then grinned. "Jenny certainly has a good-looking bridal party!"

Beth smiled self-consciously, having always been in awe of her sister's worldly best friend, but managed to introduce Mike to everyone. The others drew them into their conversation, and the half-hour drive flew by. Being away from her mother, and by Mike's side, certainly lifted her spirits, and before she knew it they'd arrived and were being guided into a small room off the side of the church.

Suddenly nervous as she peeked in and saw how many people were already inside, she looked at Mike in panic. But his kind smile, complete with the crinkling around his eyes that she loved so much, calmed her down, and when he took her hand, a warmth and sense of comfort spread slowly through her body and into her heart.

"You look beautiful Beth," he whispered. "There's no need to be nervous – I'll be with you every step of the way, okay?"

Nodding, she picked up her bouquet of red roses and followed the usher around the verandah to the front entrance. All the guests had been seated, so she motioned to Katie that they were ready to start, then she and Mike slowly walked into the church. He kept hold of her hand as they walked up the aisle, and although she should have been thinking about Jenny, the only thing she was aware of was the gentle pressure of his fingers and the amazing feeling of being so supported.

For a moment she allowed herself to imagine that they were walking up the aisle on their wedding day – but when she almost tripped over her dress, she quickly refocused on the job at hand. "You okay?" Mike whispered, and she nodded quickly, and only blushed a tiny bit.

Finally they reached the altar, and Mike let go of her hand so they could take their places opposite each other. Turning back to the doorway, Beth beamed as she watched Brandon, Phoebe and Eric make their way to the front then peel off, Phoebe standing next to her, Eric with Mike, and Brandon joining the groom at the altar.

And then all thought left her as she saw her sister silhouetted in the sunlit church entrance. Jenny looked stunning, and so radiant and filled with joy that it took her breath away. Her simple, elegant dress floated out around her, her long blonde hair cascaded down her back in soft waves, and her best friend was beaming as she held the ends of the veil and small train

Jenny had agreed on as a compromise to the full-on meringue wedding gown their mother had demanded.

Beth was overcome with emotion as she saw the look that Jenny and her almost-husband shared – their eyes were locked on each other, as though they were the only two people in existence, and she supposed, to them, they were. None of the theatrics of today were for them. It was like no one else in the church was there, and her heart almost burst as she understood, for the first time, just how much Jenny and Josh adored each other.

There really was no one else on earth for them, and she realised that the arguments with their mother over guest lists, seating and traditions, the stress of preparations, and the responsibility of having all eyes on them, meant absolutely nothing to the couple. This occasion, this day, was for them alone, and Beth finally understood why her sister had point-blank refused to have either of their parents walk her down the aisle. This walk she was on was a walk away from them, a walk to independence, and to love. The love and passion the bride and groom felt for each other was so intense she thought she might burn up in the heat of it, but it made her so happy she could barely contain herself. This was real love.

Glancing over at Mike, she saw that he could sense it too, and that he comprehended the depth of their love because he felt the same thing. He loved Violet in the same way. She could see the reflection of it in his eyes. Yet for some reason this knowledge didn't make her sad or jealous, it just filled her with hope that she would experience it for herself one day, and with gratitude that she was able to be a small part of it, with her sister today, and with Mike and Violet every other day.

Turning back to the beautiful bride, who was becoming even more radiant with every step she took towards her beloved, Beth was overwhelmed with pride and love for this girl – this woman – who she'd grown up beside, who'd suffered at the hands of their mother too, far more than she'd known at the time, but who had never let her gentle heart feel resentment or lash out in anger.

As though she felt the thought, Jenny looked up at her and smiled, then mouthed "I love you," to her.

Afraid that she would break down and start crying with the emotion of it all, Beth shifted her eyes back to the groom, and was overwhelmed all over again by the love and pride on his face as he gazed adoringly at his bride-to-be.

The ceremony was beautiful, but passed all too fast. The priest's words rippled over Beth. "Dearly beloved. We have come together in the presence of God to witness and bless the joining together of this man and woman in Holy Matrimony..."

Words of protection and promise, vows to love and obey, declarations about the bond and covenant of marriage, in God's name. Standing next to her sister, she couldn't see her, but she was transfixed by the look on Josh's face, a look of such love, such devotion. She wanted someone to look at her that way, and it moved her greatly to see it, to know it was possible.

The priest's words broke into her reverie.

"Jennifer, will you have this man to be your husband, to live together in the covenant of marriage? Will you love him, comfort him, honour him and keep him, in sickness and in health, and forsaking all others, be faithful to him for as long as you both shall live?" he asked sternly.

Her sister nodded, then found her voice. "I will."

"And will you, Joshua, have this woman to be your wife, to live together in the covenant of marriage? Will you love her, comfort her, honour her and keep her, in sickness and in health, and forsaking all others, be faithful to her for as long as you both shall live?"

His face lit up even further. "I will."

"And do you promise each other to give and receive love with faith and trust?" the priest continued. "To speak and listen with kindness and consideration, and in all circumstances of your lives be loyal to and respect each other?"

"We do."

Then, almost reluctantly, the priest indicated that they should share their vows. Josh took his bride's hand and spoke, his voice gentle, yet clear and strong, projecting to the furthest corners of the old stone building. He had no need of notes, as he'd committed his promises to memory and was simply speaking from the heart.

Darling Jenny, you are my dearest friend and my one true love, the person I trust and respect more than any other, and the one who knows me best, flaws and all.

Today I am so grateful that you have granted my greatest wish, by becoming my wife, and I am so honoured that you have taken me to be your husband.

I promise you that I will trust you and honour you. I will laugh with you and cry with you. I will love you faithfully and deeply through our life's challenges and adventures.

I promise you that I will cherish the depth and breadth of our friendship always. I will commit to the work goals we share. And I will love you today, tomorrow and forever.

I promise you that I will encourage you to explore and grow, to change if you are called to do that, to fulfil all of your dreams, and, most importantly, to always be totally yourself – because it is you, just the way you are, and will be, that I love and adore more than life itself.

Darling Jenny, I am so honoured to stand before you on this magical day, and so excited to take this next step with you on our wonderful journey of the truest love.

His eyes were shining as he finished, lit up with love and devotion, and Beth doubted there was a dry eye in the place. Well, her parents excluded, but what would they know of love? Then the priest indicated it was Jenny's turn to speak her vows.

My darling Josh, you are my closest and dearest friend, the one person on earth who knows me fully and completely, insecurities and all, and loves me despite them.

With you I feel safe, I feel supported, I feel accepted and I feel seen. Your love has changed me, has bettered me, has transformed me – you have let me see all that I can be, and you make me want to achieve it. You inspire me to be more than I am, better than I am, kinder than I am, to be the light-filled being you see when you look at me, and I hope I do the same for you.

I promise you that with every breath I take I will love you, and support you, and cherish you, and adore you.

I promise you that I will appreciate you, and inspire you, and forgive you, and trust you, and honour you.

I am so proud to stand with you today and profess my love for you to all of our friends and family members, and I'm so excited to be leaping in to our brave new adventure in our magical home, manifesting our love and passion into reality, changing the world through our commitment, our dedication, and our sense of shared purpose.

Darling Josh, you are my partner in life and my one true love, the keeper of my heart and the guardian of my soul, and I will love you through every moment of our journeys and adventures together – today, tomorrow and forever.

When Jenny finished speaking, Beth had tears streaming down her face, so touched by the beauty of her sister's words and the sentiments she'd expressed. Joy and relief swept over her, that Jenny had found someone who had healed the soul their mother had broken, someone who made her realise how worthy of love she was, someone who saw her. It reminded her so profoundly of the healing she'd had with Rose, when she had felt seen, and accepted, and loved, for the first time in her life, and she had a new respect and admiration for her sister's husband.

Her thoughts were interrupted by the priest, who was coughing for attention and looking very uncomfortable. With a stoic expression he turned to Brandon to receive the rings. Then, a sour look on his face, he held out his hand to Katie and placed the beautiful rose-gold wedding bands in her palm.

"Jennifer and Joshua want to pass these rings among the six of you, their dearest friends, to add your blessings to them before they exchange them," he stated, disapproval clear in his posture.

Panicked, Beth looked at Katie, who was holding the rings to her heart, then followed their progress as she handed them to Phoebe, who raised them to her mouth and solemnly whispered words into them, before passing them to Beth.

She glanced at her sister, not sure she was worthy of this honour, but Jenny smiled at her and mouthed "thank you," and Beth felt the warmth of her love flooding through every cell of her body.

Clutching the rings tightly in her hands, she held them to her heart. She wasn't certain that she knew the right thing to do, but her thoughts drifted to Rose and all she'd said of intention. So, closing her eyes and going within, she said a little spell, or wish, for Jenny and Josh's happiness, then handed the rings back to the priest. With a frown at her, he took them over to Mike.

Beth peered at him nervously, worried that he would feel out of his depth and not clear on what he had to do, but with a quick smile across at her, he closed his eyes, held the rings in his left hand while moving his lips slightly, then passed them to Eric. She almost laughed out loud. Of course she shouldn't have worried – Mike had been dating a priestess's daughter for years!

Finally Brandon had the rings in his hands, and he said a silent prayer before returning them to the priest, who looked relieved to have them back. Beth risked a quick glance at her parents, and it took every ounce of her strength not to roll on the floor laughing at the anger and disapproval radiating from them. Jenny caught her eye, and they exchanged a conspiratorial and elated smile of triumph, before turning back to the proceedings. They would not let their judgemental parents spoil even a second of this magical day.

"These rings will be a reminder to Jennifer and Joshua of this day you are sharing with them and supporting them in," he said to the bridal party, then turned back to the congregation with relief.

"But most importantly they are a symbol of the promises Jennifer and Joshua have made to each other before God," he concluded firmly, while Jenny rolled her eyes and Beth tried to hide her grin at his obvious dismay at their unconventional addition to the ceremony.

Again Josh stepped forward. "My darling Jenny, I offer you this ring as a symbol of my enduring love."

Smiling, Jenny moved towards him, and he slid the ring onto her finger. "My beloved, I will wear this always to seal our vows with love," she said, gazing joyfully down at the plain but pretty engraved rose-gold band. She'd told Beth that diamonds would be wasted on her while she worked outdoors and in the freezing seas off the Orkney Isles, and this ring was perfect.

"And my darling Josh, I offer you this ring as a symbol of my enduring love."

Leaning close, he extended his own hand, and she slid the matching band onto his finger. "My darling Jenny, I will wear this always to seal our vows with love," he echoed.

Looking a lot more comfortable now that they were back on familiar ground, the priest stood between the happy couple and addressed the audience.

"Jennifer and Joshua have come here today to celebrate their marriage, by committing themselves to each other, in front of us who witness their promises, and to God who seals it for them. I now pronounce them joined together in love, as husband and wife, for as long as they both shall live. You may now kiss the bride," he said, and hastily stepped out of the way as Josh pulled his new wife into his arms and kissed her passionately. Clapping and cheering, and the odd wolf whistle, echoed through the church.

After a few last words from the priest, Beth suddenly found herself walking back down the aisle in Jenny's wake, Mike holding her hand again to steady her, and the rest of the bridal party keeping step with them. First there was a short photo shoot on the steps of the church, followed by a longer, more formal one in the park across the road. Then they all climbed back into the limo and headed to the reception so they could finally let down their hair, Beth ecstatic that she'd have some glamorous photos of her with Mike – a reminder of their closeness on this magical day, and of their friendship. For a moment she even wished that Violet had been able to share it with them too.

The reception was as personal and romantic as the wedding ceremony had been. After a casual dinner, Katie and Eric both gave hilarious yet touching speeches, and had all the guests moving from laughter to tears and back again. Josh's parents both spoke as well, welcoming Jenny to their family, and sharing how much their son had blossomed since he met her. And then the groom stood up and brought the house down with a wonderful toast to his beloved, and Beth was awed again by the love he had for her sister, a love that was so clearly returned just as strongly and deeply.

A few times she cast a furtive glance at their mother, and each time she received a death stare in return. Patricia had not been happy, to say the least, that Jenny had refused to let her speak, although she suspected it was more from the perceived insult than from any real desire to wish her daughter well. Her face had been like thunder in the church too, when the priest had passed the rings around the bridal party, but Jenny clearly didn't care at all that her mother wasn't impressed by her choices.

This was her day, and Beth was so proud that, while Jenny had gone along with some of their mother's expectations, she'd put her foot down on the things that really mattered to her. She'd agreed to a church wedding, but had added the ring ritual and their own vows to make it theirs. And judging by the speeches and the toasts being made, their parents had no idea who their daughter was or what she had planned for her life anyway. Beth was discovering new depths to her sister.

Finally Brandon stood up, and tapped his champagne glass with his fork for attention. "Now, I know you all want to hit the dance floor, and the band is warming up as I speak, but on behalf of my brother and his beautiful wife, I just wanted to thank you all for coming today, and making my little brother's big day even more perfect than he'd imagined," he began.

"Josh and I spent most of our lives together – growing up alongside one another, going to school together, then to university. Holidaying, surfing, adventuring together. We even did our research in the same field, and graduated at the same time, so we could start our big, bold company together. But all that came to an abrupt end the night he met Jenny – and I couldn't be happier about that! I love you Jen. You are the sister I never had, the sweetest girl I know, and I thank you for showing all of us what real love is."

Raising his glass, he stared at the glowing couple and smiled with genuine joy. "Jen and Josh, as you undertake your united journey through life, returning to your beloved Scottish isles, may your joys be as deep as the ocean and your misfortunes as light as its foam. May you ride the waves at work and at home in harmony with each other and with nature, and always pull together, whether the tide is with you or against you. May this loving bond you share grow deeper and stronger every day, enriching your lives and the lives of those around you. You inspire us, you challenge us, you make us all want to be better, and I love you both so much – everyone here does – and wish you the happiest of lives together."

For a moment his voice cracked, but he recovered quickly. "Now, I think we all need some of that amazing cake, and then we'll hit the dance floor."

He sat down to rowdy cheers, and Jenny and Josh laughed as they stood up to cut the cake as instructed. It was a massive three-tiered confection, with the top layer angled precariously, so Beth went over to help Josh's mum serve it up, before taking two pieces and returning to Mike's side.

Part of her had been dreading this night, worried that their parents would somehow ruin it, would embarrass Jenny on her big day, and that she would feel out of place and in the way. Yet she was having the most fun she'd had in ages, and Mike was the perfect date. Not that it meant anything, she reminded herself. This was a strictly one-night-only thing, Mike on loan to her from Violet.

But when he asked her to dance, all that fell away, and she felt like she was in a dream, where all the pain and rejection she'd held so close to her melted and slipped away, and all her angst dissolved, so that the only thing she could feel was peace and contentment.

Swaying in the circle of his arms, one of his hands on her shoulder, the other low on her back, she felt safe, and protected, and perfectly content with the world.

"Did Violet mind you coming as my date tonight?" she whispered up at him, then blushed. She hadn't meant to use that word. "You know what I mean," she muttered.

He smiled at her, kindness and warmth blazing in his eyes. "Of course she didn't mind. She knew how awkward you felt about attending on your own, of not having anyone to walk you down the aisle, or sit with at dinner, so she suggested that I ask Jenny if I could accompany you."

Oh god, how embarrassing! That was even worse than Violet minding! Her thoughts must have played out across her face, because Mike stopped dancing and squeezed her shoulder. "There's nothing to be embarrassed about, silly. You haven't lived here for years, so why would you know anyone you wanted to bring with you tonight?" he asked – which just made Beth wish even harder that the floor would open up and swallow her whole.

A tap on her shoulder was a welcome distraction from the awkward moment, and she spun around with relief. It was Jenny, who asked Mike if she could cut in, then swung her sister around the dance floor. Soon they were laughing like little kids, and Beth felt another part of her starting to heal.

"I just wanted to thank you for being such an important part of my big day sis. Having you here made it complete," Jenny said, and Beth smiled, but shook her head.

"No, thank *you* for allowing me to be part of it," she insisted. "I'm so happy for you, and to see how perfect you and Josh are for each other, to know that you're so deeply loved, and so in love – it means the world to me. And I'm so grateful that I've been able to spend this time with you over the past few weeks, and reconnect with you. I guess I let my anger with Mother and the misery of my childhood spill over and taint my feelings for you, and I'm so sorry for that."

Jenny drew her into her arms. "Sweet Beth, please don't worry about that. We're both free of them now, free to live our own lives, and I want you to create the life you've always wanted, to do what makes you happy. Promise me you will?" she implored her.

Something clicked within Beth, and she felt a rush of freedom and confidence wash over her. Yes. It was time she stopped using her awful, cruel parents and her miserable childhood as an excuse for her life not being great. Time to take some responsibility and stop jumping from one thing to another, sabotaging her self and her potential career.

She knew deep down that she wanted to be a teacher, she'd always known, so she had to stop messing around, doing whatever jobs came her way, and make that happen. Melisande and Julius had got a temporary nanny in to cover her for the time she'd planned to be gone – but she would call them tomorrow and let them know she wouldn't be returning to France. Then she would call the nearest college and find out what she had to do to enrol. Term should be starting soon, and she hoped she could be in class from day one.

When Jenny hugged her again then left to thank the other bridesmaids, Beth made her way back to Mike, eyes burning with joy and passion.

"Wow, I've never seen you look so happy," he said warmly. "I'm really glad."

She threw her arms around him. "Thank you so much Mike, you and Violet, for seeing the best in me when I couldn't, and for sharing your lives with me, and being such wonderful friends," she raved, brimming over with gratitude, and exhilaration.

"I've just realised that I've put my life on hold for the last few years. I've been treading water, in some twisted attempt to get back at my parents. But the truth is, nothing I do or don't do will make them happy, and nothing I do or don't do will punish them. So I have to stop avoiding what I really want to do in an effort to spite them, and just move on and make my life work for me. I've always wanted to be a teacher, so tomorrow I'm going to find out how to get my qualifications," she said, words falling over each other as she tried to explain her new-found enthusiasm.

Mike beamed at her, then leaned over, kissed her hand, and led her back onto the dance floor.

Chapter 25

Another Storm Rolls In

Rhiannon... Today...

A few days later, Rhiannon was curled up in the lounge room reading a book – but the peace was interrupted when the front door slammed shut, making her jump, and her father barrelled inside, not even noticing her presence.

"Dad, what's wrong?" she asked, alarmed by his pale face and distracted gaze as he staggered down the hall towards her.

"Oh, hi darling." He looked surprised that she was there. "It's nothing, don't worry," he stammered. "I'm fine."

"But you're shaking! Come on, I'll make you a cup of tea, okay?" she insisted, guiding him through to the kitchen.

As she busied herself putting the kettle on, lifting down mugs, standing on tiptoe to reach up to the top cupboard for their biggest teapot, and searching for the calming herbal mix Rose had brought them, she cast sideways glances at her dad. "What's happened?" she finally asked.

"I'm okay, it's all just a bit... strange," he sighed.

"Yes, but what *happened*?" she demanded, trying hard to remain patient, but struggling.

"It's Rose, I was –"

Rhiannon's face fell. "Is she okay?" she whispered, heart in throat. "Can we do anything to help her?"

After long moments, her dad's eyes finally focused on her, and she watched him take a deep breath, straighten his shoulders, and force himself to calm down.

"Sorry love, Rose is fine. Don't worry."

Relieved, for the moment at least, she took a breath herself, then got back to spooning out the tea leaves. From experience she knew that her dad would eventually confide in her, but he wouldn't make a decision quickly, and in his current distracted state, she knew she might be waiting a while.

"I'm not sure how much you know about Rose's daughter?" her dad asked reluctantly.

Rhiannon shrugged. "Nothing really. I only found out that she'd had a child at all when you told me at Mum's memorial service. Lily? Daisy? Violet?"

"Violet." It was a tortured whisper.

"Right, Violet. But she left home a long time ago, I think it was something to do with her father, when he died?"

Suddenly she realised that she didn't actually know what had happened to Rose and her daughter, or her husband for that matter. The priest had interrupted her dad's revelation that day, and she'd been too distracted at the time to care about anyone else.

But surely she could have asked since then. God, Rose knew everything about her life, had comforted her at her mum's funeral, reassured her when she was scared she was turning into some kind of weather-controlling witch, yet she'd never paid any attention to her life. How selfish was that?

"I feel terrible that I didn't know, that I didn't ask. But Violet was your school friend, right?"

"Um, it was a bit more than that..." he said, then trailed off, reluctant again. When the kettle started whistling, he looked relieved for the respite. Rhiannon jumped up to make the tea, while Mike just sat and stared into space. But when she set the two mugs down on the bench and hauled herself up onto one of the stools next to her dad, she glared at him, wanting answers *now*. Shrugging helplessly, he picked up his cup, but his hand was shaking, and he had to put it down.

"Violet was my best friend growing up – we did everything together, spent all our time with each other, climbing the tor, making up stories, building forts, playing sport, watching the sun set and the moon rise. As we got older we started going to Rose's ritual circles together... and we were dating from the time we started high school."

Rhiannon's eyebrows rose in shock.

"Well, not just dating, that's playing it down far too much. We were in love. Totally inseparable. We had our whole life planned out. We were going to get married as soon as we graduated, and live together in the cottage at the bottom of the tor, the one that burned down. I was going to work with Dad, and Violet was going to study to be a social worker. We'd even talked about how many kids we would have, and when. It was all ahead of us." His voice trailed off, and his eyes were glazed, as though he was a thousand miles away.

What the hell? At a total loss about what to say, Rhiannon lifted her mug and took a huge gulp of tea. It burned her throat, but she hardly noticed. All of a sudden she felt as though she was sitting next to a complete stranger. How had she not known any of this?

Had she just not been listening? Surely she would have remembered if her dad had wanted to be with someone else. If her mum had been his second choice. It was a small town. Someone must have known. Time seemed to fold in on itself, as she made an effort to grasp this strange new reality.

Casting her mind back, she tried to recall any hint that her father had loved someone else, but she couldn't think of any strange moments or awkward interactions. Her parents had been totally devoted to each other, totally in love, and she'd always believed they were childhood sweethearts – yet clearly that wasn't the case. What had she based her assumption on?

They had *seemed* to be totally in love with each other and their family of four, and totally content, whether they were staying in a caravan in a rainy seaside village or driving around Brittany in France in a tiny car, or just hanging out at home, drinking tea and talking, or making dinner together, with no need for anything to distract them from each other.

And her parents had definitely adored each other. There was no acting on earth that could have faked that. They went on regular date nights – off to the movies, or out dancing, or to a restaurant for a romantic dinner. They'd also loved just being at home together – cooking, helping her and Brodie with their homework, perching on stools at the kitchen bench where she sat now to chat about their days. They supported each other through the highs and lows of life, encouraged one another to follow their hearts and their dreams and be all they could be, and were each other's best friend.

And when her mum had become sick, Mike had been the doting husband, taking time off to look after her, being totally devoted to his wife, to the exclusion of all else – even her and Brodie at times. There was no way any of that had been an act, no way the last twenty years of his life had been pretend.

But now that she thought about it, she realised that her dad never talked about his younger self. And how strange that she'd had no idea that he'd been in love with Rose's daughter. Not been aware that in another life, another universe, Rose had almost been Mike's mother-in-law. Could have been her *real* grandma.

Was fate real? Were there some events that would happen no matter what, some sort of *Sliding Doors* thing where regardless of your decisions, your actions, you would end up in the same place? Because Rose kind of *had* been Mike's mother-in-law, and her own grandmother, fulfilling the roles Patricia should have played, but was incapable of.

Most significantly of all, she'd treated Beth like a real daughter, and been the perfect maternal figure and mentor for a woman so starved of motherly love. How hard had that been for Rose? To treat the woman who'd taken her own daughter's place like a trusted, beloved child?

And oh my god, that meant… She looked up at her dad with concern and fear in her eyes. Whatever had made Rose's life so tragic must also have wounded her father. He'd planned to marry this girl, this Violet, so Rose and her husband were going to become his in-laws. They must have been really close. And then suddenly, all at once, he'd lost his true love, along with the man he'd considered a father figure.

Mike finally noticed how worried she was, and forced a bleak smile. "It was a long time ago darling, and I've made my peace with it, although occasionally it does still feel like it all happened yesterday. But Violet didn't leave us because her dad died, he killed himself because she left."

"What?" she gasped, as new horror reached out icy fingers to clutch at her heart.

"It's a long story, and old news," he began, but Rhiannon glared at him, and he laughed, a short, mirthless sound, then continued to unravel the story of his early life.

"We were seventeen, and planning to move in with each other as soon as school ended, and start our life together. Then suddenly she fell in love with someone else, an older guy, a shaman. I still don't know if he cast a spell on her or if it was all of her own free will, but she sort of broke up with me, and started seeing him. Secretly though, because she didn't want her mum to know, which was also hard for me, because I didn't like misleading Rose. Lying to her."

The love and respect in his voice as he spoke of the priestess touched Rhiannon deeply, and she wondered about the new layers she was uncovering of her father. Did everyone have secret depths and sorrows they never showed to anyone? Could you ever really know another person?

"Apart from the obvious fact that I was still in love with Violet, and wanted to be with her myself, I could never understand her attraction to him," he continued.

"Maybe it was the worldly older guy thing – most people were in awe of him, especially the girls, and he really knew how to appear charming, to lay it on thick. Although Beth saw right through him." He trailed off, warmth and love as he thought of his wife pulling him away from her again.

"Dad?"

"Sorry love. Violet tried to explain it to me. She was so disappointed that I couldn't understand how great he was, and all the reasons he'd swept her off her feet. It seemed that it was very flattering that he had chosen her, because how could he, such a supposedly 'amazing' and 'spiritual' and 'enlightened' guru, love *her*? She was just an ordinary girl, she said. He was so much better than her, she said. But she was wrong. She was worth ten of him, I can tell you that much."

Bitterness leached from his words. Even twenty years later, he was still upset by the retelling, still invested in the outcome, and Rhiannon's heart cried for him.

"It was horrifying yet strangely fascinating to watch him in action. He definitely wooed Violet, showering her with gifts and compliments, telling her she was the only person in the whole world who could understand him, and how special that made her. Yet it was all very self-centred, and cynical and insincere, because as soon as she fell for him, he began to play on her insecurities, and made her feel like she had to do exactly what he wanted in order for him to continue loving her. He was jealous and possessive and cruel, although he hid that from her, obviously."

Her father's attention wandered again, and Rhiannon wasn't sure she wanted to force him to focus back on such painful memories again. But eventually he took a sip of his tea, and started again with his story.

"The worst thing was that he convinced her that she had to leave home in order to prevent her father's death – that if she stayed in Summer Hill, Louis would die. It was ridiculous, anyone else could see that, but he'd got inside her head and knew exactly what buttons to push. And so she ran away from home, away from Rose and Louis, and didn't tell them where she was going, or even let them know she was okay."

Her dad trailed off, and Rhiannon's heart broke for him, and for Rose too. If she'd ever run away from home, she knew it would have crushed her parents, especially her mum. How did Rose survive that?

"Violet's dad couldn't handle the loss. The doctor gave him sedatives, antidepressants, but he started drinking too. He was so sad, and then really angry, which led to him losing his job, and it put a huge strain on his relationship with Rose. Within a month of Violet's disappearance he'd sunk so low that he couldn't see a way out, a way to healing, a way back to Rose. So he took some pills and drank a bottle of whisky, and drove off the local bridge."

Rhiannon gasped, and clutched at the bench, the weight of shock and grief like a punch in the stomach.

"Oh Dad."

At her heartbroken cry, he turned to her, but his eyes were distant. He was a million miles away from her, an abyss of secrets and pain gaping between them. But he tried to gather his thoughts, to give voice to the feelings he'd locked away for twenty years. "Rose not only became a young widow, but she was also no longer a mother – she never heard from Violet again."

Rhiannon felt like all the oxygen had been sucked out of the room. Shell-shocked didn't come close to explaining the emotional rollercoaster she was on. It seemed as though the earth had tilted on its axis, and everything she'd ever known to be true no longer was.

"Oh god, poor Rose," she finally stammered. "And poor you. I'm so sorry Dad."

She reached out to him, and he offered her a watery, weary smile, but his mind had drifted far away from her.

"How did you, um... I mean, when did you meet Mum?" she asked, and felt a sudden flicker of anger that she had never known this, and a shiver of fear at what she might discover. But she shook them aside, desperate now to know what had happened all those years ago.

"Beth's parents and my parents were business associates of some kind, so I'd vaguely known her and her sister Jenny since I was a child, although the girls were a bit older than us, so we weren't especially close. We didn't go to school together or anything like that," her dad began.

Rhiannon tried not to recoil from his use of the term "us", and the knowledge that he was talking about him and Violet when he said it, not him and her mum.

"Beth had left the village when Violet and I were fifteen – she lived in London for a year, studying, then spent a year in France, travelling for a while, then working as a nanny in Paris. That's why we took you and Brodie to France those times, because your mum loved it so much there, and wanted to share that with us. When she came home for Jenny's wedding, she wasn't intending to stay, because she couldn't bear the thought of being in the same town as her mother, as I'm sure you can understand."

A shiver raced up Rhiannon's spine, and she nodded. She couldn't even begin to imagine what growing up with Patricia as a mother would do to a young girl.

"We started talking at one of her family's boring business get-togethers – I think Patricia thought it would be useful for the families if Beth and I were married off – and she seemed a bit lonely, so I invited her to one of Rose's rituals, just to get her out of the house really. And Violet sensed her sadness I think, so she welcomed her into our lives and became her friend, letting her come on dates with us, and hang out with us," he recalled, smiling fondly.

"Beth couldn't understand why she did that – she told me she would never have let a pretty girl spend so much time with her boyfriend – but Violet grew up with Rose, not Patricia, and so she saw only the good in people. She saw that Beth needed love, and friendship, and opened her heart to her."

Shock washed over Rhiannon as she tried to reconcile her memories of her mother with what her dad was revealing about her. She'd always thought her mum had been perfect, the kindest and best person she knew, but maybe she hadn't always been that way. Could that be true?

"Beth was with us when Violet met the other guy. He was teaching a divination course, and the three of us went together – we thought it would be a bit of fun. Beth admitted later that she encouraged Violet's interest in him, because she was in love with me, and wanted me for herself. She even claimed that she'd cast a spell on me, but I don't believe that," he insisted. "She didn't need to use magic to make me love her."

Rhiannon's thoughts flew back to the few rituals she'd gone to with her mum. Rose would never have condoned, let alone encouraged, magic being used for selfish means, to influence someone's will or gain something for yourself. But could her mum have done something like that on her own?

When she was younger, would she have been so desperate to get away from her own family that she'd tried to ensnare Mike for herself? And turned her back on a friend? Rose's daughter sounded so sweet and kind, the type of person she'd always believed her mum to be. But if what her dad was telling her was true, and Beth had done something sneaky, how had she faced Rose all these years? Why had her mum invited the priestess into their lives, into their family?

Or had *that* been the point? Had she not only wanted Violet's boyfriend, but her mum as well? Knowing Patricia, she wouldn't have blamed her mum for wanting to swap parents, but the thought unsettled her. And as much as she wanted to reject the possibility outright that her mum could have done this, something about it just wouldn't let go.

"But, she wouldn't do that… Surely not," she whispered, turning sad eyes on her father.

"I don't know darling. She did tell me just before she died that she'd spent her whole life trying to make up for the wrong she'd done Violet," he replied. They stared at each other, unwilling to acknowledge that the Beth they had known could have had such a dark side to her.

"So what happened to Violet?"

"After a couple of months with the shaman guy, she told me she was going to live with him in London, and she hoped that I could be happy for her. She also mentioned something about it saving her dad – the stupid lie that he had convinced her to believe. And then she was gone," he said sadly.

"I had already come to terms with the fact that I'd lost her, and I'd become closer to Beth over time. But when Violet disappeared, it was your mum who helped me cope, just as friends at first, then slowly my feelings turned romantic, until finally I fell head over heels in love with her. And it was bigger and bolder and deeper and wider than what I'd had with Violet throughout school. So please don't ever think that your mum was a second choice, or a fallback plan or anything like that. She really was the great love of my life, and she always will be."

Starting to freak out, and needing to do something to distract herself, Rhiannon stood up abruptly and began pulling flour and spices out of the pantry so she'd have something to do with her hands. She was trying to get her head around this crazy, devastatingly sad story, but it was too much to take in.

"And Rose? What's happened now, after all this time, that you're both going through all of this again?" she asked gently, trying to shift the conversation away from the place where she had to embrace a whole new perspective of her mother.

Mike stared back at her, struggling to focus on her, on the question, on the present. "She got a phone call from Violet's friend in Australia today. That's where she'd been all these years."

"That's wonderful! So Rose can call her daughter and talk to her, and go and visit her in Australia! And maybe Violet will even come here at some point, so you can see her too?"

Mike shook his head, fresh tears in his eyes. "A week ago Violet was in a car accident. She died, alongside her husband, but their daughter survived."

Rhiannon gasped. "Violet had a daughter?"

"Yes. She's seventeen, and apparently she has no other family, so she's coming here next week, to live with Rose."

There was so much Rhiannon was dying to ask about this girl, but seeing her father's face, she abruptly stopped that line of questioning. A daughter didn't matter. There were more important things to ponder. "Wait, Violet died? Rose's daughter *had* been alive all this time, but now she's dead?"

A shudder rocked through Mike's body, and for a moment she thought he was going to break into a million tiny pieces. But he took a deep breath and managed to nod to her before his head sunk into his hands. Realising how much this would be hurting him, she put an arm around him, trying to offer some kind of comfort, and push away the new doubts about her mother. This wasn't the time for that.

Her heart ached for him. He was still grieving the death of the love of his life, and now he was losing his first love all over again – and would have to face the memory of that every time he saw her daughter wandering around the village. Her daughter who was the same age as she was. That was going to be very weird for her dad. And for Rose.

"Oh god, how old was Violet when she ran away?" she asked, hoping her rough calculation was wrong.

Mike gazed at her with haunted eyes, and seemed reluctant to answer the question. "She was seventeen too," he finally conceded. "So Rose will gain a seventeen-year-old granddaughter in place of the seventeen-year-old daughter she lost twenty years ago."

They both lapsed into silence. Rhiannon's mind was whirring. And while she knew it was selfish, her mind kept circling back to how this affected her. She didn't want Rose to have a *real* granddaughter. To all intents and purposes she had always been *her* grandma, and she hated the idea that she would have to share her with this stranger.

Or – *oh my god!* – would she just be completely replaced in Rose's affections? And did worrying about this now, while her dad was so distraught, make her just as bad and as self-centred as her mother, who'd encouraged her love rival to go for the other guy so she could have Mike for herself? Who had apparently used *magic* to get what she wanted?

Her mum had mentioned to her a few times that you couldn't do anything to control a person or change their free will, and if you were going to do any spellworking, you had to be very clear and very careful with your intent, and very much aware of and responsible for all the consequences that could arise. And she'd always encouraged her to be kind and selfless, to think of others and be compassionate. But was all of that simply because she was trying to atone for her previous actions? Trying to pass on the hard-won knowledge she'd acquired because she'd broken those rules herself?

Rhiannon's head was spinning, so when Brodie came running in to ask for a snack, she was relieved at the distraction. She didn't know what to feel about everything she'd just learned, so she left her dad crying in the kitchen and happily dove into playing with her brother, baking the cookies she'd begun then disappearing with him into his treehouse to play a complicated game of knights and dragons. Although compared to real life, it was a breeze.

Chapter 26

The Green-Eyed Monster

The next morning Rhiannon woke up with a smile. It was the middle of summer, and the holidays would be starting soon. She was looking forward to having almost two months off school – she needed a break from the questions, from the chaos of people, and from the pressure of study. From the pity of her fellow students, and from her own self-pity. Then she remembered the heartbreaking conversation she'd had with her father, and a wave of sadness enveloped her. Rose had lost her daughter, once twenty years ago, then all over again yesterday. The priestess was still grieving Beth's loss, and now she'd been hit again. She was the strongest person Rhiannon knew, but could even she survive this?

The oppressive cloud of gloominess reached out thicker, tighter tendrils to her as she thought of her dad's heartache. Which, knowing him, was being made even worse with an additional serving of guilt on top of his pain.

Guilt to be mourning someone else, when he should still be mourning Beth. Guilt that he'd abandoned Rose to her grief, now and then, even though that wasn't true. Guilt, she'd seen last night, that he had kept all of this from his daughter. Why had he? Who was he trying to protect – himself, or his late wife? Had Beth spent her whole life trying to pretend Violet hadn't existed? That she hadn't ever hurt her friend, or acted less than perfectly?

Selfishly though, the thing that burned Rhiannon the deepest was jealousy, and fear of her own potential loss. More than just: *Who was Violet?* – and that question continued to plague her, especially in relation to her dad's connection to her – she also wanted to know: *Who was this daughter of Violet's?* The one coming to turn Rose's life upside down? Why hadn't she ever been in touch with her grandmother before, if she wanted to live with her now?

Childishly, she pouted. Rose was *her* grandmother, not some stranger's. Would this supposed granddaughter steal the priestess away from her, turn her against her? Would Rose care more for a flesh-and-blood relation than for Rhiannon and Brodie, and lavish all her love and attention on her? Would she have any time left for them, once this new girl arrived?

It made her sound petty, she knew that, but Rhiannon wasn't sure she could cope with losing Rose too. She'd been more than a grandmother to her since the day she was born. And now it seemed as though some upstart new kid from the other side of the world was going to steal her away.

Suddenly she wished she'd gone to the rituals and celebrations when she'd been invited, when the priestess had almost begged her. She wished she'd joined the magical circle and inserted herself more fully into Rose's life when she'd had the chance.

What would she be like, this stranger? Apparently she'd just turned seventeen, the same age as her, and she shuddered to think how this would play out. Would she be lumbered with the new girl, obliged to hang out with her to help Rose? Have to show her around at school, entertain her, be her friend, when that was the last thing on earth she wanted?

Finally though, a small smile crossed her face as a flash of curiosity wormed its way into her brain – she'd never met anyone from Australia before. What would she be like? What kind of things would she enjoy doing? What would she sound like? Was she used to sunshine and beaches? What did Aussies do, throw another shrimp on the barbie? She had no idea what that actually meant, but it sounded weird and foreign. They were convicts too, weren't they, descended from British criminals?

Rolling her eyes, she scolded herself for her over-active imagination. She could hear Rose's voice in her head, telling her to give the girl a chance, to open her heart and display some empathy. Besides, Violet had been English, and had grown up right here, with Rose, in this village, so her daughter would hardly be a savage, surely, no matter how Australian she was.

And she wondered if her father had been from the land down under, or was he British too, that older guy her dad had mentioned, a shaman or something? Then again, Mike hadn't spoken too highly of him, so for the girl's sake she hoped it had been someone else. *Phew, a sliver of sympathy for the recently orphaned stranger, at last.*

With that thought, Rhiannon finally felt bad. The poor girl had just lost both her parents – and was being uprooted from her entire life and sent to the other side of the world to live with a stranger. She knew how crushed she'd been by her own mother's death, how crushed she still was, and she couldn't even begin to comprehend losing her dad as well. And all so recently. She would be a mess for sure, so she figured she could spare her a little compassion.

She was still terrified the new girl would steal Rose away from her, but something her dad had said struck her now. Violet, his girlfriend (*his girlfriend!*), had been kind and welcoming to Beth when she'd come back to Summer Hill, inviting her into her circle, both the magical one she shared with Rose, and her friendship circle, and even on dates with her and Mike, because she'd grown up with Rose for a mum, for a role model, for a friend. Whereas Beth, who'd been "mothered" by cold and cruel Patricia, which had made her careful, and suspicious, and less trusting of anyone new that she met, had apparently taken advantage of Violet's friendship, and behaved less than well.

But Rhiannon had grown up with Beth for a mum, and she'd limited her exposure to her nasty grandmother and taught her there was a better way to act and to be. So no matter how worried she was about this new girl, and how threatened she felt, she would honour her mum's memory by being kind. She just hoped the girl had inherited her own mum's good traits, since it seemed Violet had been well-loved – perhaps *too* well-loved – when she'd lived in their village. And she hoped the stranger wouldn't take Rose away from her completely.

A knock on her door brought her back to the present, and Brodie called out that she had a visitor. Stumbling out of bed, she pulled yesterday's dress over her head then opened her door – to see Rose standing there, face drawn and cheeks tear-stained, but kindness still radiating from her.

"I was just thinking about you," Rhiannon said sheepishly.

"I know, sweet girl," Rose said softly, sadly, then walked past her and collapsed onto her bed. Rhiannon followed, and sank down on the other end.

The priestess took her hands. "Dear Rhiannon, I could feel your fear, and your angst, and I want to reassure you that nothing, and no one, will ever take me away from you."

Rhiannon blushed, which made Rose's eyes twinkle. "It's normal to feel threatened by the unknown, and this situation is certainly that, for all of us, but I have room in my heart for both of you, I promise. And I'm wondering if you could help me, if it's not too much to ask of you?"

Reluctantly she nodded.

"Violet's friend told Carlie about me last night, and I could sense her terror, and an incredible anger, from the other side of the world. I don't know what Violet told her about me, but she's feeling a great deal of anguish, hatred even, when she thinks of me, and of coming here to live," Rose sighed.

Pain radiated from the older woman, and her words and emotions pierced Rhiannon's soul, before she remembered what this whole situation had begun from.

"Rose, I'm so sorry for your loss," she stammered. "I'm mortified to admit that I didn't even know you'd had a daughter, let alone lost her so many years ago. I feel so terrible that I had no idea about this. My whole life you've been like a grandmother to me – *better* than a grandmother. You've known everything about me, been so kind,

always, and I wasn't even aware of such a fundamental part of you..."
She trailed off, tears making her voice unsteady.

"Oh Rhiannon, there's nothing to be sorry for," Rose said,
scooping her into a hug. "By the time you were born, Violet had been
gone for several years, and I'd reconciled myself to life without her
– or as much as you can reconcile yourself to living with a part of you
cut away. And don't blame your dad. He didn't think there was any
point worrying you over it – and Beth was very sensitive about the
situation, feeling it was her fault in some way, so he was protective of
her because of that."

When Rhiannon inhaled quickly, panicked that this was really
true, Rose soothed her. "It was ridiculous for Beth to feel responsible,
I promise you, and I told her that over and over again. No one could
have done anything. And honestly, until yesterday, I didn't even know
what to tell anyone."

The young girl sighed. "I didn't know about Louis either," she
admitted, voice small. "I'm so sorry."

Rose patted her cheek. "Thank you sweet girl. Now, I know this is
a big ask, especially while you're feeling so vulnerable, but Carlie
is going to feel very alone when she gets here. She's lost both
her parents, and is being torn away from all she's ever known – her
friends, her home, her school, her life. Would you keep an eye out for
her once school starts, just to check she's okay? And maybe even pop
by some time to say hello, see if she needs someone her age to answer
questions or help with anything? I have absolutely no idea what a
seventeen-year-old girl needs."

The request scared Rhiannon, and she wanted with all of her
heart to say no. But she couldn't refuse Rose anything. So eventually
she nodded, and tried to grin reassuringly as the older woman stood
up from the bed.

The priestess offered a tired smile in return. "You don't have to be
her best friend, or even her friend at all – I know you have people
you're close to already, and that this is all a lot to take in. It would
just mean the world to me if she could come to you if she needed to."

"Of course," Rhiannon said, finally managing to inject some
enthusiasm into her voice. What a bitch she was, to be so loath to

provide even the most basic of polite conversation. This was a favour to Rose, who she owed so much.

"And who knows sweet girl, perhaps you'll become friends after all." A glint of mischief returned to Rose's eyes.

After the grieving priestess left her alone in her room, Rhiannon threw herself down on the bed. Why had she been so hesitant to agree to help Rose's granddaughter? Hadn't she just been complaining that she wanted a friend who understood how she felt, who had suffered her own loss, so that she recognised the pit of despair she still faced every day? And this poor girl had lost both her parents – as well as everything else – while she still had her dad and Brodie, and Rose, and her school friends, kind of, and her school, and even her family home.

God, this girl had *nothing*. She was being thrown into a whole new, totally foreign world, where nothing would be familiar, and everyone she met would be a stranger.

After nine months of thinking she was the saddest person on earth, the one who'd lost the most, she was going to meet someone who'd lost far more. Perhaps it would shake her up a little, stop her self-pity, and maybe she'd actually be able to help someone else. She'd felt so alone when she'd lost her mum, so maybe she could be there for this girl, in the way she'd wanted someone to be there for her. She wondered how it would feel, to be out-grief-stricken.

Chapter 27

A Deal With the Devil

Beth... Twenty years ago...

It was the morning after the wedding, and Beth woke with an ominous feeling in her chest. The emotional weight of her childhood home pressed down on her, and the knowledge that she was alone with her parents made her want to scream. Yet there was a spark of hope too. Last night, her newly-married sister had made her promise to follow her dreams, and follow her heart, and she intended to keep her word.

First up, calling her French employers, to let them know they would need a permanent replacement. For a moment she was sad, because she'd miss them and their two daughters. The girls and their innocent wonder and easy affection had been healing for her, and seeing the way Melisande and Julius parented them had reassured her that not all families were as dysfunctional as her own.

When she got through to the kind Parisian woman who had taken her into her home and become a friend, Melisande took the news well, and was genuinely happy for her that she had made peace with her past. Touched by the well wishes, Beth sat down and wrote a letter to her former charges, adding some local postcards so they could see where she lived, and promising to stay in touch. Being pen pals with Aveline and Joceline would bring her joy, and she knew their parents would be happy they had someone writing to them in English, since they wanted them to grow up bilingual.

Before she could slip out to the post office, her mother swept in and announced that she was required downstairs in fifteen minutes – and she'd better make herself presentable.

Sighing at the dramatics, Beth raced down the hall for the world's quickest shower, then quickly pulled the beige dress her mother so loved over her head. She wasn't going to provide any new reason for disapproval today, any excuse for her mother to ruin her excitement or distract her from her new plans. If Jenny had taught her anything, it was the futility of always arguing with their mother, always trying to score little victories, when it just meant she ended up losing the war.

When it came to Patricia, the most successful way of coping was to pretend you were agreeing with her, to let her think she was winning and that you were doing what she wanted you to, then to live your life on your own terms, quietly and with confidence. Case in point – her own efforts at petty rebellion throughout her years at home had got her nowhere but condescended to and frowned upon, whereas Jenny was perfectly happy and content. Her sister had never *lied* to their parents, she'd just... let them believe what they wanted to, and not told them the whole truth.

As she walked gracefully down the stairs fourteen minutes later, shock swept through her when she saw the large formal drawing room filled with serious, anxious-faced men in business suits. A puzzled-looking Jenny caught her eye from where she was leaning against the opposite wall with her new husband, but she shrugged. She had no idea what was going on either.

Their mother glanced at Beth as she entered the room, and gave a very uncharacteristic nod of approval as she took in her wayward daughter's neat hair, subtle make-up and bland dress. Bemused, she acknowledged her sister's wisdom – *appearing* to do what their parents expected from them really did make life so much easier.

Slipping over to Jenny's side, she stood with her against the wall while the twenty grey-haired, grey-faced men took their seats at the large boardroom table.

"Thank you for coming," their father said, his voice booming around the room. At home he didn't say much, content to let his wife do the organising and the disciplining, but Beth had been reliably informed that in business Frank Bishop was strong, ruthless and calculating – just what their mother sought in a man, a colleague, a friend, a daughter. Shame her two kids had turned out the complete opposite.

"We didn't want to distract from our eldest daughter Jennifer's wedding ceremony yesterday, so we held off this announcement until today. But we wanted you, our valued board members, to be the first to know that on Friday morning, Bishop Enterprises bought out Galen and Sons, and Patricia and I will be moving to London to run the greatly expanded operation from there, effective immediately."

A gasp echoed around the room, but it was of admiration rather than surprise. No one had ever doubted Frank would be able to pull off the deal of the decade, and the murmurs of congratulations from around the table sounded genuine.

"Throughout the day I will be speaking to each of you individually, to determine whether you will move to London with us or stay here. Our daughter Jennifer has just graduated, with honours apparently, so she will be heading up operations here. If you have any problems with that, I will be offering a generous redundancy package."

Beside her, Beth felt Jenny stiffen, and heard her indrawn hiss of shock and panic. Josh steadied his wife with a hand on her arm and a whispered reassurance, as all eyes in the room turned to stare at the new bride. Beth had paled as dramatically as her sister, knowing that she had no intention of working for their father's company, let alone running it.

Taking a deep breath, Jenny stepped forward as confidently as she could and cleared her throat. Beth could see she was shaking, yet her back remained straight and her shoulders set. She was discovering again what a formidable woman her sister was.

"Congratulations Father, Mother," she began, voice revealing only the tiniest quaver. "Your takeover is to be commended – I know it is a huge deal, and one you have been working towards for many years. I very much hope that you will treat the new employees you'll now oversee with respect and kindness."

Frank nodded in acknowledgement of her congratulations, while ignoring the exhortation to treat the new workers well, but Patricia's eyes hardened with suspicion. Beth knew there would be words later, about her implication that they treated their staff badly, but Jenny didn't seem afraid of that. And she supposed it wouldn't matter, since the newlyweds were leaving the village today for their honeymoon on the Isle of Lewis, before returning to their home in northern Scotland.

"And I thank you for your confidence in me, and the generous 'offer' to join the family company," Jenny continued, and Beth marvelled at how her sister managed to strike such a perfect balance of sarcasm and seriousness.

"However, I will have to respectfully decline. I've accepted a position to run a... company... in Scotland, so Josh and I will be remaining in our home up there."

A ripple of shock swept around the room, and Beth struggled not to laugh as she watched the faces of their parents turn a mottled purple, and the board members trying to hide their glee. Perhaps she and her sister weren't the only people in the room who disliked the Bishops – or maybe the suits just hoped one of them had a chance at the massive promotion now.

"We just came to pick up Beth for a farewell lunch, and to take her to enrol at the college. Congratulations to you both, and best wishes for the move," Jenny said to her parents, voice firm and strong. Then she turned on her heel and left the room. Beth stared after her, shock freezing her where she stood, until Josh grabbed her hand and hastily drew her with him, out into the hallway where Jenny was standing, pale and shaky, yet lit up with relief and joy.

"Quick Beth, where's your stuff? We have to go right now. Hurry!"

Flustered, Beth thought of her bag, up in her room, which had her wallet, driver's licence and everything else she might need in it. But as she turned to head upstairs, terrified her mother would come out at any moment and stop them leaving, her gaze alighted on the hall table. The small clutch she'd taken to the wedding, with money, lip-gloss and keys in it, was sitting where she'd dropped it last night. Relief flooded her as she picked it up and raced to the front door.

"Let's go!"

An hour later, the two sisters were sitting in a cafe, toasting their new freedom with large, strong coffees. Beth was enrolled in the teaching course – thanks to Jenny, who'd driven her to campus, taken her to the admissions office, and produced her passport when they'd asked for ID. Beth's heart had plummeted when they'd requested proof of her identity, until her sister sheepishly admitted that she'd grabbed her passport for her the day before, to make sure she signed up before she lost her nerve.

So, in two short weeks she would commence her studies. The admissions officer had been impressed by her employment in Paris, and pushed her into taking a couple of extra language electives to broaden her eventual qualifications. She'd also credited most of her course from London towards her degree here.

Still shaking with excitement, Beth hugged her sister again, struggling to put into words just how much she appreciated her, and her not-so-subtle push towards making her dream a reality.

"Sweet Beth, you'll be an amazing teacher, you really will."

"And you will be the most incredible eco-warrior in the country," she replied. Beth was in awe of the passion in her sister's eyes as she raved about the new environmentally-friendly energy sources her team was investigating, the promising research they'd done so far, and all the new options she still wanted to explore. She even had a meeting set up with the Scottish minister for the environment to discuss their progress and ask about grants.

It was the love her new husband had for her, a love that was so totally and unreservedly returned, that touched Beth most deeply though, and reassured her that she'd be able to find someone who felt that way about her. Clearly Andrew just hadn't been that into her – but now she had faith that someone else would be, eventually.

All too soon Josh pulled up outside and raced into the cafe, their luggage and wedding gifts all packed and ready for their journey home, and took his new bride's hand. They were both fired up with excitement that they'd soon be back in their little Scottish cottage overlooking the ocean, and getting to work in their lab.

"I'm so happy for you," Beth said, hugging her sister one last time, and trying not to cry all over her. "I'm sad that you're leaving, when we just found each other, but the love you and Josh share is so inspiring, and the fact that you're living your dreams together, working to change the world, it blows my mind, and fills me with enough strength to cope with Mother."

Jenny kissed her cheek, then took her hands. "I love you so much Beth, and I really treasure the time we've had together – it's the one thing that made coming back here to get married worth it for me. And I'm so proud of you, for returning home despite how difficult Mother is, for deciding to go after your dreams, and for allowing yourself to be transformed over these last five weeks. For letting love in, from me, from your friends Violet and Mike, and from the priestess who is helping you heal, and helping you see for yourself what an amazing person you are becoming."

It was her final sentence that made Beth break down, and all attempts to hold back their tears dissolved as the sisters clung to each other and wept. But they laughed too, and promised to stay in touch, and to visit each other soon.

And then Jenny and Josh were gone, and Beth was sitting in the cafe alone, gazing vacantly out the window. Her cheeks were wet with tears and her coffee mug was empty, but a thrill of excitement was building within her. She was going to do this. She was going to stay in this village and become a teacher. Granted the decision was much easier now, knowing that her parents were moving away, but still, she was proud of herself. After two years of what now felt like aimless wandering, she had a purpose. It felt good, and right.

Her head swam with plans. She was going to be a loyal, trustworthy friend to Violet and Mike, and let new people into her life too. She was going to join Rose's Year and a Day group and go to her rituals, now that she'd met that woman in the mists and been entrusted with the gorgeous pendant that reminded her of her connection to magic. And she was going to learn all she could, and become everything she was capable of being.

Her attention jolted back to where she was when a fresh coffee appeared on the table in front of her. "I didn't order this," she said, expecting to see the waitress standing above her. But it was Mike, his own coffee mug in hand.

"Is it okay if I join you?" he asked, and she smiled as she wiped the last tear away.

"Of course."

As he slid into the chair Jenny had just been sitting in, he looked concerned. "Are you okay?"

She smiled. "I'm great actually," she began, and filled him in on her crazy morning, from the revelation about her parents leaving town soon, and Jenny turning down the job offer, to how much she loved and admired her sister, and would miss her.

"And I've just enrolled in the teacher training course, and I start in two weeks. So I'll be staying in Summer Hill after all," she said happily, then stared at her friend.

"Are you okay though? You look a little worried."

Mike shrugged helplessly, his face sad. "I don't know. Things have been a little... weird... since we started that divination course."

"What do you mean? You don't like it?"

"It's okay, although I think Rose is way better than he is."

Beth nodded her agreement.

"But, well, I'm worried about Violet. She seems, I don't know, different?" he said, then broke off, blushing furiously.

"In what way?" she asked, heart sinking.

"She's so, preoccupied maybe? Ever since we started this bloody course," he scowled. "Has she said anything to you?"

Beth shook her head, and prayed her cheeks wouldn't turn bright red and betray her.

"It's so strange. She's usually the one who longs to go out and socialise, but she hasn't done any of our regular things since the course started. All she wants to do is practise with the cards, and do his assignments the minute we get them. Which is fine, but... Well, she seems a bit distant or something too, a bit aloof. And I have this nagging feeling that she's been to see him. But you really haven't noticed any changes in her?"

Panic swept over Beth, and she shrugged. "Um, not really..."

Mike sighed. "Maybe it's not even her so much. Maybe I'm just being paranoid or overly sensitive, imagining things. But it seems like the teacher is paying a lot of attention to Violet, and kind of, I don't know, flirting with her? Or am I just being silly?" he asked, blushing beet red at his confession.

Beth sighed. "I've noticed that too," she admittedly softly, apologetically. Although it wasn't her fault – was it? Should she have put an end to it right away? Challenged Andrew on his behaviour towards Violet? Towards herself? Should she have shot down Violet when she started obsessing over him? Confessed what she knew of their teacher at least, back on their first day?

"But Vee wouldn't –"

"She won't stop raving about him, or mooning over him," Mike complained. "How amazing he is, how psychic he is, what a great listener, blah blah blah. She really hasn't said anything to you?"

Now it was Beth's turn to blush. What could she say? Yes, Violet had gushed about their teacher to her too, going on and on and on about how hot he was, how attractive he was, how perfect at every little thing he was. But she couldn't tell Mike that, it would totally break his heart. And yet... if she did confess, would he turn to her instead? Or was that just wishful thinking? And was she only considering breaking Violet's confidence because of her ulterior motive, because of her liking of Mike? Her loving of Mike?

Oh god, what was she thinking? She didn't love Mike. *Did she?* She just wanted a love *like* Mike, right? But an ache in her heart and an incredible wave of longing rushed through her, and she realised the awful truth. She was in love with her best friend's boyfriend – and he was asking her for advice about said friend. Could this situation get any worse?

Mike's piercing stare startled her back into the present, and she took a huge gulp of her coffee before carefully placing the cup back on the table.

"Just what you said," she finally acknowledged. "He's a great psychic, he's so perceptive, so amazing, yada yada yada. But I'm with you,

I promise, I think Rose is a far more impressive teacher, and a much more intuitive reader, than he'll ever be."

Taking the lid off the sugar bowl, she scooped out a spoonful and prayed her quick change of subject would stick. "When is Rose's next ritual anyway?"

Although he remained sad and out of sorts, Mike managed to pull himself together enough to answer her question, and they talked about the autumn equinox festival of Mabon until Violet bounded into the cafe and rushed over to their booth.

"Hi guys! So sorry I'm late, I decided I need a new look, so I've been shopping all morning, and lost track of the clock. It's time I looked a bit more grown up, a bit less school girl," she announced happily. Beth studiously avoided catching Mike's eye. Wasn't that the first sign of an affair, or the contemplation of one? A total makeover, trying to look like a different person in an attempt to impress someone new.

"Tea?" she asked Violet, needing to get away from them both for a minute. "Another coffee Mike? I'm getting one."

He nodded dispiritedly, and her heart ached for him. Clearly he'd just had the same idea she had. Sighing, she wondered if she should put her own feelings aside and think of a way to get through to Violet, to let her know that her foolish crush on their teacher was a bad idea, for so many reasons. Convince her to see what she'd be giving up if she wasn't careful. How could anyone want to trade Mike in for Andrew?

The next morning, Beth caught the bus over to Smithfield to buy all the books she needed for her new course. Excitement pulsed through her as she roamed the cobblestone streets, and she felt an amazing rush of confidence about her new career path, and her new life. She knew her parents wanted her to go into the family business in some way too, but she didn't care. The sunshine and the text books in her arms filled her with positivity – things were definitely looking up for her, and all the swirling of potential managed to drown out the twinge of guilt over her growing feelings for Mike. Soon she'd be too busy studying to worry about that.

The strangest and best development was that when she'd arrived home the previous night, her parents had been supportive of her decision to go back to school and become a teacher. Perhaps Jenny's "betrayal" in studying science, then turning down her assumed position in the family company, meant she was the favoured child now. Her mother had even conceded that she could stay in the family home when they moved to London, since they had no desire to sell, and no need for the money they'd get renting it out.

And to think that just five weeks ago she'd been terrified of facing her parents, and pining away over Andrew, so desperate to see him that she'd planned to throw in the nannying job she loved in Paris to work in a cafe in London just to be near him. Shaking her head, she laughed at how silly she'd been, and sent a silent prayer of gratitude to Rose, the goddesses she connected with, and whatever destiny it was that had brought her and her sister back together.

When she saw Andrew walking towards her moments later, arguing with a woman carrying a toddler who looked just like him, she thought she'd conjured him up like a ghost from her past. She was happy to note that she felt nothing for him – although why she'd decided on a vision of him she had no idea. A reminder of what she didn't want perhaps?

And yet, it was him. She stared, trying to figure out the body language of the couple as they paused next to a blue car and he continued berating her. Finally the woman, tall and pretty, with long red hair, strapped the child into his car seat, jumped behind the wheel and slammed the door, before screeching out into the traffic and driving off.

Before she could look away, Andrew turned towards her, caught her eye, and smirked. Mike's words from the cafe came back to her, and she felt anger rising within her. Anger at Andrew's dismissal of her, and his lies and condescension on the first day of the course, burned in her veins. Fury at what he was doing to Violet and to Mike blurred her vision. And concern for the woman in the car was a black cloud hovering on the edge of her consciousness.

"Beth, it's so good to see you." Taking her arm, he marched her into a cafe and slid them both into a booth, before she'd even registered what he was doing. He was smooth, she'd give him that, even as she discerned the insincerity of his tone. When the waitress came over he ordered for both of them, and she rolled her eyes. How strange that she'd been so blind to his patronising manner when they were dating.

"So, how are you enjoying the course?" he asked smugly.

"It doesn't start for another two weeks," she replied, then as she watched the smirk slide off his face, she realised he'd meant his course. *Oops!*

Trying not to laugh, she muttered something vaguely reassuring, then noticed the wedding ring on his finger. The face of the toddler in the red-haired woman's arms came back to her, and she shivered. What the hell was going on with him? He had mentioned an ex-wife when they were in France, but that woman she'd just seen didn't look so ex. And he'd specifically told her that he had no children, yet that kid was the spitting image of him. Had it all been a lie, all this time? Not that it mattered to her now – it was Violet she was concerned about, and Mike too.

"What are you doing with Violet?" she demanded. "She has a boyfriend you know."

As their coffees were placed in front of them, Andrew sneered. "You're just jealous that I'm with someone else now."

Her face flushed red, but it was with anger, not embarrassment or envy. "I'm not jealous at all," she replied, voice strong and steady. "I deserve to be treated far better than the way you've acted towards me. I refuse to be with anyone who would raise a hand to me for starters." It still mortified her that she'd accepted his apologies, and the promises that he wouldn't do it again. But lesson learned. She would never make that mistake again.

Intrigued, she watched his face change, and his voice soften, and saw regret cross his face. But was it real? "I am sorry about that. You know that isn't the real me, I was just so stressed – my ex-wife was manipulating me."

She gazed at him, one eyebrow raised in challenge. "The *wife* you were just shouting at in the street? The one who rushed to get your son out of there because she was scared you would hurt him too?"

It had just been a hunch, that it was still his wife, that it had been his child, but as he stared down at the thick gold wedding band on his finger, his face gave away the truth, even if his words didn't.

"Okay, the divorce isn't totally finalised, but we are separated," he said through tight lips.

"And your son?"

"He's living with Louisa, but I'm a caring father," he insisted, and she could hear the first signs of panic in his voice. She rolled her eyes again, then changed the subject. His marital mess was nothing to do with her – she only cared about Violet.

"What are you doing with my friend?" she repeated. "She's in love with Mike, and he with her. They're getting married a year from now. You have no right to come between them."

"Oh Beth, still so naive," he laughed, so mockingly, and her face reddened again. "Look, she may have loved Mike once, but she doesn't any more. He was her high school sweetheart, yes, but now she wants a *real* man."

Beth wanted to throw up, or shut him up, or both, but he was on a roll now. "Violet isn't content to stay in that backwater village forever, like he is. She wants to see the world, explore everything it has to offer, meet new people. She's a free spirit, and chaining her down would break her, would make her angry and resentful, you know that. She's outgrown Mike, outgrown your village, and she wants to be with me. And she's told you as much, hasn't she, that she wants me, that she wants freedom."

It wasn't a question, and Beth had no answer anyway. But his look of triumph was making her even more frustrated.

"Even Mike knows," he continued, and with a sinking feeling she realised this was probably true. Perhaps not consciously, not yet, but he'd just confided in her about the distance between them, and Violet's obsession with Andrew.

"I could tell her about you – let her know how you treated me in the last few weeks in France. Your violence, your manipulation. I could mention your wife and child – that would surely put her off.

Who needs that kind of complication?" Her heart sank as she realised that she'd accepted the truth of his assertion, that Violet was destined to break up with Mike. Now she was just trying to bargain him into leaving Violet alone.

"But if you tell her that, she'll just think it's sour grapes, that you want me for yourself, and are trying to come between us."

She paled. It wasn't true, but would Violet believe it regardless? She'd already decided it was too late to confess her relationship with Andrew to her friend, so her threat was empty, and he knew it.

A grin crossed his face, and she shivered.

"Besides, I know you love Mike, and how much you want him for yourself," he continued. "I've seen the way you look at him. What do you think your friend would say if she knew you were trying to steal her boyfriend? What a terrible betrayal, and you just settling down here and starting your new life, with new friends. Surely you don't want them to dump you so soon?"

She gasped. "You wouldn't!"

"Of course I would," he sneered. "And it's a small town Beth. I can convince Violet to ditch you, and tell everyone that you're a backstabbing boyfriend-stealer, a spoilt drama queen who just wants to cause trouble. Just like your awful mother. But who knows, maybe I'll tell them anyway."

He laughed, but she felt like she'd been punched in the stomach. He wouldn't do that, would he? Wouldn't destroy her reputation? But she knew the truth. He would do it, would do it happily. He'd already lied, and twisted the reading he gave Violet in class, just to make her think that she should be with him instead of Mike. Which seemed to have worked.

As despair started to swallow her, his voice changed. He became conciliatory, friendly.

"I don't *want* to do that Beth," he said, voice sly. "Surely you know that I would prefer that we were all happy, that we were all friends, that we were all loved. And it would be so easy. Because surely it would be better for everyone, better for Mike, that he finds a new girlfriend? Someone who will put him first, who will soothe his heartache and help him get over Violet. Someone like you?"

A flush of hope started to spread through her chest, but she tried to shake it off. She knew it was wrong.

"How can it be wrong?" he purred. "You'd be helping your friend get what she wants and needs, emotionally *and* physically." She shuddered at his implication, but he continued, unabashed. "And wouldn't it be better to be her confidant in that, and support her decision – since the outcome is inevitable anyway?"

She shook her head, but her resolve was weakening as she started to believe the truth of his words.

"And you'll be helping Mike too, comforting him, reassuring him, offering him new love, better love. Which will make Violet happy too, of course. What a wonderful friend, to assuage her guilt in breaking up with Mike by being there for him when she no longer can be." His voice was becoming more confident with every word, and Beth was drowning in the inevitability of the picture he was painting – and trying, without much luck, to smother the small, devious part of her that was thrilled it could all work out so well, so blamelessly.

"And you'll be helping yourself too," Andrew continued. "Now that you want to stay here and become a teacher, you and Mike are ideal for each other. He wants to stay too, wants to raise a family here, and wants to love someone who doesn't want to travel, doesn't want to go off and see the world."

The vision she'd had when the woman in gold had held her hands – her with a wedding ring, her with a baby – could it be Mike's baby? Could her life really turn out so perfectly?

Andrew laughed triumphantly. "Of course it can turn out that way. The wheels are already in motion, all you have to do is continue the way you've been going. Agree with Violet, when she talks about me. Tell her that of course I could love her, of course she is worthy. And tell her that she has outgrown Mike, and her village, and deserves more from life."

Beth blanched. Could she really manipulate her friend like that? Was it even true?

"Jesus Christ Beth, she's already in love with me! She just needs someone's permission to let Mike go. That's all that's holding her back – her ties to her high school boyfriend, her guilt at hurting him if she leaves. She needs to be reassured that Mike will be okay – and he will be, with you there to swoop in and mend his broken heart."

When he put it like that, she felt a little better about it all, but still, could she trust that all of this was true? Did Violet really love Andrew now, not Mike? She was certainly obsessing over him, but was it just a harmless crush on a teacher that would pass when the course ended, or what she really wanted?

"Plus, I can help you make Mike fall for you," he said slyly. "Pair you up in class, slip you the odd love spell ingredient. It will be easy. He already trusts you as a friend – which is another reason you should help me, if you want that to stay true."

His tone was threatening again, and a shiver of fear ran up her spine. Whether Mike loved her or not, she would be totally devastated if she lost him altogether, if he wouldn't even be friends with her. And she knew the man sitting opposite her would be quite happy to make that happen.

As Andrew pulled some money out of his wallet and threw it on the table between them, his tone became impatient again. "Beth, come on. You either encourage Violet to break up with Mike and turn to me – and get all that you want into the bargain – or I tell her all the very worst things about you, and she still ends up with me, but you'll be miserable and without friends. It doesn't bother me, because I win either way. It's just up to you how you want your life to unfold." And he stood up abruptly and walked out of the cafe.

So it was blackmail then. Which made it so much easier for her to decide. It would even make her mother proud of her, that she would be dating Mike. It really was win-win.

Beth smiled.

Chapter 28

Rhiannon... Today...

Bright sunlight streaming in the window at 5am woke Rhiannon up, and she groaned. She loved summer, but the early dawns were challenging. At least the school holidays had started, so she could sleep in... Until a loud bang quickly followed by squeals of laughter from the room next to hers reminded her that she had to get up. It was her brother's birthday tomorrow, and she'd promised she would spend all day baking food for the party.

Then she groaned again, as she remembered that today had been declared the perfect time for her to spend the day with a total stranger. She'd been putting off meeting Rose's suddenly discovered seventeen-year-old granddaughter for three weeks, and her dad and Rose had grown tired of waiting.

Rolling out of bed with a sigh, she pulled on her jeans, then rifled through her drawer for a clean t-shirt. It was time to do more washing, but it would have to wait – there were only so many chores she could do in a day, and enduring several hours with the orphan girl while she churned out endless pies and cakes was going to be enough for today.

After casting a longing glance back at her cosy bed and its soft pillows, she headed downstairs for breakfast with her brother, then nervously made her way over to Rose's ivy wreathed cottage. Meeting new people was not her favourite thing, and she was annoyed that her dad was so determined for her to become best friends with the girl from Australia. The girl who was the daughter of his first love. The girl who could have replaced her as her dad's child, in a parallel universe where he had married Violet, not Beth.

She knew he was worried about her emotional state, and the fact that her relationship with Debbie and Sue had become so strained since her mum's death – but that was inevitable, surely. They couldn't understand what it was like to lose your mother when you were only sixteen, so it was awkward between them because the things they were interested in seemed superficial to her in light of her suffering. And they weren't sure how to act around her anymore, so found it easier to do things without her, which she understood. But she figured that the gulf would heal eventually, given time.

And their last year of school would begin soon, so she was okay with hiding away from people and concentrating on her studies. Not that she actually knew what she wanted to do with her future, but she didn't need a social life, and certainly not one engineered by others. While she did feel sorry for – Carlie, was that her name? – it annoyed her that somehow the girl had become her responsibility. Yet here she was.

Heart beating rapidly with nerves, she finally worked up the courage to knock on the cottage door. She'd been here a hundred times before, yet all of a sudden she felt like a stranger. Now that Rose had a *real* granddaughter, she was worried that she no longer deserved to feel such a bond with her. And despite the priestess's assurances to the contrary, she feared Rose wouldn't have time for her any more.

And what would this interloper be like? She didn't understand how she could have never once been in touch with her grandmother. Left her sad and wondering all these years. Violet and her daughter must be pretty cold-hearted, to have ignored Rose all this time – until the girl decided to play up her family connection now that she needed her. Besides, the fact that the girl's mother had been her own dad's first love? That was just plain creepy.

For a moment she thought of fleeing, but before she could, the door swung open, and Rose's face lit up as she pulled her into a hug and welcomed her the same way she always had.

The silver-haired priestess led her out to the kitchen, where a girl with long dark hair was perched on a chair in their glass-walled breakfast nook, looking embarrassed as she tried to finish her cereal. Rhiannon's heart thawed a little as she saw how uncomfortable she was. It appeared that she wasn't exactly delighted by the idea of spending the day with someone she didn't know either.

"Sweetheart, this is Rhiannon, Mike's daughter," Rose said. "We were wondering if you could help her – it's her little brother's birthday tomorrow, and she needs a hand to make all the cakes and party food. I have to go in to work, but I said she could do the cooking here, so she wouldn't ruin the surprise."

Rhiannon giggled as Carlie rolled her eyes. It looked like she'd been completely unaware of their baking date, and was just as thrilled about it as she was. But Rose's hopeful face pierced the defensive armour of both girls, and Rhiannon smiled as she watched some of the new arrival's surliness fade, until finally she shrugged her shoulders and held out her hand.

"Ever feel like you're part of a conspiracy?" the girl asked her, in a strange and unfamiliar accent, and Rhiannon nodded as she offered a wry smile in Rose's direction.

"They have our best interests at heart, I'm sure," she replied with a touch of sarcasm. "But I can do this at home, if you have other things to do. I don't want to put you out."

Carlie sighed, but shook her head. "It's okay, I didn't have anything planned for today," she conceded. "I haven't cooked for a while though, so I'm not sure how much help I'll be."

Rhiannon was amused that the girl was clearly as unexcited as she was to have a friendship forced upon her, which made her relax a bit. She'd been expecting someone needy and draining, but the defiant seventeen-year-old looked fiercely independent, and as though she would refuse any offer of help, even if she really needed it.

The thought softened her towards the stranger, and she reminded herself that Carlie was in a foreign country, all alone, trying to deal with a life-changing event that would send most people off the rails. She vowed to be a little more understanding. Perhaps sensing this, Rose left them to it and headed off to work. Both were shy at first, but slowly they relaxed and began to open up a little.

Despite her misgivings, Rhiannon found herself liking Carlie – she looked just as annoyed with the adults and their clumsy attempt to bring them together as she was, and seemed to be just as sceptical as her too, which made her feel better. And hadn't she been yearning to meet someone who understood her own grief and loss?

"I'm so sorry about your parents," she ventured, her voice shy, but kind. "Dad told me. I know how hard it was to lose my mum, so to lose both must be twice as bad, at least."

She hadn't meant to bring up her own loss, and hoped Carlie wouldn't be upset that she was changing the subject back to herself. But the other girl expressed shock – clearly she hadn't been told as much about Rhiannon as she'd learned about Carlie – then sympathy at her pain. She was genuinely empathetic, and asked her questions in a kind, compassionate way.

It made Rhiannon realise what a relief it was to be able to talk about her mum, and how she felt about her death, without having to censor her words, or worry that she was making the other person uncomfortable. But she should probably be listening to Carlie, whose bereavement was so much more recent than hers, not burdening her with her own grief. So she asked questions in return, trying to be as sensitive as the girl she was slowly getting to know.

Carlie forced a smile, but in her hesitant, halting sentences, Rhiannon could see that beneath her politeness and understanding, anger was still bubbling close to the surface. And as the dark-haired girl tried to push it back down, Rhiannon realised that a lot of her own fury had lifted. How odd, that meeting this stranger was making her understand how far she'd come on her own healing journey.

The next day, Rose and Carlie delivered the party food for Brodie's birthday gathering. Impressed by all they'd whipped up, Mike allowed the girls to hide out in Rhiannon's room for most of the day. And although she had been worried they wouldn't have anything more to talk about once they'd revealed their stories of grief and loss, she was pleasantly surprised by how smoothly their conversation flowed, and how much she genuinely liked the angry, sad, yet somehow still-caring Australian teenager.

When Mike later knocked on the door and asked them to come down and sing Happy Birthday and help Brodie cut the cake, Rhiannon was actually smiling, and for the first time in almost a year, feeling genuinely happy. She almost laughed when she remembered Rose's words – that being of service made you feel better about yourself, and that it could give you purpose when you were feeling lost. She'd doubted that could be true, yet in trying to help Carlie, she did feel a little better, a little more cheerful.

After watching her brother unwrap his presents, then setting him and his buddies up with a new game, she saw Carlie leaning against the wall looking sad, so she grabbed two plates of cake and led her outside into their back garden, seeing it through the stranger's eyes.

It was beautiful, the scent of lavender perfuming the air, apple trees offering shade down the back, and the blue sky so vibrant overhead. As Rhiannon had a vision of the black clouds and threatening skies of the storms that had followed her around all winter, she marvelled at the healing power of the sunshine and its ability to warm the heart and lift the spirits.

Sitting down on the swings and staring up at the tor, she vowed to spend more time outside in nature.

"It's strange how the tor seems to move around, isn't it?" Rhiannon said to her new friend. "The tower is definitely at the top, but from here you'd swear it was built at that first resting place, just halfway up the slope."

Carlie shrugged, her eyes focused on the hill.

"I've been stuck up there a few times when the mists have come in, and it was so strange, like being in another world," Rhiannon continued. "And I've met people up there who couldn't really exist..." she whispered, then stopped abruptly, suddenly terrified that the other girl would think she was crazy.

But Carlie just nodded, and flashed a reassuring smile. "I saw a woman up there too, all dressed in blue," she admitted shyly. "She sat down right next to me, and hugged me, and spoke to me – but I'm still not sure that she was actually there..." As she trailed off, she grimaced, just as worried as Rhiannon that her companion would think she was mad.

Voice low, Rhiannon confessed about both of the times she'd encountered the blue-clad woman, and how protected, loved and understood she had felt in the warmth of her embrace. For some reason she couldn't bring herself to reveal anything about the woman in red though, still too horrified and ashamed of the events that had led to that meeting.

Carlie listened intently, then nodded again. "I felt really nurtured too, and so much closer to my parents in that moment while she held me up on the tor. I thought I was just dreaming it all though, but maybe I wasn't?" Then she grinned. "Or perhaps we both had grief-stricken hallucinations."

Rhiannon laughed. "Maybe!"

Yet they both wanted to believe it was possible. That the comfort they'd received was real. And Rhiannon was taking the woman's vocational advice. Nervously she told her friend about the instructions she'd received that day, to rethink her career plan, then she laughed at Carlie's shocked expression.

"I know, it sounds weird, hey? And I'm still not sure what I want to do anyway – sometimes I think I want to be a journalist, other times a children's author, another day I want to be a teacher like my mum. I wish she'd been a bit more specific," she said, then giggled. "Ungrateful of me, I know."

Carlie gazed at her, face serious now. "I always wanted to be a lawyer like my mum, ever since I was a little girl, so I know this sounds a bit strange, but after yesterday, spending time with you, and you sharing your experiences and being so compassionate and so empathetic, I've been thinking that I want to somehow help people who are grieving, who have lost someone. Everything you said to me has been so helpful, so caring, and I want to be able to help others the same way, to support them and help them heal, without pushing them to go too fast. A social worker, or a grief counsellor, or something... But I don't know, is that stupid? Is that even a job?"

Rhiannon stared at her, eyes shining. "It's perfect. And my god, that's totally what the woman in blue meant, I'm sure of it. If you don't mind me doing it too?" she asked.

"Of course not, you'll be amazing. I was thinking about it for you before it occurred to me that I could maybe do it too. And it would be nice to have someone to share the journey with, to compare notes with," she said softly.

"I just... I want to do something with my life that might make some kind of sense of the loss. Something meaningful, that will help people. And I hope that in studying for it as a career, it might help me heal too. Of course I have no idea what to do or where to go or even which subjects I should take at school this year in preparation, but it feels right somehow, to work towards that."

Rhiannon's face lit up with enthusiasm. "There's a university that's only forty-five minutes from here. I'll check out their courses tonight, and ask them to send us some information."

Rhiannon hadn't wanted to like Carlie – and she sensed the feeling was mutual – but despite their vulnerabilities and stubbornness, the two quickly became close friends. In Rhiannon, Carlie found someone who had experienced loss too, someone who understood her pain, and who seemed to have come out the other side much stronger. A survivor, someone who was not afraid any more, and who was no longer crippled by her grief.

And in the young Australian girl, Rhiannon found someone more broken than she was, who made her feel wiser and more mature than the way she usually saw herself. Someone who made her feel less inadequate, less cruel, less self-obsessed.

It sounded selfish when she put it like that, and she didn't mean she *only* liked her because she made her feel better about herself. She genuinely enjoyed spending time with her, enjoyed her humour and her scepticism. Carlie was smart, and sweet underneath her grumpy facade, and despite being from such different backgrounds, different countries even, they had so much to talk about, and so much to share.

It was odd though. She knew Carlie was really grateful to her for helping her, and listening to her angry outbursts and sympathising with her grief, but Rhiannon was grateful to her too, far more than Carlie knew. Her friends Debbie and Sue struggled to understand her, to seem normal around her, and she'd felt so lonely, so isolated, when she'd tried to hang out with them and act as though nothing had changed. It was such a relief that she didn't have to pretend with Carlie, didn't have to hide her bad days or diminish her grief to make the other person feel more comfortable. It was truly a blessing.

And in a strange way, Carlie made Rhiannon feel stronger too, and more capable. She made her see that she could survive her loss and sadness, and grow – had already grown more than she'd realised – and that she could still thrive, and live a good, fulfilled life, a life not totally bereft of joy.

Yet the Aussie girl also had a calm that Rhiannon envied, and an inner strength which meant that despite her heartbreak, she was going to survive her loss too. Not that she could see it herself yet, but perhaps no one ever did.

Carlie had only met Rose a month ago – had only discovered she had a grandmother then – and while she'd imagined her to be a monster at first, due to a tragic misunderstanding, she'd emerged from her anger, and their storm of trouble, with great respect for the priestess. And Rhiannon sometimes thought that Carlie was a lot like her, holding within her some of the same composure, the same calm and confidence the wise woman had.

There was a depth to Carlie, in the way she looked at the world and saw to the heart of things. Although she considered herself weak, and believed she'd handled her grief badly, Rhiannon saw her strength, saw her heart, saw her soul, and knew she would survive and grow even stronger.

But it was the epiphany the new girl triggered in Rhiannon that rocked her to the core. As Carlie described her grief, and the way she'd acted to those still left in her life in reaction to it, Rhiannon realised how well she was finally handling her own loss. Carlie treated her as though she held the wisdom of the ages, looking up to her and longing for her self-possession, and it made Rhiannon feel stronger than she'd assumed herself to be, and to view herself in a new, more flattering light.

Seeing herself through Carlie's eyes, she was able to glimpse her own strength, her own resilience, her own progress, her own healing. She would always feel her mother's loss, but she was living with it. She was a survivor. A teacher even. It made her feel a bit better about herself, a little more healed than she'd imagined she was.

And trying to help Carlie, to lead her towards healing and acceptance, was healing for her too. In acting more maturely, she was realising that she actually kind of was. She was whole, somewhat healed, useful and wise. And now, thanks to her friend, she had a new sense of purpose to explore.

Her mother would finally be proud of her.

Chapter 29

Into the Magic

As she pulled out her mum's faery-like gold and orange layered ritual dress from the wardrobe in her dad's room and slipped it over her head, Rhiannon thought she heard the whispers of old conversations around her. Her dad still hadn't had the heart to throw out any of Beth's clothes, or even pack them away, so they all remained here, hanging in jewel-hued rows, her school teacher outfits a little plainer than the outfits she wore to work magic in, but still a good reflection of her tastes and her creativity.

She could feel ghosts in the room with her, and as she sank down onto the floor, fingers running over the lush fabrics, she remembered so many moments she'd shared with her mum in this space. Watching her get dressed up for rituals with Rose. Staring at her, transfixed, while she put on make-up for a date with Mike or experimented with new hairstyles to go dancing with friends. Feeling the sensation of her mum's hands in her hair as she'd plaited it into elaborate braids for a school dance. Laughing, as a kid, when she'd put on her dresses and bounced around the room, hem held high so she didn't fall over.

Her eyes misted as she recalled all the beautiful jewellery her mum had let her try on, and how touched she'd been a few years ago, when Beth had given her the necklace she'd worn to every ritual and celebration she'd been part of, after Mike bought her a new, even more elaborate one for their anniversary.

It was around her neck now, a string of rose quartz beads with a huge pink heart pendant in the centre, silver filigree delicately holding it in place. She loved feeling the weight of it, and the smooth surface of the beautiful crystals. Her mum had told her she'd received it from a gold-clad woman who'd emerged from the mists one night, then laughed as if it was a great joke. Of course she hadn't believed her then – it sounded crazy – yet now that she'd experienced something similar, and Carlie had too, she wondered if her mum really had met an Otherworldly being when she was young.

It definitely intrigued her, but she still couldn't believe she was actually going to a ritual. She'd been turning Rose's invitations down for almost a year, because her mum's touching farewell ceremony had been enough, had been too much. She didn't have the strength to go without her mum, to go on her own – she would feel like a fraud. She would *be* a fraud. She wasn't magical. She wasn't special.

Yet Carlie wanted to go, fascinated by the idea of her newly discovered grandmother Rose as a priestess. She was also trying to learn more about her mother, Violet, who had been a strait-laced lawyer all of Carlie's life, and yet had, long ago, before she'd somehow ended up in Australia, dressed in brightly coloured gowns and danced under the full moon right here in this village, weaving magic and casting spells with Rose and her coven.

Rhiannon sensed that it frightened her new friend, this unknown side of her mother, and this unknown side of Rose. She didn't want her grandma to know this of course, scared of offending her, or seeming to criticise her. Yet Carlie wasn't religious, and hadn't been exposed to any alternative spirituality either, so she'd confessed to Rhiannon that the idea of spells by moonlight and invocations to a strange goddess seemed a little dark, and very foreign, to her.

She was curious though, and in search of answers, so despite her fears, she was eager to take part in a ritual to find out more. When she'd asked Rhiannon if she was going, she'd said no, and meant it, not feeling strong enough for the memories that would no doubt assail her there. But when Rose implored her to accompany her granddaughter just this once, so she wouldn't feel too alone, she'd reluctantly agreed.

Rhiannon had still been nervous, so nervous that her dad had finally offered to go with her. It was a big thing for him to do, because she knew how confronting it would be for him to return to his wife's domain, to be there while her old circle worked their magic without her. And now she knew he would also have memories of performing rituals there with Carlie's mum Violet, before he'd ever met Beth. What a sad and tangled web of love and loss.

And so she and her dad walked there together, lost in their memories. Not speaking, but comfortable with the silence, with the bond that their grief and love had forged between them. When they arrived at the healing centre they paused together in the doorway, exchanging a glance that was half affection, half fear, and both pondering escape. But when another participant arrived, they each took a deep breath and followed in her wake to the stairs.

Pain stabbed Rhiannon in the heart as she took the first step, and she was terrified that recollections of her mother's memorial ceremony would descend on her and crush her. Her dad's hand on her back steadied her though, physically and emotionally. He hadn't been here since Beth's farewell either, and wouldn't have returned of his own volition, so she was grateful that he'd offered to accompany her. It couldn't be easy for him to be here either.

"Thanks Dad," she whispered, and he nodded sadly, then turned to greet Rose as she welcomed people to the sabbat celebration.

The priestess's face lit up when she saw them, and she gathered them into her arms. Rhiannon felt guilty that she'd avoided her and her magic for so long, had kept turning her down when she was invited. Her mum's death had been a huge loss for Rose too, yet she'd been left on her own to cope.

"Sweet girl," Rose admonished her, voice gentle yet stern. "The time wasn't right until now. And I'm so grateful to you for coming tonight for Carlie. She's still a little distant with me, which I understand – it's her journey, and right now her anger is keeping her going. But it means the world to me that she can open up to you. Your mum would be so proud of you."

Rhiannon felt tears welling, but there was warmth and joy as well. And as the atmosphere in the room began to weave its spell on her, she smiled and allowed her senses to absorb the soft candlelight, the sweet spices of the incense, and the beauty of the flowers on the altar. It surprised her to realise that she'd missed this, and she laughed in delight. It wasn't just Carlie benefitting from their relationship – the young Australian girl had unknowingly returned her magic to her.

As Rose slipped away to prepare, Rhiannon's teacher Laura, dressed in red velvet, hugged her and Mike, then smudged them with burning sage and ushered them into the circle. Rhiannon waved at the women she knew, but stayed by her dad's side, still feeling intimidated and in awe of it all. Flickering candle flames cast the whole room in a soft golden light, and there was a gentle energy thrumming through the room, so low as to be almost imperceptible.

Yet she *was* aware of it. She *did* feel the power being raised and the web of interconnection between everyone present, and she drew it into her body, into her heart, as desperately as she would oxygen after a breathless climb up the tor. There was the same feeling coursing through her now that she felt when she was atop the sacred hill, and she marvelled again at how tangible it was. She'd doubted that she would feel anything tonight, and yet the ritual hadn't even started and she was already swept away in the enchantment of the room, of the people, of the night.

Beside her, she felt her dad inhale sharply, and their attention shifted to the centre of the room as Rose slowly and dramatically stood up from behind the altar. It never ceased to amaze Rhiannon just how different she looked when she transformed into her priestess role – changing from her sweet grandmotherly demeanour into a wild and powerful warrior woman, a representative of the goddess and a being of such strength and mystery she found it hard to wrap her head around. The normal Rose, the familiar Rose, was still there, shimmering around the edges, but within her was a core of steel and determination and sheer will, and a connection to the deities that left Rhiannon in awe.

"Welcome to our Lughnasadh ritual," Rose announced, in a voice that was part whisper, part shout, part invocation, and all love. As she spoke of the significance of this sabbat, which marked the beginning of autumn as the seasonal wheel turned from the abundance of summer towards the cold of winter, Rhiannon felt the words and the sentiment pulsing through her brain.

And as the priestess waxed lyrical about the deeper meaning of this time of feasting, celebration and thanksgiving, of the life-giving properties of the harvest, and of the things in their own lives they should be grateful for, her heart opened wide as she realised just how much she did have to be grateful for. Yes, she had lost so much – and yet here she was, surrounded still by friends and family, by the rich tapestry of this circle and this community, a community she felt reaching out to her and holding her safe, that loved her not just because she was her mother's daughter, but because she was herself. Accepted, understood, seen.

Across the room she saw Carlie, looking around in wonder and trepidation, and she smiled when she caught her eye. Warmth spread through Rhiannon. What she'd been hoping for for almost a year had come true. Her wish for a friend who understood her pain and loss had become reality, dreamed into being and grounded right here in this room.

And in a blinding flash she became aware that she was still connected to the magic she'd been so afraid she had lost. She'd been scared she would feel nothing, that the enchantment of the rituals she'd been to was just part of being with her mum, and nothing to do with her own innate thread of connection.

Yet she could feel the energy rising around her, feel the vibration of power as it slowly built, feel the warmth and tingling as it moved up from the earth and into her, coursing through her blood, her heart, her mind, then spilling from her out into the room and to those around her.

When Rose picked up a crystal-tipped wand from the altar and stepped outside of the circle of people to cast the protective border

they would work within, Rhiannon felt the whisper of the priestess's presence as she passed behind her, and thought she saw a trail of white light being spun by the wand, swirling around them and carving out a space between the worlds. Safe, nurturing, protective.

Rose's words wove around her, filling her, expanding her heart, and connecting her to everyone in this room, and on this planet. She hoped that one day she would have the composure and strength of the priestess, and the grace, compassion and capacity for forgiveness too. The wise woman had lost so much herself, had dealt with such tragedy, and yet she was here, full of love and power and empathy, giving everything of herself to whoever needed it.

By my will a circle formed,
Between the worlds where magic's born.
Contain the energy raised within,
As the veils between these worlds do thin.
Hold us safe throughout this rite,
As we create magic together on this night.
The circle is cast, so mote it be.

Her dad squeezed her hand, and Rhiannon turned to him, seeing her own sense of wonder reflected in his shining eyes, eyes filled with tears at his loss, but also a new understanding of how loved his wife had been, and how full her life. Bringing him tonight had given him an unexpected gift, and she was grateful all over again to Rose, for still including her despite having a real granddaughter now, and for opening her circle to Mike, and honouring Beth and her role in this community.

Then she looked at the women calling the directions. Her teacher Laura, who welcomed east and the element of air into the circle. Paulette, who welcomed west and the element of water. Miri, who called south and the element of fire. And Joanna, who called north and the grounding element of earth.

She was blessed to be surrounded by such strong women, friends of her mother's, and of Carlie's mother too. What a strange small world it was, that their mums had known each other, had been – two decades ago – part of this same circle of magical women. Had both been loved by her dad too, which was a more sobering thought, and yet she no longer felt jealous or insecure about that, she just felt even more connected to her new friend.

The poor girl. It had only been a month since she'd been sent all the way across the world on her own, bereft of everything she'd ever held dear, ever known, yet Carlie thought she was weak, selfish and self-indulgent that she wasn't totally over her grief already. Perspective was a funny thing. Perhaps her friend needed to start seeing herself the way she and Rose saw her – not weak, or cruel in her grief, but strong, and resilient. Open to the world, and kind of heart.

A laugh rang out in her head, and her gaze flew to Rose.

"And you need to see yourself the way we see you, sweet girl," the priestess said. Her lips weren't moving, but it was her speaking, and there was love in her voice, along with amusement.

Shocked, Rhiannon giggled before she could stop herself. "Touche," she whispered, then tried hard to smother her grin when her dad looked at her questioningly. It was time to focus on the ritual, to be present. Heart lighter, she took a deep breath – and then she stopped thinking and allowed herself to fall under Rose's spell and into the magic.

When she woke up the next morning it was still dark, but her head was full of spells, and possibility, and for the first time in a long time she dragged herself out of bed with a sense of hope. Her mind whirred, trying to process all she'd felt and experienced the night before, and she knew she had to do something more with the magic, something more formal.

Rose had told her repeatedly that she was welcome at all her circles, the eight sabbats of the ritual year, plus the monthly new and full moon ceremonies, but she wanted more, she needed more.

She craved some kind of study, something formal, because she wanted to understand the beauty of the previous night on a deeper level, wanted to know and be and do more. Wanted to understand her mum and what she'd held so dear. That Carlie was trying to find clues and answers to the mystery of her own mother, made Rhiannon realise there was still so much she wanted to know about hers as well.

Racing downstairs, she headed into the dining room-come-study and over to her mum's bookshelf. Like everything else of Beth's, it remained as it had been when she died, neither Rhiannon or her dad having the heart to throw anything out or even pack it up and away. Gratitude swept over her when she saw that all the witchy books were still there, colourful spines enticing her over to explore.

Grabbing some paper and a pen, she started flicking through the nearest magical tome, taking notes and marking pages. It had spells for everything from how to entice a man to how to cure a broken heart, which made her giggle. It wasn't until she found a more serious one, and started delving into the history of witchcraft as well as its more spiritual modern side, that she remembered the Book of Shadows that Rose had given her, along with her mother's personal collection. Breathless, she raced up to her room and slid hers out from under the bed, then reverently lifted her mum's down from the top of her wardrobe and slowly sank to the floor.

The moment she placed her hand on her mother's book, chills shot up her arm, and she felt a flutter of anticipation in the pit of her stomach. Shocked, she opened it to the first page, and a pulse of energy rushed through her, while a shock of pain stabbed her in the heart. But as she traced over the letters on the title page, Beth's Book of Shadows, a sense of calm swept over her, and she found herself smiling through her tears. Here was her sense of connection with her mum, and she felt sad that she'd waited so long to sit with her enchanted writings and unravel their mystery.

Time flew as she thumbed through the book, and her heart swelled with renewed love for her magical mother. Within the beautifully embossed pages filled with Beth's large, occasionally messy handwriting, Rhiannon began to see a new, deeper side of her mother, and a confidence and sense of purpose she hadn't been aware of.

There were spells, of course, but also the details of simple as well as complex rituals, with invocations to the many deities and the welcoming and farewelling of the directions written out, along with the activities within each one, and recipes for the treats to be made and served as part of each sabbat.

And there were pages and pages devoted to her studies too – the medicinal and magical properties of herbs, the meanings of and uses for crystals, the timing of the sabbats, the moon phases and even the tides. And there were details of divination exercises Beth had performed for herself, showing the fears she'd held and the things she'd longed for.

So much knowledge, so much passion, which her daughter hadn't ever known about. And Rhiannon finally realised how very seriously her mother had taken all of this, her identification as a witch, her belief in the goddess, and her initiation into the coven Rose had been running in the village for decades. She'd misunderstood it completely, thinking her mum had gone along primarily for the social aspect, to spend time with her friends and catch up on gossip and their day-to-day lives, just marking the seasons on a superficial level. But her mother's words revealed a complex and long-lived connection to the world around her, to the cycles of the moon, and the rhythms of the sun, and the turning of the earth.

There was a deep and binding association with the other women of the coven too, relationships she'd never recognised, or seen revealed, relationships that had been such a crucial part of Beth's life. And throughout it all her love and respect for Rose was paramount, so clearly spelled out in each word she used, in each ritual she recorded.

Desperately Rhiannon wanted this in her life, not just to feel closer to her mother, but to feel closer to herself. Beth's book revealed a strong sense of self, and self-awareness, and she realised that witchcraft was a path of personal development, of understanding yourself and becoming a better person.

Each ritual they'd created also contained an aspect of service. Collecting food or knitting blankets for the homeless as a way to express their gratitude for their own lives. Offering healing to those in need. Planting trees in spring or protesting a harmful local development to honour their environmental concerns. Their coven wasn't about what they could get out of magic, but how they could find new ways to give to others.

Inspired by the words in her mum's book, she headed back downstairs with renewed purpose, and began searching the shelves again. Her dad and Brodie came and went, offering her breakfast, then lunch, then inviting her to the park with them, but she turned down their offers and kept reading, and scribbling down notes, until finally she had it all straight in her mind – what she wanted, what she willed, and how she would go about it.

Thrilled, she went back up to her room and changed into her favourite purple dress, put her mum's magic-infused necklace on, lit a sandalwood candle, then opened the book Rose had given her. With a silver pen, she began to write.

Dear Goddess,
Today I commit myself to a magical path, a path forged by Rose, and by Mum, a path of love, strength, giving, wisdom-seeking and exploration.
Please bless me with inspiration and courage for my journey, with patience and wonder as I dedicate myself to study, and commitment and hope as I delve deeply into the Mysteries.
I will walk this path to honour my mother, and I will walk it to be the best version of myself that I can possibly be. To repay the kindness people extended to me in my grief, and atone for the times I failed Brodie and Dad as I tried to deal with my pain.
With love, Rhiannon

A smile lit up her face as she felt herself filled with purpose, and excitement burned through her. She couldn't wait to talk to Carlie about it. She imagined her friend was just as keen as her to unravel the magic that their mothers had practised, to connect with the source of spirituality that had been so much a part of their lives – at least for a while, in Violet's case.

And through a strange quirk of fate, the more one of them learned about her own mum's magical journey, the more the other would learn too, since Beth and Violet had once been friends, had once been students of the same wise woman, had once loved and been loved by the same man. The parallels were spooky, yet it seemed fitting that she and Carlie would embark on this journey into the Mysteries together, each as innocent as the other, as cheerfully unenlightened and unaware, but with the same priestess to mentor them as their mothers had been blessed to have.

For a moment she wondered how this was affecting Rose. It must be unnerving to see dark-haired Carlie and blonde-locked Rhiannon in the circle together, both looking so much like their mothers. How had she found the compassion to love Beth as a daughter all these years, when she'd expected her own flesh-and-blood child to marry Mike?

Yet the priestess had made it very clear that discovering her biological granddaughter would not change how she felt about Rhiannon, who she'd loved as family since the day she was born, and she had been true to her word. With a sigh, she wondered how she could ever have doubted that Rose had enough love for all of them.

Then her thoughts turned to Carlie. It must be so overwhelming for her, to have suddenly discovered a grandmother she didn't know existed, then to learn that her mum had once had a whole other side to her, a whole prior life that she'd never seen any sign of, never glimpsed a hint of.

The Aussie girl had revealed to Rhiannon that she'd had a secular upbringing in Sydney – so it would have been quite a shock to have been launched into a magical ritual, surrounded by women in floaty velvet dresses with flowers in their hair and a cloud of incense misting around them as they honoured nature and the goddess, and all of them drawn together by her own priestess grandmother.

A few days later, too curious to wait any longer, Rhiannon knocked on Rose's door. She was still a little shy, and unsure of Carlie and how she felt about the magic. What if she was just being polite that day at Brodie's party, and didn't really want to be friends? What if the ritual had totally weirded her out? What if she didn't want to have anything to do with her, or with magic?

Before she could wimp out and go home, Rose opened the door, hugged her, and ushered her inside. "Sweet girl, hello. We just started brewing a pot of tea, so come in and join us," she said, leading her out to the sun-filled kitchen.

Carlie looked up from the book she had open in front of her and smiled. "Hey Rhiannon, how are you? Are you already dreading the end of the holidays?"

Rose bustled around, bringing another cup over to the table and pulling a tray of cinnamon cookies out of the oven. Rhiannon raised one eyebrow. "Were you expecting guests?" she asked, anxious again. "I can come back later if that would be better?"

Rose's eyes twinkled. "Only you sweet girl. Come, sit down. I was just heading out to the garden." Rhiannon highly doubted that she'd really been on her way outside, since she'd been brewing tea, but she played along, making small talk until Rose left the girls alone.

"So what did you think of the ritual?" she asked Carlie the moment the back door had closed.

"I really enjoyed it," she began, eyes alight with enthusiasm, but voice still hesitant. "It was very strange though, and I'm still trying to get my head around so much of it, because it doesn't make sense that I could feel all those things with just the power of someone's words..." She trailed off, then quickly changed the focus. "What about you? Did you like it?"

Rhiannon smiled, warmth filling her as she thought of standing in the circle with her dad, and feeling the sense of connection with her mum. "I loved it. I was really nervous, I must admit – I'd been to a couple of Rose's rituals with Mum before, so it was tough to walk in there without her. I felt her absence from my life so strongly. But it also made me feel a little closer to her."

Pausing, she bit into a cookie, trying to think of how to proceed. "To be honest, I wasn't actually sure that I'd feel anything, but I really did."

Carlie grinned. "Me too! But it's so hard to reconcile that with my logical brain. I know you're familiar with all this stuff, but it's so strange to me. And the fact that my mum used to go to these circles, but I had absolutely no idea, that was tough. How could she have cut that part of her life off so completely? Did she miss it? And I couldn't help feeling just how much Rose lost in a magical sense as well when she lost Mum – not just her daughter, but a part of her witchy circle."

Rhiannon frowned as she tried to work out what to say. She couldn't admit that her own mum had stepped in and taken Violet's place – as Rose's student, as her fill-in daughter, *and* as Mike's wife. But Carlie seemed... not totally unaware.

"I know Gran still wove her magic with the rest of her circle, and that it included your mum. And she still misses her so much," Carlie offered, and Rhiannon felt such gratitude, that even while her friend was grieving her own parents and trying to come to terms with this strange new world, she was sensitive to everyone else's feelings too. She knew Carlie thought she'd been mean to everyone after her parents had died, but she disagreed. She was as thoughtful as she would expect from a granddaughter of Rose's – very.

"Had you been to many rituals before?" she asked.

Rhiannon shook her head. "Just those few with Mum before she died, but only the more social ones. I never did any serious ritual work, because she thought I was too young, and I probably was. Then after she died, Rose kept inviting me, but I just couldn't bring myself to go on my own. And to be honest, deep down I wasn't sure I'd feel anything. I wondered if I'd just imagined it before, or felt something because I knew Mum wanted me to. And I was worried it would make me too sad, be too much of a reminder of what I'd lost." Then she grinned. "But it was amazing, I really loved it!"

Carlie nodded in agreement, and poured them more tea.

"I loved it so much that I've been doing some research over the last few days, reading Mum's old books on magic, and trying to work out the best way to learn more, and do more…"

Excitement sparkled in Carlie's eyes. "Me too! I've been poring through Rose's books, trying to find answers. And I've started reading my mum's Book of Shadows, which is blowing my mind – it's not just all the amazing research she did, on herbs and crystals and divination and spellcasting, which is absolutely fascinating, but it's also a strange adventure into rediscovering my mum, and what she used to be like, before she went to Australia. It's like meeting a brand new person. Some of the things I'm learning about her are a little disturbing, but it also makes me feel really close to her."

Flabbergasted, Rhiannon stared at her. "I have my mum's Book of Shadows too! Rose gave it to me on New Year's Eve, but I threw it on top of my wardrobe and forgot about it, until the ritual the other night. I felt guilty about that, but maybe I wouldn't have appreciated it as much if I'd looked at it earlier. After the ceremony the other night though, I woke up so inspired, and it was amazing to dive right into her work – it was so personal, but in a really beautiful way."

Carlie smiled. "Same! So do you have any ideas about what we should do? Is it something we can learn at a workshop or course, or do we need to study via books and articles or something? Or just keep going to Gran's gatherings?"

Drawn to the window, Rhiannon smiled as she watched Rose tending her herb garden. "Well, I don't know about you, but I felt a bit overwhelmed the other night, and definitely a *lot* underprepared. I'd really like to do some independent study before the next ritual, so that I feel more confident, and can appreciate it all on a deeper level."

Sighing with relief, Carlie grinned. "Me too."

"So I was thinking that maybe we should create our own little working group, so we can discover things together, and ask all the questions we want to without feeling like we're holding anyone back, or revealing our ignorance."

Her friend nodded. "That sounds wonderful!"

And it did. When Rose came back in from the garden, cheeks red from the early autumn sunshine, they peppered her with eager questions. And the priestess was overjoyed that the girls were getting along so well, and were so willing to dive into the magic that had sustained her through so much loss.

Chapter 30

Beth... Twenty years ago...

In the darkness of a moonless night, Beth tiptoed down the stairs and let herself quietly out the kitchen door, creeping across their huge yard to the gate in the back fence. Holding her breath, she carefully unlatched it, praying it wouldn't squeak, then slowly swung it open. Sighing with relief that it had remained as soundless as her, she turned in to the laneway and made her way quickly down the darkened path, heading away from the village.

She stumbled a few times, her eyes not used to the pitch black outside her small, weak circle of torchlight, and swore under her breath, but she kept walking. It would have been easier to do this when there was a moon to illuminate her way, or if she'd taken the main road, which had a few street lights on to pierce the darkness. But she'd timed her ritual so she could make use of the most potent energies, so no light it was.

For the past week, since her encounter with Andrew in Smithfield, she'd been furiously studying all the books of magic and the occult that he'd dropped off at her house. They were books Rose didn't stock in her healing centre, and she suspected that was because the priestess wouldn't approve of their content, or of her planned spell – to the binding of another person to her, and interfering with someone's free will.

But it seemed to her that Rose's magic was far softer and more gentle than some witches employed, more about enriching and empowering everyone to be more fully themselves and to help others, than changing circumstances and creating what you wanted, consequences be damned. It was enticing, and tempting, this new view of spellworking.

Finally she reached the woodland on the edge of town, and gingerly made her way into the trees, along the narrow winding path she'd memorised in the daylight hours, until she reached the small clearing. Slipping the coat from her shoulders, she gasped as the cool air touched her naked flesh, but her shivering was more from desire than the cold, from the sensuality of the wind caressing her body, making her feel so alive, and at one with the world and with herself.

Body, mind and spirit they said, and she grinned. Rose's magic was safe, and sweet, but too much about the mind and spirit, and not grounded enough in the body, in the reality of flesh and carnal pleasure. That's what she'd discovered in the books Andrew gave her – a whole other realm that embraced power and the self, so different to the magic Rose shared with the villagers at her rituals.

Goosebumps rippled across her skin, and she let the sensation awaken her to the magic of the night, to the passion burning within her heart and her body, and to these darkest moments before the dawn. It was the dark moon now, the time for banishing and binding. Then when the sun rose in a few hours, so too would the new moon, which would fuel her spell and help her manifest her wishes and grow the relationship she was so intent on.

Feeling her way through the bag she'd brought with her, she pulled out the thick golden pillar candle, placed it in the glass lantern, lit a match and held it to the wick. Then, invigorated by the cold air on her warm skin, and the headiness of her will, she carefully began to step out the boundary of her sacred circle, the way Rose had done it at the rituals she'd attended. Although the priestess hadn't ever done it skyclad. She giggled at the thought.

Rose was too tame, too afraid of sensuality, and sexuality. Too content with words and metaphor. But it seemed important to Beth, if she wanted to capture Mike's interest, and his body as well as his heart and mind, that she offer up all of herself to the gods and goddesses – not just her words, and her wishes, and these herbs she would burn, but her vulnerable heart and her brave and naked self as well. She wanted all of him, and she wanted him to want all of her.

And how could he resist her, she thought, lips curving in a triumphant smile as she gazed down at her full breasts and the curve of her hips, caressing with her eyes what she wanted him to caress with his hands and his mouth. She was far more worldly than sweet, innocent Violet was, far more of a woman than she'd ever be, and she was determined to convince Mike of that truth.

With the wand she'd bought in Rose's store raised in her left hand, she carved out the etheric world between the worlds she would create and form her ritual within, while her right hand drizzled a handful of salt crystals infused with crushed rose petals in its wake, to add a circle of physical protection to her spellworking, and the emotional energy of love that this flower held.

Then she sank down onto the cold ground in the centre of her small circle, at her makeshift altar, and lit the three candles, one pink for love, one red for passion, and one white for eternity. For a moment she recalled the image of the silver-haired woman from Rose's healing, who had handed her three coloured roses that represented forgiveness, joy and innocent love, but she shook it off. Tonight was for passion, not innocence.

Inhaling the scent of the rose-vanilla wax pillars, she took out a small velvet pouch, and carefully arranged the rose quartz crystals within it into a heart shape that framed the edges of her altar and mirrored the rose quartz heart nestled against her chest, a gift from the woman of the mists to prove her connection to magic – a connection that now infused every cell of her body.

The crystals represented the earth, and love, while the candles symbolised the element of fire, and the power of passion. She added a small dish of spring water, to represent water and the flow of inspiration, then lit a cone of patchouli, known for its aphrodisiacal properties, and representing air. Breathing in its scent, she slowly stretched her arms skyward. Sinuous, seductive. Reaching up to the last twinkling stars before the dawn would begin its slow dance. The flickering light of the candle flames cast shadows on her naked skin, and she smiled. She felt powerful, aware of the strength of her body, the sensuality of it, and the beauty of her self and her soul.

For a moment she felt a pang of regret, as her thoughts turned to sweet, trusting Violet, who had surprised her by becoming a close friend. She was kind, considerate, selfless, and no doubt above spellcrafting to get what she wanted. But she had Andrew now, and didn't need Mike, so really she was doing this to *help* her friend, so Violet wouldn't feel guilty about hurting Mike with her obsession over their teacher. And she was doing it for Mike too, so he would no longer mourn his lost love, with her to soothe his heartache.

It was a win-win situation, she told herself.

A vision of Rose's compassion-filled face flashed into her mind when she closed her eyes, and she felt a sliver of guilt, but she turned away from it. She was doing this for the good of everyone involved. *Really, it was almost selfless. Right?*

Tentatively at first, she invoked the elements and directions then the god and the goddess, her voice gaining in confidence with every word she spoke. Lastly she reached back into her bag and pulled out the small bottle of jasmine oil, a flower known for enhancing and amplifying love and desire.

Pouring a few drops onto her finger, she anointed her forehead, then dabbed a few more drops between her breasts, then on her solar plexus. She shivered, but it was from desire and anticipation, not the cold. Despite the wintry temperature of the woods in this pre-dawn hour, from the moment she'd stripped off her coat she'd felt warm and toasty, at one with the elements and the spirits of the trees.

Taking a deep, centring breath, she sat and focused on her breathing, just as the spell book had instructed, deepening each inhalation and exhalation until she felt the sharp and rigid controls of her mind slacken, then blur, and a dreamy haze descend.

Joyfully she acknowledged a moment of triumph as the trance state she'd read about settled over her. She'd been worried about not being good enough, not being magical enough, to make this work, but already she could feel the enchantment dancing around her, and the desire building within her. It felt as magical as any of the rituals she'd done with Violet and Rose at the healing centre, it was just that this time *she* was offering up the intent and controlling the outcome. *She* had the power.

Holding on to the swirling sensation of mystic awareness that swooped around her, she poured the herbs she'd crushed earlier into the small clay dish she'd borrowed from her mother's garden, and mixed them gently with her finger, pouring her intent in as she worked.

Picking up the little witch's knife she'd also bought secretly, she sliced into the ring finger of her left hand, into the vein said to run directly to the heart, and dripped several drops of her deep ruby red blood into the dish, mixing it with the herbs. Then, unrolling a thick piece of parchment paper and taking up the beautiful, expensive quill pen she'd invested in, she dipped the nib into the still-dripping gash on her finger, and wrote out her invocation in her own blood.

> *Gods and goddesses, hear my plea,*
> *Bring my greatest wish to me.*
> *With my blood I bind his soul,*
> *With our love, both become whole.*
> *Mike and Beth, both true of heart*
> *In love forever, 'til death do us part.*
> *So mote it be.*

Glancing up at the sky, she marvelled at the beautiful wash of colour just starting to appear along the eastern horizon, and the thinnest sliver of the tiny crescent moon that could just be seen as it peeked over to begin its slow climb to the heavens. Her timing could not have been more perfect.

Clutching the parchment to her heart, she spoke her fervent desire aloud, repeating the rhyme three times, and imploring with every molecule of her being, every yearning of her soul, the gods and the goddesses to grant her wish as she whispered it to the universe.

It was at this point that one of the books suggested raising energy to fuel the spell through sexual release, but at the last moment she lost her nerve. The still-dark woods were secluded, but the day was now beginning, and the first rays of the sun were illuminating the top of the trees around her. For today she would settle for using the transformative power of fire to take her words and her wishes to the deities. There was time enough for sex magic later, when this spell had bound Mike to her.

Already she was planning to enact the Great Rite with him – and she would do it properly, in the body, flesh to flesh, the way it used to be done. Not just placing an athame into a chalice as a symbolic representation of the ritual, as Rose did, but undressing Mike as he undressed her, then leading him into the sacred circle and raising energy and power through real sex. Through making love.

That was the way it was done in the past, the high priest and high priestess embodying the god and the goddess and joining together in the sacredness of sex during the ritual, blessing the lands with their physical bonding, and balancing the energies of their coven, their village and their whole country if need be.

She was starting to like this magic business.

Finally shivering from the cold in the pale dawn light, Beth carefully unwound her circle, then gathered up her ritual tools and placed them reverently back into her bag. She had felt the exact moment that her spell had been sent out into the universe, and the wonder of it still warmed her heart.

Her body was exhausted though, totally drained from the intensity of her ritual focus and the fuelling of the spell with her own energy and will. As she reached out for her clothes, she wobbled slightly, then collapsed onto the cold ground, light-headed and dizzy.

Remembering Violet's instructions at her first ritual, that after working magic you must eat in order to ground yourself, she reached a shaky hand into her bag and felt around for the container of biscuits she'd baked the night before. Her cheeks blushed red as she recalled her mother's terse words when she'd made them just before Jenny's wedding as a test run. Patricia had stormed into the kitchen, drawn by the apparently devilish scent of butter and sugar.

"How dare you cook biscuits this close to the wedding," she'd thundered. "I always knew you wanted to sabotage Jennifer's ceremony. I don't know why you even bothered coming back for it – or was it just to wreak havoc?"

Beth had been flabbergasted, and speechless in the face of such an awful accusation, but Jenny had reached over to the tray of still-warm shortbreads, picked up the biggest one she could see and crammed it into her mouth.

"I asked her to make them for me Mother," she'd said, with a wink at her sister. "A few cookies are not going to ruin anything, no matter how much that would secretly thrill you. Besides, Josh loves me for me, don't you get it? I don't have to be stick thin to keep his interest, not like *some* women," she'd added, and there was a stab of malice woven into her sister's words that Beth had been shocked – but impressed – by.

Biting into a biscuit now, she felt the energy sweep back into her tired limbs, so she could reach into her bag for the clothes she'd thrown in earlier. She slipped a dress on over her naked body, then buttoned up her long coat over the top. Grinning, she decided that she must look almost normal again. Not that it mattered too much – she was pretty sure she wouldn't see another soul as she stumbled home in the early morning light, but she knew how angry her mother would be if she was spotted by anyone looking less than immaculate – and wearing no underwear, no less.

The image made her giggle, then she sighed. Had she always been so scared of and yet so angry with her mother, or was this combination a new thing? Fury and fear. It was no way to live. But she comforted herself with dreams of Mike – and her new life in her hometown, now her parents were definitely leaving. A week from now she would begin her journey to become a teacher, which she'd always longed to be, and soon she would have her heart's desire too.

As she walked, her thoughts returned to Mike, and her eyes lit up in anticipation. She wondered how her spell would work. Would he all of a sudden realise that it had always been her that he loved, or would it take a more subtle path, a growing awareness of his new feelings for her that were revealed to him over time?

Weakening for a moment as an image of Violet floated into her head, she tried to shake off the guilt, but the sudden grey storm clouds gathering overhead matched the pessimistic mood she'd begun drowning in, and she quickened her pace.

The first drops of rain fell as she opened the back gate, and she ran the rest of the way to the kitchen door, making it just seconds before the heavens opened. Breathing a sigh of relief that she'd managed to stay dry – and that her parents weren't up yet – she tiptoed upstairs and into her room. Mission accomplished, she thought, with a sense of joy and satisfaction that managed to eclipse any glimmer of guilt that still lingered about Violet. She flopped down onto her bed and fell into a deep, trance-like sleep.

Two hours later her mother barged in, complaining that she was sleeping the day away, and furious that she wasn't already up and helping the cleaning women she'd booked in preparation for their move to London. Yep, Patricia was still fulfilling the wicked stepmother to her Cinderella role.

It would normally have bothered her, and perhaps led to a shouting match, but today Beth just smiled, feeling surprisingly calm and magnanimous, and jumped out of bed and started packing up all the books and business ledgers in the study.

It didn't even bother her when her mother criticised the way she was packing, or complained about the speed, because all day the memory of the enchantment she'd woven that morning stayed with her, shielding her in a protective bubble that deflected all of her mother's bitter barbs and poisoned arrows.

Once or twice Patricia looked at her questioningly, surprised that she hadn't snapped at her or lost her temper, but Beth really did feel that the magic she'd worked and the spell that she'd cast had permeated her body, her mind and her soul at a deep and powerful level, and was making her more likeable to herself, and far less irritable with her mother. Had her anger these past few weeks, these past few years, been because she hadn't liked herself?

Chapter 31

Into the Mists

Rhiannon... Today...

As the mists rose up around her, Rhiannon smiled. She'd always loved the mists. There was something so magical about them, so cleansing, as though she could travel through them to another world, another time, another place. One where her mother was still alive, and she didn't have to look after her father and her brother. Not that she minded, not really, but every now and then she felt so hemmed in it made her cry. So weighed down by her responsibilities that she wanted to scream. So lacking in magic that she felt bereft.

Sighing, she tried to pull herself together. She loved her dad, and adored Brodie, and it was a privilege to be able to help, especially as she'd been emotionally absent for three months after her mum died. And she still had her dad and her brother – Carlie had lost her whole family. She needed to get a grip.

Taking a deep breath, she allowed her mind to still, and concentrated on appreciating the magic of this moment. Tonight she and her friend were consecrating their newly formed coven with a dedication ritual, and she was excited, and happy, and just a little bit nervous too.

The girls stood at the base of the tor together, ready. The sky was already a gorgeous lavender-gold in the west, where the sun was preparing to set, while the eastern sky, where the full moon would soon rise, was coloured with the faintest hint of pink.

Rhiannon felt Carlie shiver beside her, and she glanced at her, seeing the fire of the candle she held reflected in her eyes. They'd decided to take different paths to the top of the tor, to symbolise their separate lives before now, then meet on the summit, to represent the deepening of their friendship and the shared magical journey they were embarking upon. She turned to begin her climb.

"Wait," Carlie called out. "Maybe we should swap our flowers, so we have something of each other's to bring with us on our climb, to lend each other a bit of strength and support?"

Rhiannon nodded, impressed with the suggestion, and glad her friend had found the courage to speak it. They were both still shy about this magic they wanted to weave – worried that they were frauds, that they were somehow making it up, that they were only pretending they could feel the power of the energy they were drawing up from the earth, and breathing in from the trees and the moon and the stars.

Awkwardly they exchanged their bunches of flowers, then whispered a blessing and turned away from each other again. This was it. Carlie set off, weaving her way along the more gentle, winding pathway to the top, while Rhiannon headed around to the back of the tor, to the place where she could start her journey up the shorter, much steeper trail.

Lost in thought, in enchantment at the beauty of the sunset and the magic of the approaching twilight, she tucked her flowers into the bodice of her dress to keep a hand free, so she could dig her fingers into the earth of the hillside when necessary, to pull herself up, or grab on so she wouldn't fall when it became especially steep. It seemed fitting somehow, that she had chosen the more difficult path, the most challenging climb.

And she was determined to conquer it, because in some way she felt that this physical achievement could be symbolic of the emotional battle she was waging in her mind. That proving she was stronger physically would translate to her being stronger mentally, and thus allow her to conquer those demons.

So lost in thought was she that she didn't notice the mists that were thickening around her, although she was grateful for the cool air that was soothing her hot cheeks, which were already red from the exertion of the first half of her climb. But suddenly she almost stumbled into something, and her eyes flew upward from the grass of the hill to the face of a woman who had appeared right in front of her. Her heart beat a mile a minute. She'd thought they would be alone out here tonight, and her shoulders drooped in disappointment.

Would their ceremony be ruined by the interruption of others? Should they give up now and go home, maybe do their ritual inside, rather than out under the full moon? The thought saddened her, because nature was so much a part of the path they were committing to, but she knew that intent was important too, and if they had to change venue they should just roll with it and make the best of things. But still she sighed… until her heart started hammering again.

As she peered more closely at the woman, she realised that parts of her were still as insubstantial as the mists, and the blue gown she'd thought she was clothed in was actually transparent in some places. Was she a ghost? For a moment fear thrummed through her, but the being smiled at her, with a look of such love and comfort that her terror slowly faded away.

"Ah Rhiannon, my brave and shining one," she said, as she moved forward and enfolded her in a hug. A sense of joy and peace came over her as she melted into the embrace, and she smiled. Was this the blue-clad woman, the same one who had held her close while she cried that long-ago day on the tor? The one who had shown herself again a few months later, and taken her hands and encouraged her to reconsider her career plans?

The figure before her inclined her head regally in acknowledgement, and Rhiannon bit her lip to stop herself pouring out a diatribe of questions, challenges and comments. She wasn't sure that would be welcome right now.

"We are so happy you are taking this step with your friend, committing to your magic, and to your own growth and inner peace," she said, although her lips didn't appear to move, and Rhiannon wasn't sure whether the sound she was hearing was coming from within her own head or outside of it. Could she be making this up, thinking something magical was happening because she wanted so badly for it to be true?

But the woman kept speaking, words of love and hope, of the power of nature and the wisdom of their circle and all the potential it held. Rhiannon's heart lifted, and her excitement grew – until the message changed, and cryptic words of warning were added, of the possibility of betrayal, and the need for her to trust even when it seemed undeserved.

Panic rose in her, and she started to wonder what it meant, and whether it was Carlie she couldn't trust. But within moments a calming sensation enveloped her, and the blue-clad woman smiled at her so sweetly, so reassuringly. All her worries fell away, and Rhiannon took a deep, steadying breath, focusing again on the beauty of the sky and the magic of the mists swirling around her. When she turned back to the woman in blue, she saw that she had a silver chalice in her hands, and was holding it out to her.

"For you, when things get hard," she explained, and there was love, compassion and understanding in her voice as she leaned over and placed it in the velvet bag slung over Rhiannon's shoulder. "And for your friend," she added, slipping a small object into her hand.

"It's beautiful," she whispered, entranced by the way her candle flame glittered on the chalice's surface. She looked back up at the woman to thank her, but there was no one there, just the mists that continued to dance around her and in front of her. She shivered.

People said this hill could get into your mind and your heart, could play tricks on you, and it seemed as though she had fallen prey to it too. Yet nestled in her palm was a silver ring, with a delicate silver butterfly on it, and wings that were made from sparkling aquamarines. And in her bag was the beautiful silver chalice, complete with inlaid moonstones. These things were real, even if the woman of the mists was not.

Eventually she shook herself. She couldn't stand here forever trying to puzzle it out. Carlie was probably up on the summit right now, wondering where she was. Quickly she resumed her climb up the steep grassy slope, and by the time she got to the top, she was breathing heavily, her cheeks rosy with the effort, but eager to begin, and relieved that Carlie was alone up there. No one would interrupt them tonight.

Her friend's face was flushed with excitement, and before she had even put her bag down, Carlie had presented her with a gorgeous silver ring with a dragonfly on it, its wings formed from tiny pink rose quartz crystals – twin to the one she'd been given for Carlie. Thrilled, she handed that one over, then they both shared the stories of their encounters.

While Rhiannon had been listening to the blue-clad woman, her friend had been conversing with a woman dressed in green – the beating heart of the tor, she'd explained, and of the nature and landscape of this country, someone they could call on when they needed to ground themselves and connect back to the earth.

"Maybe this means they're happy for us to be here, to be making magic in this sacred place?" Carlie asked hopefully.

Rhiannon nodded. "The one I met said that she's glad we're doing this too, which was a nice confirmation."

Both were quiet after that, lost in their own thoughts, and Rhiannon suddenly wondered if Carlie had received a warning about *her*. Would she fail her new friend in some way? The idea that she might betray someone worried her, but she pushed the fear aside so they could start their dedication ceremony.

Kneeling together on the lush grass at the top of the tor, the girls set up their altar. Rhiannon placed two large candles in pretty glass jars in the centre, to represent the god and the goddess, then poured the blend of lunar herbs she'd mixed that morning into a small dish in the east, to represent air, and set a golden candle in the south to represent fire. Carlie added a large piece of clear quartz in the north to represent earth, and a small cup of lavender-infused water in the west for water.

Then she carefully unwrapped an athame from its green velvet pouch – a gift from the green-robed woman, and pair to Rhiannon's chalice – and raised her eyes to the darkening sky. Inhaling a deep, centring breath, she slowly paced out a circle, with the ritual knife tracing the lines of its border as her words cast their intent and manifested the protected space between the worlds they would work within into being.

> *Within this circle, that our intent will form,*
> *Between the worlds, a safe place born.*
> *Ancient beings of this sacred hill,*
> *We call to you with our deepest will.*
> *Please hold us close throughout this rite,*
> *Reveal the magic on this full moon night.*

The air seemed to shimmer as she came back to the place where she'd started, and Rhiannon gasped as golden sparks danced around Carlie's head, just as the moon began to rise slowly above the horizon. She felt a sensation of warmth and power slide over her shoulders, warming her, and lending her the confidence for the next step. It was her turn to speak, to welcome the elements and the directions, so she filled her new chalice with spring water, then raised it above her head as she turned to face the north.

> *Guardians of the north, and element of earth,*
> *Please ground us with your strength and nurturing,*
> *and watch over our sacred rite.*

> *Guardians of the east, and element of air,*
> *Please grant us your intuition and clarity,*
> *and share your wisdom with us this night.*

> *Guardians of the south, and element of fire,*
> *Please burn away our fears and doubts,*
> *and flood us with your power and might.*

> *Guardians of the west, and element of water,*
> *Please wash away all we no longer need,*
> *and allow us to soak up this magical moonlight.*

They stood opposite each other in the centre of the circle, one on each side of the altar. Gazing skyward again, Carlie raised her arms and invoked the goddess, looking as though she was gathering all the energy of the universe within her.

Then Rhiannon raised her hands and eyes to the sky and called on the god, and for the blessings of all the deities on their ritual of dedication. She felt the magic weave around her, comforting her, strengthening her. And she felt a huge release, a softness of sorts, soaking into her very bones, and leaving her calmer, and stronger, and more complete.

When she closed her eyes, she saw the woman in blue before her, wreathed in mists and with a smile on her face, and no matter the message she'd received or the warning within it, her heart lifted. She felt peace and contentment coursing through her blood as she thought of the steps she and Carlie were taking tonight, formalising their coven and declaring to the world, to the gods, to themselves, that they were serious about their magical studies and their journey into the Mysteries.

Smiling, she sank down onto the cool grass, and inclined her head in Carlie's direction. Her friend nodded, then lifted a small, thin gold candle, and bent forward to light it carefully from the central flame. Somehow managing to keep her cascade of long dark hair away from the tiny golden light, she held it to her heart, then looked towards the horizon as the huge glowing ball of the full moon continued to rise slowly in the darkening sky.

I light this flame to symbolise the growing flame in my heart, as it awakens to the magic that flows within me, and the sense of ancestry that runs through my blood and connects me to this land. I come before you, goddess and spirits of place, humble in your presence, to commit to learning more, understanding more, sharing more. I am grateful to Rhiannon for allowing me to share this with her, and I promise I will work hard, research well and often, remain open minded, be supportive, and commit wholeheartedly to our Tuesday night study circle.

Carlie seemed to be buzzing, energy coursing through her as she spoke. When she finished, she secured her candle in a small glass holder and smiled over at Rhiannon. She nodded, then took her own thin gold candle and lit it from the central pillar too.

> *I light this flame to be a beacon of hope and love, to illuminate the darkness so that Mum can see me from wherever she is. Tonight under the silvery beauty of the full moon, I promise to honour the Old Ways, to step where my mother once walked, on the path of the goddess, and to pledge my support, my time and my heart to the coven that Carlie and I are consecrating tonight. Blessed be.*

"Blessed be," Carlie echoed. A cool breeze set their candles fluttering, and the girls collapsed back onto the grass, suddenly feeling light-headed and spaced out.

After gratefully farewelling the elements, the directions and the deities, then closing their circle, the girls grounded their energy with fruit juice and spicy moon cookies, then headed back down the hill for their sleepover.

That night Rhiannon dreamed of the woman in blue, who repeated her messages from the tor. She was trying to warn her, to prepare her, for a coming war, or a battle of wills, and of the potential of her friend to betray her. There was a test to come, she kept repeating, and Rhiannon would have to hold close to her faith, hold close to her trust, no matter what.

"There are things you cannot see, things you cannot know, that will make you doubt the ones closest to you," she said urgently. "Remember your faith in them, even when it seems no longer deserved. This will test you as much as them, believe me. And you will pass, if you stay true to you."

The next morning when she woke there were tears on her pillow. The words betrayal and trust echoed through her mind, but she couldn't latch on to any of the other words in order to make sense of it, so finally she shrugged her shoulders and dismissed her worries. School was starting the next day, and she had to get ready.

When the alarm shocked Rhiannon from sleep on Monday morning, she groaned and pulled the covers over her head, before remembering that it was the first day of school. The first day of her final year. And she was surprised to find that she felt a lot more positive about it than she'd expected. Before she'd met Carlie she'd been dreading returning, but having a friend who understood her, a friend who needed her, made all the difference.

Jumping out of bed, she headed for the shower, then made sure Brodie was up before skipping downstairs to make breakfast for them. Their dad had already left for work, but he'd made them both lunches, and left a little note with each one. Grinning as she read hers, she hurried Brodie along so they could walk to school together.

"Rhi-Rhi, are you going to move away and leave me?" he asked plaintively.

Shocked, she stopped and knelt down so her eyes were level with his. "Why would you think that?"

"Ben said his sister can't wait to finish school so she can escape this crummy village and move to London," he said, lip quivering. Admittedly the thought had crossed her mind too, but that was a while ago. Now she was actually excited about staying here, of learning more from Rose, and studying to be a grief counsellor with Carlie at the nearby university.

Grinning at Brodie, she shook her head. "No buddy, I'm not going anywhere, I promise."

Face brightening and voice stronger, he took her hand again. "And will Carlie keep coming over to our place?"

Curious, she stared at him, trying to understand where the question was coming from. "Probably, because we'll be studying together, at school and out. Why, is that okay?" she asked, suddenly worried her brother didn't like her friend.

But Brodie nodded vigorously. "Yes, I like her," he said. "You've been happier since you met her. And it's like she makes you stronger or something, more content."

Gobsmacked, she stared at her little brother. Her little brother who wasn't so little any more. And she realised that for some reason she'd frozen him in time as the innocent child who hadn't understood what it meant when their mum died, the one who couldn't comprehend her sadness and despair, didn't realise just how much they'd both lost. And yet, he was growing up, and he was seeing her and their dad and how they reacted to things. She'd have to keep that in mind.

Suddenly she felt a stab of guilt. Had their dad been right to not let him come to Rose's memorial ritual for their mum? Was it wrong that they hadn't taken him to their mum's grave yet? To act like it was perfectly normal to lose a mother so young, and try to hide their own anguish from him? And even if they'd been right then, perhaps things had changed, and they should include him in their remembering of Beth now?

"I'm glad you like her," she finally said, and ruffled his hair affectionately. This was definitely something to talk about with her dad when she got home tonight.

When they reached the primary school she leaned down and hugged him before she let him go. A ferocious hug, in which she tried to convey all her love and affection for him. And he let her for a moment, until his friend Ben came towards them, and he quickly squirmed out of her arms and ran off onto the playground. She grinned. There was still a lot of the kid in him, which made her happy. She would hate for him to have lost all of his innocence.

Hurrying across the road to the high school, she made her way to the assembly hall just in time to get her class schedule for the term. She felt a twinge of guilt when she saw the relief on Carlie's face that she'd finally arrived, then disappointment when they saw they were in different classes for the first three today. But fourth period finally came around, and they filled each other in on their mornings before their teacher arrived.

They were both shocked, yet excited, when Laura, Ms Henderson, explained their assignment for the coming term. They would be studying pre-Christian gods and goddesses, and would each choose one to do a project on.

"No prizes for guessing who you two will do," she said to the girls as she handed a list of deities around the room. They stared at her in confusion. Carlie had recently discovered that her mum had named her for Kali, the goddess of life, death and destruction, but Rhiannon?

They ran their eyes down the list, then raised their eyebrows as they saw her name there too.

"Rhiannon is the Celtic goddess of healing, inspiration and the moon. And she's especially associated with this area," Ms Henderson revealed. "Your mother named you well. You'll be honouring her memory as you research this project, and you may come to know her even better too."

Rhiannon felt a fluttering in her tummy, a sense of excitement and possibility. That's what she wanted to do, learn more about her mum, learn more about the goddess, and it was being handed right to her.

When she got home from school that afternoon, she settled Brodie at the kitchen table with a glass of milk, some crackers and a colouring-in book, then pulled out the beautiful Book of Shadows Rose had gifted her with. She was determined that it would be every bit as magical as her mum's was.

I found out today that Mum named me for the goddess Rhiannon, a deity of transformation and inspiration, and an example of love, grace and beauty to many. She's connected with birds and horses, and with the cycles of the moon and the stars, and is considered by many to be a faery queen, dwelling in the Otherworld. I wonder if she knows our friends from the mists?

She is a goddess of love, of fertility and of dreams, and is associated with the horse deity Epona, the ancient British goddess Rigatona, and the Lady of the Lake. The moon and the winds are sacred to her, and she reputedly possesses great magic.

Also known as the night queen, she was falsely accused of a terrible crime by her people and unjustly treated by her husband, but she endured her punishment with patience and love, grace and dignity, confident that truth and balance would eventually prevail — and she forgave all those who'd wronged her once they did.

Her symbols include birds, horses, horseshoes, the moon, gates and the number seven. She's a goddess of healing and forgiveness, and she and her birds sing songs that heal, that mend, that rescue people from trouble, that grant sleep to humans and awaken spirits. Oh how I wish to connect with her — maybe she can sing a song for me, heal my hurt, heal my pain, or wake Mum's spirit so I can speak with her again...

Oh! This all reminds me of that moment up on the tor, when I saw the white birds, which the blue-robed woman called angel terns, or faery terns. What did she tell me? "They represent peace, and hope. And they have come to whisper to you of magic, and of healing. Sweet Rhiannon of the birds, of healing and inspiration, they are a part of you, a reminder to you that you hold all that you need within you. That you are stronger than you think." Maybe if I work with this goddess, I will feel stronger, feel healed. Or maybe it will help me heal others. She also sounds like the perfect deity to invoke while Carlie and I are studying to be grief counsellors.

To start working with this goddess, I'll need to pick up some supplies from Rose's shop this weekend – her gemstones include moonstone, quartz, amethyst, garnet and silver. And I'll visit the nursery, as her plants include daffodils, pansies, narcissus, bayberry, rosemary, sage, cedar and pine trees. Her colours will be easy to incorporate though, by wearing white, silver, dark green, maroon, grey or red clothes, which I already have thanks to Dad, or even just ribbons in those hues in my hair.

Most of all, I love that you can invoke her to help you work on issues of self-trust, self-knowledge and inner strength, and that she also inspires people to discover their own ways to survive, and to survive with joy, after a situation that seems terribly bleak. I'm not sure I'll ever be at the joyful stage regarding the loss of Mum, and I don't need to be, but I'm feeling more hopeful now that at some point I will feel that I'm not just surviving, but will eventually thrive.

Classes at school the next day seemed to go on and on, because all Rhiannon could think about was their first coven meeting that night. Excitement and nerves battled within her all day – excitement that she and Carlie would begin working magic together, just like their mums had so long ago, and nerves that she would get it wrong, or be exposed as a fraud. Yet it went off without a hitch.

Her friend was impressed by the circle of tiny tealight candles she'd laid out, marking the physical border of the liminal place between the worlds they would work within, as well as the small altar she'd set up in the centre, and the blend of sandalwood, lemon and lavender oils she was burning to cleanse and clear the space, and help them stay focused for their evening of magic and mysticism.

Rhiannon was impressed too. Although she suspected Carlie was hesitant about being in a coven, she had researched and written an essay on athames, the ritual tool she'd received at their dedication ceremony on the tor, which was as in-depth as the one Rhiannon had written on chalices. It seemed they were even more in synch with each other than she'd hoped.

They talked about the Great Rite, which was performed in covens using the athame and chalice to represent the marriage of the god and goddess, the joining of the high priest and high priestess, and the combination and balance of masculine and feminine that is at the core of the earth, of people, of all of life.

"Perhaps that's why we were given these two gifts, rather than anything else, so that our dedication incorporated the god and the goddess in a really deep way?" Carlie pondered. "I also found a reference, in a very old book, that talked about the Lady of the Lake gifting a chalice and a sword to someone worthy of those gifts. Perhaps that's who you met, the one who gave you the chalice. Lady of water, of lakes, of blue."

Rhiannon's face lit up. "It's such an awesome mystery, isn't it? I mean, who are they? Are they even real? The things they gave us are certainly real, but I can't work out how a person could materialise like that, or have such knowledge about us."

They went back and forth for a while, but eventually they paused, acknowledging that they might never understand, but content for now to leave it as a mystery.

The following Tuesday night, Rhiannon went to Carlie's. When she knocked on the door she was out of breath, and hastily trying to compose herself, but she laughed when Luther started weaving around her ankles. She'd always loved Rose's black cat, thinking him especially perfect for her witchyness, but now it seemed he'd adopted Carlie. Which was a good thing. His purring was especially soothing, and he had a wisdom that was hard to explain, but definitely felt.

She'd been surprised when Carlie had told her she hadn't had an animal companion back home in Australia, because the love she felt for Luther was visible and real. And it cracked her up that Luther was the archetypal, stereotypical witch's cat, green-eyed and shiny black, with a grace unusual in a cat so old. He'd been with Rose for as long as she could remember, so he could be… fifteen years old? More?

He stared up at her, his eyes assessing, and she giggled. "Oh Luther, you don't have to be suspicious of me! I love Rose and Carlie, and I know you do too."

Why was he was eyeing her like that? Or was she just imagining it? Ever since their coven dedication, when the woman in blue had warned her that Carlie might betray her, she'd been feeling a little paranoid. Foolish of her, really. She was in charge of her own fate, and her own actions. She wasn't going to do something she didn't want to do, just because a woman of the mists had told her she would, and nor would Carlie. *God, sometimes she thought too much!*

Relief washed over her when her friend finally opened the door, and she could stop thinking, stop second-guessing herself. It was time to start doing…

The two girls sat in the kitchen drinking tea with Rose while she shared stories with them about Mabon, the next sabbat in the Wheel of the Year, which celebrated the autumn equinox. The priestess told them the history of the festival and then revealed the literal and metaphorical meanings attributed to it, and helped them delve into the herbal correspondences and foods associated with the sacred day. They scribbled all of it down in their Book of Shadows, eager to catch and capture every piece of wisdom the wise woman was prepared to offer them as they soaked up the magic.

"All the festivals have a traditional meaning, rituals that have been celebrated for hundreds of years, but the meaning you attribute to it is just as important, and just as valid, as anything someone came up with last year, or last century, or wrote in a book. Whatever you feel is right, is right for you, so don't ever let anyone tell you that you're wrong. The magic you create and send out into the world, that comes from you. That's why a spell you dream up will be far more powerful than any you find in a book, because it's imbued with your energy, your intent, and your power," she explained.

Rhiannon's face lit up with happiness and hope. She had always been in awe of Rose and her wisdom, and now she was inspired as well. To be told it was her own energy and intent that would make magic happen, that would give a spell or ritual its power, filled her with joy and enthusiasm, and fired her up with passion. And she vowed to dedicate herself even more fully to her magical studies.

A few days later, Rhiannon took one of her spell books to school, and she and Carlie flicked through it in their lunch break, rolling their eyes at some of the more bizarre inclusions, but bookmarking others to add to their own Book of Shadows so they could try them out later.

"It's the new moon this Sunday – which is the perfect time for casting love spells," Rhiannon said, sneaking what she hoped looked like a casual sideways glance at her friend. Carlie seemed nervous, but agreed they could give it a go.

"Do you want to cast a spell for love or lust?"

Carlie blushed, and Rhiannon giggled. She'd just been teasing her friend – she only wanted love herself, but there were plenty of spells for both. Agreeing to change their upcoming coven night to Sunday to take advantage of the lunar energies, they got ready for their next class just as the bell rang.

"Don't forget to work on your list of things that you want in a guy!" Rhiannon called out, as she waved goodbye and rushed off to chemistry. The irony wasn't lost on her, and she spent the whole class considering a very different kind of chemistry, and what qualities she wanted in a potential boyfriend.

When Carlie climbed the stairs to her friend's bedroom on Sunday evening, Rhiannon was physically prepared for the ritual – a sweet incense blend she'd crafted that morning was burning on the altar, pink and red candles were positioned around the room, flickering warmly against the fading sky outside, and on the altar a large piece of rose quartz sat in the centre, surrounded by pink and white rose petals. Emotionally though, she was a bundle of nerves. She'd never done a spell before, and she was scared she'd mess it up. And while she'd been flippant when she'd spoken about it at school, trying to pretend she didn't care about true love, trying to pretend she was far more worldly than she actually was, the truth was that she was a novice at relationships, just like she was a novice at magic.

There had been a guy she liked last year, before her mum got sick, but that had fallen by the wayside after Beth's diagnosis. And when her mother died, she'd been a total mess. For a year, romance had been the last thing on her mind. At the Lughnasadh ritual she'd started to feel a little less fragile though, a little more likeable, a little more worthy perhaps, so she tried to convince herself she was ready to open her heart, and that she deserved to be loved.

Not that there was anyone at school she was interested in, but that was the thing with spells, wasn't it – you sent what you wanted out into the universe, and trusted that you would attract it to you. Of course there was more to it than that – the spell was just the beginning, and you had to work diligently towards the outcome as well, not just sit back and wait for it to be handed to you.

So how would that translate with a love spell? Her mind raced. Maybe she'd just have to remain alert and aware. Prince Charming didn't know where she lived, so he was hardly going to come around and knock on her door, begging for a date. She would have to go out into the world so she could meet him. Start to interact with people again. Leave the house.

For a moment she quailed at the thought, but becoming friends with Carlie was important. She was letting someone in. Being vulnerable. Opening up to opportunities. Helping someone in more pain than she was in. Becoming more sociable. And she was starting to have fun again.

The thought hit her with the force of a blow. Since she'd been hanging out with Carlie, she'd actually been laughing again. Having moments of light within the darkness. So now seemed to be a good time to start focusing on love. There was no way anyone would have been interested in her surly, angry, grieving self, even if someone *had* come to her door, and she'd been in no fit state to accept love either.

But her heart had been lighter of late, and that was a good first step. It also helped that she wasn't desperate or anxious – she could be patient. For now she was quite happy having fun with her friend.

Then guilt slammed into her. Was it bad for her to be enjoying life again? Making friends? Should she be obsessing over love, now that her dad was a widow? Should she even be contemplating boyfriends when her mum was dead?

"Thank you for convincing me that I still deserve love," Carlie said, breaking in to her thoughts. "Deserve to love someone, even when everything I loved is now lost, and deserve to *be* loved, even though I was… well, not so nice to people."

Rhiannon's attention snapped back to Carlie, and she gazed at her thoughtfully. Here she was, thinking she didn't deserve love, after almost a year of grieving – yet she'd told Carlie that *she* deserved it, just a few months after her parents had died. Why was it always so much easier to see things for other people? She wasn't just being nice to her friend either, she genuinely thought she deserved love. So it was about time she started taking her own advice.

"Are you okay Rhi?" Carlie asked gently.

Oops! Time to be present, in her body and in this room. Smiling at her friend, she nodded, then handed her some matches to light the candle, while she lit the incense. Instantly the magic swirled around them, and her heart lifted as she felt a hand on her shoulder. Could it be her mum? Here to reassure her that it was okay to move forward? It was a nice thought.

She anointed Carlie with jasmine oil, then watched as she cast the energetic circle they would work within. Then it was her turn, and she welcomed the goddesses of love to their rite. Branwen, Celtic goddess of love and beauty. Aine, Irish goddess of love and fertility. Venus, Roman goddess of love and beauty. Aphrodite, Greek goddess of love and fertility. Ishtar, Babylonian goddess of love and procreation. Freya, Norse goddess of love and magic. Hathor, Egyptian goddess of love and beauty. Inanna, Sumerian goddess of love.

As the air seemed to shimmer around them, with whispers of voices and echoes of fragments of songs, the two girls sat in the middle of their sacred circle, each with a red and a white candle, which they anointed with jasmine oil then carved love hearts into with a white-handled boline.

A shiver ran up Rhiannon's spine, and she felt the presence of the goddesses standing behind her, steadying her, letting their warmth and acceptance settle around her shoulders, around her heart, and holding her close.

Inspired, she took a piece of paper and a pink pen, and wrote down all the qualities she wanted in the person she was welcoming into her life, while Carlie did the same.

> *Goddess, thank you for the blessings you have bestowed on me, and the precious gift that I still have my dad and my brother. I miss Mum so much, but I know it is time for me to open my heart again, to let someone in.*
> *I want to meet someone who will understand me, and cherish me, and allow me my moments of sadness and despondency, knowing that it is not a failing on their part that I am like that, but a part of my journey.*
> *Someone who is strong yet soft, confident yet caring, interested but not obsessive, intuitive, kind, and understanding. Someone who will love me just the way I am...*
> *With much love and gratitude, Rhiannon xx*

At the exact same moment both girls put their pens down and looked up at each other, the candlelight sparkling and dancing in their eyes, and together they began to chant:

> *As a new lunar cycle starts with today's new moon,*
> *We ask that you send new love to us soon.*
> *Someone whose heart and soul we can fill,*
> *Someone who comes of their own free will...*

As they said it for a second time, both girls gently held a corner of their parchment into the flame of their candle, and watched as their lists curled up and started to smoke, their wishes released into the cool night-time air and sent skyward to meet the tiny crescent moon.

Just before the paper burned down to their fingertips, they dropped the remains into the small cauldron on the altar, then held hands and chanted their invocation for a third time, ending with the witchy equivalent of Amen, "So mote it be."

Rhiannon wasn't sure if it was the heady scent of the jasmine oil or the wafting smoke from the incense, the presence of the deities they had called on or even the spirit of her mother, but she felt a tangible shift in the energy surrounding her, felt a lightness, as though a weight was lifting from her shoulders, and a bolt of pure energy slammed into her heart.

And when she slept that night she dreamed of a tall blond guy with broad shoulders and a kind smile.

Chapter 32

Embracing the Magic

Excitement pulsed through Rhiannon as their train pulled up in London and they jumped off, two people in a sea of strangers pushing towards the exit. It was a week after they'd cast their love spell, and she and Carlie were in the capital to spend the day at the Body Mind Spirit Festival. Rhiannon grinned. Not only had she found someone who understood her grief, but her new friend was as intrigued by spirituality as she was. She was so excited by what the year ahead might bring for them.

When they got to the convention centre and entered the huge concrete halls, Rhiannon felt a thrill rush through her. She absolutely loved the wall of heat, light, colour and sound that hit them as they walked through the doors, and it was all overlaid with the scent of sage and sandalwood – the scent of magic. Her face lit up with joy, and she turned to Carlie with a laugh. But her friend looked shell-shocked, and Rhiannon felt a pang of remorse.

She had assumed Carlie would enjoy it as much as her, but she seemed terrified, which was odd, since she'd lived her whole life in the huge metropolis of Sydney. Then again, the festival was its own little world, carved out of the city, not part of it. As her eyes flashed over the rows of stands and the crystals reflecting beams of light in all directions, and she became aware of how loud and intense it all was, she realised some people might find it overwhelming.

"Are you okay?" she asked gently. Carlie stared at her, trying to hide the emotions flashing across her face, and managed a hesitant nod.

Rhiannon giggled, but took her hand. "Come on, I'll protect you," she promised, pulling her into the middle of the first aisle. "Do you want to book a psychic reading first, so we can plan our day around that, and then maybe we can go and check out the seminars and see what's on?"

"Sure, whatever you want, I'm in your hands. Just don't lose me," Carlie pleaded, only half joking.

Smiling, Rhiannon led her into the safety of a book stand and left her there while she organised appointments for that afternoon. When she got back to Carlie she tried not to laugh at the relief that she'd returned emblazoned across her face. Then her eyes widened as her gaze rested on the stand opposite them.

"Oh, it's Rowan! Do you want your spirit guide drawn while we wait?" she asked her friend, dragging her over to a stand where the walls were covered with beautiful paintings of various animals, druids, shamans, and what looked like faery people.

"Hi Rowan! We'd love to have a spirit guide drawing done today – both of us if you can fit us in?" Rhiannon said, voice a little breathless. "You can do my friend first."

He glanced at Carlie, and his face paled for a moment, before he quickly recovered. "Okay," he said. "You first though. Your friend can come back in half an hour."

Turning nervously to Carlie, she raised an eyebrow in question, scared she would say no to having to wander off on her own, but her friend just shrugged and said she'd be back soon, and headed off down the aisle. Rhiannon breathed a sigh of relief and turned back to the young druid artist.

She'd had a crush on him ever since she'd seen him teach a seminar at a festival she'd gone to with her mum a year ago, and she'd read as many magazine interviews with him as she could find, and seen photos of his incredible artwork, each one speaking to her in a profound way. She could feel the magic of each piece, no matter what the subject matter was. He was amazing – so talented, and so charismatic. And, well, he was gorgeous too, she thought with a grin.

She knew from reading about him that he was a very well-respected healer too, admired even by older, more experienced wisdom keepers, and he was also inspiring a new generation of young people to explore spirituality. It was an honour to be able to have a session with him, and she couldn't believe her luck that they'd found him before he got booked out.

"You can come in Rhiannon, and take a seat," he said softly, and she stared at him, embarrassed. Had she just totally zoned out and been ignoring him?

He grinned. "It's fine. The energies are always a bit weird here," he offered, and gratitude swelled within her, that he was putting her so at ease. "Now just relax, and breathe," he said, voice gentle, and she felt her body becoming softer, more languid, as she lowered herself into the chair at the back of his booth. Her mind started drifting, and for a moment she wondered if he was working some magic on her.

"Nothing specific, but I'm connecting with your guides, asking them what you need to know, so they are around you, cocooning you, holding you safe while you lower your guard to reveal your inner self and inner heart to us."

Making the decision to let go, she allowed herself to float upwards. For a moment she was afraid, as she gazed down at her body, and at Rowan standing at his easel watching her, but eventually her whole body seemed to sigh outward and then relax into it, and she rose up out of the exhibition hall, above the city, and flew, following the curves of the river, then relaxing on a fluffy white cloud. Soon she was darting this way and that with an eagle, then diving back down to the water and landing on the back of a gorgeous white swan.

It was crazy, but she felt a kinship with the proud white bird, and she leaned into its neck, cuddling up against the softness of its feathers. Then, with a shock, she felt its mind reach out to her, and open up to her – and then it began to speak, and she almost fell off into the water.

"Dear girl, I am here to remind you that you must figure out how to balance your family commitments and school work with friendship and play, and find a way to recover and re-energise, so that you do not lose yourself."

Before she could wrap her head around the concept of a talking swan, she was suddenly drawn down under the water, under the ground, into the centre of the earth. She wasn't scared though, because she felt strangely at home, and very much at peace, and was soothed by the nurturing darkness.

After what felt like hours, she rose up, above the surface, and was flying again, but she was no longer in London. In an instant she'd been transported to a beautiful green meadow. A small white horse stood in the corner, under a shady tree, and it lifted its head and whinnied softly before trotting gracefully over to her, lowering its head so she could pat the velvety nose. Leaning towards him, she closed her eyes and placed her brow to his, and felt a cascade of golden light flashing before her darkened eyelids.

"Perfect trust," the horse said softly, and inexplicably she understood him. "You are safe beloved, and you are worthy of love." Happiness washed over her as the words lodged within her heart, until she felt her body dissolving, transforming into golden sparkles, and for a while she and the horse's essence danced together in the sunshine, their souls merging, and her consciousness lifting with the sheer joy and sense of freedom she felt. Time stopped, and the whole world slowed as she swooped around the glade, free of her body, of physical pain, even of grief.

But then a fierce wind surrounded her, enveloping her completely. Panic jolted through her and her heart raced, until she felt a soothing hand on the place where her shoulder would be, if she had a body anymore, and slowly the sensation of peace returned.

"Rhiannon," said a chocolate-smooth voice, and she felt it guiding her back to London, back to the hall, back down into Rowan's booth, and back into her body. Slowly she opened her eyes, blinked, and saw the artist peering at her, his hand on her shoulder, a gentle smile on his face. "Welcome back."

She blushed, worried about how she'd looked and what she'd done when her whole soul, her whole consciousness, had deserted her physical self. But he was gazing at her calmly, as though nothing out of the ordinary had happened. Perhaps he was used to people vacating their bodies while he worked.

Worked. Her drawing. What would it look like? Eagerly she stared at the back of his easel, desperate to see it, and he laughed. "Don't panic, it's all done," he said, and she blushed again at her impatience. It was weird, that he knew every single thought she had. Kind of creepy, if she thought about it too hard. Although, oops! Would he have heard that as well?

Hiding his smile, he turned back to the easel and lifted the sheet of paper, then held it up for her.

She gasped, genuinely shocked, and impressed, and delighted, all at once. "Oh my god, Rowan, it's gorgeous!"

In the centre was a vision of Rhiannon in a flowing white dress, her long blonde hair floating around her, and her body merging somehow with a proud white swan, the details of the feathering so intricate, so subtle, that at first you didn't realise that she was half bird. The words of the swan echoed through her mind, and she stared at Rowan in awe. How had he known?

He shrugged, dismissing what an incredible feat it was, and she turned back to the drawing, her gaze sweeping upwards to the top right corner, where a small white horse was depicted, with a trail of golden stars travelling from the middle of its brow to the middle of Rhiannon's forehead.

Her mind whirled as she recalled the sensation she'd felt when the golden sparkles of her soul had merged with the white horse she'd met, and she actually felt teary as she gazed on its wild, innocent beauty. But they were happy tears.

"The wild, innocent beauty is yours Rhiannon," he said softly. "What you saw and experienced, it was all just a reflection of you."

Her heart swelled, and she looked at him with gratitude.

"The swan will be with you whenever you need strength, and will remind you of your purpose when you feel lost. It represents beauty, balance, commitment, dignity and grace, and is all about finding balance between work and play in your life, letting go of pain, and focusing on hope. It wants you to be fearless, and to defend what is right," he explained.

"And the white horse is one of the goddess Rhiannon's animal companions, and is a symbol of love, grace and dignity, and enduring through hardship. Surviving pain to gain wisdom."

Shaking her head, she tried to take it all in, but it was tough. Had he somehow seen her visions?

"Not your visions, but the swan and the horse came to me, and shared with me what they wanted you to know, so I could incorporate it into the artwork, to remind you always of what they told you, and what they mean to you. They want you to see and recognise your own grace and beauty, your own strength. They want you, not to forget your pain and your grief, but to let it transform you, let it push you forward, and open you up to a whole new level of understanding and of compassion."

Nodding, she tried to commit every word of his to memory, but when she glanced again at the amazing picture, she knew she would remember every time she looked at it. That was the power of his art, she guessed, that the symbols were worked so deeply into his illustrations, so that simply glancing at them brought back the immensity of what she'd experienced.

She was still floating, submerged in the images, when her friend returned, and her time was up.

"Wow, it's beautiful," Carlie conceded, clearly surprised at the incredible skill and depth of emotion expressed in the artwork.

"I know, it's amazing!" Rhiannon said excitedly. "Thank you so much Rowan, I really love it!"

He inclined his head graciously in acknowledgement, and she handed over the money, then wandered off so Carlie could have hers done. For a while she wandered aimlessly, head filled with swirling visions of all she'd experienced, and eyes skipping over all the colourful stands without being able to focus on any of the details. Until she stopped abruptly at one that sold dresses, drawn by something she couldn't explain. Curious, she ran her hands over the velvety fabrics, which felt as delicate as swan down to her heightened senses.

When the woman running the stall saw Rhiannon, she gasped, then pulled a dress from the rack behind her and handed it to her. "This one is for you sweetheart," she said, ushering her into the tiny cubicle. And as soon as she pulled the soft, flowing white fabric over her head, she realised with surprise that it was. It swooshed around her ankles, caressed her legs and her arms, and felt as light and delicate as feathers.

Grinning, she came back out and paid for the dress, then glanced at her watch. Time had mysteriously flown again, and it was time to return to Carlie. But no matter how well she recalled the stands at the top of Rowan's aisle, she just couldn't find her way back to his stall. Fear jolted through her, and her mouth went dry. God, would Carlie think she'd abandoned her? Finally, totally flustered, she found a way through, but her watch said she'd been gone for an hour.

"I'm so sorry Carlie, I don't know what happened," she cried, panic and confusion in her voice. "I started heading back after twenty-five minutes, but I just couldn't get here – it was like this whole aisle had disappeared. And I know that sounds crazy, but I promise, I wouldn't just leave you here."

Carlie smiled at her. "It's okay, I think time went crazy everywhere. And Rowan only just finished my picture, so you're not late."

Rhiannon wondered what they'd been doing for the extra half hour, but she forgot her suspicions when she caught sight of Carlie's drawing. "Oh wow, it's beautiful," she gasped, awestruck as she took in the swirl of colour, of faces, of buzzing bees. "You get better every year," she gushed, turning to Rowan in astonishment.

Again he shrugged off her compliment, seeming a little flustered himself, then turned back to Carlie. She was trying to pay him, but he refused, and after another attempt and a moment of indecision, she finally nodded and held out her hand to shake his.

Instead, he took her hand, drew it towards him, pressed his lips to it and kissed it, then turned away. Rhiannon's eyes widened with surprise, as she took in Carlie's blushes and Rowan's discomfort. What was going on between them?

After they'd pushed through the crowd to the cafe, and placed their order, Rhiannon stared at her friend. "What was all that about?"

she demanded, a question in her voice. Carlie squirmed in her seat, and blushed, but she was saved from replying when the waitress brought their tea and scones to them.

As she added honey to her cup, Carlie changed the subject and asked about her reading. Rhiannon smiled, feeling the sensation of freedom and peace wash over her again as it had while she'd been communicating with the swan and the horse. She tried to put it into words, then gave up and showed Carlie the gorgeous swan-inspired dress she'd bought instead.

Once they'd finished their tea, they got back to shopping, wandering up and down the aisles, stunned by the beautiful clothes, crystals and jewellery on display, and intrigued by the many alternative healing methods on offer. When they saw a past life therapist's stand, Carlie hesitantly asked if she believed in them, and Rhiannon nodded.

"I love the idea," she began cheerfully – then noticed that Carlie was blushing again. "Wait, why do you ask? Do you believe in them?"

"I don't know, I'd never actually thought about it before. But Rowan said something about us knowing each other from a past life..." she admitted shyly.

Rhiannon stared at her. "What did he say? Come on, spill!"

Hesitantly she revealed that Rowan had told her that he was once King Arthur and she was Morgaine, his soul mate and magical partner in Camelot, and before that they'd been high priest and high priestess in Avalon together. Then she laughed.

"He was just being nice, trying to make me feel better after I broke down and cried on his shoulder," she insisted.

"You cried on his shoulder?"

Her friend shrugged. "Sure, I started crying when he was asking about my parents, and he gave me a hug."

"I think he really likes you!" Rhiannon exclaimed. "He never touches people, let alone claiming that they've been lovers throughout time," she added, her voice a strange mix of disbelief, admiration and jealousy.

Carlie scoffed. "That's ridiculous!" she insisted – but she looked relieved that the beep of Rhiannon's watch halted their conversation.

"Oh, it's time for our readings with the psychics," she said, excited again, as she fished out their tickets from her bag.

"Yours is with Isabella, and mine is with Carmen," she added, as she grabbed her friend's hand and excitedly dragged her through the crowd to the back of the huge hall.

They split up, Carlie finding her reader near the front of the room, while Rhiannon walked to the back, where a cheerful-looking woman wearing a gorgeous purple scarf over her hair and holding a deck of tarot cards sat.

"Welcome child," Carmen said, her voice low yet commanding. "How can I help you today?"

Pulling out the small chair, she lowered herself gingerly, and folded her hands on the table. "I'm not sure what I need to know, or hear," she began, voice a question.

"Or perhaps you don't know how to ask what you want to know?" Carmen suggested, and she nodded uncertainly.

"We can start with a general reading, how about that? Here, take a deep breath, calm your mind and shuffle the cards," the psychic said, handing over a well-used but beautiful deck.

Rhiannon took them reverently, closed her eyes and let the feeling of freedom and peace course through her again, then she carefully shuffled them and handed them back.

Sadness crossed Carmen's face for a moment as she held the cards, then it brightened as she turned the first one over.

"Oh child, you have lost so much, and yet you haven't let that defeat you. You haven't stopped believing in the good of the world, and the potential for goodness in your own life."

Rhiannon stared at her, perplexed, thinking back to just after her mum had died, when she'd been so selfish and thoughtless. But the psychic shook her head.

"Do not dwell on that. It is the past, and you did what you could with what you had and what you were faced with at the time. You need to let that go now. It doesn't mean you're forgetting your mother, she will always be with you, but she wants you to start living your life."

Rhiannon paled. How did this woman know her mother had died? She hadn't said a word about anything – not about losing someone, and definitely not about who she'd lost.

"She is with you child," Carmen said, her voice so confident, so reassuring, that Rhiannon felt the words wrapping around her, soothing her heart, and filling her with a sense of potential and an urgency to start making a difference.

Carmen smiled at her. "Yes child, now you're starting to get it. And as you see, so will you be seen."

Puzzled, Rhiannon stared at her, trying to understand.

"New love," the psychic said. "I see a tall, fair-haired and handsome guy sweeping you off your feet by Christmas."

A smile slid across Rhiannon's face, and a sliver of hope lodged in her heart. She wondered who it could be, and whether she'd already met him, or if he was so far a stranger. Could he be an existing student at their school, or maybe someone who would transfer there next term? Or would she meet him out somewhere? But where would she be going? Where could she go? She barely socialised.

For a moment she felt frantic, panicked that she would somehow squander her chance, but she tried to rein it in – and then she was hit by a wave of guilt. The same question came back to her. How could she be worthy of love, when her mum was dead? Surely she should be grieving too much to crave the respite that love would bring her?

"Oh my child, of course you are worthy, and you have no reason to feel guilty about it, I promise. It will be a nice distraction from your pain, and a well-deserved one."

Rhiannon's mind whirled, flitting from doubt to belief and back again. She'd been battling this duality for a long time, and she couldn't help but feel it was too hard a balance to strike – living her life, trying to plan for the future and enjoy the good things that came along, while still honouring her grief and not wanting to forget the one she had loved and lost.

"You are stronger than you realise," Carmen said. "You will know what to do when the time comes. And he will help you. He has very kind eyes." A memory of the blond guy from her dream flitted into her mind, and she smiled.

When the girls met up back at the cafe afterwards, Rhiannon hesitantly shared what her psychic had said, alternating from excitement that she would meet somebody soon, guilt and grief over her mum, and anger that Beth would miss everything, from her school ball to her wedding day to meeting her grandchildren – not that she was anticipating the last two happening any time soon.

Carlie's reading hadn't gone quite as well, with Isabella first telling her that she would have resolution with her mother, and then that her migraines were caused by the mercury in her fillings, and would stop if she had them all removed and replaced. Which might have been useful if she had any fillings.

They both collapsed with laughter, and the high emotion of Rhiannon's reading dissipated as they walked around the stalls again, arm in arm, looking at all the pretty things, and losing themselves in the colour and vibrant sound of the festival. When they saw that Rowan was running a seminar at 4pm, Rhiannon eagerly asked Carlie if they could go.

They headed upstairs and found seats in the rapidly filling room, but Rowan soon had them on their feet, hands joined as he went around the circle and blessed each person.

Rhiannon felt the golden light swirling around her again, and revelled in the sensation of peace that filled her. On her left she felt Carlie squeeze her hand, and a warmth spread up her arm, making her grateful for their friendship. A smile crossed her face, and for a moment she felt genuinely happy and content.

Once they were seated again, Rowan explained that they would be going on a journey to meet their animal spirit guides, so after they closed their eyes, he took them through a meditation, guiding them as they went into their own hearts and minds, then travelled to a place deep within the forest, where a series of animals came to aid them with their emotional and physical attributes.

Rhiannon watched herself walking through the lush forest, and was shocked to feel the physical sensation of the ground beneath her feet, the cool breeze through the tree branches over her head, and the golden sunlight piercing the leaf canopy and warming her shoulders. The path before her twisted and turned, and she followed it, curious, until she came to a small stream, where she was overjoyed to see the swan from her earlier vision.

Stepping closer, she crouched down at the edge of the clear, cool water, and it glided over to her, extending its head when she reached out her hand, and allowing her to pat the smooth glossy neck. It told her, in a strange garbled string of words she could somehow understand, that it would assist her with clarity and purpose, and seeing the truth of what she was.

"I will guide you to the healing you need, and remind you of the possibility within you to transform – transform your grief to wisdom, your pain to experience, and your loss to purpose. I offer you deep peace, balance and inner healing, and I hope you will accept my gifts into your life, and into your being, and remember to connect with me when you are feeling most down," the swan said kindly.

"Whenever you feel that way, simply stop what you are doing and drop into the stillness of the moment, and the beauty of your surroundings, and feel my presence soothing your heart." As golden light surrounded her again, she smiled and nodded at the swan. She felt so peaceful, and so right with the world.

Then a huge condor swooped down, who wanted to help her deal with her sense of loss, and see how it could transform her into someone willing to help others, to share the wisdom she'd gained in order to not only heal herself, but others too.

"I will guide you to new heights of awareness, show you a new perspective, and help you rise above your pain," the condor told her. "I am with you to show you how you can take other people under your wing, like you have with your new friend, and as you will with your future career, and guide them through their journey of grief to healing, and through the cycles of life, death and rebirth."

Then the massive bird carried her across the stream, and she followed the cool, leafy path he indicated until she came to a green meadow. In the centre stood a huge ox, who ordered her to start sharing the burden of her family with others, and stop insisting that she could handle everything.

Embarrassed, she shook her head, denying that was an issue, but the hulking animal pawed the ground, stomped his foot, and told her that he knew she'd taken on a huge amount of responsibility since her mum had died, and it was time she handed some back. She felt the truth of the statement deep within her, but still she resisted. Her father needed her, and Brodie needed her.

"You need you," the ox said sternly, and she felt Carlie next to the animal, next to her, nodding in agreement, yet her energy was softer, more accepting and understanding. "I'll help you," she whispered, and reached out her hand to her.

Before she could feel her touch, the sound of a rattle sent her flying out of the forest and back into the room, and she gazed around in a daze. Turning to Carlie, a question in her eyes, she saw her friend smile, the same smile she'd given her in the vision with the ox, then focus back on Rowan.

He was telling the class he'd recently had an oracle deck published, which explored the magical and medicinal purposes of a range of healing herbs. He shuffled the cards, then handed one to each person, and told them that the plant on it had a message for them.

Carlie got tansy, a plant associated with the dead, which was used in rites of death and rebirth. It was a great card, symbolising rebirth of the self. Rhiannon got wood betony, a herb of grounding, of home and hearth, of responsibility, which tied in with what her animal guides had been saying – to stop taking on so much responsibility. She laughed. That would be nice, but she wasn't sure how her dad would take it.

When the seminar ended, Rhiannon stood up and headed for the door – but she stopped abruptly when she realised Carlie wasn't with her, and made her way back to where her friend was talking to Rowan. He smiled at her in welcome as she approached, then asked the girls if they'd like to come to the after-party once the festival had closed, where lots of the presenters and exhibitors would be, chatting and catching up with friends.

Carlie shook her head, but Rhiannon ignored her. "We'd love to!" she said, excitement dancing in her eyes as he handed them passes to get in. "We have an assignment to do on goddesses for school, so we can pick your brain!"

Then she put her arm through Carlie's and waltzed her away. "Oh my god, this is so cool! He must really like you."

Her friend shook her head, refusing to accept that, and insisted that they head home now so she could help Rose in the store the next morning. But Rhiannon was determined, and swiftly batted away all Carlie's protestations. She wasn't going to take no for an answer.

"My cousin was hoping we'd stay with her tonight, so I'll call her now and let her know we'll be over later. This is so exciting!" she raved, ignoring her friend's pained expression. "And who knows, maybe we'll meet the objects of our affection – the ones we called forth with our love spells," she grinned, and Carlie finally gave in.

When they arrived at the party a few hours later, both wearing pretty new dresses, Rowan was waiting for them at the door, clearly overjoyed that they'd actually come. He quickly introduced Rhiannon to a Celtic wizard, Kevin, then spent the whole night at Carlie's side.

Rhiannon was excited to learn that Kevin had been working with goddesses for years, and had written a book about the deities of the British Isles. She also loved that he treated her as an equal, never talking down to her, but engaging her in discussions that made her dig deep within to define what it was she actually thought and believed, about life and love, magic and death. Some of the revelations surprised her, and she was really grateful to him for inspiring her to unravel and reveal her hidden thoughts and desires.

He was a wise and lovely man, and so funny and irreverent, in between the more serious stories of gods and goddesses. He introduced her to another author too, who brought a new perspective to their discussions, and he also gave her a long list of books that would help her with her assignment, as well as with her own personal journey through life.

By the time she and Carlie left to catch the train to her cousin's place, her mind and soul were filled with magic, and a sense of potential and promise that lifted her heart with hope. The next morning the girls woke up happy and excited, and raced over to the biggest spiritual bookstore in London, stunned by the shelves and shelves of fascinating tomes on everything from shamanism, vodou and spirit guides to angel therapy, crystal healing and herbalism.

They spent two hours there, wandering around, flicking through books, shuffling the beautiful oracle deck cards and gazing admiringly at the stunning jewellery and ceremonial pieces. Both of them spent every last cent they had, and on the train home Rhiannon threw herself into reading, while Carlie stared out the window, daydreaming about her time with Rowan, and finally realising how disappointed she was that she'd never see him again.

Back in the village, the girls each headed home to prepare for Rose's Mabon ritual. Rhiannon breathed in the cool air and smiled. The middle of autumn was her favourite time of year, with its crisp, chilly mornings, bright blue skies and world aflame with colour, and she giggled as she skipped back to her place through the crackling red-orange-gold leaves that covered the bare earth.

The things she'd talked about with Kevin the night before swirled around in her mind, and she started to feel the truth of them. He'd added a new depth to the sabbats they were celebrating too, and she was eager to talk more about them with Rose.

He'd explained that the autumn equinox was when the world was poised between summer and winter, when day and night were in harmony. It was a time of equal dark and equal light, equal day and equal night, and she could feel it reflected in the earth's energy in this moment, as well as within her self.

When she climbed the stairs of Rose's healing centre that night and entered the sacred space above the shop, she felt even more awe than usual, understanding so deeply that she was entering a magical realm, a place of the unexpected and the mystical. Standing on the threshold, she breathed in the heady scent of incense and the darkened mystery of the room, her eyes drinking in the flickering candlelight, the smoke weaving skyward and the four altars that had been set up with magical ritual tools and a sense of reverence.

As she was welcomed into the circle and anointed with a blend of autumnal oils, she felt a deep reverence within her, and a deep connection to the women in Rose's circle, a feeling of maternal energy wrapping around her and soothing her in a way she hadn't experienced since her mum had died.

And as Rose stepped forward to invoke the god and the goddess, Rhiannon saw her in a whole new light. She was a priestess who had become a maternal figure to all of them, but she was also a mother who'd lost her daughter, a potentially tragic figure who had channelled her loss in a new direction and emerged a survivor, a love-filled and caring woman who chose healing and service over bitterness and defeat. A longing to be like her swept over Rhiannon, and she made a promise to take this magic seriously, vowing that she would focus on the light, and the joy, and stop falling into the darkness that so often circled her. She could choose, and she *would* choose.

"Vibrationally Mabon is a season of withdrawal, of being quiet, of meditating, recharging, reassessing and pondering where you're at in life," Rose began, her voice rich and powerful.

"The energy of the earth retreats and goes within at this time, as does your personal power, but you will emerge from this cycle with immense strength and wisdom. This is the period to honour your achievements, experiences and growth, and to ensure balance by integrating all parts of your self. Acknowledge and celebrate what you've reaped in your own life. Feel fulfilment from each goal reached, releasing what no longer serves you in order to move forward."

Rhiannon gazed around the room, stunned by the pulsing of electricity that she could see joining them all.

"And on this day, when all is balanced, witches traditionally renewed their magical commitments, so you can renew any vows you've made or pledge a new one, be it to do with magic, love, friendship, career or anything else that you dream of."

Feeling a jolt of recognition, Rhiannon was proud that she'd vowed to continue working with magic just moments before.

"As the shadows lengthen, it's also a good time to scry for insight into your future, so we'll light the cauldron fire in the centre of the room and stare into the flames," Rose continued. "Just allow your mind to go blank and your vision to blur, and see what messages and symbols are revealed to you. Look deeper, into the very heart of the mystery you are seeking wisdom about, and try to discover what you need to bring into your life, what you are harvesting, what you are saving and what you are letting go."

As Laura lit the twigs and kindling in the cauldron, and the heady scent of the scrying herbs wafted around the room, Rhiannon inhaled deeply, and approached the fire hand in hand with Carlie. Staring into the flames, she could have sworn she saw her mother in them, dancing joyously, free of pain.

A constellation of tears trembled on her lashes, then spilled over and slid down her cheeks. But the heat of the fire made them evaporate – and as they dissolved, she realised that it was only the worst aspects of her grief she had to let go of. As she had that thought, she felt another weight lift from her shoulders. She almost laughed in delight. This sabbat was leaving her lighter in so many different ways.

After the fire ritual, Miri, one of Rose's priestesses, stepped forward and led them through a guided meditation based on the myth of the Greek harvest and fertility goddess Demeter and her daughter Persephone. Using a small drum to create a rich heartbeat that underpinned her chant, she welcomed them down into the earth, into the heart of the planet, grounding them with her words and her rhythm, and reassuring them that they were safe. Her voice was beautiful, and filled with power, strength and love.

"Tonight we align ourselves with Demeter the mother, who cared so deeply for her daughter that she tried to change the world. And we connect also with Persephone, the daughter split between maternal and romantic love."

As the exercise began, Rhiannon felt a moment of panic, not sure she wanted to drown in memories of her mother in so public a place. But as she listened to Miri's words and absorbed the tone and vibration of her voice, she finally felt soothed and safe, and sensed the presence of the goddess amongst them.

Later, when they were gently brought back from their journeying, Miri asked if anyone wanted to share their experiences. Her face wet with tears, Rhiannon shook her head, not willing to be vocal right now, but she felt that she could have spoken, and that one day soon she might, which was progress. She no longer felt like a child, or a fraud, or a pretender, but a potential member of this circle of magic that had been so important to her mother. She felt close to these women, and to their experiences, even though hers were so different.

And she knew that at some point she would be able to reveal herself, be vulnerable, take part, and the realisation filled her with joy.

There was an electricity in the room, a sense of healing, and of shared possibilities and magic. Tonight, together, they had created a place between the worlds. Nurturing. Inspiring. Balanced. And Rhiannon wanted to be a part of that always, to bring the magic they'd woven back into her "normal" life.

After the ritual ended, it took a while for her to anchor herself back into her body, and into the room. When Carlie started speaking to her, she still felt distant and out of focus, and for a moment she couldn't form words to reply – although she laughed when her friend dragged her over to the table of food and sternly told her to eat. It wasn't that long since she'd been instructing Carlie to have a biscuit to ground herself after her first ritual.

The spread was beautiful, with wedges of bright orange pumpkin, a bowl of yellow corn, and a centrepiece of red apples, ruby-hued pomegranates and purple grapes laid out on a golden cloth. Towering plates of muffins, slices of fresh bread with jam, dark rye and pumpernickel cakes and sweet potato pie held the heavier energies of the season, and reflected the importance of grains at this time of year, alongside the root vegetables that grow within the earth.

A bowl where people were leaving money to be donated to the homeless shelter sat at the end of the bench, and was filling rapidly, because the awareness of the coming winter was a rich thrum beneath each word that had been spoken tonight, and there was great sadness in the knowledge that even today there are many people who struggle to survive the cold season, or to find shelter and food and warmth.

Rhiannon felt the chilly pull of autumn's power, and the heartache of the upcoming anniversary of her mother's death, but she also felt the hope of spring, and new beginnings. Had Carlie brought that with her from the southern hemisphere, where the seasons were reversed? She giggled. It wouldn't surprise her if that was the case – her friend might be new to witchcraft, but she had an innate sense of magic that pulsed through her, no doubt helped by living with Rose. Or maybe it was in everyone, and just needed to be shown how to emerge.

Rhiannon smiled. Tonight she had summoned the courage to come to the ritual on her own, without needing the security blanket of her dad, or the urging of Rose. After three weeks of magic and coven work with Carlie, it was starting to feel natural to her, part of her, and she was sad that she'd waited so long to return to the circle. But all in the right time she supposed – maybe without her friend to accompany her, she would have felt too paranoid or insecure to let herself step in and soak up the magic. She might have gone once and been too overwhelmed to ever go again.

Mabon was about balance, and today, finally, she felt that. Balanced between grief and hope, the past and present, anger at what she'd lost and gratitude that she'd had it at all. She glanced at Carlie. It was only six weeks since the Lughnasadh ritual, and three since their coven dedication, but her friend had blossomed, growing more confident of her own inner strength, and her potential. And she supposed she had too.

Casting her eyes over the women assembled in the ritual space, she marvelled at their gentle auras, and at their power and steeliness. They were her mother's dearest friends, yet it had taken losing Beth for her to really learn about the circle of friendship and support she'd so loved. Rhiannon's heart swelled with gratitude for them, and she hoped that one day she would find a circle of friends like this, women who accepted her for who she was, and also encouraged her to be more than that.

Until then she had Carlie, the perfect magical partner, and she was very grateful for that – the Australian girl was what she'd always wanted in a friend, and she could see that they were going to push each other to be so much more than they presently were. Strength in numbers, and in shared experiences…

Chapter 33

How To Break A Heart

Beth... Twenty years ago...

Nothing dramatic happened in the week after she cast her love spell, and Beth tried her best to be patient. She also tried hard to maintain her new, unruffled, more accepting and magnanimous attitude towards her parents, since she'd become so aware of the futility of her old responses, her old arguments. Jenny's advice, and the example her sister set through living her authentic life despite their parents, had kicked off this new way of seeing their familial relationships. The protective bubble she'd erected with her spell in the woods had stayed with her too, and she still felt shielded from the worst of her mother's vicious barbs by the layer of magic she'd woven that morning.

And it didn't matter now anyway. She no longer had to defend herself, or try to prove herself, or attempt to "win" in their battle of wills – her parents had bought a huge house in London, and her father was already living there, with her mother to follow shortly, as soon as she'd finalised the last of the removalists.

It couldn't come soon enough for Beth. Now, finally, her real life was about to begin. She felt like she'd been treading water until now, marking time, but this was it. The dress rehearsal was over, and she was terrified and excited in equal measure. The career she'd always dreamed of was going to be a reality, she had wonderful friends, and she was in love with a man who treated her with kindness and respect, the way she should be treated. Granted, he wasn't aware that he loved her yet, but life was going to be perfect very soon – she just had to wait for everything to fall into place.

Then, the day before she started at college, Violet knocked on her door. Her shoulders were hunched, her face was pale, and she was fidgeting nervously. Beth ushered her inside and put the kettle on, then sank down into the chair opposite her.

"What's wrong?" she asked, voice sharper than she'd intended. "Are you okay? Is Rose okay?"

Violet smiled wanly. "We're fine. No need to panic."

Relieved, Beth grabbed some biscuits and pulled out the teapot. Everyone in her house drank coffee, but she'd bought some tea leaves after the last time Violet had been over, and now she spooned them into the pot, grateful for their soothing scent.

"So, your course starts tomorrow, right?" Violet asked her. "And you're definitely staying in Summer Hill?"

"Yes, and I'm so excited about both those things! I'm so happy that I'll be able to see you and Mike so much too, and go to rituals with you, weave magic..." She trailed off as she was flooded with a vision of herself, naked in the woods as she'd cast the spell to make Mike want her. Her cheeks flamed red, and she fervently hoped that Violet wasn't as psychic as her mum Rose.

Fortunately her friend was too distracted to notice her discomfort. She sighed, and Beth reached out a hand to her. "What is it?" she asked gently, and this time Violet's face crumpled, and a tear traced a path down her cheek.

"I feel so terrible. You've only ever been kind to me, such a good friend, and I've kept something from you," she said softly.

Trying not to laugh, because really, what could be worse than falling in love with your friend's boyfriend – and casting a spell to lure him from her side – Beth tried to muster her most understanding face. And it must have worked, because as she poured out the tea, Violet started pouring out her heart.

"You've been busy with your sister's wedding and stuff, so I haven't really seen you much alone, to talk about this, but... well, Andre and I... oh god! Um, I'm breaking up with Mike," she finally blurted, her last words tumbling out lightning fast, like she had to spill her secret before she changed her mind.

Beth stared at her, mouth dropping open in shock. "Why? What happened? When?"

"Well, we've been drifting apart for a while now, ever since that first day at the course..."

Beth tried not to roll her eyes. That was what, all of five weeks ago? Violet had still been desperately in love with Mike that morning, until the so-called spiritual teacher did his fake reading and told her she should be with him instead.

"And I've been spending a lot of time with Andre. The night you couldn't come to class, he asked me if I could stay back to help him with something. Mike was mad, and said I couldn't because he had to drive me home, but Andre said he would do that, so Mike reluctantly left. And we just sat there together and talked, and laughed, and he was so amazing, telling me all the things I could achieve, all the places I could go."

"But you wanted to stay here after school," Beth protested. "You're going to marry Mike, and be a social worker, and help your mum with the healing centre."

Violet's eyes flashed with – was it anger? "Andre helped me see the truth, that I've outgrown Mike, and outgrown this village. You know that – the first night we met I was so desperate for you to tell me all about France, all about the world, because I want to experience it too! I want more than this, more than a life toiling away in the same village where I was born, surrounded by the same people. No offense!"

Shrugging, Beth stared at her friend. "None taken," she muttered, although she wondered what Violet thought of her, the former rambling girl, now that she was so happy to *not* be travelling, so happy to be settling down in this village, surrounded by the same people Violet seemed to all of a sudden despise.

"Andre said you would understand, that you'd support me."

The accusation hung in the air, and Beth paled. So this was what Andrew had meant, when he'd told her she had to play an active role in their situation. She had to encourage Violet to leave, convince her that she'd outgrown this town – and her beloved boyfriend – and let her know that it was a great idea to dump Mike and be with him instead. *But was it?*

Against her better judgement, she decided to at least try to be supportive, while hopefully hiding the knowledge of the situation Andrew had fed to her, since she didn't trust him. So far Violet had only said she wanted to break up with Mike, so she would start there.

"So, you want to be single for a while? Travel the world on your own, meet new people?" It was the best she could do, with guilt still breathing uncomfortably down her neck.

Violet shook her head, and her face lit up. "No silly, I'm in love with Andre, and he's in love with me! I want to be with him! We want to be together!"

Although she'd known it would be this, the confirmation of it still slammed into her, a punch in the guts. She might be over Andrew, but it still hurt to see how quickly she'd been replaced.

"Wow," she burst out, voice hoarse with the shock of it. "But how well do you know him? I mean, it's been so *fast*. You've only seen him a few times, in class, and that one night after class..."

"We've been spending lots of time together, secretly, whole days here and there when Mike was working – thank god it's still school holidays! And last weekend when Mum and Dad were away, he stayed at my place the whole time."

Beth gasped, but Violet was oblivious to her consternation.

"It's amazing. *He* is amazing. I've never been loved like this, so totally and fully. And I've never loved anyone like this either."

Eyes shining, and needing no encouragement at all, Violet launched into another passionate rave about their teacher – how clever he was, how loving, how spiritual, how sexy. How incredible kissing him was. That thought turned Beth's stomach, but she couldn't help noticing just how radiant Violet became when she talked about him. She really did seem to be transformed by his love, by loving him. Had *she* looked like this when she'd been with him?

"So you're going to break up with Mike to be with Andre?"

Violet nodded confidently, then bit her lip, and a little of her fear was revealed. Whatever she was going through now, planning to do now, Beth knew Violet was kind and sweet at heart, and it wouldn't be easy for her to break Mike's heart. They'd been best friends since they were kids, and high school sweethearts for years.

"What are you going to tell him?"

A blush stained Violet's cheeks, and she stared into her tea, as if she'd find a less painful answer at the bottom of the cup. "I'm just going to explain that I need some space, and that as it's our final year of school, I have to focus on that."

"And you think he'll believe you?"

Violet glared at her, gaze sharp. "Why wouldn't he?"

"Oh Vee, you've been going on and on about Andre for weeks, and he's been unashamedly flirting with you in class, doing readings that pretty much order you to break up with Mike and be with him instead, and now he's been getting you to stay back with him at night, which Mike knows about, even if he is oblivious to the rest."

Shoulders slumping, Violet sighed, and Beth actually felt sorry for her. The last thing the poor girl wanted to do was hurt Mike, although his devastation was inevitable. But would lying about why she was doing it make it any less brutal?

"What should I say?" she pleaded.

A scream sounded in Beth's head. This wasn't fair, on any of them. Mike's whole world was about to crumble. Violet was going to break her best friend's heart. And perhaps worst of all, *she* was going to encourage Violet to do it, *help* her to do it, without revealing her own ulterior motive.

She sighed. Andrew had a lot to answer for. She could just picture him, grinning sadistically as he stood above the three of them, pulling their strings, making them dance to his tune.

"Beth?"

She picked up her cup and took a sip. *Tea.* Bloody hell, she needed coffee for this conversation. Groaning, she tried to put herself in Mike's shoes, and ignore her own vested interest in the outcome. And it became surprisingly clear to her.

"If you're really certain about this, and you can't stay with Mike, I think you need to tell him the truth. You owe him that, surely, because, romantic relationship aside, you've been best friends since you were kids. He deserves the truth."

Rebellion and denial flashed in Violet's eyes, and she tried to interrupt, but Beth held up her hand and continued. "Not just for his sake, but for yours too. It's a small town, so he'll know right away that you're dating Andre, and that's going to be awkward if you've lied about why you're breaking up with him. Also, you're not a liar Vee. You are better than that. Don't compromise your principles and your integrity by being untruthful. And you still want to be Mike's friend, don't you?"

Reluctantly Violet nodded.

"Besides, it doesn't matter what reason you give, what lie or half-truth you tell, he will still be heartbroken. A lie won't make it any easier for him. And I don't say that to talk you out of breaking up with him – you sound like you are very sure of your decision – but a lie will just make it worse for both of you. It will create trouble, and complications, and terrible pain, for you and him. Respect Mike – and yourself, and your friendship with him – enough to be honest with him about this."

Violet offered a small smile. "As much as I hate this, you're right Beth, thank you. Andre said not to worry about telling him, to make it easier for me, but that's not fair. I do owe Mike the truth. And I agree with you, it won't actually be easier if I lie, for either of us, not in the long run. Although I'm terrified about telling him," she confided, face contorted with emotion.

"Are you absolutely sure you want to end it?" Beth asked, breath held in anticipation. "Is there really no way back for you both?" For Mike's sake, she wanted her friend to deny the latter, to say of course there was a way back, and this whole Andrew thing was just a strange summer flirtation she would soon put behind her. But in her heart of hearts, Beth had to admit that mostly she wanted Violet to say yes to the former. And it looked like her wish was coming true.

"I'm sure," Violet said, simply, and strongly. "But thank you so much. I really appreciate you being so honest with me, and having the guts to tell me that. I know it can't have been easy, because you're just as close to Mike as you are to me. But it means so much to me that you took the difficult path, that you are looking out for me, and for Mike. I'm not sure I deserve a friend like you, but I am so blessed that you're in my life."

For a moment Beth wanted to tear her hair out, or her tongue. She felt like such a traitor, and it was even worse because Violet was so damn grateful to her, and thought she was being so selfless, when really she was just as bad as Andrew.

God, could that be true? Was she really that selfish? Her heart quailed at the possibility. Thoughts and doubts swirled around her, chasing each other from mind to heart and back again, but finally she shook it all off and smiled, relieved that she could say, with a clear conscience, that she hadn't talked Violet into ending things with Mike. That had been a fait accompli long before her friend had knocked on her door today.

It was strange that Andrew felt he required her help to convince Violet to be with him though. Her friend was all in – she hadn't needed any encouragement at all from her. Hmm, had he cast a spell on Violet? She shivered. The way she'd cast one on Mike? She felt so guilty about that, and about this current situation, yet she *had* challenged Violet about breaking up with Mike, and made a case for her staying with her long-term boyfriend too.

"Will you help Mike?" Violet asked hesitantly, voice so quiet that she had to repeat herself before Beth realised she'd spoken.

"What do you mean? What can I do?"

"He's going to need a friend, a real friend, and he's grown so close to you, we both have. I know he enjoys your company – he had a great time at Jenny's wedding with you – and I know that you care about him, right? I'd feel so much better about breaking it off with him if I knew he would have your shoulder to cry on."

Beth paled. Had Andrew suggested that to Violet? Maybe this had been his plot all along. He just wanted to get Mike set up with someone else, so Violet wouldn't feel as guilty about breaking his heart. Still, if it would make Violet happy, and help her feel less callous about her choice, she would have to find a way to get over her guilty conscience and be there for Mike.

"Of course." She smiled at her friend. "Are you okay?"

Violet nodded.

"When are you going to tell him?"

Shrugging helplessly, Violet took a deep breath, and seemed to physically and emotionally brace herself. "Now, I guess. It will only get harder the more I obsess over it. Besides, the three of us are having dinner together tonight, which could be a good thing. Will you still come?"

Pouting inside, and wondering how on earth she'd got herself into this mess, Beth nodded. Violet smiled with relief, then stood up. "Wish me luck!"

The crunch of autumn leaves underfoot and the soft pink of the sky almost distracted Beth from the heaviness of her thoughts, but the chill of the early evening breeze reflecting the chill of her heart kept her present, and she wondered how she had ended up here. She'd been so excited about her new life, about starting college tomorrow, about her friendship with Mike and Violet – but now she was doubting her decision to stay, when she could be living so free of drama back in Paris.

As much as she knew she was falling for Mike, did she have the strength to nurse him through the heartbreaking split he was about to endure? Did she really want to be the one who patched him back up and soothed his hurt? And how long would it take before she was confident that he really cared about her, and it wasn't just a rebound thing, finding comfort with a friend after his real love had dumped him?

Sighing, she pushed open the door of the cafe and walked inside, eyes instantly drawn to their usual booth, where Mike and Violet were already sitting, not quite as animated as they usually were, but not hostile either.

"Beth, thank god, I'm so glad you came," Violet said, then blushed. "I mean, hi."

Mike turned to her with eyes a little red from crying, but they filled with gratitude when he saw her. "Hey Beth, how are you?" he asked, forcing a smile. "Here, come sit with me."

She looked at Violet, who shrugged, then nodded to her, but despite the permission, she still felt awkward. Her two friends had always sat next to each other, holding hands, leaning into each other, sharing their food. It was so strange to see them sitting opposite one another – and even worse that now she had to take sides, physically at least. As she slid in next to Mike, she hoped they would never make her choose emotionally.

The waiter bustled over to take their order, and Beth said she'd have whatever Mike was having – she had no energy for making decisions tonight. And yet, aside from sitting in different places, it seemed that nothing much had changed between the three of them. As they ate dinner, they still discussed their usual topics, and Mike even brought up Andre's course, then asked Beth if she'd be going the following night.

"I'm not sure what time I'll get home from college," she replied apologetically, although that wasn't the reason. While she'd never admit it, she just wasn't sure she could handle being in the same room as the happily coupled Violet and Andre, with a sad-faced Mike looking on. Unless she hadn't actually told him yet?

Her head snapped up and she gazed at Violet, a question in her eyes, but her friend nodded again, and indicated their changed seating arrangements with a flicker of her eyes. Beth almost laughed, that yet again her younger friends were displaying so much more maturity than she was capable of.

"I'll be in Smithfield tomorrow afternoon, picking up some stuff for Dad, so I could meet you when your classes finish, and we could head over together?" Mike suggested. He smiled as he said it, but his eyes were pleading. Poor thing, it was going to be so awkward for him to turn up tomorrow night – yet probably just as awful if he didn't go at all.

"Sure, that sounds great."

"Now it's time to celebrate," Violet said with forced cheer. She slid out of the booth, returning a moment later with three huge slices of chocolate cake, and the waiter on her heels bringing another pot of tea for Violet and Mike, and a large coffee for Beth.

"What are we celebrating?" she asked, as she stared at the flickering candles on the cake wedges.

"You, silly," Mike laughed. "We're both so proud of you, that you've decided to follow your heart, and we think you'll be an incredible teacher. So, happy day one for tomorrow!"

Sadness crossed his face – no doubt realising as he'd spoken that there was no more "we" between him and Violet. But with an effort he shook it off and raised his cup. "To you Beth. Have the best time tomorrow. I know you'll be fantastic."

Her heart hurt, that this beautiful, kind, compassionate man considered her a friend. Even if it never went any further between them, she would be content. Just knowing him, knowing that he existed in the world, made her happy, and hopeful. Although she'd be even happier if they were dating.

Violet echoed his well-wishing sentiments, and the three of them enthusiastically ate every crumb of their sweet treats, slurped down their hot drinks, and chatted like nothing had happened to change the dynamics of their group.

But finally Mike made his excuses and headed home, and Beth turned to Violet, curiosity burning her up. "Are you okay?"

It was a sad smile, but a smile none-the-less, that was offered in reply. "I'm okay, and Mike will be too, eventually. And you were so right Beth, that I should tell him the truth – he said he'd suspected there was something going on between me and Andre, and he appreciated me being brave enough to be honest about it." She sighed, but continued.

"He also said it was a tiny bit easier knowing that I was leaving him for someone else, rather than if I'd just wanted to be without him. Dumping him for no one, like even being alone would be better than being with him. So thank you for your advice, and for having the courage to challenge me."

"You're welcome."

"And thanks for agreeing to meet Mike tomorrow so you can go to class together – he'll be so grateful that he doesn't have to walk in alone after, well, you know..."

As it turned out though, it was Violet who struggled the most on entering the classroom the following night.

After a brilliant, exhilarating first day at college, Beth was brimming over with excitement when Mike met her at the end of the day, and her mood bolstered his. After an awkward: "So I guess Violet told you our news?" and a sympathetic hug, they grabbed a coffee and a sandwich while Beth waxed lyrical about her course, then they made their way into Andrew's classroom and took their usual seats next to Violet...

Violet who was thoroughly miserable. The class began as soon as they sat down, so they couldn't ask her what was wrong, but something clearly was, because Andrew ignored Violet all night. Even when she put up her hand to answer questions, which she did a lot, he chose someone else. Compared to the over-the-top praise and flirting he'd lavished on her every other time, his abrupt change of behaviour was blatantly obvious. By the end of the night, Violet looked like she was going to cry, and Beth's heart broke for her.

What the hell? Had Andrew just been playing a game this whole time, wanting to break Violet and Mike up for the sheer sadistic pleasure of it? Wanting to see how much he could make Violet fall for him? Or was he wanting to get at *her* for some reason, thinking she would be jealous of his interest in her friend? She swapped worried glances with Mike, but he shrugged helplessly.

As they were walking out the door at the end of the night, Andrew finally spoke. "Violet, could I see you for a moment?"

She froze, but didn't turn around, gazing at her two friends in shock and indecision. Mike stared back at his former girlfriend, with no idea what to say, so Beth knew it was up to her. *Great.*

"Find out what he wants, and why on earth he was being so rude to you tonight," she said briskly. "We'll wait for you in the car for fifteen minutes, in case you need to come home with us, okay? But if all is well we'll go, and leave you to it."

Violet smiled, relieved and grateful. "Thank you."

They ended up waiting half an hour, just in case, then Mike sighed and started the car, before pulling out onto the road and heading for home. "Guess they worked it out," he muttered.

Beth placed a hand on his arm in comfort. "Are you okay? Can I do anything?"

He smiled at her, but shook his head. "I'll be okay. I guess it was inevitable, right? They always say you shouldn't marry your childhood sweetheart. And how can I compete with him, all swarthy good looks and older-man intrigue, and 'so spiritual, so intuitive, so amazing,'" he sighed, echoing Violet's tone as she'd raved to them about their teacher over the past few weeks.

Grimacing, Beth tried not to roll her eyes. "I could handle never hearing *those* sentences again."

She was surprised when Mike laughed. Taking it as a good sign, she spoke quickly, before she lost her nerve. "I think she's crazy, to be honest. I'd choose you every time." Then she held her breath. Had she gone too far? Spoken too soon?

"Thank you for being here for me Beth, I really appreciate it. And thanks for being there for Violet too. She told me you were really supportive."

"I tried to convince her not to break up with you," she blurted out, then slapped a hand across her mouth. Maybe she should have kept that to herself.

But Mike just nodded. "She mentioned that. You're very sweet. I have to admit, I was a little surprised that Patricia's daughter could be so kind and thoughtful, so unselfish. And I just want you to know how glad I am that you decided to stay in the village. Not just for my sake, but for yours too. I'm really proud of you, that you've started your degree, and are following your heart, and your dreams. You'll be a wonderful teacher."

She blushed, and stammered her thanks, then there was silence for a while. It wasn't awkward though, it was just the two of them lost in their own thoughts, pondering the huge changes in both their lives. Companionable silence.

"Will you still come to Rose's rituals?" Beth finally asked. "And oh god, what has she said about all this? I can't imagine she's thrilled by Violet's decision – I know how much she cares about you, how much she loved that you were together."

Mike turned to her, alarmed, and the car swerved wildly. "We can't tell Rose!" he said urgently.

"Why not?" Beth asked, shocked. "Surely Violet wouldn't keep something like this from her mum, they have a wonderful relationship. She wouldn't lie to Rose, would she? And keeping it a secret hardly seems fair on *you*."

"Or you," he conceded, brow furrowed. "But we can't tell her. Violet doesn't want to upset her parents, and she's worried that they won't approve, that they won't like that Andre is older than her, or has been married before. So we're going to pretend we're still together, for a while at least."

"But that's crazy! How can Vee expect you to do that for her? How can she think it's okay for you to have to *pretend* to be in love with her, when you still are? To kiss her and hug her in public, but never be able to touch her in private? Surely that's taking your friendship, and the feelings you still have for her, way too far."

He shrugged again. "I don't mind, I'm happy to help her out," he said, although he sounded a little less sure this time. Maybe he hadn't quite thought it through when he'd agreed to this acting gig. "For a little while at least. It was actually me who suggested she not reveal her new... whatever it is... until she's sure about it. There's no point worrying Rose or Louis if it doesn't really go anywhere."

"Wow, you are a much better person than me, Mike Stark," she said, equal parts admiration and surprise. A better person than Violet too, she thought, but held her tongue.

He laughed, but there was little mirth in it. "We've been part of each other's lives for so long, I guess it will take me a while to get used to us not being completely entwined. It didn't even occur to me not to offer to help. I guess I'm going to have to learn how to be my own person now. We've been Mike-and-Violet for as long as I can remember..."

He trailed off, and in the headlights of an oncoming car Beth saw his face, shadowed and twisted as he clutched the steering wheel with white-knuckled fingers. "I guess I have no idea, no reference point, for how to act after a break-up. Violet is the only person I've ever been with."

"I can help you with that," Beth said sternly. She was worried now that he hadn't actually taken it all in, that he still had hope it would work out, and they'd get back together. That he was in denial about the devastating blow he'd been dealt, and would fall apart the moment the impact finally hit him.

"First on the list – it's totally inappropriate that she's putting you through this, expecting you to continue a charade for Rose's benefit. But it also says so much about who you are," she added, voice gentler. "You will make some woman very happy one day Mike."

He looked over at her and grinned, that gorgeous smile that lit up his face. "You're too kind."

Shaking her head, she wondered how in all of this drama, *she* had ended up as the one considered kind. How ironic. The spell caster, the storm bringer, the drama queen.

Chapter 34

Un-Happy Anniversary

Rhiannon... Today...

Rhiannon woke up shivering, feeling the ice seeping, creeping, into her heart. Today was the one-year anniversary of her mother's death, and she felt completely numb. She had no idea how she was going to get through the day. Intellectually she knew that this day shouldn't affect her any more, or any less, than yesterday or tomorrow, and yet it did. Idly she wondered if her father would let her stay home from school to wallow in her pain, but the knock on her door made her think that was a definite no.

"Come in," she called hoarsely. God, what had happened to her voice? Her whole body had tensed, the pain seeming to have tightened around her throat as well.

Her door opened, and Mike poked his head in. "Darling," he began, his voice broken and hollowed out. She gazed at him expectantly, but it seemed he was unable to say anything more, and her heart squeezed in pain at the obvious agony he was still suffering.

"Laura is picking Brodie up in a minute to take him to school," he finally said, and her brow furrowed in bewilderment.

"I thought we could take the day off, and do something together?" he suggested. It was so unlike him that she almost laughed.

Surprise washed over her, and she opened her mouth to say no – her first instinct was to turn him down and run off to spend the day holed up somewhere on her own – but slowly she warmed to the idea.

"What did you have in mind?"

He shrugged. "I thought we could take some flowers to your mum's grave, then maybe drive over to Smithfield, see a movie, have a picnic in the grounds of the historic home there, like we used to…"

A brief smile crossed Rhiannon's face as she remembered the afternoons they'd spent there as a family, munching on sandwiches and cupcakes, drinking coffee, feeding the regal swans, crunching through the autumn leaves or taking shelter from the summer sun under the huge old oak trees.

God, she felt so alone. Finally having a friend who understood her was amazing, yet the contrast from the joy of that to her self-imposed exile today meant she now felt even more isolated. Which wasn't Carlie's fault by any means. She hadn't told her that it was the anniversary of her mum's death – her friend's grief at losing her own parents just three months ago was still so raw, so present, and she didn't want to burden her with any more pain.

But she didn't want to be alone today either, so she nodded to her dad, then jumped in the shower while he went downstairs and put the kettle on. After a quick breakfast, they stopped in at the florist, and she marvelled at the strange floral link between love and death. Her dad bought long-stemmed red roses, as he had on every wedding anniversary they'd celebrated, while Rhiannon created her own bouquet, choosing white lilies, white roses, white poppies and white chrysanthemums, echoing the funeral flowers she'd chosen a year ago at Rose's memorial of farewell.

And now they were at the entrance to the cemetery – but neither one of them was ready to walk inside. Finally an over-enthusiastic dog took the decision out of their hands, bounding over to them, jumping up on Rhiannon and licking her face, then pushing the pair through the gate.

It felt strange to be there with someone else. Grief was such an intimate thing, and she felt raw and exposed standing beside her mother's grave with her dad right next to her. She was too shy to speak to her mum in his presence, and for a moment she wished they hadn't come together. Perhaps shifts would have been better.

Her dad looked at her and smiled as if he'd heard her, then sank down onto the grass beside his beloved wife's resting place and closed his eyes, head bowed. Rhiannon felt as though she was intruding again, and took a step backwards, preparing to slip away and give him some privacy.

But before she could, he reached up his hand to her, and she reluctantly took it.

"It's okay darling," he said, voice surprisingly calm. "You're not intruding at all. This is our place, and I'm so glad you're here with me now, to help me through it. I'm not sure why it's so much harder today, but it is."

His echo of her thought from that morning almost made her smile, but she was stuck on what he'd said first.

"I'm helping you?" she asked, incredulous.

"Oh darling, of course you are. Every day. I don't know what I would have done if I'd lost you too, and had to face your mum's loss without you. I couldn't cope with Brodie on my own either, and *he* wouldn't be able to cope with me alone. We both need you so much, and I am so grateful that you're here for us. I can't even begin to imagine how hard it is for Carlie, to have lost her entire family."

"I've been no help," she insisted, but her dad drew her down beside him, put his arm around her and held her close.

"I promise you love, you are absolutely a godsend to me. And even when you were being all surly and thinking you hated the world and it hated you, I was still so grateful to you when you did make the time to be with us."

His words filled her with shame, and regret, but also with hope, and she looked around with new eyes.

The cemetery was beautiful, in a tragically lovely way. Sometimes, when she was here on her own, she wandered for ages before she even approached her mum's resting place. There were graves from hundreds of years ago, most of them in various states of disrepair, but a few were kept in good condition, well tended and with flowers regularly left on them. There must be families in the village who went back generations, who grew up knowing about their ancestors, and honouring them even though they'd never met them.

There was one in particular that really fascinated her – it had a rosemary bush growing on it, just like her mum's did, although this one was much older. There were always fresh flowers in the vase there, although she'd never seen anyone leave them, along with several small crystals scattered around the base, a variety of red, yellow and purple ribbons tied into the sprigs of the rosemary, and tealight candles in glass containers. Often she arrived to find them burning, yet there was never anyone in sight.

It saddened her, yet also filled her with longing, that these people were remembered so long after they'd lived, that they had family who honoured them, and that they were still connected to people today. It made her acutely aware of how little she had in the way of family.

Her mum was gone, and her mother's parents were no longer in her life – not that they ever really had been, and not that she missed them at all. Beth did have a big sister, Jenny, but she lived in Scotland with her husband, on an isolated northern island, and rarely visited. She had stayed with Jenny's daughter, her cousin Millie, in London the night of the festival, but she was older than her, and often travelled to Spain for work, so they weren't in regular contact.

Her dad had been an only child, and while his father died before she was born, she saw his mum, her Nanna Anne, and his stepfather, her Grandpa William, a few times a year. Mike's grandparents had died long ago though, so she didn't know anyone any further back on that side of the family tree either.

Did it matter? If family was made up of the people you cared about, who cared about you, then she had her dad, she had her brother, and she had Rose, who had been the predominant "grandmother" figure to her for her whole life. And yes, she was okay with admitting that she'd been jealous of Carlie at first, when she'd feared that the Aussie teenager would replace her in Rose's life and affections, but the priestess had been very clear that there was enough love in her heart and space in her life for both of them.

So she had nothing to complain about – and yet the longing still clung to her whenever she was at the cemetery.

Today though, during her first visit with her dad, she felt soothed, and more satisfied with her lot than she had since her mum died. They sat by her grave for an hour in companionable silence, before Rhiannon rose and wandered over to the older part of the graveyard, leaving her dad to commune with his wife in private. Then something unspoken passed between them, and Rhiannon started walking back just as her dad stood up from his position on the grass, and so they headed back out to the road, even sadder than when they'd arrived, but glad that they had shared this time together.

Once they were in the car, they didn't feel up to a movie, but with no better plan they drove over to Smithfield, grabbed lunch from a cafe, then wandered through the grounds of the manor house they used to visit with Beth and Brodie.

For Rhiannon, her brother's absence was everywhere. In the family sitting on the banks of the stream, munching on hot chips and slurping back chocolate milk. In the sound of laughter that rang out from a passing car. In the grace of the swans gliding past on the river. In the small boy running ahead of his parents through the trees, a small dog yapping at his heels.

A dog. Brodie had asked for a pet the night Beth died, but they'd been distracted by Rose's phone call, and their own grief, and then by the funeral preparations, and had forgotten about it. Hastily finishing her sandwich, she wandered over to where her dad was sitting, under a big old oak tree, listlessly feeding his crusts to the pigeons.

"Dad, remember how much Brodie wanted a dog? Just after mum died?" Pausing, she marvelled that she was able to say that sentence without choking on the words. It was progress of a kind.

Mike looked up at her, puzzled.

"That first night, when we got home from the hospital. Just before Rose rang, to say she'd cancelled the restaurant."

Pain crossed his face, but he nodded.

"Well, maybe we should get him one. He's old enough now, to look after it and take it for walks – to be honest, I've been stunned, over the last few weeks, at just how mature he's become. He's certainly not the same little kid who couldn't grasp what it all meant a year ago, when mum didn't come home. And I'll help him."

For a moment she thought he would refuse, but finally a small smile flashed across his face – and his eyes smiled too – and he nodded again. "Where would you suggest we get one?"

Funny he should ask. When they'd been in the cafe earlier grabbing lunch, Rhiannon had noticed a flyer for a local rescue shelter on the noticeboard, with a heartfelt plea for good homes for their precious animals. So they made their way back there, Mike ordering coffees while she called the place to find out whether they had a dog suitable for a young boy, and what adoption would involve.

Her eyes were shining when she came back to the counter and picked up her cup. "They were just about to close for the day, but they're happy to wait for us. They said they have the perfect dog for Brodie – he's a young beagle, well trained, and he's been the beloved companion of a six-year-old, who only surrendered him because his family is moving overseas."

When they drove up to the shelter, a gorgeous little dog was waiting outside the front door with one of the staff, and Rhiannon fell in love the moment their eyes met. The cute canine was very well behaved, sitting down as they approached, but with eyes filled with curiosity, and a hint of mischief.

She knelt down a short distance from him and slowly offered her hand for him to sniff. He gazed up at the man standing with him, and at his nod he moved closer to Rhiannon and gently licked her palm. A moment later, he put his paws on her legs, then with only the slightest encouragement, fell into her arms, hungry for pats.

By the time Mike emerged from the shelter, weighed down with a bed, blanket, collar, lead, food and toys, the two had become firm friends, and the cute dog eagerly followed Rhiannon to the car and jumped into the back seat with her.

And so, on the night Rhiannon had long been dreading, the house was filled with laughter, the occasional excited bark, and unexpected but most welcome joy. Brodie's face as he saw the dog leap out of the car when they picked him up from school was a picture of happiness, and his delight when Rhiannon told him that the puppy was his to care for moved her deeply. He squealed even louder with excitement when she said he could choose their new family member's name.

When they got home, Brodie proudly attached the lead to the pooch's collar and took him for a walk around the block with Rhiannon, overwhelmed with joy even though his arm was almost pulled out of its socket several times by the excited pup. Once that was complete, and the little dog had investigated every smell he could find, Brodie led him out into their backyard and played with him as the sun set and the sky dimmed.

And when Rhiannon tucked her brother into bed later that night, with little Baxter curled up on his feet, just as exhausted as his new carer, she felt so much love for her brother, and a warmth and sense of hope for all of them that she hoped would stay with her.

Chapter 35

Eye of the Storm

The next morning, Rhiannon was woken by loud, excited yapping, and she surprised herself by laughing. As bleak as her world felt, especially after the crushing darkness of yesterday's anniversary, there was new hope too. It was hard to stay miserable when you shared a house with a sweet, kind-hearted and curious six-year-old brother and his new, equally curious, best friend.

Dragging herself out of bed, she played with Brodie and Baxter, then made them all breakfast, before settling down with boy and dog in the lounge room. Carlie was coming soon to study, and she knew she should jump in the shower and get ready, yet this precious time with her brother was one of those rare and perfect golden moments, and she wanted to soak it up and breathe it in for as long as she could. File away the memory to cheer her up on the next not-so-bright day.

By the time Carlie knocked on the door, Rhiannon had also watched a movie, made lunch, washed the dishes and cleaned the kitchen, and was starting to worry. Her friend was flushed and out of breath, and full of apologies for her tardiness, yet she looked radiant and bursting with happiness.

Intrigued, Rhiannon quickly brewed some tea and grabbed some bikkies, then ushered her upstairs where they could talk in relative privacy, away from the curious ears of her dad and the constant interruptions of Brodie and the puppy.

Carlie curled up in the window seat and gazed out into the garden, hands wrapped around her mug, eyes shining, and a huge smile lighting up her face.

"So, spill!" Rhiannon urged, and was shocked and delighted by her friend's news. That morning Carlie had woken up way earlier than usual, with a strange urge to climb the tor. Not even sure why she was doing it, she'd crept out of the cottage, stumbling through the darkness as she made her way to the top. When she saw there was already someone sitting on the summit, she'd been disappointed, and had turned to go – until she realised it was Rowan.

"Rowan Rowan? Rowan from the festival? Tall, dreamy eyes, gorgeous and *amazing* Rowan?"

Carlie nodded.

"And you've been with him since before dawn?" Rhiannon shrieked. "What–? Where–? How?"

Shyly, as though she couldn't quite believe it herself, her friend filled her in. Rowan said he'd been thinking about her all week, but all he knew was that she lived in Summer Hill, so he'd driven over and climbed the tor, then sent his spirit out to summon her – a call, he said, that her soul had answered.

They sat atop the sacred hill in the cool pre-dawn and watched the sun rise. When other people approached, they headed down the grassy slope, hand in hand, and wandered around town, talking and laughing, and sharing glimpses of their stories, and parts of themselves. Later he took her to his favourite place, in a beautiful meadow on the banks of a stream, and pulled out a picnic basket and rug, and they continued their conversation, and their slow revealing of themselves to each other.

As Carlie tried to impart every sight, sound, word and glance she could recall, her friend listened, rapt.

But finally Rhiannon held up her hand. "What aren't you telling me?" she asked, eyes narrowing with mock suspicion.

"What do you mean?" Carlie tried – and failed – to look innocent.

"I know you're holding something back. Out with it!"

Her face turned scarlet. "Um, he kissed me – and it was really lovely. I really did go weak at the knees, as cliched as that sounds."

Rhiannon hugged her, thrilled. "When will you see him again?"

"Tomorrow morning. But shouldn't we start our assignment?"

Rhiannon laughed, and finally agreed to stop pressing her for details so they could get some work done. But all day she felt really happy, and finally realised it was because she could almost taste the possibility swirling around her. If Carlie's love spell had worked, and brought an amazing guy like Rowan into her life, then there was no reason why she wouldn't meet someone too, now she was ready.

That night, as she curled up on the couch with Brodie to watch a video, Baxter sleeping between them with his nose on her lap, she looked up at the photo of her mum on the mantelpiece, and silently thanked her for watching over them.

As their first term progressed, Rhiannon was shocked to find herself enjoying school so much more than she could have imagined. She was working extra hard to keep her grades up, now she had a goal to aim for, and several of their teachers praised her for her continued diligence and successes. It still mortified her, how close she'd come to throwing it all away in the aftermath of her mum's death, but she was proud that she'd managed to turn her grades around earlier this year, and determined to stay on top of it all.

She especially adored her history class, and their goddess project. Their teacher was right – all the research was helping her feel closer to her mother. Many nights she pored over Beth's Book of Shadows, and the wisdom and breadth of knowledge within the pages astounded her. She felt sad that she hadn't known more about her mum's passion for magic, and her many esoteric interests, while she was alive. She also felt cheated. Her mum had taken her to a few rituals, but said she was too young to be a member of Rose's circle. Now she was old enough to be part of it, she was angry that it was too late for them to do it together. Foolish and pointless as it was, she felt such a longing to be able to share all of this with her.

At least she had managed to join her for a few ceremonies. Poor Carlie – her mother Violet had inexplicably turned her back on magic and ritual long ago, so it had been a total shock for her friend to discover that her non-religious, non-spiritual, most conventional and conservative lawyer mum had once worn purple velvet and danced under the full moon with other witches.

She felt sad for Violet too. When she'd first learned her dad had loved someone else before her mum, she'd been angry and jealous – and she'd resented Carlie for it, as unfair as that was. But from the little they'd managed to figure out about Violet's early life, it seemed she'd had a terrible, soul-destroying relationship with a manipulative guy, who had convinced her to run away from home. It was a tragedy that led her dad to take his own life, and left Rose a childless widow.

Eventually, somehow, Violet had managed to escape that situation and find true love, and a new life. And while she'd never returned to magic, or to her home town, she'd had Carlie, who was healing her grandma Rose's heart – and helping Rhiannon heal too.

Her excitement at having a friend to share her magical exploration with was pure and intense, and she was so happy they'd formed their own coven, so they could learn more about the nature-honouring spiritual path their mothers had both followed. And all their magic was deeply healing. Even the smaller rituals she created with Carlie as they nervously, shyly, experimented, made her feel better, made her feel more whole. Not fully whole yet, and maybe she never would be, but she was gathering little pieces of herself with every spell and every sabbat. The rituals were healing her, expanding her, and filling in some of the pieces she'd lost.

There would always be a gaping wound within her, but she was slowly coming to accept that, to love it even. It was where her mum could reside, could visit her, could live. It gave her strength, a beautifully fragile strength, to know her mother was there, within her if not physically with her. That she would always be a part of her soul, a wisdom that flowed through her heart, a presence that was carved into her bones.

That night, at Rose's full moon ritual, Rhiannon sensed her mother. Felt her winding her way around her heart, swirling around her shoulders to protect and comfort her, holding her close then tingling within her, as the priestess invoked the goddess and drew her down into their circle and into her own body. Afterwards, Rose asked if she could help her pack up the altar tools.

They talked for a while, then Rhiannon screwed up her courage and asked what she'd been longing to know. Her voice was soft, tentative, apologetic. "How were you not destroyed by what happened when Violet disappeared all those years ago?"

It felt strange speaking the name of her daughter aloud, now that she knew her dad had been in love with her – like she was being disloyal to her own mother in acknowledging it. But Rose had been through far more pain than she had, and remained the kindest, most compassionate person she'd ever met. If she could transcend all the tragedies of her life, maybe there was hope for her too.

"How do you know I wasn't destroyed?" the priestess asked her, and a vulnerability Rhiannon had never seen in her before bubbled just below the surface of her calm.

"Oh my god… um, I'm sorry, you're just, well –"

Rose forced a smile, which hid the pain again, but Rhiannon knew she wouldn't be able to unsee the shadows that had haunted the eyes of the woman who had always been like a grandmother to her.

"Sweet girl, we have a choice, every day. We can let ourselves be destroyed, and in our bitterness destroy the rest of our lives – becoming destructive and hurting others, and ourselves, far more than the original pain did. Or we can pick up the shattered pieces of our broken lives, and try to glue our hearts and our minds back together." She gazed across the room to where Mike stood talking to Carlie, her eyes wistful.

"I choose every day to believe that the world is good, and people are redeemable, because I couldn't function if I saw it any other way. Offering healing where I can, helping others, that helps me too. A wise man once told me there's no such thing as altruism, that we do good because it makes us feel good, and there is some truth in that. Being able to help others deal with their pain and grief and illness gave meaning to my life after Louis and Violet were taken from me, when I thought all meaning was lost."

"So time really does heal all wounds?"

Another shadow flitted across Rose's face. "No." She was emphatic. "Time changes things, but it will never totally heal them, and you wouldn't want it to. The wound is a badge of honour, a badge of love, a badge of memory. The grief won't ever leave you completely, but you're no longer crippled by it, right?"

Rhiannon nodded, shocked to realise this was true.

"And it's a good thing, because you'll want to remember. You'll want to hold on to that wound, to the scar deep within. Others will stop seeing it, but it will always be there. It never leaves. It sits below, beneath, within, and it will resurface occasionally, when you least expect it, and you'll feel the pain all over again. But sweet girl, that wound is also where the light gets in. The scars are where new hope can break through." A sad smile flickered across Rose's face.

"And the pain reflects the depth of the love you shared. It broke my heart to lose Violet and Louis, but I would never wish I hadn't had them in my life, hadn't loved them and been loved in turn, just to avoid that. In some ways I think the pain is what reminds me to go on living, and so I embrace the pain that I imagine has made me stronger. That I have to believe has made me stronger." Her voice was a whisper, was a sigh, was a wrenching ache of emotion and yearning.

"But not everyone can survive it," she continued. "My Louis couldn't. His grief when we lost Violet was a huge black storm cloud that sat above him and around him, ominous and threatening. Drowning him, and drowning my words and my love and all hope that I had of getting through to him. He collapsed under the weight of his personal storm, shrivelled up and shrunk down to a husk, until it was as though he was no longer there, so reduced was he by his grief and his pain, by the burden he felt that he alone must carry."

Rhiannon watched, horrified, as Rose seemed to fold in on herself, bowed down by the weight of her own suffering. And she saw the faintest glimpse of the scars that the tragedies of her life had inflicted on her, saw the pain that was always there. Usually it was buried deep, but for a moment she saw it rise, ready to bubble back up and suffocate the priestess in the pain of her memories. She couldn't begin to comprehend how much losing her daughter again, after all these years, was devastating her now.

But Rose smiled at her. "I'm okay. The sadness is part of me, and I welcome it because it reminds me not just how much I lost, but how much I had. How much I loved, and was loved. And it reminds me of the blessings I still have – the blessing of you and your family, the blessing of the women of my circle, the blessing of Carlie, sent here to heal my heart, and to help you too, as much as we will help her."

Rhiannon nodded, accepting the truth of that, and realised how much stronger Rose had become in the months since her granddaughter had arrived. Not that she'd ever been weak, but now there was a new breath of life that animated her, a new fire. And if Carlie could help the wise woman heal, maybe there was hope for her too, that some day she would be able to help people heal from their grief.

"Everyone has tragedy in their lives, *everyone*," Rose said, breaking into her thoughts. "But when we suffer, we can choose to find purpose in our pain and be inspired to help others, or we can choose to remain bitter and broken and inflict our pain on those around us, and on ourselves. It saddens me that some people continue acting out their pain by hurting others, because it doesn't help. Lashing out doesn't ease our pain, it just causes more suffering, and perpetuates that vicious circle. And so I choose to radiate healing and peace outwards from myself, in the hope of radiating it inwards as well."

Sadness and defeat swelled up in every cell of Rhiannon's body. "I don't know how to do that," she complained.

Rose leaned over the altar and hugged her. "Oh sweet girl, that's not true! You and Carlie have already figured all this out on your own, in choosing to find a purpose from your loss, in deciding to become grief counsellors so you can help others going through what you suffered, and endured, and survived." She beamed at her.

"I'm so impressed with how you have handled your grief. You knew that you had to go into the storm to heal, and you did it, unflinching. I saw you with the same black clouds above you that my Louis had, battling the same furious conditions that drowned him. You felt all of the pain, and all of the anger, and you allowed it in. You shirked nothing, avoided nothing – you dove into the storm, and you made your way through, and now you've come out the other side. I'm so proud of you. There will be cloudy days ahead, of course, but you've let the sunshine in. You are a remarkable young woman."

As Rhiannon blushed, she sensed her dad approaching her. And as he folded her into his arms, she smiled.

Storm above, storm within, storm without.

She had stood in the storm, arms outstretched and face turned to the sky, and felt her body and soul battered and bruised and torn apart by its cruel power.

She had been the storm, been the might of its eye, and the chill of its ice, and the howling of its winds, and the drenching of its rains, and the crack of its thunder, and the flash of its lightning, and the swirling press of its magical, mysterious mists.

She had caused the storm, wreaking havoc and instilling fear in others.

She had been broken inside and out by the storm – lightning splitting her mind as it split the sky, thunder shaking her to the very core, leaving her unmoored and unanchored.

Words had been carved into her heart by the storm, words of love and of loss, and of the futility of trying to stand up to its power and fury.

It taunted her: "You cannot withstand this storm."

But Rhiannon roared back: "I am the storm!"

She knew it, deep in her bones in the throes of her pain and the rain that poured down on her. Windswept and broken and dashed on the shore, then left, bereft.

Shattered, then rising from the fire, from the ashes.

Scattered shards eventually glued back together and made whole again. Except for the scars etched so deeply into her body and soul. Scars that would always remain. That she would wear as a badge of honour. Of endurance. And as a place to let the light come in.

Her heart had broken wide open.

Wings tattered and torn, and brought undone.

Rhiannon of the birds. The angel terns circle, with their hungry beaks and their hungry eyes.

Then the goddess speaks, and the darkness seeks, wanting to drown her in its inky black, lose her in the constellation of stars on a moonless night, hide her within a shimmering light, stretched out across the black highway of the sky, of the road to hell and to pain and to loss, made real and twisted inside with the lies, with the pain, with the well of shades she was drowning in.

Shadows and light, and the ferocity of the storm splitting her heart and her soul and her self.
Holding the wind in her hands and the inky blackness in her heart and the echo of hope flung around her shoulders like a cloak.
Seeking the heat she cannot find, the flame in her heart, in her very being. The star that will guide her home.
Torn from the shore and floating, drifting, drowning.
Hammer to heart and darkness in bloom.
A planet within, starlight without, the dying breath of a dying dream and a universe too large to contain.

But the magic was bringing her back to life. Waking her up inside.
Fusing the shards of her shattered soul, returning what had died and gone, and bringing it back.
The rituals were a path to reveal her hidden light.
The friendship was a beacon calling her home.
She was still a riven soul, raw and broken and torn asunder.
And yet it would be the broken pieces of her that would be her strength, her power, her beauty, her knowing.
Carved by loss. By cold and rain, and fire and flame.
Heat and ice that froze her inside, and then released her...
Finding her strength again. Her self again.
She was the balance in the eye of the storm, and finally she was home again.

Chapter 36

A New Storm Breaks

Beth... Twenty years ago...

The week passed in a haze of classes, study and helping her mother pack, then seeing her off. The relief Beth felt when Patricia finally drove off to London for the last time was palpable, and she spent the weekend wandering through the house from empty room to empty room, enjoying the beauty of silence and the freedom from criticism and fear.

A huge weight had been lifted from her shoulders, and from her heart, and there were moments when she couldn't quite believe that she was free of her parents, and that at last she was working towards her dream vocation and her dream life.

Just eight weeks ago she'd reluctantly dragged herself home for her sister's wedding, dreading every moment she would have to spend in the village, spend with her family, and desperate to head back to Paris and resume her real life the second she could. Instead she'd become close to her sister, and healed a piece of her heart through their new relationship. She'd been shocked to develop a real friendship with Mike and Violet – the closest she'd had since... well, ever. How sad, that she hadn't even realised how surface-level her travelling friends had been. Even Priya, who she'd shared a house with for a year, didn't actually know her, not the way Violet and Mike had seemed to do as soon as they'd met her.

She'd been shattered to realise that the man she'd thought she loved had lied to her and manipulated her – but her heart was being put back together by the hope of her feelings for a better man. She'd been healed by the priestess Rose too, and discovered the magic she'd always had within her, thanks to the beauty of the rituals she'd been invited to take part in, and a few mysterious encounters within the mists.

Now, rather than taking jobs just because she fell into them, even though they weren't exactly what she wanted to do, she was studying to become a teacher, the career she'd always dreamed of. Life couldn't get any better.

She wasn't even worried any more about whether or not she and Mike would end up together, because she was finally happy with her life and her self. Now that she knew herself, and knew her heart, she was confident that she would meet the person she was destined to be with when the time was right. Maybe it would be Mike, maybe not, but her impatience had evaporated, and her stress was gone. Life was good, just the way it was.

When she met Violet for dinner on Sunday night, she felt at peace and at ease with herself, and was glad that her friend was bursting with happiness too. Quickly she revealed that everything was fine with Andre – his cold demeanour in class had simply been because he didn't want anyone to know he was dating a student. It had to be their secret, he'd said – "how cool is that?" Violet grinned – as apparently it would seem unprofessional if anyone knew, and he didn't want people to think he was favouring her because they were in a relationship.

Her eyes shone. "He said we're in a relationship!"

Beth tried not to gag. "Did you tell him it actually made it *more* obvious that there's something going on between you two *because* he ignored you? Especially compared to all the flirting and the extra attention he's always given you?"

"No, I didn't think of that, but I'll mention it tomorrow when I see him." Violet grinned again. "I'm spending my last day of freedom from school with him, and we won't leave his room all day. So I'll meet you and Mike in class, is that all right?"

"Sure."

"Mike mentioned that he'd pick you up after college again, like last week, if that's fine with you?"

Beth nodded, and tried not to dwell on the thought of Violet and Andrew in bed all day. "That sounds like a good plan. How are you and Mike getting along anyway? Have you seen him much this week? Is he okay?"

Violet forced a smile. "He will be. And he's really grateful to you, for going to class with him the other night, and listening to him vent, and just being there for him. I think he really likes you," she said, voice teasing and eyebrows raised.

Beth blushed, and quickly changed the subject. "How is your mum coping with the knowledge that Mike won't be her son-in-law now?" she asked, figuring two could play at the unsettle-your-friend game.

Sadness crossed Violet's face, and Beth felt a pang of regret in asking. "I haven't told her yet."

"Why not? She's the perfect mum, and she's so understanding," Beth began, but Violet impatiently cut her off.

"Oh my god, no, I can't tell her, not yet! Please Beth, promise me you'll keep this between us!"

"But surely she'll be happy for you, if you're happy," she argued. "She loves you so much Vee, she only wants what you want, only wants you to be happy."

"Maybe she's like that to everyone *else*," Violet snapped. "But when it comes to me, she mixes up what I want, and what's good for me, with what she wants. She adores Mike, and thinks we're perfect together, so she'll be devastated. So I'm putting it off for as long as possible."

"But if you love Andre, surely she will too," Beth insisted. "If he's so wonderful she'll see that, and think so too. Or are you having doubts about him?"

Panic raced across Violet's face and flashed through her eyes, and she picked up her glass of water and took a huge gulp. "No, of course not," she said hastily, almost angrily, but Beth stared at her, eyebrows raised in question.

"I promise Beth, it's so wonderful. I love him so much – and it's so much deeper and more grown-up and amazing than what I had with Mike. I'm actually just worried that you or Mike will let something slip to Mum, before I'm ready to tell her."

Beth's expression revealed how she felt about that insult, and Violet reached across the table and took her hand. "I'm sorry, I didn't mean that how it sounded. I just, I want to wait until it's a little more concrete before I tell anyone else. Not that it isn't, we've been together over a month now, so I'm sure, I promise. I know that he's the love of my life, and he swears I'm his –"

"A month?" Beth cut in, voice almost a shriek. "You've been cheating on Mike all this time?"

Her friend blushed. "Well, five weeks, but it was really slow at first, just friendship. They weren't real dates, just, well, meeting for coffee to talk about the course... and, um, getting to know each other, and... stuff..." She trailed off, wilting in the heat of Beth's angry gaze. "I'm sorry," she whispered.

Beth held up a hand. "It's not me you have to apologise to."

Violet sighed. "I know. I feel terrible about Mike. I never wanted to hurt him, but I couldn't stay with him once I knew I loved someone else. That I wasn't in love with him any more."

"That's not the issue Vee. No one thinks you should stay with Mike just because he still loves you. But you do owe him the respect of being honest with him, surely, and treating him well, and fairly. And it's *not* fair that you're making him act like he's still your boyfriend in front of Rose, then expecting him to turn it off when you run off to be with Andre the minute she's not looking," she said passionately.

"And worse, Mike won't be able to move on while he's pretending to be your boyfriend – and no one will want to go out with him when they think he's still with you."

She tried to dial back her disapproval, but it was tough. She couldn't believe that Violet didn't see how unfair she was being to her poor dumped boyfriend. "I will keep your secret for now, but you can't keep lying to your mum, and you can't keep putting Mike in such an awful, soul-destroying situation."

"You care about him." Violet sounded almost surprised.

"Of course I do Vee, I care about you both."

She didn't blush, or get tongue-tied, and she marvelled at her composure. Yes, she did love Mike, but she wanted him to be happy – and not to be hurt – more than she needed him to be with her. She no longer felt the previous desperation for him to like her, to want her. Had it only been Andrew's words and manipulations that had led her to cast that love spell? Had he cast one on her?

Scanning back over the past few weeks, she realised that she hadn't actually been obsessing over him until after that conversation in the cafe with Andrew, when he'd asked her – no, blackmailed her – to encourage Violet to break up with Mike. Had given her those books on binding magic. Had threatened her, then suggested that he would help her win Mike over in return.

Of course she'd say yes if Mike asked her out, she wasn't that noble, but she really was content to just be his friend, especially right now, when he was dealing with so much, and she wanted to focus on her studies. Huh, maybe she was becoming mature at last. The thought made her giggle.

Violet gazed at her quizzically.

"Sorry, it was a train of thought thing. I was just thinking, with my studying and all, perhaps soon I might be as grown-up and sure of my place in the world as you and Mike are."

A laugh erupted from her friend, and the surprising sound lifted the mood. "Really? Us? Whatever made you think *that*?"

Beth laughed too, and they moved on to safer topics, like the upcoming Mabon ritual. Violet told her that it was a celebration of balance, harmony and gratitude, which honoured the loving yet challenging relationship between the goddess Demeter and her wayward daughter Persephone.

"But what if your mother is more she-devil than goddess?" Beth asked, only half joking. Her friend explained that you could also honour your mothering of yourself, your maternal feelings towards a person or situation, or any projects you wanted to grow and develop, and nurture into being.

As she walked home afterwards, Beth thought hard about that. Maybe wanting to be a teacher was her way of nurturing children in the way she'd never experienced, but had always wished for. Perhaps it would somehow address the imbalance in her own life, which perfectly complemented the seasonal festival they were about to celebrate.

By the time the ritual rolled around, Beth was excitedly looking forward to it, and she spent a long time getting ready. A soothing bath, scattered with dried rose petals, apple blossoms and ground orris root, settled her into an almost-trance state, opening her up to whatever the night would bring. After gently drying off, she got dressed in a long floaty gown, the rich colour of autumn leaves, then she wound thin gold ribbons into her hair. Once she was almost ready, she twined a garland of ivy leaves on her head like a crown, and slipped her magical rose quartz pendant around her neck.

As she climbed the stairs to the sacred space above Rose's healing centre, a woman in a long blue dress, her wavy red hair flowing loosely around her shoulders, was coming down. She paused in front of Beth and smiled at her, then reached out a hand and held it over her heart. A flood of warmth flowed into her, and she felt enveloped in love and peace.

"Beloved, trust. You are surrounded by love, and you always will be." The voice was a whisper, was a song, was a spell.

By the time she could find her own words, the woman had gone, sweeping past her down the stairs in a cloud of apple blossom scent. When she heard the bell over the front door tinkling, she assumed it was the mysterious stranger exiting the store, but a moment later Violet was standing behind her on the stairs.

"Hi Beth, are you okay?"

Beth turned to her, gaze soft, thoughtful, dreamy. "Did you see a woman in a blue cloak leaving as you came in?"

Eyes crinkling with curiosity, Violet stared at her friend. "No, it was just me. Why?"

"Huh." Beth shrugged. "How strange. A woman just came down from the ritual room, and placed her hand over my heart, and it was so comforting, so healing. But maybe she wasn't really there. God, am I hallucinating now?" She tried to keep her voice light, jokey, but she felt a shiver of fear.

Violet smiled reassuringly and took her hand to lead her upstairs. "Stranger things have happened around here," she giggled. "Maybe one of those mysterious women from the mists that people claim to have seen came to offer some maternal love to you. It's the perfect day for it."

"You've seen them too?" Beth asked, voice incredulous.

Violet shook her head. "No, but I've heard people talk about them. And I must admit, I always feel jealous when I hear the stories. I'd love to meet an Otherworldly being one day!"

"Maybe they only show themselves to those people who really need them, need the comfort," Beth muttered. How weird that super-spiritual Violet hadn't met one.

"Girls!" Rose called from the top of the stairs. "I'm glad you're both here. Mike is already inside, and we'll be starting soon, so come on up."

Violet gazed at Beth, a question in her eyes, and her friend sighed. "I'll keep your secret, for now," Beth whispered. "But tell her soon, please. Promise me?"

"I promise."

When they reached the landing they hugged Rose, were smudged with cloying sage smoke by Laura, who'd just started the same teacher training as Beth, then joined Mike over by the window as the last rays of the setting sun shone in on him, softening the pain on his face. He kissed them on the cheek, then they chatted about their plans for the following weekend.

They'd decided to go up to London for the day, and Beth was looking forward to showing them some of her old haunts. She knew they would both love the Chelsea Physic Garden, and Violet had talked them into going on a river cruise up the Thames as well. She also regaled them with stories about the psychic readings she'd done for several customers that day, to help Rose out.

And then it was time to focus on the enchantment Rose was weaving for them. The whole ritual was so beautiful, so magical, and the priestess's meditation journey about mothers and daughters was very healing for Beth. It made her realise that she was slowly letting go of her bitterness towards her own mother – and even beginning to see their struggles over the years as character building.

Of course she'd still swap parents with Violet in a heartbeat – she adored Rose, and found Louis kind and considerate, with a softness that belied his strength – but she was starting to understand that while her miserable childhood had been a huge influence on shaping her into the person she was, that wasn't necessarily a bad thing. She was finally content – even, maybe, happy – with who she was, and who she was becoming. And who knows, if she'd had a better, easier childhood, and less-cruel parents, less expectations, would she be the same person she was now?

Certainly she knew that if she ever had children she would be a much kinder, more demonstrative and more empathetic parent, the total opposite of her own mother and father. And just knowing that made her feel that she had broken the cycle, and was moving forward from her bitter darkness into the light.

Later, as they drank coffee while Mike grabbed them some oat cookies to ground themselves after the magic they'd woven together, Beth turned to her friend.

"Are you okay Vee? You seem, I don't know, sad? I didn't upset you did I, trying to convince you to tell your mum?"

Violet smiled. "No, not at all, I promise. I'm just really tired, and one of the readings I did today has stuck with me in a strangely heavy way. But a quick cord cutting and a good night's sleep will fix that, and tomorrow evening I'll come over and we can plan more of our London adventure, and that will get me excited again."

Beth leaned over and hugged her. "I'm excited too."

The following night, Beth was sitting downstairs in her lounge room, course notes spread over her lap and across the cushions and the nearest table. Her mother would have a fit, to see the chaos she'd created, but she was feeling free, and so productive

– it made her incredibly happy to be getting so deeply into her studies, and discovering the ways that worked best for her to learn the new material, all of which she was soaking up like a sponge.

And Patricia need never know just how much she'd transformed the formal room into a relaxed and casual place of learning, right? Then she glanced at all the coffee cups and the half-eaten sandwiches strewn amongst the text books. Hmm, she supposed she could tidy those up at least, but the rest was fine. It was beautifully organised chaos.

For a while she lost track of time, diving in to her current research assignment, until a hammering at the front door brought her abruptly back to the present. As she went to answer it, she realised that night had fallen, and she tried to shake off her foggy study brain as she switched on the lights, just as another furious hammering broke out. She laughed. Violet must really be desperate to discuss London.

"Geez, what's the hurry Vee?" she grinned, as she pulled the door open.

But it wasn't her friend standing there on the front porch, lit up by the golden light spilling out into the darkness. It was Mike, and his eyes were wild, his hair a dishevelled mess and his clothes crushed, as though he'd dressed in the dark. He pushed past her and paced down the hallway like a caged animal.

"Mike, my god, what's wrong?"

"Have you heard from Violet?" he demanded, looking almost angry as his vivid eyes burned accusingly into hers. "Do you know where she is?"

Shrinking back into the couch she'd sunk down onto, Beth held a cushion to her chest defensively. She had no idea what was happening, or what she'd supposedly done to upset him, but he was worrying her with his strange misplaced rage.

"Mike, slow down, what's going on?" she asked, trying desperately to understand what he meant. "I haven't seen Violet since the ritual last night. She said she was going to come over tonight, to talk about our trip to London, but she hasn't shown up yet."

She looked at her watch. "She didn't mention what time, but maybe she's having dinner with Rose and Louis first, then coming over for a cup of coffee afterwards? Did she tell you what time she planned to be here? Mike?

"*Mike!*"

When she repeated his name again, he finally stopped his pacing and looked at her, as if seeing her for the first time and suddenly realising where he was. The nervous energy that had been fuelling him until then seemed to slide right out of him, and he stopped pacing and threw himself down on the couch next to her. She watched, horrified, as he seemed to unravel before her eyes.

"Rose came over to my place a little while ago – Violet's gone," he said, voice bleak, and flat, almost dead-sounding.

"What?"

"She's disappeared. Packed a bag and run away."

And then he broke down. Beth put her arms around the beautiful, compassionate man she loved, and held him close as violent sobs racked his body and his heart shattered into a million pieces.

Epilogue

Out of the Storm

Rhiannon... Today...

She was climbing the tor with her mother, golden light trailing behind Beth as her laughter dipped and wove around them. Rhiannon spun around, her long meadow-hued dress swooping and weaving and floating around her ankles. Turning to her mum, she was surprised but not alarmed to see that Carlie had taken her place. Her friend smiled at her, respect and love in her eyes, and motioned to the summit of the sacred hill.

Beth and Violet stood there together, silhouetted against the vivid blue sky. Beth's cascading blonde waves of hair spilled around her shoulders, shining like gold against the deep red of her dress, while Violet was the mirror image of Carlie, long dark curls flowing down her back, and an emerald green cloak lifting gently in the breeze.

Together they gazed back at their daughters.

"Thank you Rhiannon, for supporting Carlie in her grief," Violet said softly.

"And thank you Carlie, for helping Rhiannon so much," Beth added, voice tender.

Then the two women stepped into the crumbling old stone tower on the top of the hill and disappeared, dissolving into a blur of golden light that blinded their daughters for a moment, but left them wrapped up in warmth, love and comfort.

Rhiannon awoke from her dream with a smile on her face and a lightness in her heart. She knew she would never get over the grief she felt at losing her mother, and she didn't want to. But for the first time since she'd lost her, she was filled with hope for the future.

After feeling so isolated and alone, she had found a friend, a sister of the heart, and they were inspiring each other to dig deep to discover their own strength. She'd started her final year of school, and thanks to Carlie, she now had a career goal to work towards, the perfect way for her to give back, and at the same time continue her own path towards healing, and a companion to undertake the long years of study with.

The love she shared with her father and her little brother was growing ever deeper, and despite fearing she would lose the grandmotherly relationship she'd long had with Rose once her flesh-and-blood relative arrived, she now knew that nothing could break their bond, and that the priestess's love was unconditional and without limit.

And she had a new, inspiring and potent relationship with magic that she knew would be a huge part of her life, a way to connect with her mother, and to deepen her connection to nature and the earth, as well as herself.

When she heard her little brother knock at her door, she jumped out of bed and hurried over to let him in. Through her sadness she had gained strength, and an intense gratitude for the family that she did have, and the friends who cared so deeply for her.

Despite the storms she'd endured, she knew now that it really was an enchanted life.

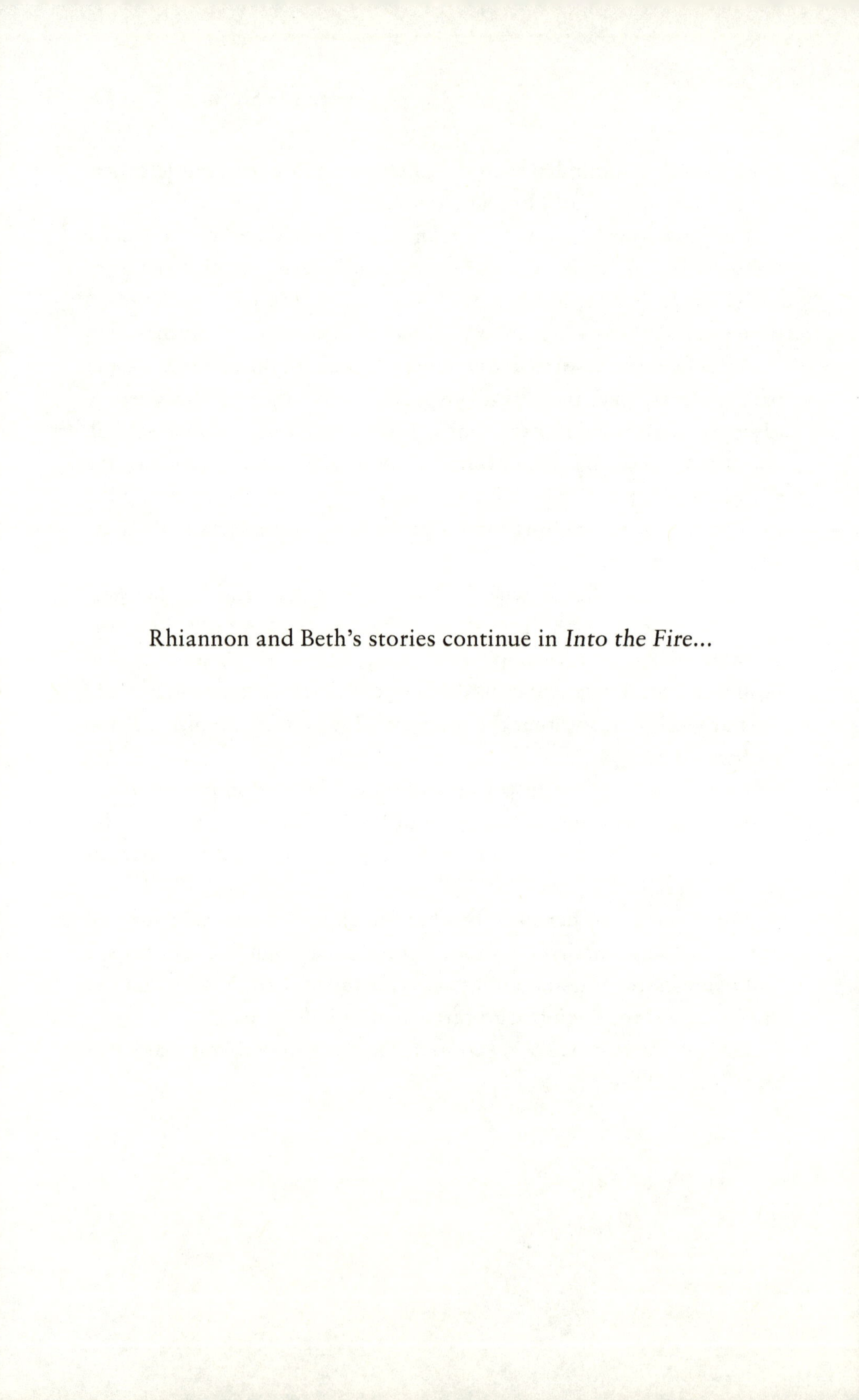

Rhiannon and Beth's stories continue in *Into the Fire*...

"I am not afraid of storms,
For I am learning to sail my ship."
Louisa May Alcott, American author

Thank You!

Thank you so much for reading this book, and
sharing the magic of Rhiannon and her mother Beth's stories.
As an indie author, I rely on word of mouth and reader reviews
to get the word out. If you enjoyed *Into the Storm*, I would be
so grateful if you could take a moment to leave a review on
any book site. Reviews help improve sales and ranking,
and are of immense help to all indie writers.

If you'd like to stay in touch and receive free exclusive content,
be the first to hear about book news and events info, giveaways
and more, you can sign up for my newsletter at

www.sereneconneeley.com/subscribe.

(And don't worry, you can unsubscribe at any time...)

With love and gratitude,
Serene xx

"Say not in grief that she is no more,
but say in thankfulness that she was.
A death is not the extinguishing of a light,
but the putting out of the lamp
because the dawn has come."
Rabindranath Tagore, Bengali poet

With Thanks

I am so grateful to my sweet husband, for his love, support, encouragement and belief in me. For making me countless cups of tea as I write. For being patient when I'm on deadline, and when I want to quit. For wanting me to tell Rhiannon's story, and believing in her, brainstorming plot points and debating her life with me. This one is for you. I love you so much, always...

I'm indebted to amazingly talented, kind and generous artist Selina Fenech, for the stunning cover image for this and all the Mists books, and for sharing the hard work and hilarity of so many festivals with me. I can't wait to bring our project to life!

Love and gratitude to my wonderful author friends Selina Fenech and K. A. Last for invaluable feedback on this story, and cover design inspiration. To Gabrielle Baker, narrator of the Mists audiobooks, for giving a voice to my characters. To my sweet hubby and my faery friend Daniella Spinetti for the illustrations. And to Margie for her love and support, and help with the French conversations, Petie for the laughter and political raves, and my beautiful family in the west.

Love and blessings to my writer friends, Kylie Matthews, Lucy Cavendish, Felicity Pulman, Elisabeth Knowles, Nigel Bartlett, Cheralyn Darcey, and L. L. Hunter and the Story Queens, for sharing the book launches, festivals, writing retreats and sprints, and the craziness and wonder of our trials and triumphs.

Love and thanks to my workout buddies Janine and Claire, and our fun fit group friends. Working out every day keeps me sane, and there's nothing like punching my way through a Combat session, upping my weights in Pump or letting Jillian Michaels kick my butt to gain a new perspective on a plot dilemma.

And love, honour and gratitude to beautiful Annalie, whose bravery, kindness and wisdom added an extra dimension to Beth. My heart aches for your gorgeous family left behind, but I'm trying to do as you asked and not be sad at your loss, just grateful for your friendship and happy we got to spend precious time together...

With much love, Serene xx

"There are some things you learn best in calm,
and some in storm."
Willa Cather, American author

About the Author

Serene Conneeley is an Australian writer with a fascination for history, travel, ritual and the myth and magic of ancient places and cultures. She's written for magazines about news, travel, health, spirituality, entertainment and social and environmental issues, been editor of several preschool magazines, and contributed to international books on history, witchcraft, psychic development and personal transformation.

She's the author of the Into the Mists Trilogy – *Into the Mists*, *Into the Dark* and *Into the Light* – the Into the Storm Trilogy – *Into the Storm*, *Into the Fire* and *Into the Air* – and the non-fiction books *Faery Magic*, *Mermaid Magic*, *Witchy Magic*, *Seven Sacred Sites* and *A Magical Journey*, and creator of the meditation CD *Sacred Journey*.

Serene is a reconnective healing practitioner, and has studied magical and medicinal herbalism, bereavement counselling, reiki and many other healing modalities, plus politics and journalism. She loves reading, drinking tea with her friends, working out and celebrating the energy of the moon and the magic of the earth. Her pagan heart blossomed as she climbed mountains, sat in stone circles, climbed into ancient burial mounds and stood in the shadow of the pyramids on her travels, and she's also learned the magic of finding true happiness and peace at home.

www.SereneConneeley.com

THE INTO THE MISTS SERIES

Into the Mists is healing, empowering, inspiring and magical. I loved every single page. I haven't enjoyed a book this much since I read *Heart's Blood* by Juliet Marillier. Can't wait for a sequel!

Julia Burdock, healer

Into the Dark is darker than the first book, but it also portrays the sweetness of love, and the power of the magical. This is a compelling novel, which haunted my dreams while I was reading it, and lingered in my mind long after I'd finished it.

Felicity Pulman, author of the Janna Chronicles

Into the Light is a wonderful story and a stunning conclusion. I'm absolutely blown away by this series. It is truly beautiful from start to finish – magical, realistic, gentle, harsh, sad and joyful...

Kylie Matthews, book reviewer

Into the Mists: A Journal is *divine!* The lovely quotes are very inspiring, and the feel of the journal is heart-warming. It sits on my bedside table for writing in during quiet times of reflection. Just beautiful.

Cheralyn Darcey, eco-artist and author of Flowerpaedia

The Into the Mists Trilogy: Hardcover Omnibus is a mystical, magical tale of forgiveness and love. I couldn't stop reading once I started – I had to know what happened next! I recommend this to anyone.

L. L. Hunter, author of The Legend of the Archangel Series

The Into the Mists Trilogy audiobooks will sweep you away with the melodic voice and magical story. It was written and narrated beautifully, capturing the character and captivating the reader.

Rebecca Bosevski, author of Enchanting the Fey

Into the Fire is powerful, heartbreaking and intense. So beautiful.

Beta reader

COMING SOON...
Into the Air: Into the Storm Trilogy Book Three.

THE MAGIC SERIES

Faery Magic is the ultimate guide to all things faery; entertaining, informative and enthralling. A charming book with much to offer, from history and legends, magical gifts and sacred sites and the unique beings found around the globe, to recipes and crafts to keep you busy while you explore this magical world.

Larissa Chapman, book blogger

Mermaid Magic is a wonderfully inspiring read. It really made me want to shed my twenty-first century shackles and dive into the ocean to embrace its wonderful healing powers. Mixing magic, myth and history with nature and environmentalism, it is clear, practical, well researched and written with real passion.

Sabina Collins, book reviewer

Witchy Magic is a definitive reference for the would-be witch, and entertaining and enlightening for the witch-curious. This beautiful book is for everyone, from the history buff, ritualist and nature lover to the magician, pagan and spiritualist.

Kylie Matthews, book reviewer

THE SACRED SERIES

Seven Sacred Sites is a rich and lovely, very wise and tender friend, with good advice and insights to inspire you in your travels, be they physical or imaginary. I wish I'd had it years ago.

Lucy Cavendish, author of Spellbound and White Magic

A Magical Journey is a gem for the adventurers among us. What distinguishes it is Serene's emphasis on enchanting the writing process. A fascinating concept, and gorgeous to the touch.

Joanne Lock, Spheres magazine

Sacred Journey is a treasure. Serene is a gentle, loving, wise teacher of great wisdoms, and this meditation CD takes us on a sacred journey not only into the earthly and heavenly elements and realms, but into history, spirituality and self-love.

Lucy Cavendish, creator of As Above, So Below CD

9 780099 459 3382